THE DARKER ARTS

Oscar de Muriel was born in Mexico City, where he began writing stories aged seven, and later came to the UK to complete a PhD in Chemistry. Whilst working as a translator and playing the violin, the idea for a spooky whodunnit series came to him and 'Nine-Nails' McGray was born. Oscar splits his time between the North West of England and Mexico City. *The Darker Arts* is the fifth book in the Frey & McGray series.

Also by Oscar de Muriel

Strings of Murder
A Fever of the Blood
A Mask of Shadows
Loch of the Dead

THE DARKER ARTS

OSCAR DE MURIEL

ORION

First published in Great Britain in 2019 by Orion Fiction,
an imprint of The Orion Publishing Group Ltd.,
Carmelite House, 50 Victoria Embankment
London EC4Y 0DZ

An Hachette UK Company

1 3 5 7 9 10 8 6 4 2

A CIP catalogue record for this book is
available from the British Library.

ISBN (Hardback): 978 1 4091 8762 2

Typeset by Born Group

Printed and bound in Great Britain by Clays Ltd, Elcograf S.p.A.

www.orionbooks.co.uk

The fifth one is for my very dear sis Olivia.

Finally!

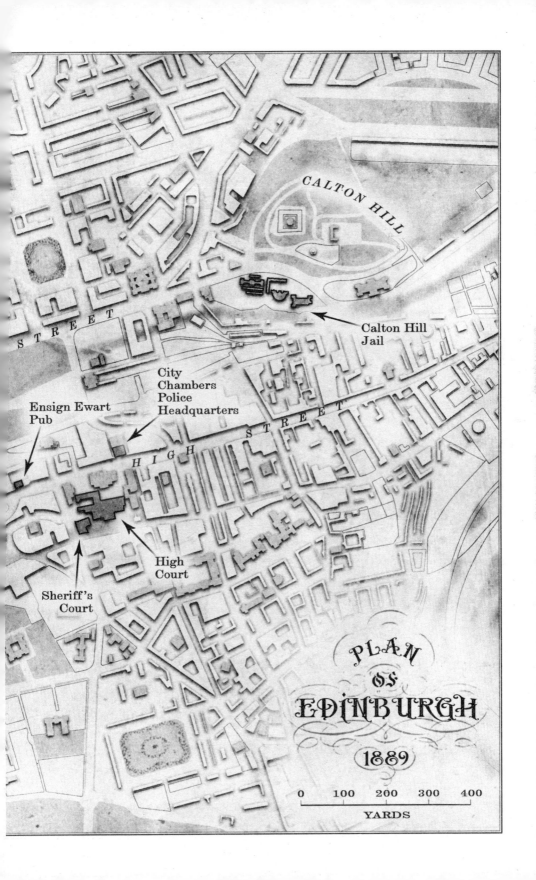

CALTON HILL

Calton Hill
Jail

City
Chambers
Police
Headquarters

Ensign Ewart
Pub

S T R E E T

H I G H   S T R E E T

High
Court

Sheriff's
Court

PLAN
OF
EDINBURGH
1889

0   100   200   300   400
YARDS

I have seen my death.
I saw myself hang.

I saw the crowd around me cheering.
I felt the noose around my neck;
the strangling grip;
the tearing skin.

And you were there.
I saw your tears.

You were always there . . .

A. K. Dragnea

1883

[1]

2 *July*

Public enquiry held at Dundee's Sheriff Court,
following the deaths of Mr James McGray esq.
and his wife Amina McGray (née Duncan)

Doctor Clouston stepped ahead hesitantly, his footsteps deafening amidst the deathly silence of the courtroom. His hands trembled, and he had to clench them into fists to conceal his anxiety. All eyes were fixed on him, all hostile, as if he had committed the murders himself.

He took his seat at the witnesses' box, his chin held high, took the oath, and then waited until the procurator fiscal came to him.

The man, completely bald and with a scalp as smooth and pale as polished marble, took his time, rearranging and revising documents as everyone waited in tense silence.

Clouston looked at the young Adolphus McGray, who had just given his statement. The twenty-five-year-old stood out in the rows, taller than most, broad-shouldered and with raven black hair. He also had the palest face, staring down at his bandaged hand, pressed against his chest. The wound had not fully scarred yet.

'Doctor Thomas Clouston,' said the procurator suddenly, making more than one at the court jump. 'Of Edinburgh's Royal Lunatic Asylum.'

He approached with an odious grin as he read the credentials. A lead tooth caught Clouston's eye.

'That is correct,' said the doctor, taking an instant dislike to that man.

'Can you recount the events of the evening?'

'I am only here to testify as to the mental state of Miss McGray.'

'Oh, indulge us, doctor.'

He spoke in grumbles. 'I received a telegram telling me that Mr McGray and his wife had been attacked. That they were sadly dead. That their son was injured and their daughter had had to be locked up in her chambers. When I arrived—'

'No, no, doctor,' the procurator interrupted. 'Before that. I would like to know what happened earlier that day.'

Clouston snorted. 'I only know what I heard from Mr McGray's son and servants. I do not know how a third-party statement might—'

'*Please*,' the sheriff intervened from his higher bench, 'answer the procurator's question.' His 'please' was rather a growl.

Clouston cleared his throat. The sooner he obliged, the sooner this would be over.

'From what I was told, Adolphus and Amy, Mr McGray's son and daughter, left the house in the early evening. They went horseback riding since the weather was pleasant despite the hour. After some time they stopped to allow the horses to rest, and they sat by the small lake that borders their family's estate. They chatted for a while before Miss McGray said she felt indisposed, and—'

'Indisposed how?'

'Again, I can only repeat what—'

'How?'

Clouston ruffled his moustache with impatience. 'Her brother said she complained of a headache and shortness of breath. She decided to return to the—'

'On her own?'

4

'Yes.'

'What time was this?'

'I must assume it was before dusk.'

'You said they went out in the early evening. Do you believe they managed to have a ride long enough so that the mounts required rest, and then a chat, all before sunset?'

'Are you not familiar with midsummer, Mr Pratt?'

The entire courtroom laughed, and upon the very mention of his own name, the fiscal's lip trembled in an uncontrollable tic.

'I simply find it odd,' he said, ominously, 'that a young lady would decide to ride alone, in the middle of the wilderness, when the day must have been coming to a close.'

'It was their family's land. The girl had probably ridden alone there countless times.'

'And she insisted her brother stayed behind?'

'You just heard him say so himself.'

'A young lady, feeling ill, refuses to be accompanied back home, despite the gathering darkness. And the next thing we know is that she went berserk and killed the only two souls in the house. Do you not find it slightly suspicious?'

'Suspicious?'

'She was perfectly healthy when she left her brother, was she not?'

'Yes.'

'And mere minutes later she'd become an uncontrollable murderess?'

Adolphus stood up at this, glaring at the fiscal. The corpulent guard posted next to him pushed him back on the seat. It was not the first time the young man had lost his temper today.

Clouston took a deep breath. 'It is an extraordinary shift, but not unheard of. The mechanics of the mind sadly remain a mystery.'

The fiscal nodded, albeit with a sardonic side smile. 'So you sustain the plea of insanity?'

'Indeed. The girl is under my custody now.'

'When did you take her to your – ahem – very honourable institution?'

'The very next day.'

'Indeed?'

'Yes. She was a danger to herself and others. She attacked me when I first encountered her.'

'Oh, yes,' the fiscal said, turning back to the audience to face Betsy, the McGrays' stumpy, ageing maid, and George, the weathered butler. 'As these servants said, you arrived and subdued Miss McGray without any trouble.'

Clouston inhaled, smelling a trap. 'Yes. I did.'

The fiscal chuckled. 'The girl managed to kill two healthy grown-ups, mutilate her brother, who, as we can see, is hardly a featherweight . . . yet you, doctor, never came to harm.'

Clouston stroked his long, dark beard. 'That is true. When I arrived, Miss McGray was famished and dehydrated. The servants had locked her in her bedroom and nobody dared go near her. The poor girl had not eaten or drunk in a day. She only managed to lift a blade for an instant. She hurled herself onto me and then collapsed.'

Clouston looked at the jury with the corner of his eye. Several heads nodded.

'Did she say anything?' asked the fiscal. 'Before collapsing?'

This was what everyone had been expecting. People stretched their necks and strained their ears. Some did not even blink. There were rumours already, but Clouston was the only one who'd heard the girl's last known words.

'Remember you are under oath, doctor,' the fiscal pressed.

Clouston looked at Adolphus. They'd talked about this before. There was a tormented, pleading look in his blue eyes. *Don't tell them*, he seemed to beg.

But he was under oath . . .

The doctor gulped and then spat the words.

'She said *I'm not mad . . .*'

There were gasps and murmurs in the crowd. The fiscal walked triumphantly to the bench of the jury.

'The girl herself said she was not mad! And if she was not mad, then these murders must be treated as—'

'*Oh, what a stupid statement!*' Clouston roared, jumping to his feet. His booming voice silenced everyone present. 'I have treated hundreds of patients in the past twenty years. Nine out of ten will claim they're not insane. Do you want me to believe their word and release them all at once – Mr Pratt?'

There was another wave of laughter, which turned the fiscal's scalp bright red.

Clouston went on before the racket receded. 'Miss McGray also said, right afterwards, that it was all the work of the devil.'

In a blink, the laughter became gasps and cries of shock. That was what people had been craving to hear. That was the statement all the papers in Dundee and Edinburgh would publish the next day.

Clouston cast Adolphus a troubled look. The young man was falling apart, clenching his bandages with his healthy hand. Clouston felt so sorry for him his heart ached – and yet, the truth had to be told . . .

He looked straight into the jury's eyes. 'Miss McGray, a dainty girl of sixteen, turned against her mother and father, whom she *adored*, and killed them. She became wild and had to be restrained and sedated. There is no doubt she was not herself. She . . .' Clouston looked down, his voice infected with sorrow. 'She may never be herself again.'

His words hung in the air for a long while, until the fiscal clicked his tongue.

'A very sad tale – however inconclusive. The girl must attend court.'

7

'*What!*' Adolphus howled in the distance.

There were claps and cheers in the crowd, and some men were lasciviously rubbing their hands. A young woman at court always promised a good spectacle.

The procurator saw the fidgety members of the jury, whispering at each other, and he sneered. 'I am afraid the girl's insanity must be properly—'

'*Her insanity has been proven!*' Clouston asserted, now addressing only the sheriff and the jury. 'My report is comprehensive. I have submitted it this morning and you can analyse it at once. A colleague from Inverness is on his way and I am certain he will only corroborate my findings. They will comply with the requirements of the Lunacy Act.'

The fiscal approached him like a stalking wolf. 'And in the meantime you will hide a potential murderer in your institution?'

Adolphus jumped up again. '*Ye fucking cretin!*'

At a sign from the sheriff, another two guards rushed to drag him out of the courtroom. Clouston spoke even as they did so.

'What would you have us do, Mr *Pratt*? Bring the girl here so she can be made a spectacle of? Nothing shall be gained other than your morbid desire to see a helpless creature publicly humiliated.' He turned to the sheriff and jury. 'The law *is* being followed. That girl has no business here. The court must show her some human compassion.'

'Did she show any compassion to her own kin?'

There was uproar at this. People stood up, clapped, whistled and demanded the girl appeared at court. They wanted her blood; her dignity.

Clouston felt tears of rage build up in his eyes. He pictured himself and the McGrays as caged prey, surrounded by a pack of thousands of hounds, only kept at bay by leashes that were just about to snap.

[II]

The gypsy stood by the pub's door, swathed in a dark cape and hood. She pressed her hand, armed with curved nails painted in black, against the door, but she hesitated before going in. She looked left and right, scrutinising the Royal Mile. At this hour the cobblestoned street was deserted. Even the public house was quiet.

'D'ye want me to go in with ye?' her manservant asked, still at the cart's driver seat.

'No,' the gypsy mumbled. 'Wait here.'

She stepped in quietly and looked around. The place was very dark, lit only by the golden glow of some dying embers, and the air stank of cheap ale – the gypsy recognised her own brew.

There were only a few patrons left; a mixture of the drunkest men in Edinburgh, stooped over their pints and their drams, and those plagued by disgraces no amount of drink could drown.

The McGray heir was easy to spot. Her contacts had told her he'd taken to dress in showy tartan, but even without those mismatching trousers and waistcoat, she would have recognised his tall, well-built frame from the newspaper reports.

She was expecting him to be distraught; a sad, red-eyed figure nursing a bottle of single malt. Instead, the towering man was all over the pub's landlady.

They were in a darkened corner of the room, locked in a tight embrace like a pair of octopuses.

The gypsy walked closer, her cloak brushing the knee of the drunkest man in the establishment.

He stared at her, his head swaying, and whistled. 'Oi! I like a pair o' those!'

She did not look back or break stride.

'I'd curse you – if you had anything left to lose.'

Her well-chosen words, delivered in a strange accent from somewhere in Eastern Europe, struck her enemy's most delicate nerve. The man looked down, attempting to hide his flushed, leathery face.

The gypsy stood firmly by the couple's table and let out a cackle.

'You don't waste your time, my dear. Well done!'

The young landlady jumped up, her cheeks as red as her mane of curls. 'Madame Katerina!'

The gypsy smiled.

'Oh, don't blush, Mary! At least you're moving up in the world; this one's much more fetching than the wretch you asked me to jinx last month.' She lowered her voice. 'By the way, those warts must be sprouting nicely as we speak.'

She installed herself on Mary's chair, and the young McGray, indignant, snapped his fingers at once.

'*Oi!* I didnae say ye could sit.'

They exchanged stares in a silent duel of wills. His were light blue, hers bright green. Both cunning.

She spoke first. 'I think you'll like to hear what I have to tell you.' And she unbuttoned her cloak and let it fall around her shoulders.

McGray's eyes went directly to her protruding breasts, the largest in Edinburgh, and sported proudly under her low cleavage.

The gypsy smiled. Her attributes always threw her enemies off guard.

'Would you like a drink, madam?' Mary asked, before McGray managed to close his mouth.

'Yes, my dear. But the good stuff, not the piss I sell you for the clients.'

Mary winked at her. 'I'll bring ye a single malt from the McGrays' distillery. They know their trade.' And as she made her way to the backroom, Mary exchanged a look of complicity with McGray.

He was not amused at all.

'I don't mean to be rude, hen,' he said, 'but ye should really piss off.'

'Oh! Are you busy, my boy?'

'Aye. I'm polishing my fuckin' nails, don't ye see?'

The drunkard laughed from the distance. 'Och, ye'll finish sooner now!'

McGray gulped down the remains of his dram and then threw the tumbler at the man. It landed right in-between his eyes and smashed to pieces. The drunkard yowled, jumped up and attempted to make a fist, but then staggered, swayed, and looked at his hand as if it were the first time he'd seen it. He shouted some vulgarity and clumsily made his way out.

'Adolphus!' Mary grunted, coming back with a new bottle. 'That's the third good client ye've scared away today! He could've downed one more bottle!'

'I'm sure my custom will pay off, my dear,' said Katerina, pouring herself a very generous measure. 'And I promise you I won't scare this one away.'

'Yer about to do just that,' McGray snapped.

Mary squeezed his forearm. 'I'll be right back, Adolphus. Do listen to Madame Katerina.' And she scuttled into the backroom, in clear collusion with the generous-breasted gypsy.

McGray sighed. 'What the fuck ye want?'

He interlaced his fingers. He'd only just lost the bandages, but the stitches on his finger stump, the one chopped off by his own sister, still made a grisly sight.

'Ring finger, right hand,' the gypsy said with a note of melancholy. 'Just like the papers said.'

'Aye. I'm glad I didnae lose this one – or these two.'

The gypsy smiled. 'I like you already.' She swirled the tumbler, sniffed the liquor and took a good swig. She winced. 'Ahh, good stuff indeed!'

'I hate asking things twice. What the fuck ye—?'

'I believe your story, my boy.'

McGray looked up, his eyes catching the glow from the hearth, the blue gone a fiery amber.

'Don't toy with me,' he warned, placing a hand on the table and slowly making a fist. 'I've already met many quacks like ye. Youse are all after the brass with cheap tricks and lies.'

'Don't compare me with them, boy. I am so sorry for your losses.'

'What d'ye care?'

She smiled wryly. 'I know what it feels like. I lost my parents when I was very young. You're lucky.'

'*Lucky!* Aye.'

'You have your fists and your townhouse and your distilleries . . .' she indulged in the aroma of the drink. 'I had none of that. I was a pauper girl with a funny foreign voice, all by herself. I traded anything you can imagine for a loaf of mouldy bread or a night indoors. Sometimes—'

She went silent, suddenly swallowing whichever words she was about to say. She took a long sip and cleared her throat.

'But I made my way up in the world. I'm not desperate or helpless and I never will be again. Believe me, I'm not here to beg or take advantage. I'm here to help, even if nobody helped me when I was on the streets.'

McGray twisted his mouth in a mixture of compassion and annoyance. The gypsy smiled at that faint glimpse of empathy. That was her chance; a crack in the young man's shell.

'You think you saw something,' she whispered, her voice entrancing, like the hiss of a snake. 'Something you can't explain . . . You have even thought you might be mad yourself.'

McGray said nothing. He stared at her, not blinking, his chest swelling slowly.

'You saw the devil, didn't you? You saw his horns and his burned flesh. You saw him running away. Didn't you?'

McGray drew in a troubled breath. 'How can ye tell?'

The gypsy displayed both hands on the table, her nails like the talons of an eagle.

'I see these things, my boy. I see that something terrible happened to your little sister. Something dark and too horrible to bear.'

A draught came in then, pushing the door ajar and making the embers quiver.

'These things leave a trail, my boy,' she insisted. 'They reek. This all reeks of demons.'

McGray's lips parted. By now everyone in Edinburgh talked of nothing but Clouston's statement. Pansy had mentioned the devil; it was all over the papers. He wanted to say so, to grab the woman by the arm and throw her out; however, there was something in her eyes he could not ignore. She was looking at him with a rather motherly gaze.

She leaned closer and whispered. 'You saw what really happened, didn't you? You saw what I see.'

The cold from the street began to creep into McGray's bones. Hardy as he was, he could not repress a slight shiver.

'And there's something else I see,' the gypsy said at once, as if that brief tremor had lowered McGray's guard. She smiled, but it was a warm, relieved smile. 'Your little sister may not be lost. Not yet.'

McGray tensed his entire body; that stiffness felt like a shield that somehow kept the gypsy at bay. Here was this woman, telling him the very words he so desperately yearned to hear. All the more reason to remain cautious.

He said nothing, and the woman leaned closer. Her eyes too were like embers.

'I can help you.'

McGray raised his chin, clenching his fist more tightly. And yet, he could not look away.

The gypsy smiled wider.

'We can help each other.'

1889

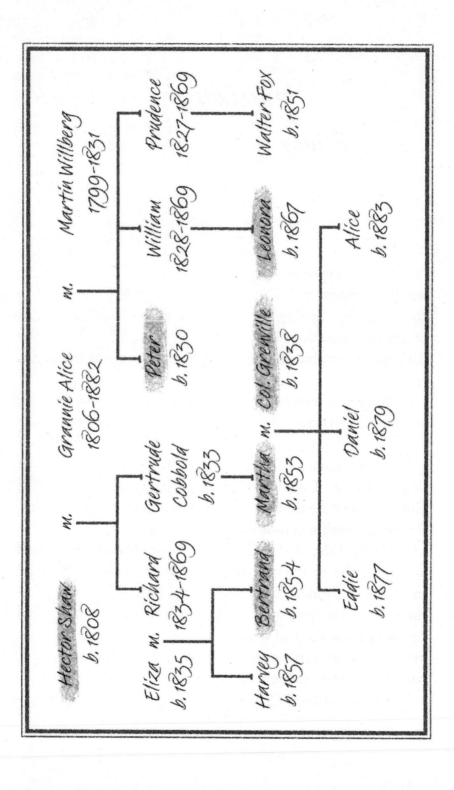

PROLOGUE

Friday 13 September 1889

11.30 p.m.

'Your damn gypsy is late,' Colonel Grenville barked, staring out the window at the gloomy gardens. His teeth had been clenching the cigar so tightly his mouth was now full of bits of crushed tobacco. He spat them as he turned back to the darkened room, but the sight of the others only worsened his temper.

Leonora was hunched over her blasted book of necromancy and related nonsense, and the many candles on the round table cast sharp shadows on her gaunt face.

'She will come,' said the twenty-two-year-old with her dreamy airs, as if intent on looking like an apparition herself. Colonel Grenville thought the silly girl deserved a good smack, fancying herself a consummate fortune teller.

Mrs Grenville, at the edge of a nearby sofa, fanned herself anxiously, the insistent ruffle of the feathers the only sound in the tense parlour. She cast a fearful look at her husband – the colonel had seldom been made to wait. Even when asked to marry him, she had been shaken and forced to provide an answer with military promptness. She'd thought it so romantic back then. Now, though . . .

She let out a tired sigh.

The old Mr Shaw, her grandfather, sat rather stiff by her side. The man's white beard and whiskers, and the golden frames of his round spectacles gleamed under the candlelight, but little else of him could be seen. Like a spectre, he brought an infirm hand to the light and grasped his daughter's wrist, forcing her fan into stillness.

'Thanks, Hector,' said a hoarse voice from the depth of the shadows. The voice of a man the colonel despised: Mr Willberg, clad in black and almost invisible standing in a darkened corner. The man took a few steps into the light, as if materialising from nowhere, and began pacing. Peter Willberg was almost a decade older than the colonel, and the only man present who'd dare challenge him. Colonel Grenville knew this, and glared at Willberg's bushy beard, which was curly and jet black, even if the hair on his scalp was thin and growing white.

'You'll have to ask someone to clean that,' Mr Willberg told the colonel, nodding at the flakes of tobacco on the red carpet.

'Go to hell, Pete,' snapped Colonel Grenville. 'This is my bloody house!'

Mr Willberg sneered. 'Oh, is it now?'

Nobody spoke. They simply waited for the colonel's reaction. Leonora was the only one who moved, stretching an arm to squeeze Mr Willberg's. Her eyes pleaded for his composure.

Defiantly, the colonel tossed his cigar onto the floor and produced a new one from his pocket.

'The last thing we need is more bloody smoke, you fool!' Mr Willberg snapped.

In that at least they all agreed. The air in the small chamber was thick, with wafts of sickly smoke floating in-between the flickering flames.

The colonel roared, 'Then tell your bloody niece to put those damn things out!'

'We need to cleanse the room!' Leonora cried just as loudly, raising her arms as if readying herself to defend the set of candles. The same ones her grandmother had blessed so many years ago, which were – according to the gypsy – key to their success tonight. 'We need them to talk to the dead!'

'There, there,' said the old Mr Shaw, applying an already damp handkerchief to his forehead. 'We are all . . . we are all very tense.'

They all sensed the fear in his voice, and at once fell silent. If the séance succeeded, the poor old man was about to face demons none of the others could even imagine. Mrs Grenville placed a hand on her father's, but the man twitched and pulled it away.

'Is that scaredy-cat Bertrand ready?' the colonel asked.

At once, a tiny voice came from the parlour's door. Bertrand had been standing next to the door frame.

'A – aye. I'm here, sir, sorry. The room is stifling.'

The colonel snorted as he cast him a derisive look. Bertrand embodied everything he hated in men: he was weak, sheepish, soft in the knees, with a squeaky voice and fidgety hands he always rubbed by his chest. Many times the colonel had remarked on Bertrand's apparent lack of gonads – more than once to his face, but the stupid fella simply giggled as if it all were a joke. His manners might be childish, yet the chap was not even young; his oily hair, always parted and flattened with obsessive care, was already going grey at the top. The colonel's wife was Bertrand's first cousin, and it still infuriated him that his three children shared blood with such a gritless oaf.

'Here she comes!' said Mr Willberg, peering through the window.

Bertrand squinted, for he'd feared the prospect all along. He was present only because his Aunt Gertrude had backed down that very morning and, according to that gypsy woman, the ceremony needed seven souls.

Mrs Grenville stood up, fidgeting with the pearls of her choker, and saw the light of the coach approaching through the gardens. The night was so dark, the sky lined with clouds so dense, that it looked as though the carriage floated amidst an endless void.

She went closer to the window. Her shoulder accidentally rubbed Mr Willberg's, and they both flinched. She'd never seen the man thus altered, his customary stench of ale stronger than usual.

The colonel brusquely pushed her aside to have a look, and saw Holt, his fleshy valet, jumping off the driver's seat and helping down what looked like a bundle of extravagant curtains.

Soon enough, Holt entered the parlour, and when the gypsy came in, everyone froze still. It would take them a moment to scrutinise the woman, and even the colonel had to admit there was something unnerving about her.

She was squat, solidly built, wrapped in countless multicoloured shawls, scarves and veils. Nobody could see her face, shrouded in black tulle trimmed with cheap pendants, which tinkled softly at her every movement. The many layers of fabric gave off a pungent herbal smell, strong enough to overpower the parlour's mist. Her hands were wrapped in black mittens, so all that could be seen of her were the tips of her stout, pale fingers, each one armed with curved nails – she moved them slowly, as if drumming on an invisible table.

The young Leonora jumped to her feet and ran to the woman, reaching for one of those menacing hands.

'Madame Katerina, it's an honour! I knew you'd come.'

'I always go to those who need me,' she replied with a hoarse, foreign voice.

'Or who pay you,' the colonel said between his teeth.

Leonora turned to him, ready to retort, but the gypsy grasped her arm.

'Leave it, child. This room is already quite disturbed.'

'Oh, but I cleansed it as you said, madam! Like Grannie Alice herself would have done.'

The colonel went to Holt and barked at him. 'What took you so long?'

Holt had barely opened his mouth when the gypsy answered herself.

'I was in the middle of something else.'

The colonel let out a loud 'HA!' which the gypsy ignored. She pulled off one of her mittens, rested a palm on the wall, and leisurely ran her hand on the oak panelling. Her long fingernails, painted in black, shimmered under the candlelight. She then turned to Leonora.

'You did well, girl. We can do the rituals here . . . but only just.' She came closer to the table and candles, and the light went through her veil's thin material. They all managed to see the twinkle of her cunning eyes, going from one person to the other. She only spoke again once she had studied them all. 'Yes, only just. There's too much guilt here.'

Those words caused more than one gulp.

'The chairs, Bertrand!' snapped Mr Willberg, and the fidgety man, after a jump, began dragging seats from the adjacent dining room. The screech of the wood proved unbearable for the old Mr Shaw, and his grandaughter had to go to him and hold his hand.

Leonora led Madame Katerina to the little round table. 'We dispatched the servants, ma'am. They were all gone before sunset, just as you requested.'

The woman assented, casting an approving look at the table.

Bertrand placed the seventh chair and Leonora offered a seat to the gypsy, as reverently as if addressing Queen Victoria. The woman sat down as Bertrand brought a tripod and installed it clumsily by the window.

'What's that for?' she said. 'A camera?'

Leonora sat by her side, her eyes burning with excitement. 'Oh, do, *do* humour me, ma'am. I want photos of this session. I read the spirits sometimes show in the plaques.'

The gypsy remained silent, her face inscrutable. 'I never heard such a thing.'

'Do you not like to leave evidence behind?' said the colonel, sitting next to the clairvoyant. He puffed at his cigar with an insolent look.

The gypsy set her hands on the table, as she liked to do to prove she was in command of the situation. 'No more than you do, little man.'

The colonel made to stand up, dropping his cigar on the floor. It was Mr Willberg's hand that pushed him back down.

'Will you *stop* it, Grenville? You of all people here—'

'Oh, save it, Pete!'

Mrs Grenville sat next to her husband but did not say a word. She knew any attempt to calm him down only enraged him further.

'Do you have the offerings?' the gypsy asked.

'Of course,' replied Leonora, already rushing to a side cabinet. She brought a cut-glass decanter that made Holt shudder. It seemed to contain blood.

As if feeling his agitation, the clairvoyant turned her head towards him. 'He has to leave.'

The colonel let out an impatient sigh, rose and dragged Holt out of the parlour. The middle-aged valet could only be relieved.

'Here,' the colonel said as he pulled a generous amount of notes from his pocket. 'More than I promised. If you intend to spend it on beer or women, make sure it is not tonight. I need you here in the morning.'

'Of course, sir,' replied Holt, barely repressing the urge to count the money. 'What time do you need me back?'

'Break of dawn,' he said, and he then clasped Holt's collar. 'Not a damn minute late. The sooner I get all these vermin out of my house, the better.'

Holt had always wanted to spit on the man's face, but the colonel paid too handsomely, so he simply bowed.

'I won't fail you, sir.'

Colonel Grenville straightened his jacket, casting Holt a warning stare, and went back into the parlour.

As he shut the door, Holt strived to catch a last glimpse of the young Leonora, setting up the photographic camera. He also saw the nervous faces gathered round the table and the dark liquid in the decanter amidst the candles.

He pocketed the money and went straight to the carriage. Just as he crossed the garden gates, Holt cast a last look at the façade. He saw a flicker of intense light coming from the parlour's window, surely from the camera's flash powder. After that, the room went as dark as a grave, like all the others in the empty house. Holt thought he'd heard a hoarse, deep growl coming from the parlour, and felt a shiver.

The colonel had told him nothing about that meeting, but Holt knew the family far too well. Something monstrous was about to happen within that room. Something far too horrible to be spoken out loud.

The less he knew, the better.

PART I

The Crime

Cut out from *The Scotsman*

Saturday 14 September 1889, afternoon issue

THE DAWNING HORROR OF MORNINGSIDE: SIX DEAD

The genteel neighbourhood of Morningside awoke to sheer horror when Mr Alexander Holt, personal valet to the illustrious Colonel James R. Grenville, walked into his master's house to a most gruesome spectacle.

Six bodies, his patron included, lay dead in the house's main parlour. The discovery was made at approximately 7.45 a.m., when Mr Holt returned to attend his master's morning necessities.

Upon being notified by a dismayed Mr Holt, police officers hastily made their way to the site. There were no signs of violence or mutilation, and the police are still unable to ascertain the cause of the deaths. All bodies have been transported to CID headquarters, and a forensic investigation is pending.

More intriguing still is the fact that a seventh person, a middle-aged female foreigner, lay unconscious amongst the six deceased. Initially thought a seventh loss, the well-built lady recovered her senses and, as if by the most unlikely of miracles, turned out to be unscathed. This very correspondent saw the woman in question walk out of the Grenville residence, unaided and without any sign of injury or illness.

The identity of the lady was confirmed as *Mme Katerina* of No. 9 Cattle Market. She is well known in Edinburgh's less reputable circles for her flourishing business as a fortune teller. It is understood that the honourable Colonel Grenville and his fine guests were attending a séance conducted by the aforementioned woman. Mr Holt refused to confirm this.

The peculiar foreigner, now sensibly regarded as chief suspect for the deaths, shall remain under police custody whilst this heinous crime is investigated.

Cries for justice can already be heard amongst the neighbouring residents. Colonel Grenville was a much-admired member of the community, best remembered for the gallantry and valour shown during the recent military campaigns in Southern Africa. The full list of the victims' names has not yet been made public, but it is presumed that amongst the other fatalities were the good colonel's wife and some of his extended relatives. Colonel Grenville leaves three young children, aged between six and twelve.

Robert Trevelyan, CID's recently appointed superintendent, refused to provide any further details, but this correspondent heard from a very reliable source that the case may fall under the purview of local detective Adolphus McGray, more popularly known as 'Nine-Nails'.

I

Sunday 15 September 1889

04.45 a.m.
Gloucestershire

I knew the carriage trip was going to be dreadful, but the corpse made it all the worse.

Propped up next to me, his pale hands resting on his lap, his bowler hat still on his head, he could have passed for another passenger. I looked at his face, slightly bent forwards and swaying softly, following the erratic movements of the carriage. His cheeks were grey and dry, even veiny, and blue rings darkened his shut eyelids. Other than that, he looked as though he were simply dozing off; resting his mind and waiting to alight, ready to jump off and demand a cigar and a warm bath.

I wrapped myself in my coat, feeling as cold as him, my own skin only a little less pale. I even felt tempted to wrap him in one of the blankets kept under the seats, but realised how foolish that would be.

In the end, I only leaned a little closer, stretching my arm to straighten his scuffed hat.

And then he opened his eyes.

*

I jumped up at once, panting and feeling the cold sweat running down my temples.

My bedroom was as dark as my dream, with only a ray of moonlight filtering through a fine gap between the curtains. I could still see my uncle's glazy eyes, as clear as if they were floating right before my face, so I rushed to the gas lamp and let out a relieved breath when its gentle glow lit my chamber.

I saw the preposterous hour on the mantelpiece clock and rubbed my eyes in frustration, knowing I would not be able to sleep again. I thought of asking Layton for some tea, but preferred not to; my old valet had had very difficult times too. Besides, hot beverages had done very little to improve my general mood in recent days. I rose nonetheless, and pulled the curtains aside to peer through the window. Mile after mile of darkened fields and woods opened before me: my uncle's – *late* uncle's – large estate.

It was a peaceful, starry night, and the moonlight drew the landscape in beautiful shades of blue and silver.

Just like that terrible night at the Highlands. The night Uncle met his demise, surrounded by those ghastly torches.

I shook my head and turned away from the view, or those images would make their way into my head like they'd done almost every night ever since.

I looked at the pile of half-read books on the bedside table and made to pick one up, but gave up even before touching them. I was sick of staring at the same page for hours, unable to take in the words, or all of a sudden finding myself ten pages ahead without the faintest memory of what I'd just read.

With nothing else to do, I paced for the next hour.

'This is what Nine-Nails must feel like every night,' I mumbled at some point. I wondered if he too had nightmares, if he might still dream of his dead parents, or the moment when his deranged sister had cut his finger off.

I'd been ignoring his correspondence, not even opening the letters and telegrams, secretly hoping that he'd become tired of my apathy and dismiss me. I knew I would never be so lucky.

Just as the sky began to clear, there was a soft rapping at my door. It was the tall, bony Layton, already bringing my morning coffee. The bags under his eyes told me he too had had a sleepless night. No wonder – before working for me, he had served Uncle Maurice for more than ten years and had also been terribly affected by his death.

As he displayed the service on the table, and before I could remark on the early hour, he pointed his long, aquiline nose at the window.

'It appears you have visitors, sir.'

I went back to the window and saw a carriage approach at full speed. It was pulled by four horses, so it must be a real emergency. The carriage soon reached Uncle's manor, and just as Layton passed me a cup of coffee, I saw an unmistakable figure emerge.

'Damn my luck!' I grumbled.

'Shall I let him in, sir?'

'He will make his way in even if you refuse,' I predicted, and the moment I finished the sentence, I saw Nine-Nails climb up the entrance steps and push the main door open.

'Tell the staff I want them to start locking that door,' I told Layton. I could almost hear my late uncle cry, *Lock the doors? This is England!*

A moment later, Layton was showing McGray into my chamber.

I should be used to his scruffy stubble, his clothes garish and creased, and his hair as messy as if he'd galloped through a blizzard. However, surrounded by my quaint rugs and furnishings, he looked as out of place as a bristly grouse tossed into a basket of fine linen.

'You look positively dreadful,' I said.

McGray frowned. 'Och, I've been travelling all night! *Ye* look much fucking worse in yer silken shimmy and freshly out o' bed.'

It would have been pointless to argue; my dressing gown was indeed silk damask.

'Enough of the niceties,' I said. 'Have some coffee.'

He wrinkled his nose at it. 'Anything stronger?'

'McGray, it is barely after six in the morning.'

'And yer point is . . .?'

Layton bowed then and went to fetch him some liquor.

McGray lounged in one of the two armchairs, stretched his long legs and arms, and cast an evaluating look at the oak panelling and four-poster bed.

'Nice pile o' rubble ye've been sleeping in, Frey! Sort o' gives grounds to yer bloody snobbery.' He clicked his tongue. 'Sort of.'

I half smiled, sitting down and sipping my coffee.

'I have spent many happy Christmases here,' was all I could say.

McGray nodded. 'So . . . is this all yers now?'

That was a fair guess. Uncle Maurice had never married, and the only child he'd fathered (as far as he'd told me) had died very young.

'Uncle said so more than once, but knowing what he . . . *was* like, he may not have left his legal affairs in proper order. My brother Laurence may litigate to get his cut.'

'Laurence? The same twat yer fiancée left ye for?'

I clashed my cup on the saucer. 'Do you always have to remark on that? You know very bloody well who he is.'

'There, there! Nae need to snap. What about yer younger brothers?'

'Elgie and Oliver were not his blood relatives.'

'Och, right! Their mum is that bitch o' yer stepmother.'

'Indeed. And even if they had a claim, I doubt they'd be interested in managing an estate like this. Elgie is too artistic to be practical. Oliver is . . . just Oliver.'

Layton came back then, bringing McGray a decanter of single malt, a good measure already poured in a tumbler.

'Yer done with the funeral, I guess.'

I let out a long sigh. 'The saddest affair you could imagine. Elgie was the only other relative who attended. The rest were Uncle's creditors and tenants, all more interested in asking whether his death would disturb their businesses.'

Layton discreetly walked out, perhaps affected by my words.

I put my coffee on the table and rubbed my forehead. 'McGray, I have a million matters to deal with right now. I am sorry you had to come all this way, but you will understand it is impossible for me to go back to Scotland after this.'

I did not look at him at first, expecting one of his typical outbursts. He, however, said nothing, and when I did turn my eyes to him, I found him biting his lip. The coarse, unsinkable Nine-Nails McGray looked shy and uneasy for the first time.

'Am afraid ye have to.'

A deeper silence followed, each moment increasing my anxiety.

'What – what do you mean?'

McGray could not have sounded more sombre. 'The prime minister wants to keep our subdivision open. And us handy.'

'The most illustrious *Commission for the Elucidation of Unsolved Cases Presumably Related to the Odd and Ghostly*?' I cried, the interminable name rolling off my tongue at speed. 'Why on earth would *anyone*, let alone the prime minister, want to keep that pit of manure open?'

I was expecting Nine-Nails to pounce on me. That subdivision was his baby, created for the sole purpose of finding what had driven his sister insane, and almost entirely funded from

33

his own pocket. He, however, remained silent, giving time for the answer to creep slowly into my head.

I hunched forwards, mumbling as I buried my face in my hands. 'The Lancashire affair?'

'Possibly . . .' McGray downed his drink in one gulp. 'Dammit, I cannae lie to ye. I am certain. I spoke with the new superintendent. He received a letter from the PM himself. Lord Salisbury didnae give explanations; he just told him that our department must stay open.'

At once I stood up and began pacing.

The previous January, whilst following another case all the way to Lancashire, we had accidentally discovered that the prime minister's son had turbulent dealings with a coven of so-called witches – well, McGray called them that. To me they were nothing but crafty smugglers and charlatans, so dangerous and influential the Borgias would have envied their organisation. It was clear now that Lord Salisbury himself owed them 'favours'.

McGray tried to soothe me. 'It might be nothing, Frey. Salisbury maybe just wants us handy as a precaution.'

I let out a strident laugh. 'Oh yes, nothing! Believe that, McGray, if it makes you happy.'

Somehow I already knew that Lord Salisbury and his dubious affairs would come back to haunt us, and it would turn out to be one of the worst nightmares of our lives. However, it would not happen for a while.

'Frey,' said Nine-Nails, if possible looking more sombre, 'there's another reason I came.'

'Another reason!' I reached for the decanter and 'strengthened' my black coffee. Sod the time. 'An even worse emergency? A bout of the bubonic plague, perhaps?'

He was searching in his breast pocket.

'This is a proper emergency. The clock's ticking.'

'Oh really? Who is about to die?'

Nine-Nails grimaced as he produced a piece of newspaper. 'Madame Katerina.'

I had downed half the cup before he said that.

'Why, your swindling clairvoyant?'

'Aye.'

'Who also happens to brew toxic ale to render pedlars blind? Is she in trouble? My, oh my, how bloody unexpected!'

'It's really delicate, Frey.' McGray grumbled, unfolding the sheet on the table. 'They might take her case to the High Court. She may hang!'

I snorted. 'A miserable and squalid life followed by early death? Well, that is just what happens when you move to Scotland.'

'Frey . . .'

'And when they put you in a box and bury you, that is the warmest you will ever be.'

'Och, I forgot ye can whine like an Ophelia when ye set to it!'

'And six feet underground is also the safest—'

'Frey, can ye shut it for a second and read this?'

I grabbed the cut-out, ready to toss it into the dying fire. However, even before I could crumple it, the headline's obnoxiously wide lettering caught my full attention.

2

'Have you questioned her?' I asked as we walked out of the manor. I was still astonished as to how fast I'd managed to sort out my luggage.

'Nae, they took her straight to—'

'Did you go to this Grenville man's house?'

'Nae yet. I'm—'

'Did you at least manage to have a word with that valet? Or the officers he called?'

'*Nae!* Frey, I'm—'

'Oh, for goodness' sake, Nine-Nails! What did you do then?'

He slapped the back of my head. 'I'm fucking trying to tell ye I didnae get time to do anything at all! The new blasted superintendent wanted me to come and get ye first. His very words were, *Bring Ian Percival Frey here, else—*'

'What? He asked you to come here when there is a crime like this to investigate?'

He cupped both hands like a pair of scales. 'Urgent letter from the prime minister . . . Saving a dubious gypsy's life . . .'

'I see. Do you at least know if the corpses are properly—?'

'Frey, what the hell! Are ye bringing yer entire new buggery manor brick by brick?'

He made a sensible point. The servants were bringing three more of my chests to the already laden carriage.

'I parted Edinburgh with all my belongings. I had no intention of going back. I even settled my rent with your beloved Lady Glass.'

McGray's jaw dropped. 'Ye were leaving for good, ye wee trickle o' slimy snot?'

'Lady Anne might call me the same when I tell her I want the property back. And I am sure she will try to treble the price.'

Layton came to me then. 'Sir, what shall we do with your mare? The stables man says it will take him a while to—'

'Ye brought Philippa too?' McGray squealed.

'I just told you I had no intention of—'

'Och, forget it. Ye can send for her later. Ye won't be able to mount her a lot anyway. The weather's already turning for the worse.'

I blew inside my cheeks. 'In more ways than I can tell . . .'

I knew the carriage trip was going to be dreadful, but McGray's unease made it all the worse. He kept reading the cut-out over and over, every time emphasising a different passage and voicing a new speculation. Thankfully, the ride to Gloucester's train station was not too long, and from then on it became much easier to ignore Nine-Nails, even if we did miss the day's last service to Scotland.

We spent the night in Gloucester to ensure we'd catch the first train in the morning. McGray was of course keen to talk, but I categorically rebuffed his offer of drams and locked myself in a separate room. At least the station's inn was clean and very comfortable.

The following day, the service to Scotland set off with considerable delay. Then we had to change trains in sooty Birmingham, having to run for dear life to catch our connection.

One of my trunks was even dropped onto the rails and very nearly burst open. And the second leg of the journey was worse: our train sat still for three full hours in the outskirts of Carlisle, no explanations given. By the time we made it to Edinburgh, the sun was already setting.

As soon as we stepped off the wagon, I saw that autumn was setting in with annoying punctuality; the trees of Princes Street Gardens were already shedding their leaves, and the winds brought gelid chills from the north-east. I looked bitterly at the uniform layer of grey clouds, which might not let through a single stream of sunlight until April. The thickset castle, atop its craggy mount, made me think of a chubby old man in brown, sooty tweed, lounging in an armchair and smoking a pipe as he watched the ages go by.

'Here I am again,' I said in a resigned sigh, wrapping up tighter in my overcoat. 'Against all expectations . . .'

I sent Layton to Great King Street with all my belongings, and paid a young boy to deliver a note to Lady Anne Ardglass.

'Begging that auld bitch to let yer valet in?' McGray asked. He carried no luggage at all, and I envied his light pace.

'Indeed. I would try some other lodgings, but she owns all the respectable properties in this tattered town.'

'If she kicks ye out ye can come to Moray Place for a wee while. Joan will be glad to have ye there.'

I could not contain a sigh at the mention of her name. Joan had been my maid for eight years, before meeting McGray's elderly butler George and deciding she wanted to live in sin with him. I still missed her coffee, her delicious roasts and sometimes even her irreverent gossip.

The station's clock struck seven right then.

'It is too late to go to the City Chambers,' I said.

'Indeedy. Nae chance we'll get anything meaningful done today, but we still have time to see Katerina.'

I sighed, for the prospect of meeting that woman – again – did not thrill me. And in the following weeks I would be talking to her much more than I'd ever wished for.

'We better hurry, then.'

'Nah, it's fine. I've made a few agreements with the laddies at Calton Hill.'

'*Calton* – is she already in Calton Hill Jail?'

'Aye, for her own safety. They took her to the City Chambers, but as soon as *The Scotsman* published the story, we had a mob of dribbling idiots trying to catch a glimpse. A couple o' drunken sods even threw stones at the building.'

'Dear Lord. We have to be careful or this case will become a spectacle.'

'Might be too late for that, Percy.'

Calton Hill Jail was a deceptive building.

With a set of rounded towers that looked more like a painting of Camelot, enclosed by sturdy walls, and with a gate surrounded by medieval-style battlements, anyone would have mistaken it for a fairy-tale castle. It also stood proudly on the craggier edge of Calton Hill, and even its address – Number 1 Regent Road – sounded prestigious.

Nothing could be further from the truth.

The kingly towers were the residence and offices of the governor, and were indeed lavish; however, the cell wings were dingy, damp and overcrowded, understandably feared by those on the wrong side of the law. Some of those sentenced to death were still chained to the walls while they awaited execution.

I'd been there only once, in February, when a pathetic prisoner claimed that the mysterious hole on the floor of his cell had been opened up by a stone-eating gnome. Even McGray had laughed at the tale – I both laughed and retched upon hearing that a steel spoon had miraculously appeared in the prisoner's ablutions.

I recognised the gloomy esplanade at the front. Hangings were carried out there, and even though executions were no longer public, people still climbed to the top of Calton Hill to have a peek. I looked north and saw the steep slope of the mount, its edges blurry behind the mist. From there, the mobs possibly had a better view than their morbid fellows a century ago, when hangings took place at Mercat Cross, in the middle of Edinburgh's High Street. More comfortable too. I imagined people sitting on the grassy slope, maybe even drinking and picnicking, as they watched a miserable wretch writhing in the gibbet.

A guard came to receive us, greeting McGray with deference. The man had a weathered face and a deep scar running all the way from his temple to his chin. His eyes, however, had a benevolent air.

'I thought ye were nae coming, sir,' he said as he led us through the darkened corridors.

'Delays, Malcolm,' McGray answered. I saw that he discreetly passed him a one-pound note.

Malcolm took us to a small questioning room.

'Please wait here. I'll fetch her right away.'

We stepped in and sat at a battered table. The air somehow seemed to become colder and colder as we waited. A moment later, Malcolm came back, Katerina by his side.

'Oh, God . . .' I let out when I first saw her.

I was expecting the tingling mass of multicoloured shawls, veils and pendants, the cunning green eyes and the mordant smile. Instead, the poor woman was clad in a ragged grey dress, handcuffed and walking in a stoop.

Without her thick layers of mascara and fake eyelashes, she looked at least a decade older. She was not wearing any of the studs or rings that usually decked her nose, eyebrow and earlobes, and the empty piercings looked like wrinkly slits on her saggy skin. Her hair was wrapped tightly under a faded black cloth, a few blonde and greyish locks sticking out like the bristles of a brush. Her menacing fingernails had been cut short, and the black varnish was flaking off the jagged edges.

There was something else missing, and it took me a moment to realise it. Her protruding bosom, famous throughout Lothian and most of the time scantly covered, now could only be described as empty woollen stockings under the jail dress.

'I know,' she said, for I must have stared open-mouthed. 'I don't look as pretty as that night you came to my divination room with a bottle of wine.'

McGray gasped. 'He did *what?*'

I rolled my eyes. 'Could we please focus on the case? This is hardly the time to—'

'Och, ye dog!' he said, elbowing me at the ribs.

Katerina was sitting down then, smirking. It was as if she had no energy left for one of her usual cackles.

She squeezed McGray's hand. 'I'm so glad to see you, my boy. I've not laughed in days.'

Judging from how hoarse her voice was, it appeared she had not spoken to anyone either.

'How are they treating ye?' McGray asked. His blue eyes were full of concern.

Katerina clicked her tongue. 'The food is rat's shit. Looks like it too.' She nodded in my direction. 'Your English rose here would be dead by now.'

'Don't tell me they've beaten ye, or I'll kick them in the arse so fuckin' hard they'll be able to taste my boots.' He said it looking straight into the guard's eyes. Malcolm gulped.

Katerina managed a brief chuckle, and for a moment her green eyes glowed with their usual cunning. 'Thanks, Adolphus.

They were a little rough on me at first, but they haven't dared hit me. They're afraid I'll cast a curse on their pricks or something.'

Malcolm gulped again.

'Ye can go, lad,' Nine-Nails said, and the guard was only too happy to leave.

At once I lounged back, letting out a tired sigh.

'What a fine quandary you've got yourself into.'

Katerina simply looked at Nine-Nails.

'Why did you bring him? He'll tell me I'm a mad hag.'

'He's not a complete waste o' space,' said McGray, kicking me under the table. 'And contrary to his looks, he did pick up a thing or two about the law in his Cambridge college for petunia-sniffing dandies.'

'Thank you,' I said, looking directly at Katerina. 'Now, I need to ask you this, madam. Did you do it?'

'Did I . . .?'

'Did you kill them?'

I might as well have slapped her in the face. She looked up, astounded, and McGray slammed both hands on the table.

'Of course she didnae!' he yelped. 'She—!'

'*Let the bloody woman speak!*' I shouted over him, with a roaring volume that surprised even me.

As the silence lingered, Katerina bit her lips, lowering her head.

'I didn't harm anyone,' she mumbled.

I nodded. 'Very well. In that case, we need you to tell us exactly what happened.'

We were in for a riveting tale.

3

'This young woman, Leonora Willberg, sent me a letter a month ago. She and her aunt are good clients. Well . . . they *were*.'

'Did they both die that night?' I asked.

'No, just Leonora. Her aunt passed on a few years ago, her father too; but the girl kept looking for me. She was very interested in my arts.'

'Was she?'

'Yes, all her life. She told me her grandmother also had the eye.'

I looked into my breast pocket and produced my little notebook, struggling to keep my face neutral. 'Why did they ask you to perform the – session?'

'Were they trying to contact anyone in particular?' McGray added.

'Yes. The grandmother, I just told you. They called her Grannie Alice.'

'Ye ken what for? Was it just to talk to her? 'Cause they missed her?'

I thought that would be the reason, as séances had become very popular in recent years. Even Queen Victoria was rumoured to hold them frequently, to chat with her beloved Albert (McGray and I knew for a fact that the rumours were true).

Katerina's answer, however, was rather unexpected.

'That's what Leonora told me, but she lied.'

'She what?' McGray said.

Katerina lowered her voice. 'They needed to ask her something. Something very specific.'

I sighed as discreetly as possible. 'Who told you so?'

'Nobody. They didn't have to. I felt it.'

McGray jumped in exactly as I was about to blurt out my best sarcasm.

'Tell us more.'

Katerina shook her head. 'Oh, it was all over the place, Adolphus. In Leonora's note, in the valet they sent to fetch me, on the tablecloth, in the parlour walls . . . Oh, that house!'

'Did ye visit before the séance?'

'Yes, you know I always do when people ask me to work in their houses.' She shook again, this time her entire body, as if suddenly hit by an icy draught. 'There is something floating there, my boy; it's like a stench I could sense even before I walked in. There's hatred . . . Guilt . . . A lie . . . Something hellish that stained that air years ago and hasn't faded.'

There was a long silence: Katerina apparently recovering from a strike of emotion, McGray meditating with an expression worthy of St John upon writing the Book of Revelation, while I gripped my pencil.

'I had to ask Leonora to cleanse all the rooms with blessed candles,' Katerina went on. 'It barely did the job. And I had to take precautions I rarely do.'

'Precautions?' I asked.

'Protect my soul; my spirit. A séance is so . . . So . . .'

She struggled to find the right word, so McGray stepped in.

'Intimate. I ken. Crudely put, it's almost like getting into bed with someone. If they have – let's say, *lice*, yer goin' to catch it.'

I raised an eyebrow. 'So . . . You protected yourself from catching spiritual syphilis?'

'*Dammit!*' she cried, standing up and banging both palms on the table. I was glad her fingernails were no more, or she would have ripped my eyes out. 'Yes! You may laugh if you want, but that protection saved my life. My life and my soul! Those six other bastards are burning in hell now.'

I raised a conciliatory hand. 'Very well, let's not linger on that right now. There are still many details we need to know.'

McGray nodded at her. Katerina took a few infuriated breaths, but then sat down again.

'You mentioned that this Leonora contacted you over a month ago, yet the séance took place last Friday?'

'Yes. You have to wait for the stars to align. The best conjunction is different for every soul.'

My scribbling stopped, I took in the words, and then resumed the writing. 'Can you name the people who attended?'

She looked sternly at me. 'You mean the people who died?'

That required no answer, so I said nothing, and Katerina began counting with her fingers.

'There was Leonora . . . the uncle who moved into her house after her parents died . . .'

'What was his name?'

'Everyone called him either Willberg or *Mr* Willberg.'

'Who else?'

'I recognised the grandmother's widower, a really frail old man . . . Mr Shaw. Hector Shaw.'

I wrote it down. 'Go on.'

'There was also this bossy gent everyone kept calling Colonel . . .'

'That would be Colonel Grenville,' I said, recalling the newspaper. 'Was he a relative?'

'An in-law. His wife was present too; another granddaughter of that Alice woman.'

'That makes her Hector Shaw's daughter?'

45

'Yes, she called him Father. I think her name was Martha. Lovely jewellery she wore. And there was also a mousy, lanky man. Leonora's uncle ordered him around all the time. His name was Bertrand.'

I counted. 'Very well, that accounts for all the bodies found. Did any of them look odd to you?'

'I told you already, they were all damned souls.'

'Even the young Leonora, so interested in your arts?'

'Oh, yes! She was always asking more than she ought to. On the night, she even brought a camera.'

'*There was a photographic camera?*' McGray cried. I too was surprised, and underlined that in my notebook.

'Yes,' Katerina replied. 'Leonora said spirits sometimes show in the pictures.'

She snorted at that.

'Ye don't think that's possible?' McGray asked.

'I wouldn't know. Only rich folk can afford those damn things.'

'Yet you do not seem to like the idea of photographing the dead,' I remarked.

'Too right. It's a violation! The souls of the recently deceased sometimes get trapped in glass and mirrors. If it's true that spirits appear in photographs, perhaps it's because the machines can catch them too.'

I simply stared at her with my lips slightly parted. I could not believe that such rampant ignorance still existed in our times. Nevertheless, the presence of a camera offered tantalising opportunities.

'Were any photographs taken on the night?' I asked.

'Yes.'

'How many?'

'Oh, I don't know exactly. I was focused on my job. Several, I think. Before and during the session.'

I underlined that too, while McGray rubbed his hands in excitement.

'We must look for that camera, Frey. It must still be at the—' he had to bite his lip not to say *crime scene*. 'At the parlour. They told me the house was locked. Everything there should still be untouched.'

'I bloody hope so,' I said, followed by a sigh as I turned to Katerina. 'Now to the point, madam. Describe the séance itself.'

Her expression darkened and she took short, sharp breaths, readying herself to tell us the tale. The one newspapers would have cheated and killed for. The one everyone in Edinburgh was so desperate to hear.

4

'I could tell we would be successful, even before I set foot into the house. The spirit was angry. Angry and keen to meet her relatives.

'I checked the walls, the air. Everything seemed fit enough for the communion. Barely, as I told them, but the spirit would overcome any barriers.

'That so-called colonel dispatched his servant and we were left alone. Leonora took a photograph of everyone before we gathered at the table. I could feel this angered the spirit – the girl's frivolity; her keenness; her disrespect; the fact that she only wanted those bloody photographs to show them off later . . . *Spirits have to cross worlds to commune with us!* That's painful to them!

'I said nothing, though I should have. We moved on. I told them to lock the doors and turn all the lights off, except for the candles.

'I had asked them to prepare an offering too. You always need something to tempt the spirits. Sometimes it can be anything the poor souls liked in life – their favourite scent or drink or food. Sometimes they are so keen to see their loved ones their mere presence is enough . . .

'Not this time. I knew the spirit would demand the most precious sacrifice. Grannie Alice wanted their blood. I had told them so.

'Before I arrived, they had all cut themselves and poured a little of their blood into a decanter. We all held hands in a circle, and I began my work.

'Either that colonel had not bled enough, or Alice wanted a greater sacrifice from him. I let them know. Leonora and the man's wife gasped, and this other man – Leonora's uncle – smirked, all smug. The colonel didn't even protest. He went for the . . . He went for a knife, and bled himself again. Much more than needed and without as much as a flinch. He wanted to show off his strength.

'And then we were ready. I could feel Grannie Alice was so keen, *so* keen. She was like this horrible oppression growing in my innards. Cold. Malicious.

'I closed my eyes, called her name . . . told her we had all gathered there to meet her.

'The room went cold right then. I had shut my eyes, but I could see the flicker of the candles. It was as if a draught was about to blow them off . . . Yet we could feel nothing; nothing other than the deathly cold.

'Then we waited. She was there, ready, but she didn't speak to me immediately. I felt she was watching them.

'She . . . I don't know how to describe it . . . It felt as if she was – *feeding* on their fear. It was a revolting sensation, Adolphus. Like watching a wild dog devouring bloody entrails.

'I tried to calm her down, but Alice was pure fire. The room got colder and colder, and then she spoke through me.

'She said, "*How dare you?* How dare you summon me?"

'I hardly recognised my own voice. I felt her anger as if it were mine, bursting out through my throat.

'They had all jumped. Someone knocked the table and I think I heard some of the candles fall over. Then the old man asked if it was her. When she said yes, he choked. I thought he was about to faint.

'He asked her if she was in peace, but she cackled . . . Well, *I* cackled for her.

'She said, "I'm burning. Like you all will too."

'The old man babbled some words I didn't understand, but Alice did. He was begging for her forgiveness.

'She said, "You're all wicked! Perverse! You're all damned!"

'Then Leonora broke the circle. I didn't see her, but I felt it. I thought the connection would break and Alice would leave, but she didn't. Her grip was so strong.

'I heard the bursts of the powder flash. Leonora was using that damn camera, the foolish girl! Alice was furious. But not as furious as she got when the colonel opened his mouth.

'He said, "Ask her where it is! Ask her what she did with it!"

'I wish he hadn't said so. She wanted me to spit out the most vulgar, horrible cursing, but I resisted.

'I began shaking. I was holding the colonel's hand and the hand of Leonora's uncle. I could feel how hard I grasped them; they were grunting in pain. Thank goodness I wasn't holding the old man's hand or I would've crushed his bones!

'The colonel insisted, and so did the other man.

'I felt Alice pushing me forwards. Some noise came out of my mouth, like – a growl. Something horrible. The colonel's wife was weeping in horror.

'Alice made me say, "I'll never tell. *Never!* You're all doomed. You'll all die."

'Everyone gasped then. They couldn't even scream.

'I thought she was lying. She wouldn't be the first spirit I caught telling a lie. When evil souls want to cause harm, the easiest way is just by telling lies. I think Alice read my thoughts, because she said it again, and this time I knew she meant it.

'She made me roar, *"You'll all die tonight!"*

'I've never been possessed like that. She was about to harm us all, my body first of all.

'I opened my eyes, which usually breaks the link, but she still wouldn't leave! She clutched my heart and my guts in a grip of fire. I couldn't even see properly; everything was shrouded by my veil.

'I wanted to scream and shout, but all I could do was blurt out her cursing.

'And then I saw something right in front of me. It was like a shadow taking shape in-between the candles; something solid sprouting from thin air. I could not believe it at first, but there it was . . .

'The hand of Satan.

'I . . . didn't *want* it to be true, but the others saw it too. They were screaming and pointing at it.

'There were his fingers, all twisted and charred. And his skin stank like sulphur . . . It was the devil coming from fire itself. The fire was bringing him to life.

'I leaned forwards to blow out the candles, but the two men wouldn't let go of me. They were petrified.

'And then the hand leapt down, those horrible fingers clasped the tablecloth, and it crawled in my direction.

'Alice's voice was everywhere. Everyone was screaming. There was an explosion of light . . . and . . .

'And then . . .

'I saw no more.'

5

Katerina was exhausted, so we let her go then. As the guards took her, McGray once more threatened their manly parts if they mistreated her in any way. Right before she left, Katerina grasped McGray's four-fingered hand, and looked at him with misty eyes.

'Help me, my boy. I beg you. We go a long way back . . . You know me. You know I *couldn't*—'

She could not finish the sentence, and McGray also seemed too affected to speak. He simply patted her on the shoulder and let her go.

Again we walked across the jail's esplanade. This time, I looked more intently at the flagstones, and saw the clear marks left by the gallows poles. They clearly had been installed at the very same spot for the past seventy years, ever since the jail had been built.

McGray spoke as soon as we were out of the officers' hearing range.

'What d'ye think happened?'

'I have no idea. I can think of a dozen ways six people can be killed at once in a locked room, but the fact that only *one* lived to tell the tale . . . No wonder everyone in town is scratching their heads. No weapons, no injuries, and the only living witness is – *her*.'

'Ye don't believe her story, do ye?'

'Do you even have to ask?' I opened my notebook. 'Allow me to summarise her statement. *An evil spirit killed everyone but her. Her charms and rituals and talismans saved her* . . . McGray, this sounds as ridiculous as that drunken farmer who swore he was possessed by the devil when his wife found him frolicking with the milkmaid.'

McGray anxiously looked for a cigar in his pocket. 'Percy, d'ye really think she killed six people?'

I grunted. 'Well, she may be a trickster, a fraud, a charlatan, a roguish lowlife, a—'

'But?'

'But no, I do not think her capable of murder. And she had no apparent motive to—'

'See? What she says is true. I've studied those things. Everything she said about spirits' behaviour is true. Everything.'

'Oh, for goodness' sake, McGray!' I snapped, startling the officers who were opening the gates for us. 'It's not me you have to convince! Let me remind you this is an indictable offence. Unless we find something blatantly obvious in that room or those bodies, Katerina will be tried at the High Court. How do you think the judge and the jury will react to her story?'

It was McGray's turn to snort. When he lit his cigar, his hands shook with frustration.

'If you really want to help her,' I resumed, 'I suggest you stop thinking of evil spirits and start looking for a proper explanation. Something that will stand up in court.

'And if that fails, claiming insanity might be her best choice. Perhaps you should go to the asylum and talk to Dr Clouston. He might be willing to sign a certificate for her. Only, remember you will need two. And he might be stuck with her in the asylum for the rest of her life.'

McGray shook his head. 'Clouston will never agree to that. He's all duty and morals.'

I chuckled. 'Is he? He has signed questionable certificates before.'

'*One!* One certificate. And that sod was clearly mad back then!'

I did not have the energy to debate our older cases. 'I am trying to give you alternatives.'

McGray puffed at his cigar as we descended the steep Calton Hill. I could tell he was doing his best to keep his temper. He understood I was still mourning my dear uncle, and how fragile my patience was.

At last, he took a deep breath. 'I'll go see Clouston if we come to that, even if I ken what he'll say. Right now—'

'Right now, we have to plan our course of action, prioritise the evidence and discuss our theories. *Real* theories. I have a couple already.'

As I said so, we made it to the intersection at North Bridge; to the left was the shabby and medieval Old Town, to the right the wealthy New Town.

'Fancy a dram and a plate o' stovies at the Ensign?' McGray said. 'I'm starving and I've nae had a single drink since yesterday. We can ponder there.'

'No. I am going to the New Club. I need a decent meal and I do not want to eat it from a sticky table.'

'Frey—'

'*I will rephrase,*' I said with a raised voice. 'I *am* going to the New Club. If you want to discuss the case this evening, you can follow me. And if you are in anyway unhappy about it, you can file a complaint to whichever bloody clown is leading your blasted Scottish police these days. See how much I care.'

And I stepped faster towards the emerging lights of Princes Street.

'Och, I liked ye better before ye grew a pair!'

In his gaudy tartan trousers, ragged overcoat and grimy shirt, and seated right at the centre of the New Club's main dining hall, Nine-Nails was like a flashing beacon. And his eating was as sordid as his clothes: squelching, smacking his lips, hacking at his teeth with his fingernails . . . and when he was done butchering his steak, he let out a mighty belch that almost shook the windows. I had to move my wine glass away from the path of debris.

'Nae bad, this coo,' he said. 'A wee bit raw, though.'

I sipped my wine and said nothing, enduring the reproachful stares of the other diners, all dressed in black and white. I could tell how worried McGray really was; despite his outward nonchalance, he could not repress a nervous flicker in his eyes.

'So, Madame Katerina mentioned you two go back some years,' I said as soon as the waiter cleared our plates. 'I've never asked how long you have known her.'

McGray drank half his pint of ale (which the waiters had had to fetch from a nearby pub) before answering.

'Five years, I think. She was one o' the first clairvoyants I ever met. After my sister's . . . troubles.'

He stared at the stump of his missing finger, and I saw no need of bringing up the Amy affair one more time.

'How did you first hear of her? About Katerina, I mean. She hardly strikes me as the sort of *professional* that advertises her services in *The Scotsman*.'

Nine-Nails smirked. 'She came to me. She'd heard my story and she offered help. I doubted her at first, but then she told me her list o' fancy clients. She still works for many preening new-towners.'

'Is that so? We have been to her . . . premises several times. I have never seen one respectable client around.'

'Oh, that's 'cause she's brilliant. She either goes to them, or only receives them at certain times, when she's sure nobody's watching. I bet even the Lord Provost has consulted her at some point.'

'I remember you telling me once that she was different from all the other seers . . . How so?'

He half smiled, at once with sourness and nostalgia. 'Ye believe I'm a gullible halfwit.'

'Oh? What have I *ever* said to make you think that?'

'Och, shut it. I could see when fortune tellers were trying to swindle me. They went straight to the money or said they could feel my tragic past. Of course they fucking did! It was all over the papers and people wouldnae stop talking about it. Remember it was all fresh news back then.'

I preferred not to add that he was a local legend even today. Tomorrow, everyone at New Club would be commenting on the visit of the crass Nine-Nails McGray.

'Katerina was different,' he said. 'She was the only one who admitted she heard my story from gossip. And then – she . . .'

He stared at his ale for a moment.

'She divined something . . . Something that happened on the night my sister did this.' He tapped at the small stump. 'Something only *I* had seen.'

I very nearly gasped.

'You mean she knew that you . . .' I leaned closer and whispered, 'That you thought you saw the devil?'

'Aye.'

I nodded. Katerina indeed had an annoying history of telling things she could not possibly have known.

'She described what I saw in detail, and she said that the . . . *vision* was key to bringing Pansy back. She said I should dig deeper and I might find a means to cure her.'

'Is that how your obsession with the occult began? After Katerina's suggestions?'

My tone betrayed me. Had that woman simply manipulated him? She *was* clever. She would have seen that McGray was a wounded wreck, prompt to believe anyone who offered him some hope. The woman herself had told me she had a talent for knowing what people wanted to hear and that she used it when it suited her; nothing to do with *inner eyes* or otherworldly energies.

McGray stared at his drink. Either he was looking for words to express something or was struggling to decide whether to talk or not. In the end, he twitched.

'I was researching witchcraft and the occult already, but I went much deeper after I met her. Katerina herself helped me source books and passed me useful contacts. And if ye think she only did so to rip me off, let me tell ye she's never charged me a penny to tell me things about Pansy. I only pay her when we need help for police matters.'

To me that would be reason enough to doubt her motivations. We had consulted her many times in the past year, and from the department's books I knew exactly how much she received for her 'consulting' services. Most of that money, predictably, came from McGray's pockets.

I kept all those thoughts to myself, otherwise we would have argued until dawn.

'I'm curious about one thing,' said McGray, sneering. 'Did ye really have a wine and candlelit supper with her?'

I huffed. *That* would take some explaining. Fortunately, the waiter refilled my glass right then.

'You can hardly call it that. I did visit her in July, in the thick of the Henry Irving scandal. I wanted her to tell me – well, whatever she could.'

McGray arched an eyebrow, his lips slowly stretching into a grin. 'Ye consulted her! Ye really consulted her!'

I snorted. 'This is precisely why I did not tell you back then!'

His grin reached maximum width. 'And the bottle o' wine?'

'I thought some drink might loosen her tongue.'

'Aye ye did, ye dog!' McGray let out something between a laugh and a joyous growl. 'Am surprised she even let ye in! What did she tell ye?'

I sighed. I knew Nine-Nails was not going to like this.

'She . . . She admitted to lying.'

He choked on the ale. For a second I thought he'd spray it all on me, but luckily he managed to grasp his napkin and, for the first time ever, I saw him cover his mouth.

'*She what!*' he squealed after coughing and clearing his throat.

'Sometimes,' I clarified. 'She admitted to lying – *sometimes.*'

McGray looked at me in utter disbelief. Then he called the waiter with a loud muleteer's whistle. 'Oi, laddie! Start making yer way to the pub. I'm goin' to need another one very soon.' Then he leaned closer to me, his face stern. 'What d'ye mean? Who does she lie to?'

I must admit I savoured the moment.

'Are you afraid she may have lied to you?'

He banged a fist on the table and everything on it rattled. 'Answer the fucking question!'

I was somewhat glad to see that, all and all, McGray was still far more irritable than me.

'She assured me she has never lied to you,' I said, my tone telling just how much I doubted her. 'I asked her how she did her divination tricks. She admitted she often observes and guesses, or asks seemingly unrelated questions, very much like we do with witnesses. She also admitted that most of her clientele are "simple" folk who crave to be helped.' I raised a hand before McGray protested. 'Nevertheless, she insisted she has "the eye", and that she inherited the gift from her grandmother.'

Again, I said all that with blatant incredulity, but it seemed to quieten McGray's temper.

'So, what d'ye think happened last Friday?'

I pondered for a moment. I had said earlier I could not believe Katerina could be responsible. This little chat, however, had made me wary.

'I would like to hear your theories first,' was my evasive reply. 'Skip the ones that involve evil spirits, please.'

McGray shrugged. 'I can only think of two options. Either one o' those sad bastards decided to kill him – or herself along with the others, or someone set the whole thing to murder them and frame her.'

I nodded. 'My very thoughts, though I am more inclined to believe the latter.'

'How so?'

'I am not ruling it out entirely, but if this were the doing of a suicidal person – or group of persons – it strikes me as odd that they would summon Katerina. Or care to let her live.'

'Perhaps they needed her as part of a ritual.'

'Some suicidal rite of passing?' I ventured. 'Atonement for sins, perhaps?'

'Aye, and that would explain what Katerina heard. I need to look into my books.'

'And I must think of the nuts and bolts . . . something that killed them but not her . . . That should be – I hope – evident from the bodies and the crime scene.' I took a sip of wine. 'We should also look at the people connected to the six victims. Anyone who might have wanted them dead.'

McGray stroked his beard. 'The colonel's valet . . .'

'A logical assumption. He was the last man around and the first one to arrive. And he could only have found the bodies if he took a set of keys with him, so he had full access to the house at all times. We must question him, and soon. But even before that, I want to see those bodies.'

McGray began counting with his fingers. 'Morgue, séance parlour, the valet . . . Anything else?'

'Not that I can think of right now.'

'Good, I'd run out o' fingers. With a wee bit o' luck, we might be able to squeeze them all in one day.'

'We better do. We must present a good case at the inquest if we want to avoid a full trial.'

Nine-Nails nodded and downed his pint. Just as he put the glass back on the table, the waiter approached with a jug and refilled it.

'Drink at your leisure, sir. We brought you plenty.'

McGray grinned. 'Good service here. I might join.'

'Please, do *not*. I beg you.'

6

I cannot tell you how relieved I was to find all of the windows of my former house lit up. Layton was pleased to tell me he had received the keys, along with a note from Lady Anne. Exhausted as I was, I forced myself to read it.

The nasty old woman was reprimanding me for my 'abrupt and most inconsiderate' request for lodgings. Her lengthy treatise on acceptable manners was followed by a succinct paragraph in which she agreed I spend the present night at *her* property, but only out of her boundless Christian charity. Her postscript, however, demanded we signed a 'new and amended contract' as soon as my 'petty duties' allowed, or she'd be forced to send her men to evict me.

I did not have the energy to think of any of that. I went straight to bed, so dreadfully tired no nightmare came to haunt me.

In the morning I thought I'd walk to the City Chambers – already regretting I'd left my white Bavarian mare back in Gloucestershire. However, an insistent rain was falling all across the city, so I opted for a cab. It turned out a wise choice, for I made it to the Royal Mile precisely as all the pauper tenants of those shabby buildings were emptying their chamber pots onto the road.

I made my way into the City Chambers, barely thinking of my surroundings. By now I could have found the way to our 'office' blindfolded. However, once there I found a surprise waiting for me.

The cellar's usual clutter was no more. Instead, there were piles upon piles of crates, all crammed with McGray's preposterous books and odd paraphernalia. I recognised his gargantuan Peruvian idol, nearly as tall as me, hastily wrapped in brown paper. Nine-Nails must have been packing his mountains of rubbish, preparing himself to be kicked out of the police buildings as soon as the new superintendent took charge.

Inexplicably, I felt a wave of warmth finding myself back in that damp, dingy place.

Like many times before, I caught Nine-Nails listening at the walls with a stethoscope, expecting to hear the ghosts that were said to haunt the underground passages of Mary King's Close. According to McGray, only a thin wall separated us from those tunnels, and he alleged he'd occasionally heard footsteps, and once even a high-pitched laugh. I had offered him a plethora of sensible explanations – after all, a few sections of Mary King's Close remained inhabited to this day; even a tanner and a shoemaker still had their businesses there. Nine-Nails, of course, paid no attention to that detail.

'I found this auld lad in Grass Market,' he said with unabated excitement. 'He sold me that wee map. It has all the streets o' Mary King's Close! This very basement was part of it!'

I barely glanced at the piece of yellowy paper on his desk.

'Did you walk here under this rain?' I asked. His overcoat was quite damp, and strands of wet hair still stuck to his forehead. Tucker, his faithful golden retriever, was drenched too, and lay belly-up at a corner, a puddle of mud all around him.

'Aye. It's only water. It's clean.'

'Have you not bought a new horse yet? It has been nine months now.'

His last mount, a magnificent Anglo-Arab specimen, had been killed in January. A gift from his late father, McGray had not had the heart to get a replacement. Today he simply ignored my comment.

'Glad yer here. Dr Reed left me a note. He can only see us this morning.'

I had to laugh at that. 'The snotty child telling us we need an appointment?'

'Aye,' said McGray, already walking to the door. 'He's really busy with that other murder at the Deaf and Dumb Institution.' He poked my chest. 'I ken ye don't like the lad, but don't upset him today. We'll probably have to ask him to rush his work for our case.'

I only sighed and followed him.

The morgue occupied an adjacent basement so that the corpses remained cool, and was only a few steps away. There we met young Dr Reed, who at twenty-four was already Edinburgh's chief forensic physician (not because of his astounding talent, but because a fresh graduate was all the Scottish police could afford).

We found him at the morgue's small reception room, sorting out stacks of paperwork – reports to be presented at court, from what I could see. The chap was responsible and he learned fast, I must admit; however, the strain of his duties was beginning to show on his face. He still had the plump, slightly reddened cheeks that always reminded me of a baby's rump, but his eyes, which used to look like those of a nervous cocker spaniel, were now stern and encircled by darkened, puffy skin.

'Good morning, inspectors,' he said with an already tired voice. He pulled a surprisingly thin file from between the neat piles of paper.

'What have ye found, laddie?' McGray asked, attempting to sound jovial.

'Nothing so far.'

'*What!*' I cried. 'How long have you—?'

McGray had to elbow my ribs, even if his own tone was not much kinder. 'What d'ye mean?'

Reed yawned, though looking daggers at me. 'I *have* looked at all six bodies. I found nothing that might suggest the cause of death; no obvious signs of poisoning, no fatal wounds, no—'

'Were you absolutely thorough?' I interrupted.

'Oh, no, not at all, inspector. I barely glanced at them so that you could step in and remark on my incompetence.'

I clenched my fists while McGray laughed hard.

'Och, the laddie's become a baby, Frey!'

We both looked at him with unifying hatred.

Reed turned a page and went on, utterly unamused. 'They all presented a deep cut in the arm joint. It looks as though they bled themselves in the hours preceding their deaths.'

'The offering,' McGray mumbled, recalling Katerina's statement. 'Did they bleed themselves to death?'

'No, inspector. The officers found a decanter with the stuff at the site. From the volume, I'd say each person lost the equivalent of a tablespoon. The colonel, however, presents two wounds; the other one on the palm of his left hand.'

I looked sideways. 'They could have been poisoned from the knife, directly into their bloodstream.'

'That may become evident after I run the chemical tests,' said Reed.

'Good. Make sure you start with the Reinsch—'

'The Reinsch and the Marsh tests, of course. I've already collected samples of blood and tissue.' Before I could interrupt again, Reed turned another page. 'I also found another thing you two might find interesting.'

'Yes?'

'One of the bodies does show some signs of violence, even if it doesn't seem related to the deaths. Let me show you.'

We followed him into the morgue. The place was as sterile as always, with its icy air and its smells of ethanol and formaldehyde, and its white tiles opaque after having been cleaned with vinegar for years on end.

The six corpses were lined up neatly, all covered in white sheets. Not a speck of red tainted the pristine fabric.

Reed went to the second table, where one of the smaller bodies lay. He uncovered the face first, to reveal an apparently well-to-do lady. Her curly brown hair was still braided in an intricate French plait, and her face, quite beautiful, had plump cheeks and a tiny, rather girlish mouth.

'Mrs Martha Grenville,' Reed read from his report. 'Thirty-six years old. Quite healthy, except for—' Reed lifted the sheet further to reveal the rest of the body.

As usual, I could not repress a faint blush. There is nothing more intimate and vulnerable than an exposed body, and the lifeless ones, unable to defend themselves, make me feel like a voyeur. Still, I had to look carefully.

The post-mortem's Y-shaped suture, running all across her chest and stomach, was hard to ignore, even if Reed had done a very neat job with the stitches. The sight made me feel a tingle creeping all over my spine, just as an image of my dead uncle forced itself into my mind. And that of a rotting dead man refusing to be buried. I believe I swayed, but fortunately Reed and Nine-Nails were staring at the body and did not notice.

All I could do was grasp my lapels, discreetly take a deep breath, and confront that sad corpse.

Mrs Grenville, despite being dead, looked like a delicate porcelain doll. Her skin was firm and smooth, her hands soft and without blemish. I could picture her bathing in milk every night and then rubbing in all manner of oils and creams. However, amidst her abdomen's ivory skin stood out a cluster of ghastly bruises. Smudges in all the shades of black and purple and green. The sight made me squint.

'These are at least a few days old,' said Reed. 'Quite severe, but not life-threatening.'

I bent down to look at a particularly dark spot. It was a perfectly round mark; almost like a seal, its contours marked as sharply as if done with ink.

'Is this—?'

'Her husband's signet ring. He was still wearing it when they brought him here.'

I felt an instant compassion for that poor lady; keeping herself prim and pretty, perhaps to please a husband who in return punched her in the stomach.

I looked at her hand, still sporting a wedding ring. No wonder – the gold had grown into her flesh.

'Was she wearing any other jewellery?' I asked.

'Oh yes, and very expensive pieces.' Reed consulted the report. 'Pearl choker, diamond and sapphire rings, matching earrings. None of that was taken from the scene.'

'Did the others also have valuables on them?'

'All but the youngest man and lady. All the other men had pocket clocks, cufflinks, wallets with money and so on. We have all that in the storeroom if you want to have a look. If something was taken, it was not obvious.'

'We still cannae rule out theft,' said McGray. I was glad he was following my advice and looking for reasonable explanations.

I made a note as I said, 'You are right. We should find out if that colonel had an inventory of valuables in his house, and—'

'And I am afraid I must leave now,' said Reed, shoving the file in my hands. 'I'm already late. I am expected to testify at court.'

'We need you to carry out those tests as soon as possible,' I said as he made his brisk way out.

'I'll see what I can do,' said Reed over his shoulder and then he shut the door.

I felt fire in my stomach. 'I'll see what I— *I'll see what I can do?*'

'There, there, Frey. I'll talk to him. Now let's focus. Who's next?'

We moved on to the next table, as I flipped the page. 'Hector Shaw. Eighty-one.'

'Bloody hell! Why even bother living that way?'

'Why even bother killing him?' I added. 'I assume he was the *ghost's* widower?'

'Aye, according to Katerina.'

I uncovered the body and found an old man with a large nose, a wiry white beard and very messy hair. From the marks on his nose, I could tell he'd worn heavy spectacles for years.

I poked one of the old man's calves. 'Well, he looks reasonably healthy. I'd say fit enough to look after himself.'

I looked thoroughly, but Reed had been right. Other than the cut on his arm, there were no wounds. The only sign of illness were a few rashes on his forearms – eczema, perhaps – which none of the other bodies shared.

Next in line was his grandson-in-law, Colonel Grenville. Fifty-one.

He was a tall man, with a brawny body perfectly suited for the military. His face was cleanly shaven, and though weather-beaten, he was a remarkably good-looking man. Prone to furious outbursts, though, suggested by the deep furrow on his brow. I recalled Holt's statement, saying that this man had looked terribly angry, even after death. On the other hand, even his wrinkles and locks of grey hair appeared to have been placed by a dexterous hand, only to add more character to his

67

features. His hands were large and sturdy, and he too had a wedding band which Dr Reed had not managed to remove. His signet ring had left a noticeable mark on the small finger. I looked more closely at the wound on the palm of his hand. That coincided with Katerina's account. His knuckles, I noticed then, were grazed.

'From beating the missus?' McGray suggested.

'I . . . I don't think so. He *broke* his skin. Bad as they are, her bruises would have looked far worse. And his knuckles have barely healed. I'd say he was punching something solid – a wall, maybe. And most likely just a few hours before his death.'

'The valet might've seen,' said McGray, and I made a note. 'It might not be important, but still . . .'

We moved on.

'Bertrand Shaw,' I read. 'Thirty-five. Martha . . . Mrs Grenville's first cousin.'

He shared the lady's dark, wavy hair, and other than a flimsy face and a very thin body, he too appeared to have been in perfect health. The only remarkable features were the tips of his fingers; chapped and reddened from insistent biting.

'A nervous chap,' I said.

The next victim was a rather chubby man with a bulbous nose. His almost white hair contrasted starkly with a jet-black beard, bushy and scruffy. Like Colonel Grenville, this man looked like he'd spent his entire life frowning.

'Peter Willberg. Fifty-nine. Grannie Alice's son.'

'Her son, ye said? How come he's called Willberg instead o' Shaw?'

'Well spotted,' I said, looking back at the corpse of old Hector Shaw. 'Grannie Alice must have married twice. I will draw a family tree when we are done here.' Then I looked at Reed's report. 'It says here he was a heavy smoker and drinker.'

I pulled the man's lips and saw a set of yellowy teeth. 'And a keen walker.' His feet were all calloused, and his thick calves were those of a seasoned hiker.

'So the last one,' said McGray, going to the next body, 'is Katerina's client.'

'Leonora Willberg, yes. Twenty-two years old. By far the youngest of the group.'

She could not have been called handsome. Her round nose was the same as Mr Willberg's – her uncle – and she even had a receding hairline, perhaps from braiding her hair very tightly since childhood. Besides, there was something strange about her. I could not pinpoint what, but it had much to do with the darkened skin under her eyes and the slight creases that already ran from her nose to the sides of her mouth. Even in death she exuded some sort of – malice.

'What ye thinking, Frey?' McGray asked, startling me a little.

I cleared my throat. 'I was hoping we'd find something glaringly obvious. One common symptom.'

'Are ye puzzled now?'

'To say the least. We have a very heterogeneous group here. I cannot think of anything terrible enough to kill an eighty-year-old man, his young step-granddaughter *and* a sturdy military man, all without leaving clear marks.'

I saw Nine-Nails biting his lip, struggling not to insist that it all looked like the doings of an evil spirit.

'Heart attack?' McGray ventured. 'Frightened to death after the hand of Satan appeared?'

I flickered through the pages as I spoke. 'Reed does not mention anything about it.'

'D'ye think he forgot to check?'

I chuckled. 'I thought you trusted the chap beyond all—'

'Och, shut it!'

I tapped my chin with the file. It would be hours before Reed came back. 'Bloody hell, I cannot wait. I will have a look myself.'

McGray giggled. 'Ye handling guts? That's something I want to see.'

I cast him a murderous look as I took my jacket off and rolled up my sleeves. I would have told him that I had performed many dissections while studying at Oxford, but preferred not to. McGray never tired of reminding me I had abandoned the degree. And I would very soon remember why.

Reed kept his instruments in a nearby chestnut box, from where I retrieved two forceps and scissors. I chose to look at the colonel first, since he looked the least likely to have died of a fright.

Very carefully, I cut the stitches and then pulled a fold of flesh with the forceps. The squelching noise nearly made me retch.

'Hold this,' I told McGray, and I used another pair of pincers to pull the pleat of skin on the other side of the man's chest. As I expected, the colonel had very little body fat; barely a thin layer of yellowish tissue.

'What ye looking for?' McGray asked.

'If they died of an attack, the heart muscle will have gone black. It is usually very easy to see.'

With my free hand (and after a very deep breath), I probed at the ribs and realised Reed had indeed cut them around the sternum. I pulled the bones aside and, nestled between the lungs, found one of the leanest hearts I had ever seen.

'It looks really healthy,' I said, though my voice sounded constricted. Again, I had to take a deep breath, past caring what McGray thought, and forced myself to pull up the heart. Reed had also cut the arteries, so I had no problem lifting it for a closer look. 'Healthy indeed.'

The organ was red and firm, as if about to come to life and beat again. For an instant, I marvelled at its design; the strength of the muscle, the perfectly placed arteries, the fine, branched-out veins. What I held was an elegant, efficient propeller, built to last for life. I suddenly remembered why at some point I'd thought medicine was the path for me. Facing this on a daily basis, however, would have driven me completely insane.

I put it back in place, followed by the ribs, and stitched back the skin – not as neatly as Reed, it pained me to admit.

'Don't ye want to check another one?' McGray asked when he saw me rush to the ewer and basin.

'No, I am satisfied Reed did it.' And I could not stand that moist and slimy feeling on my hands.

McGray covered his brow, exhaling in a grunt that infected me with his frustration.

I reached for a rag to dry my hands. 'If the bodies do not tell us much, perhaps the scene of the deaths will.'

Still massaging his temples, McGray nodded. 'Aye. The day's nae over yet.'

He went hastily to Reed's desk and left him a note requesting he carried out the chemical tests as soon as humanly possible, and then we set off for Morningside.

I was frustrated the bodies had not yielded any new information yet; however, little did I know that the case was about to become an ever more puzzling, unsolvable tangle.

7

As soon as we stepped out, and despite the insistent rain, three journalists blocked our path like a colony of vultures.

'Are you in charge of the Morningside deaths?'

'Have you talked to the gypsy?'

'Do you think a demon did it, Inspector Nine—?'

McGray raised a hand and pointed directly at the man's face, his index half an inch from the reporter's nose. He had no need to speak. There was an instant of utter silence, and the chap gulped and stepped back, but once at a safe distance, he continued to shout out impertinencies.

McGray walked on impassive, as I called a nearby cab. Before I could jump in, one of the hacks seized my arm, babbling some nonsense about the deaths happening on Friday the thirteenth.

McGray grabbed him by the back of the collar and pulled him out of the way, using him as a dead weight to push the other two men back. We got on the carriage at once.

'Friday the thirteenth!' McGray grunted indignantly as the cab gathered speed.

'Oh? Do you also think it is nonsense?'

'Course it's damn nonsense! Katerina chose it for the moon phase.'

I only sighed as the driver took us south.

By the time we made it to Morningside, the rain had become even worse.

The Grenville house was the last one on Colinton Road, right after its intersection with Napier Road. That was the very edge of Edinburgh, where new money erected their mansions these days.

The house was surrounded by extensive grounds, and the land was delimited by tall sycamores still in full leaf, so it was impossible to catch a glimpse of the property from the road. It would be useless to ask the neighbours if they'd seen anything.

The cab passed through the gates and took us through some overgrown lawns. We then heard a distant sound, high-pitched, coming and going at regular intervals. Only when the cab stopped by the house did we realise it was the howling of a tormented dog.

The poor animal, an enormous black mastiff, sat by the main entrance, drenched to the marrow and letting out the most harrowing laments towards the sky.

I stepped down, landing straight into a brown puddle, and opened my umbrella.

'A tad too . . . ostentatious,' I said, looking at the wide façade with a grimace. The house had a mismatch of inappropriate features, some of which would have looked out of place even in Buckingham Palace: a turret, Greek columns far too thick for its portico, and two overgrown lions guarding the front steps. Carved in cheap sandstone, the weather would erode them within a few years.

McGray was patting the dog's head with one hand and scratching under its ear with the other. The animal stopped howling, instead letting out soft whimpers.

'What happened to yer boss, ye wee brute?' McGray said warmly. He looked at the collar and found a little nickel tag. 'Yer name's Mackenzie. Nice. And ye belonged to Peter Willberg! It has his address here, Frey.'

'Good. That will save us some questioning. Do you have the keys?'

Nine-Nails gave a last pat to the dog and came to the stone steps, pulling the set from his breast pocket.

'Wait here,' he told both the driver and the dog with a single gesture, and then unlocked the heavy oaken door.

The hinges screeched and the sound echoed in an otherwise sepulchral interior. The air felt very cold and the clumsily placed windows let in very little light.

'Did they live here?' I said, for the place already felt like a dwelling abandoned long ago.

'Aye,' said McGray, his steps resounding throughout the hall as we went deeper into the house. 'The colonel, his wife and the auld man.'

There was something in the air. Something – hostile. It felt almost as if an invisible hand had rushed to the entrance and was now pushing my chest, bidding me to leave. I forced the thought out of my head.

'So all the servants left,' I said. 'Before the séance?'

'Aye. Katerina requested it. And no one was allowed in after they took the bodies, so everything should be—'

I nearly tripped on something and had to lean against the wall.

'Blast! I wish we'd brought a lantern,' I grunted. Only then I realised that I had tripped over a floorboard. Several had been pulled out all across the hall.

'I don't think they were redecorating,' said McGray.

Indeed, we looked into one of the side rooms, a small seating parlour, where both floors and walls had been partially stripped. There were wooden boards and chunks of plaster and wallpaper strewn on an expensive mahogany table.

'Apparently they *were* looking for something,' I mumbled. 'So . . . where did it happen?'

'McNair said they found them on the first floor.'

We climbed the broad staircase, dodging pieces of ripped carpet and nearly having to grope about to find our way.

A draught hit my face then, but it felt almost solid, like a ghostly hand. I stopped for a second and pinched my septum. The instant I shut my eyes, I saw the fire of a thousand torches reflected on the choppy waters of a loch, all coming to get me.

In the garden, the dog was howling again.

'Ye all right, Percy?'

I shook my head and gripped the banister, the touch of polished wood bringing me back to the here and now.

'Yes,' I assured, but McGray gave me a look of understanding that only managed to annoy me.

'Frey, right after my sister—'

'Let's move on,' I snapped, taking the lead. 'Which room?' I asked when I reached the landing.

'Front parlour. It must be that one.' He pointed at an ajar door, which allowed in a thin strip of sunlight. McGray opened it slowly, and the hinges, like those of the front door, screeched.

I readied myself to see something dreadful, but for once that would not be the case. Nine-Nails and I stepped in as if treading on eggshells, saying nothing while our eyes took in every detail. The window was south-facing (my stepmother would be appalled) and the curtains wide open, so we had very decent light.

That was the only room that did not look half-stripped; the carpets, the wallpaper and the wood panelling still in place. There were a couple of book cabinets and a drinks trolley which also seemed undisturbed.

Everything looked domestic enough. It was just the centre of the parlour that spoke of death.

There stood a round table which clearly did not belong in this room. It was surrounded by seven rather ugly chairs in

75

the Chippendale style, two of them on their sides. The white tablecloth had been pulled, a spot still creased by a clenching hand. I pictured a dying person clinging to it while sliding onto the floor.

I walked closer and saw seven silver candlesticks, only two still standing. The rest had been knocked over and lay in disarray. Molten wax had dripped, puddled and hardened all around, dotted with black specks of charred wicks. Underneath, the tablecloth looked singed; the candles had set it on fire, but the wax had clearly stifled the flames. Quite fortunate, or the entire room might have burned to ashes.

McGray leaned closer and placed a careful hand on the table, next to a stain I had not yet seen – a dark rim, left perhaps by a decanter.

'The blood offering stood here,' he said. 'That was the one thing the lads took away.'

I looked around. There were still two half-finished drinks on the little trolley, next to the perfectly tubular ashes of a cigar left to consume completely, and a china cup that still held dregs of tea.

'It looks like it happened all at once,' I muttered. 'Within minutes, I'd say. Otherwise it would be more of a wreck.'

McGray nodded, looking rather frustrated. Like the bodies, the room was not offering any immediate clues. We could tell where people had sat, what they had drunk and smoked; we could tell which chair Katerina had taken, for her long fingernails had left deep marks on the tablecloth; we could tell someone had dropped a cigar on the carpet; we could deduce Mrs Grenville had had tea from the marks of lipstick on a cup . . .

But there were no weapons, no suspicious little vials; nothing that spoke of struggle or violence. The only trace of destruction was half-hidden behind the table. There, we found a very expensive photographic camera lying on the floor.

The tripod was intact, but the bellows were crushed and the lens had been ejected. The glass plate – or plates – were smashed to smithereens.

'Looks like someone fell on it,' I said, squatting down next to Nine-Nails.

'Must've been that lass Leonora. Katerina said she took several photos. That last flash o' light she saw might have come from here.'

I examined the camera carefully. The debris around it was undisturbed; a perfect circle of glass and bent parts. It looked as though Miss Leonora had simply dropped dead, and none of the other attendants had been able to come to her aid.

We then saw a wooden box sitting against the polished oak panelling of the nearest wall. It was large and sturdy, with a little brass key still in the lock.

'The plaques?' McGray asked with excitement.

I went to the box and opened it carefully, suspecting it might contain exposed plates.

'Blast,' I said as I opened it fully. 'These are all new plates.'

They were stacked neatly in their own compartment, which was only half full. Lined with green velvet, I could still see the marks left when the plaques had been pulled out, visibly in a rush.

Another compartment, smaller, contained chemicals, lenses and tins of flash powder.

McGray cast them a frustrated look, and stared at the mess on the carpet. He picked at the shards of glass with a dejected look. 'Pity . . . Only *one* bloody photograph could've told us quite a—' McGray abruptly turned his head. I knew that expression far too well now. He'd heard something.

He rose to his feet slowly, staring at the ajar door. I looked intently at the narrow gap, but only saw darkness.

'Look at the window,' McGray said loudly, but shaking his head and pointing at the door. 'What d'ye think o' those lawns?'

Then I heard a faint sound; something rubbing against the corridor's carpet. There was someone out there.

McGray was reaching for his gun just as we both caught a glimpse of a grey sleeve. Nine-Nails hurled himself forwards and kicked the door open.

'*Who the fuck are ye?*'

His holler made me jump and I nearly dropped the box of plaques. I put it down and ran to the door.

A plump, grey-haired man stood in the darkened hall, his face fixed in sheer terror. He'd been dragging a huge cloth sack, tied up with burgundy curtain ropes he was still grasping.

'Who the fuck are ye?' McGray repeated. '*Answer me!* Before ye pass a turd.'

When he spoke, his voice was so guttural, I feared he'd just done precisely that.

'Ser-servant, sir.'

'Whose?'

'Colonel Grenville, rest in peace.'

McGray pointed at the sack.

'And what are ye doing with that?'

The man looked at the bag, let go of the ropes and then looked back at us. After a moment of stammering, he smiled stupidly, like a child caught with his hands on somebody else's cake.

And then he ran.

Nine-Nails growled. 'Och, why do they always—'

And then he dashed after the servant, gun in hand, and I followed.

We ran down the stairs, McGray shouting at the man to stop. He shot at the ceiling and pieces of plaster fell on the entrance hall, just as the man pushed the main door open.

I saw him run across the lawns like the wind, splattering mud as he dodged our carriage. McGray and I raised our guns, making the driver crouch and shriek.

The instant before I pulled the trigger, a dark shape sprinted ahead. The huge mastiff, carrying its weight with disturbing speed, reached the servant in just a few strides and then pounced on him, throwing him onto the ground with a big splash of mud. The man thrashed and kicked about, but the dog pinned him down firmly with its thick paws.

We rushed towards them – I feared the dog might rip the man apart. McGray, on the other hand, patted the animal as if it were his own.

'Good Mackenzie! Now let the miserable sod go.'

The dog stayed put, growling, until McGray pulled it by the collar.

I was glad to see that, besides being covered in dirt and dribble, the servant looked unscathed.

'Look at that!' McGray said triumphantly, lifting the man by the lapels as if he were another dog. 'Nae even my birthday!'

'*I can explain!*' the chap whimpered, covering his face as if still threatened by the mastiff. '*I can—!*'

'Och, shut it! Ye'll have plenty o' time for that.'

'Who are you?' I asked.

'H-Holt. Alexander Holt,' he stuttered.

'The colonel's footman?'

'His valet, actu—'

'Frey, take him to the City Chambers. I'll look at the rest o' the house.'

I was about to suggest the reverse (after all, brute force has always been McGray's strongest suit), but a glance at the house deterred me. I could not possibly admit it, but I did not want to roam around those darkened rooms on my own.

What was happening to me?

8

The blasted reporters were still prowling around the City Chambers when I returned. Miserable as they looked after hours in the rain, their eyes glowed in excitement when they saw me escorting the battered servant.

'Mr Holt!' they cried at once. 'Did you do it? You said it was the gypsy!'

Constable McNair came to my aid just in time, and extricated me from the pushing and shoving.

'The police forces used to be respected, I'll have you know!' I grumbled at McNair as soon as we made it in. The rangy ginger officer was already taking Mr Holt to a cell. 'There is a heavy sack still in the cab,' I told him. 'Have someone bring it to my office.'

I rushed to the cellar and went directly to McGray's desk. I knew he kept whisky there, and I had a long swig directly from the bottle. I could swear I still felt that nasty chill that struck me at the Grenville house, and only the burn of the spirit managed to take it away.

I heard someone come in just as I held the bottle high.

'Never mind this,' I said, clearing my throat before a second drink. 'It is medicinal.'

I turned then, only to find a thin, middle-aged man with auburn hair and deep creases around his eyes. His hands were serenely interlaced just below his chest, like those of a priest, and he was looking at me with a hooked eyebrow.

'Inspector Frey, I assume?'

Right then a young clerk walked in, bringing Holt's bounty. He left it on McGray's desk and walked away, but before leaving he bowed at the other man. 'Superintendent.'

Just as I faced the new head of the Scottish Police, a drip of whisky trickled down the side of my mouth. Slightly blushed, I wiped it with my handkerchief and put the bottle aside.

'Superintendent Trevelyan,' I said, also bowing, but not bothering to sound too deferential. 'Pleased to meet you.'

He cast an evaluating look at the whisky, but said nothing.

'Evidence?' he asked then, nodding at the sack.

'Yes. And we caught another suspect.'

'Good. Not another fortune teller, I hope.' It was not said as a joke. That man, serene as he looked, did not seem designed for laughter. 'I asked one of the clerks to prepare those documents for you,' he continued, pointing at my desk. Only then did I notice the stack of files. 'Legal documents of all the victims. Birth certificates, marriages, so on and so forth.'

I was astonished. A helpful Superintendent – *and* Scottish – stood against all my existing paradigms.

'Thank you, sir. How did you know that we—'

'It is my job to know. And I want you to take good care of this investigation. The affair is becoming far too public for my taste. I had to send a couple of officers to disperse a crowd in Cattle Market. People were flocking to that gypsy's brewery as if it were some sort of shrine.' He sighed. 'We can expect a circus at the inquest tomorrow. I trust you can handle that.'

I nodded. 'It would not be my first time, sir. You might have seen in my files, I was in charge of the prosecution of the serial killer nicknamed—'

'Good Mary Brown,' he interjected. 'Yes. Though I had it from several officers, who remarked how much you revel in telling the story.'

Again, if there was any humour intended, his face did not show it. He took a short step closer, and despite his relaxed demeanour, I could sense his underlying tension.

'On other matters,' he said, his voice a smidgen lower, 'has Inspector McGray told you why you two are still here?'

I sighed, preparing myself for what might be gruelling questioning.

'He has.'

I said no more, despite the superintendent's expectant face. He waited patiently for a while, but eventually he had to get to the point.

'I suspect you will not be able to shed more light on the motivations behind such a request? Or why the order came from – such person?'

So he would not even dare mention the prime minister's intervention. I remembered having had a similar conversation with the former superintendent. It had not been a full year ago, but it already felt like another lifetime. My attitude, for instance, could not have been more different. Only a few months ago I would have attempted to offer at least some sort of an answer; today I no longer cared, and even if I did, the prime minister had spoken, so this man had no authority to sack me.

'That would be accurate, sir,' was my unadorned, yet honest reply. I was not going to give him a lengthy account on the murkier details of the Lancashire affair.

Trevelyan stared at me, scrutinising. I wondered if he'd given McGray the same treatment. Surprisingly, he would not attempt to probe any deeper. Once more, he lowered his voice a little more.

'Though I ignore the details of the matter, if the time comes I can be of any assistance . . .'

We looked at each other in utter silence. How strange that dialogue had been; so few words said, so many unknowns, yet so much implied.

'You know where to find me,' he concluded.

He did not say those words as if talking to a subordinate. Upon leaving, Trevelyan nodded at me like one does an equal.

I decided I liked him.

I first looked at the goods Mr Holt had nearly stolen.

There were a couple of pocket watches, some fine leather items, a couple of thick overcoats and some hunting gear, which accounted for the bulk and weight. Though not mere trinkets, those objects did not strike me as particularly valuable. I was expecting to see money, bonds or Mrs Grenville's jewellery. This looked more like a bag of mementoes.

I nearly tossed the bag aside, but then something caught my eye. A little black pouch, almost lost within the sack's folds. It contained a fine chain which held a rather unusual pendant: a simple gold nugget, the size of a thumbnail. Rugged and opaque, it could have been freshly dug from the mine.

After examining it for a moment, I put it safely aside. I'd have plenty of time to assess it.

I looked next at the family documents. The files turned out to be much more comprehensive than I expected, and it was very easy to sketch out the family tree. Once I traced it, I put a mark on all of the deceased, and circled the six who had died on Friday. Things began to take shape.

Grannie Alice had indeed married twice and had given birth to five children – three from the first marriage and two from the second. Of those five, only *one* remained alive; Mrs Grenville's mother. From the records, she must be fifty-six, and I assumed she'd be the one looking after the colonel's three young orphans.

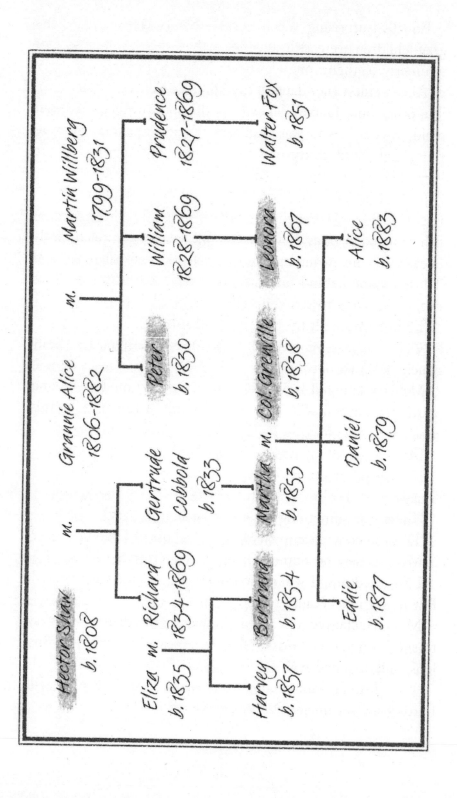

Equally surprising was the fact that only two of Alice's grandchildren were still alive, and there was an odd sort of symmetry to them: one was named Walter Fox, the only son of Alice's eldest (her daughter, who had died a few years ago). The other one, Harvey Shaw, was the son of Alice's *youngest* child, Richard, who was deceased. Walter and Harvey were thirty-eight and thirty-two respectively. I thought we were very likely to see them at the inquest.

Just as I took one last look at my work, Nine-Nails burst into the office. He was drenched in rain and brought a huge piece of fish wrapped in greasy newspapers. The smell made me instantly queasy. To my wonderment, the two dogs, Mackenzie and Tucker, came behind him, jumping about with their tongues out, as McGray tossed chunks of fish at their muzzles.

'Did you walk all the way from Morningside?'

'Och nae, are ye mad? Just from the Ensign. It's really chucking down out there.'

McGray lounged back at his desk, putting his feet up and shoving a handful of chips into his mouth. 'I forgot to eat this morning. I was fucking ravenous!'

I had to cover my nose. 'Did you find anything?'

He looked at me with that portentous stare of his, which usually precedes his sillier statements.

'There was something eerie in that house, Frey.'

'Did you come face to face with the ghost of Grannie Alice?'

McGray saw no humour in that. 'Ye felt it too. I saw ye.'

I breathed out. 'I will not deny I was . . . somewhat altered. But it was not because of spooks at large.'

McGray chewed on and had the unprecedented courtesy to speak only after he'd swallowed. Again, his understanding look only irritated me.

'Frey, I don't want to force ye to admit it, but I ken yer still hurting for yer uncle. Did ye feel ye were reliving it?'

I turned my face away, but McGray went on.

'Some spirits can do that to ye. Bring out yer worst—'

'*I don't give a damn!*' I snapped. Even the dogs, now lying on the floor in a bundle, got startled. 'That is all nonsense! All I need to know is if you found anything of consequence in that house. If not, just stuff your mouth with that ghastly—'

'All right, all right! Nae need to burst out o' yer stays! Aye, I found something. And yer goin' to love this.'

He searched his breast pocket and tossed something onto my desk. It was a filthy rag wrapping a small, thin object.

I unwrapped it warily – for it was covered in fat and bits of soggy batter – and nearly gasped at the contents. A short knife.

'Is this the knife they used for their *offering*?'

'Must be.'

Though compact, the blade was as sharp as a scalpel, and the handle was carved ivory. Its light colours contrasted with the deep red of coagulated blood all over its edge.

'An expensive item,' I mumbled, lifting it carefully. Just as I did so, McGray came closer and lifted the sheet with the family tree.

'Where did you find this knife?' I asked him. 'I did not see it.'

'Right underneath the camera. The thing must've fallen on top.'

I sat back, interlacing my fingers. 'According to Katerina, the colonel bled himself again during the session. So he must have dropped the knife right before that girl Leonora fell and knocked the camera over. The colonel then probably was dying while she was still— Nine-Nails, would you mind not smearing half your nauseating dinner on my work?'

I snatched the already soiled family tree.

'Och, what sodding difference does that make?' and he snatched it back to read at leisure.

In the meantime, I began to wrap the knife again. 'We should keep this with the rest of the evidence. I am not sure what we—' And then I stopped, tilting my head and bringing the knife closer to my eyes.

'What?' McGray asked. He caught me staring at the sharp end of the knife. I was holding it an inch from my eyes.

'Do we know if they all used this knife?'

'Dunno, but that would explain why only those six poor sods died. What could've done it? Arsenic?'

I nodded. 'Amongst many other things. We need Reed to perform those tests soon. If he is too busy, I can attempt to do them myself.'

'Nae,' said Nine-Nails, taking hold of the little bundle. 'There's too much at stake. I don't want a finicky bloody prosecutor questioning the results because ye fucked something up. I'll talk to Reed right now. I'll make him see the urgency.'

'As you wish,' I said, partly relieved.

I was going to follow him, but McGray stopped me.

'Nah, ye wait here, Percy. Just the sight o' ye puts the laddie on edge.'

Again, I agreed with relief.

Nine-Nails came back not ten minutes later, looking insufferably smug.

'Sorted. He'll try to give us some results tomorrow morning, hopefully before the inquest.'

I was not in the mood to hear him boast his success, so I promptly changed the subject and briefed him as to the contents of Holt's loot.

'We still have the chap in a cell,' I concluded. 'Do you want to question him now?'

McGray rubbed his hands together. 'Och, aye. He might be Katerina's salvation.'

9

The questioning room was usually a depressing sight, with its bare brick walls, meagre and battered furniture, and the narrow window that barely provided any light. Today, the rain lashed the grimy glass, adding to the general gloom.

When we walked in, we found Holt biting his nails and sweating profusely. Behind him sat a clerk, ready to record the man's statement.

McGray sat down, facing Holt. There was a third chair, but I preferred to stand behind Nine-Nails as I took notes. I have seldom permitted any of those nasty chairs touch my clothes.

'Mr Holt!' said McGray. Even though I could not see his face, I knew Nine-Nails was smiling. 'Do I need to tell ye yer deep in shite?'

'I can explain,' Holt said once more.

'Oi, ye better. From the state o' the colonel's bedroom and the stuff the dandy here found in yer bag, I'd say ye had yer eye on yer boss's belongings: watches, clothes, a handsome Italian gunshot. Why did ye take them?'

Holt pressed his hands on the table, attempting to control his trembles. 'I was entitled to all those things. The colonel knew I loved them. He said many times I could have 'em if something ever happened to him.'

Nine-Nails cackled. 'Aye right, he did.'

'*I swear!* He—'

'Can you prove that?' I intervened. 'Did someone reliable ever hear him say so? Did he leave it in writing?'

'Aye! Well . . . I think he did. He said he would write it in his will.'

That could be easily checked, but I did not mention it right then. I simply gave him my most dubious look. I have learned that a stare can be more effective than hostile questions.

'There are many things much more valuable in that house!' Holt finally cried. 'I only took what I was entitled to. I swear.'

I nodded, still playing the doubtful act. 'Let us assume you are telling the truth. Why did you take these items now? Why not wait until the will was effected? That would have saved you—'

'I know how long those things can take,' he interrupted. 'I'm up to the neck in debt! I've a family to support! I have a wee daughter and no job now – if I can't pay the tenement, she'll have to go to the orphanage.'

He buried his face in his hands, perhaps to conceal tears, and I felt a surge of sympathy. Even if it was all true – and again, a couple of brief enquiries would be enough to verify it – his actions remained very suspicious.

'You had another set of keys to the house,' I said. 'Why did you not surrender them to the police?'

Holt rubbed his grey beard. 'I kept a spare set at home. I didn't have it with me when the peelers first came. And I didn't say a word 'cause I wanted to get my stuff.' He looked pleadingly at McGray. 'But I went straight to my master's room! I'd never dare steal from his house, let alone from the room where he died!'

'Ye sure? Ye sure ye took nothing from the séance parlour?'

'*Course not!*'

McGray cast him a stabbing stare and Holt whimpered from the bottom of his throat.

'Nothing at all?' McGray repeated.

The whimper became a little louder, and I pictured Holt's head like a hot-air balloon about to burst. In the end it did.

'I . . . did – but . . . I didn't!'

Nine-Nails and I spoke over each other: 'What the fuck ye prattling about?' and 'Will you care to explain?'

Holt looked down. 'Well, I . . .'

McGray banged a hand on the table. 'Oi! My eyes are up here.'

Holt did look at him, though barely lifting his head.

'I didn't walk into the parlour, I swear. I didn't dare! Not after—'

'Then what?'

The man moistened his lips. 'I was going to my master's room. I walked past the parlour door. It was half open. I . . . saw Miss Leonora's chain, the one with the wee gold nugget, on the floor . . .'

McGray and I nodded at each other, both recalling the piece.

'So it was just lying there,' said McGray, all suspicion.

'Aye. The peelers must've dropped it when they took . . . the young miss away.'

'Why did you take it?' I asked. 'You said you would not dare steal.'

Holt blushed profusely, and for an instant I thought he was about to shed tears.

'It . . .' he started, and then covered his mouth with a fist, like one does to repress vomit. 'It seemed easy.'

McGray's eyebrow rose slowly. 'How did ye ken it was Miss Leonora's?'

The blush intensified. 'She always wears it. Well – she always did.' His voice then reduced to a whisper. 'I thought . . . she's not gonna miss it now.'

McGray was going to enquire further, but I stepped forward.

'I think we have heard enough about today. I am more interested in last Friday. And also the preceding days.'

Holt cleared his throat. 'If I can help youse—'

'Why did they call the gypsy?' I said promptly.

'A family matter.'

'Which was . . .?'

Holt shook his head. 'I don't know. They never told me.'

McGray chuckled. 'Oi, please! Ye must have heard something.'

'I don't like to eavesdrop my—'

'*You must have heard something!*'

My quickness to raise my voice surprised me. Holt recoiled at my shout, then gulped.

'They . . . they needed to find something.'

'And what was that?'

Holt's eyes went from McGray's to mine. 'What did the gypsy tell youse?'

McGray leaned forwards. 'We're asking *ye*.'

'I . . . I – I don't know. I—'

'Looks like yer master was looking for something in that house. What was that?'

'I told youse, I don't know!'

McGray clenched his fists, ready to beat the man to a pulp. I had to pat his shoulder like one does an enraged hound.

'You were the colonel's valet,' I said. 'For how long?'

'Five, six years.'

'Preparing his clothes, helping him dress, fetching his meals . . .?'

'Aye.'

'So you *must* have seen them searching. We saw the stripped floors and walls. That did not happen overnight. My guess is you even did some of that for them.'

'No! My masters searched. I didn't.'

'And yet you have no idea what they were looking for.'

'I told youse, it was a family matter! They didn't share their secrets with the likes of me. I respected that.'

I half smiled. 'In my experience, Mr Holt, servants usually find things out. Even if they don't mean to.'

He chuckled. 'Then you've only been served by nosy gossipmongers.'

'Very well,' I said with a sigh, 'let's talk about Mrs Grenville.'

'What about her?'

'We found terrible bruises on her. Did you ever hear about the colonel being . . . harsh on his wife?'

Holt shrugged. 'Aye. A few times, but all marriages have their highs 'n' lows. She seemed happy most of the time.' He looked sideways. 'Although I can tell youse, the lady's mother didn't like them fighting.'

'What did she think o' the colonel?' McGray asked. 'Did she like him?'

'Oh she didn't. She always looked uptight when my master was around.'

I recalled the woman's name: Gertrude. Still alive. I made a note to question her.

'Moving on to what happened that day,' I said, 'we also found grazes on your master's hands. Did you see him fight?'

'No, sir, but I wasn't near him for most of the day.'

'How so?'

'I was the one who fetched most of the guests, including the gypsy.'

'I see. Do you remember the times and the order in which you fetched them?'

'Aye. Miss Leonora was the first one. I picked her up from Mr Willberg's house, her uncle. It must have been midday.'

'So early?' I asked.

'Aye. She needed to buy some stuff for her camera, so I took her to Princes Street first. From there I drove her to

Morningside, and she began setting the parlour at once. I was helping her, but the colonel told me to go to Mrs Eliza's house.'

'Mrs Eliza?' said McGray.

'The family call her that, although she ought to be Mrs Shaw now that her grandma is dead. She's the mother of Master Bertrand, first cousin of Mrs Grenville. He still shared a house with his younger brother and their mother. God, poor Mrs Eliza must be distraught!'

I looked at my previous notes. 'I assume the old Mr Shaw did not need fetching, since he shared the house with the colonel and his wife.'

'Aye.'

'So the last person you fetched was this other man, Peter Willberg.'

'Aye.'

'Why did you not pick him up along with his niece, Leonora? I see she had lived with him since her own father died.'

I noticed Mr Holt's lip quivered. 'Mr Willberg wasn't home. Miss Leonora told me he was busy and I should come back for him. I did so and left him in Morningside just after eight.'

McGray whistled. 'Long drive for a single day! Mr Willberg lived nearby the botanical gardens – I saw it on the dog's tag. That's on the other side of Edinburgh.'

Holt showed his palms. 'That was my job, inspectors.'

'And then you went to Cattle Market,' I continued.

'Aye. I was supposed to pick up the gypsy at half nine. I was there early, but her footman – or whatever she calls the fat lad that sells beer for her – told me she was busy with another client. I waited for almost two hours. My arse got numb in the seat. She finally came out just after eleven. I remember the time very well. I knew my master would be really annoyed.'

'Did Madame Katerina offer any explanation?'

'None, sir. She just jumped in and asked me very bossily to

93

hurry up. I couldn't even see her face. She had it covered with this black veil. And she stank. I think she'd been drinking.'

McGray clenched his hands at that. I wrote the detail down – as did the clerk – and underlined it before my next question.

'Did you notice anything unusual in any of the guests?'

'No . . . well, Miss Leonora was very excited, like she always was when she was up to that kind of occult stuff. Mr Willberg was a wee bit put out, but that was usual in him . . . They all looked very tense before I left them.'

I asked him to describe the room in detail, and what he told us matched what we'd seen ourselves.

'So you left them then,' I said.

'Aye. My orders were to leave and come back first thing in the morning, before all the other servants.'

'What did you do that night?'

His answer was confident enough. 'I went to my local for a few drinks, and then straight home to the wife.'

'Can anyone vouch for that? Other than your wife and the drunkards at your *local*?'

'Aye! The pub's owner will remember. And – o' course, my landlord. I had a quarrel with him when I got home.'

'That late?' I asked. 'That must have been in the small hours.'

Holt again blushed. 'Erm . . . You might call it early, sir. Just past five o'clock, I think. He was hoping to get his rent. I've . . . I've been hiding from him for a few months now. He threatened to evict us. I just told him I had no money.'

'Because ye had spent it on pints and drams,' McGray added, making Holt look down.

'I . . . I also owe money at the pub.'

He barely managed to utter those words, his hands tight on his lap.

I asked for his address, the name of the public house and the address of his landlord.

'And then you went back home?'

'Aye. Had a wee rest – as much as the wife allowed, with her whining – then washed myself and went back to the house.'

'I see. Did you find it locked?'

'Yes, sir.'

'But only you and your masters had the keys.'

Holt gulped at this, and only managed to nod. I took note and moved on.

'Did it look as if anyone had been and gone?'

'No, not at all, sir.'

'Are you sure?'

'Y-yes! I was looking down, sir – I had a mighty hangover, you see – and I remember I only saw the tracks of my carriage. It was very muddy; the wheels going so deep caught my eye.'

I frowned. That would be impossible to verify. Then again, why would Holt admit there had been no other intrusions? That only incriminated him further.

'Now,' said McGray, leaning forwards, 'tell us how ye found the bodies. Who was where? And don't spare any details.'

Holt gulped. His face changed from red to green and he began rubbing his hands. It looked as if he were trying to scrub off his own skin.

'Poor Miss Leonora . . .' he began, on the verge of tears, 'was lying on the camera. It was all smashed to pieces. And there was this horrible look on her face, like . . . like she'd seen hell itself.'

The man pressed his eyelids, attempting not to cry, but doing it so hard I feared he'd squash his eyes. He then cleared his throat and looked back at us, his expression slightly ashamed.

'Young Bertrand was lying right next to her, the same expression. His chair was knocked back. I think he fell backwards.

'On the other side were Mrs Grenville and her grandfather, both on the floor. The poor lady was still clutching the old man's sleeve. I don't know why, but she had this look . . . like a wee child trying to reach for her father . . .

'The colonel and Mr Willberg were on each side of the gypsy. They . . . they were also on the floor, but . . .' Holt stared on, and for a full minute he said no more.

'But what?' McGray prompted.

Holt twitched, as if suddenly reawakened. 'Everyone else looked scared, but not them. They looked angered.'

'Angered, ye say?'

'Aye. They were frowning. Their jaws were closed tight.'

I took note of that. 'What about the gypsy?'

'Oh, she was still on her seat. The only one still on her seat.'

'But she had fainted, aye?' McGray jumped.

'Aye . . . her head bent backwards. I . . .' Holt shuddered. 'I thought she was dead. Nobody looked more dead than her. She had her mouth open, that black veil on her. I don't remember seeing her breathe . . . She looked . . . like a corpse.'

'And you found no signs of violence. Something that suggested there might have been a skirmish or an intruder?'

'Not at all, sir. Not even today. Everything in the house was as I had left it.'

'So . . . you'd say they simply dropped dead? Just like that? Killed by an evil spirit?'

He only managed a nod, his eyes misting up, and remained silent. I spoke as soon as I finished taking my notes.

'And you went to the police straight away?'

'Yes, sir. Immediately.'

'It must have taken you at least a few moments to react.'

'It's . . . it's all a blur, sir. I think I retched . . . I . . . I did freeze for a wee while, but as soon as I recovered I ran out o' there and called for help.'

'Did you touch anything?'

'N-no! Course not!'

'Did you not even stir the bodies? See if anyone might still be alive?'

'No! I . . .' he gulped, more and more anxious. 'I touched no one. I didn't dare!'

'It is all right,' I said, as conciliatory as possible. 'It was a terrible sight. I would not blame you if you ran to the bodies and—'

'*I didn't!*' he roared, banging his fists on the table and then covering his face. He wept miserably for a while, and we gave him time.

McGray was the first one to speak. 'We'll have to keep ye here, I'm afraid.'

'*What?* Are you mad? I just told you I have a—!'

'Yer the mad one if ye think we're goin' to let ye go after this. Ye broke in, tried to steal goods, resisted arrest, took an item from a potential crime scene . . .' He gathered breath for dramatic effect. 'There's nae way to prove ye didnae mess with that room before ye called the peelers . . . And, to be honest, I feel like yer a filthy liar.'

I sighed. 'McGray . . .'

'A scrounging, thieving, scheming sod. I think ye did it.'

Holt again changed colour, this time to pure white. 'What?'

'I think ye killed them all.'

'*What?* Why would I kill my master? I told youse, I'm up to the neck in debt! And everything I said can be verified! Ask the people who saw me that night. Ask Mrs Eliza or—'

McGray leaned forwards. 'I ken there's something yer nae telling us. I can see it in yer face.'

Holt went silent at once, faster than if Nine-Nails had punched him straight in the stomach.

I was about to give him the benefit of the doubt, but that expression alone rekindled my suspicions.

'The inquest is tomorrow morning,' I said. 'You will have plenty of opportunity to talk then.'

10

I was appalled to see it was still raining when I finally left the City Chambers. It was very late, so at least the reporters had given up for the day, and I had a quiet ride home.

McGray and I had agreed to meet directly at Calton Hill Jail the following morning, to escort Katerina to the Sheriff Court. That would also give us a chance to give her some advice. I could only wonder what might be going through her mind that night.

Layton received me with a large brandy and told me that Joan, my former housekeeper, had just left. She'd brought me a delicious roast chicken, but her duties at McGray's house meant she could not wait for long. I'd not had a proper meal throughout the day, so I ate three quarters of the bird before going to bed, which I would regret.

As soon as I laid down, I felt as if the bed and the entire room swayed. It was like lying face up on a boat, and disturbingly familiar. That sensation had been very frequent since our tragic trip to Loch Maree – the one that had cost my uncle his life – and it felt like the worst land-sickness I'd ever experienced.

Again I closed my eyes, and a wave of unwanted images came back to me – the torches, the lonely islands, the dead . . . I had to light the oil lamp, fearing I'd see my late uncle's face again.

I then realised I had been all right during the day. Other than the brief episode at the colonel's house, I had not even thought of the matter. The work had kept me blissfully focused, but now, as soon as I found myself alone, in my dark and silent bedroom, it all came back to me.

How childish I must seem. Suddenly I pictured everyone at the Sheriff Court laughing at me, the gutless inspector who could no longer sleep without a little lamp on his bedside table.

Again, I woke up at an ungodly hour, and again Layton came with my morning coffee and breakfast. The lack of sleep had made me quite hungry, so I had a few extra pieces of buttered toast and extra sugar in my coffee.

Still, I could not help yawning all the way to Calton Hill. McGray was already there, waiting at the jail's esplanade, and he whistled when he saw me.

'Ye look terrible, Percy.'

'What an ironic remark,' I grumbled, gesturing at his entire persona, and then we walked towards the building. 'Is Katerina ready?'

'Aye. I asked the lads to bring her to one of the questioning rooms. I think she—'

'Inspector McGray!' cried a young officer, coming from the gate.

'Aye?'

'There's a lass here that wants to see ye, sir.'

'What?'

'I told her to piss off, but she won't stop nagging. Asked me to tell ye she's *Mary from the Ensign*.'

McGray's face changed at once, and impatient as I was, I had to follow him back to the front gate.

The officer let in a chubby young woman, whose hair was an explosion of distressingly ginger curls, the same colour as her thousand freckles. She had to elbow her way through three reporters, all trying to catch a glimpse of the interior. I recognised her as the landlady of McGray's favourite pub.

'*Mary!*' cried Nine-Nails with a smile as soon as the gate was closed. 'What ye doing here?'

She was carrying a wide basket, which she dropped on the floor as she flung herself to cry over McGray's shoulder. He held her and patted her back with scandalous familiarity.

'There, there! What's wrong, lassie?'

'Is she well? Have ye seen her?'

'Madame Katerina, ye mean?' McGray asked.

The young woman was sniffing and sobbing, so she only managed to nod.

'Aye, we've seen her.'

'Do you know her?' I said, rather surprised.

'Course I do!' Mary wiped her tears and blew her nose thunderously. 'She was *so* good to me when my auld man died. I was just sixteen. I was a right mess. But she came to me 'n' she told me my dad was in heaven looking after me.'

I chuckled. 'How much did she charge you to—?'

Nine-Nails silenced me with a jab at the ribs.

'Oi, she charged me nothing, sir. She heard I was in trouble 'n' she came to me. I was broke with the funeral, then someone looted the Ensign . . . I was in there all the time, but all I could do was hide behind the barrels! Madame Katerina loaned me some money, and then for months she supplied me ale on credit. I would've lost the Ensign without her.' She rushed to pick up her basket and pushed it into my arms. 'Here, sir. Please give her this, I beg youse. I brought her some bridies 'n' cheese 'n' sweetmeats. Also, a blanket, some soap, 'cause . . . youse know. Oh, 'n' some nice clothes she can wear at the Sheriff's, 'n' the make-up she loves so much.'

'Oh . . . madam, I do not think it will be appropriate that we—'

'Please! These lads say I cannae see her. I wouldnae be troubling youse if . . . if . . .'

'Course we'll do it, hen!' McGray interjected, seeing that Mary was struggling to speak. 'We'll tell her ye came.'

'Thanks! *Thanks*, Adolphus! Please tell her I'm praying for her.'

McGray pinched her rounded cheek as though she were a young child, and then bid her goodbye.

As we walked to the building, I tried to put the basket in his hands, but he would not take it. From the barred windows, some of the prisoners began shouting flirtatious vulgarities at me.

'You seem awfully . . . familiar with that young woman,' I said, and McGray grinned, a twinkle in his eye. 'Are you and her . . .?'

'Occasionally. We scratch each other when we're itchy, if ye ken—'

'I know, I know,' I grunted.

'But the lassie likes her life as it is – her own business, answering to no one . . .'

I nodded. The rules that applied to women like Mary were very different to those that constricted high-society ladies.

The guards took us to the questioning room again, but we had to wait for a few minutes, while Katerina changed into the clothes Mary had brought her. I was pleasantly surprised when she finally emerged.

She was wearing a plain grey dress, buttoned all the way to her neck (her admirers would be disappointed to see). She had not put on the two-inch long fake eyelashes, she'd restrained her use of mascara to human decency, and wore her hair in a simple plait underneath a small, unadorned hat. With the shawl around her arms she looked almost respectable.

'This good enough for your bastard jury?'

I blinked a few times. 'And the illusion is shattered.'

'That'll do, hen,' said McGray after a laugh.

'Tell Mary I'm really grateful. She's a very good girl.'

'She remembers,' said McGray, a grave look on his face. 'A lot of folk remember.'

There was a deep silence then, far too emotional for my taste.

'Shall we talk about court matters now?' I said after clearing my throat. 'It is getting late.'

'Aye,' said McGray. 'Katerina, I want ye to listen to the dandy here. A big sodding ask, I ken, but these juries are more his arena than ours.'

I got straight to the point. 'Today's session is not intended to judge you. The jury will simply decide if there is enough evidence to consider those deaths as murder, which—'

'Of course they'll think it's murder!' she snapped. 'I hear the bloody pricks shouting from the street, baying for my blood.'

I sighed, knowing that the public outcry was likely to influence the minds of the sheriff and jury, but I preferred not to confirm the fact just then.

'We will claim that the evidence is insufficient at the moment,' I said. 'Which is only temporarily true. It would be better, of course, if we had those post-mortem results . . .' I looked accusingly at McGray.

'Reed said he'll meet us at court. He promised he'd have the full report then.'

'I bloody well hope so,' Katerina and I said in unison, and we both winced.

'If the jury thinks there is sufficient evidence to suspect murder, the sheriff will have to remit the case to the High Court, given the gravity of the crime. They will then decide whether or not there is a case against you.'

'What d'you think will happen?' she asked. 'And don't coat it in sugar, son. I can handle the truth.'

I looked at McGray, and he assented with a brief nod.

'I will do my best today,' I assured her, 'but since we have failed to find conclusive evidence so far, I think it is almost unavoidable this will proceed to a full trial. However, there is a chance we can . . . *partly* clear your name. The colonel's valet, Mr Holt, is in a very awkward position. I believe the sheriff will see a stronger case against *him*. You, madam, are likely to remain as a suspect, but I hope they will at least let you go home while we wait for the trial.' Katerina let out a sigh, interrupted when I raised a finger. 'That shall happen if, and only *if*, we handle the situation well.'

She arched an eyebrow. It looked odd without its usual pendant. 'What do you mean?'

'Try to keep any mention of ghosts and spirits to a minimum. In fact, do *not* mention them at all, unless directly asked to. And even then, answer as succinctly as possible.'

'They called me to commune with old Alice!' she cried. 'And I did. And she wanted them all dead. That's the truth! Do you want me to lie under oath?'

'Gosh! Do you *honestly* believe that—?' I rubbed my brow and decided I was done humouring people. 'Well then. Tell them what you wish. Let's see how the jury and the sheriff react when you say you think those six people were murdered by the Bloody Phantom of Cripplegate!'

I made to stand up, but McGray pushed me back down.

'Oi, don't get so tetchy, Percy. And, Katerina, it pains me right in the arse to tell ye this, but ye better listen to the sissy dandy here.'

Katerina and I remained silent, sulking like scolded children.

I took a deep breath. The clock was ticking.

'Is there anything,' I said, 'anything at all, you think we should know before we go out there? Anything you have not told us yet?'

Katerina shifted in her seat. 'No.'

'Nothing you did or said that might be seen as suspicious?' I insisted. 'It is better to be prepared.'

She looked at me without blinking, drumming her fingers on the table but rather clumsily, as if she could not quite co-ordinate their movements without her preposterously long nails.

'No,' she answered at last, but there was something in her cunning green eyes that betrayed her, regardless the resolution of her voice. I think even McGray knew she was not being completely honest.

II

The Sheriff Court had its own dedicated courtroom; a detached building just behind Parliament Hall, on George IV Bridge. We rode past St Giles' Cathedral and its blackened spire, and when we turned around the corner, we found a small crowd already gathered at the gates. Not only workers and washer-women, but also many better-off young men and ladies who had nothing better to do. Two boys were making a juicy profit reselling last week's papers; the ones that told the specifics of the case in the most elaborate detail.

Those boys were the first ones to realise whom we brought. They shouted and pointed, and by the time we halted there was a handful of onlookers clustering all around us, pushing themselves against my door so I could not open it. On the other side of the cab, McGray gave his door a decided kick, sending half a dozen men on their backs as he alighted.

He and a handful of officers came to aid us, and they surrounded Katerina as we rushed into the building. She wisely covered her head with her black shawl, for a couple of thugs threw unidentifiable rotten vegetables at her. I blush when I recall what Nine-Nails shouted at them.

I was the last one to get inside, pushing and shoving, only to find an equally crowded hall. The officers took us through a side corridor, not open to the public, and from there to a small sitting room.

'We have to leave ye here,' McGray told a visibly distressed Katerina. The woman was panting, a trembling hand on her bosom, the other attempting to straighten her little hat. 'But we'll be at the front row. It'll all be all right.'

'Thanks, Adolphus,' she mumbled, squeezing one of his hands. 'I know you'll do everything you can.'

She looked at me with a combination of anxiety and deepest sadness. I wanted to say something comforting but found myself speechless, so I gave her a short nod and made my way to the courtroom.

Never, since my days back in London handling the case of Good Mary Brown, had I seen such a crowded place. Not an inch of the wooden rows could be seen, people packed against each other snugly like sausages in a crate. The bench reserved for the press was just as crammed, with reporters already jotting down frantically and chatting with the enthusiasm of college boys. This might as well have been a public ball; on the furthest pews I could even see a very chubby man selling pies less than discreetly.

'Is that Katerina's manservant?' I whispered at McGray. He just let out a cackle and I shook my head. 'Well, if anyone should be profiteering—'

'There's Nine-Nails McGray!' someone shouted from the back, followed by a wave of laughter and cheering.

'*I can still show youse this one!*' he howled, which only worsened the clamour.

'Inspectors!' I heard a voice say from the front row. There I saw Constable McNair, who had reserved us two seats.

'Where is Dr Reed?' I asked him as soon as we sat down. We had to shout amidst the racket.

'Still at the morgue, sirs. Says he'll try to bring youse some results before the session ends.'

'*What?* How can it be taking him so bloody long?' and for once Nine-Nails shared my indignation.

'There's a few folk I should warn youse about,' said McNair, looking back. 'See that lady there? Huge black hat with the ostrich feathers?'

'It would be impossible not to,' I said. In a matching black velvet dress, she stood out like a fattened crow. Even from a distance, her irate features struck me as very familiar.

'That is Mrs Grenville's mother,' McNair told us. 'Gertrude . . . something-something.'

It instantly made sense; the dark curls, the rounded cheeks. She looked like a larger, angrier, more weathered version of her now-deceased daughter, whom I'd seen at the morgue.

'What's she doing here?' asked McGray. Indeed, the woman looked very uncomfortable, as if fancying herself out of place. Although many refined ladies have taken to attending court proceedings to amuse themselves with the misery of others, they very rarely do so when the cases involve their own families. On those occasions, staying at home sniffing salts is the appropriate thing to do.

She was talking at the ear of a man seated next to her. That chap, most likely in his late thirties, was very thin, his skin mercilessly tanned, and his expression fixed in a deep frown. He looked at everything and everyone with a belligerent countenance, clenching his black top hat with restless hands. He too was in mourning clothes.

'The lad she's talking to is called Walter Fox,' said McNair. 'The eldest of the surviving grandchildren.'

'From Grannie Alice's first marriage,' I recalled, and as I said so, Walter Fox gesticulated exaggeratedly at the front.

'Who's he winking at?' asked McGray.

'Ah, that's how I know them,' said McNair. 'They came asking to talk to the assigned prosecutor.'

'Prosecutor?' I repeated. 'This case is not yet—'

'He's there,' McNair interrupted, pointing at a well-built man in his mid-forties, yet completely bald and with a scalp as shiny as a freshly polished shoe. He was gesticulating back, moving his arms in overdramatic waves, almost flinging the bundles of documents he held in his hands.

Nine-Nails went livid the instant he saw him, baring his teeth in a gesture that would have made the mastiff Mackenzie look like a tender puppy.

'Do you know him?' I said.

McGray was opening and closing his fists as if ready to slaughter him. He had not even heard my question.

'That's George Pratt, sir,' McNair told me. 'He—'

'Aye, I know him. George *twat* tried to get my wee sister tried for murder,' McGray at last managed to spit out. 'The bastard wanted her to come to court and parade her around to demonstrate she'd never lost her—' McGray growled; his face had gone red. 'Dr Clouston himself had to testify. Pratt was like a hungry fuckin' vulture, encircling 'n' trying to break the good auld doctor. He wanted him to confess Pansy was nae mad. That she'd killed—' He could not finish the sentence, his eyes burning with a rage he barely managed to contain. 'Poor auld Clouston nearly broke in tears.'

'Clouston?' I echoed. I could not picture the head of Edinburgh's asylum thus intimidated.

'I heard him tell Mr Fox and that Gertrude woman that the gypsy is as well as hanged,' McNair said, nodding at the gallery. 'He's already been told the case will go to him if the sheriff sends this to the court.'

'Fuck,' McGray blurted out, so loud nearly everyone around heard him.

Pratt noticed our stares across the courtroom, and gave us a petulant nod.

It looked as if he was going to approach us, and I prepared myself for carnage. Luckily, right then the jury and the sheriff walked in, and the officers shouted for silence. There was the clatter of people standing up, but it quickly subsided.

The sheriff was a robust man, short and broad-shouldered, and he walked with heavy strides, almost as if his body were made of lead. His face was very pale but reddened at the cheekbones and the tip of the nose, the rouge highlighted by his wiry beard and mutton chops, which were snow-white. As we sat down, he combed the courtroom with absolute boredom. His eyes had the unmistakable weariness of a man who knows he has missed every chance of further promotion and has only a meagre retirement to look forward to.

He introduced himself as Sheriff Principal Blyth (with a deep, throaty voice far more energetic than his looks) and commenced to the hearings.

To the disappointment of those keen to hear the juicy details of the Morningside deaths, three cases were heard before Katerina's. They had to sit through them in solemn silence, but went mad as soon as Sheriff Blyth summoned 'the gypsy defendant' (perhaps unable to pronounce her name).

Madame Katerina emerged from the waiting room, escorted by two officers. She looked dwarfed between them, and even though she managed to keep her chin high, she could not help wincing at some of the abuse people shouted at her.

Sheriff Blyth immediately cried for order, overpowering the crowd.

'I will remind you all in the gallery,' he boomed, pointing at the rows, 'that this is a *legal* precinct. I will not tolerate any puerile remarks, indecent language or any form of disorderly behaviour.' He then lowered his voice to a normal volume. 'Administer the oath to this lady.'

A clerk went to Katerina with a Bible, and as she took the oath, a man at the gallery shouted something I could not quite catch.

Katerina turned in that direction, incensed.

'Of course I know what the Bible is, you soiled imp!'

'*Order!*' cried the sheriff, making more than one audience member jump. He cast another murderous stare before looking at the paperwork. 'What is your name, madam?'

'Ana Katerina Dragnea.'

Sheriff Blyth sneered blatantly at her. 'Curious enunciation. Place of birth?'

Katerina, to my surprise, blushed more than if asked the size of her undergarments.

'Dumfries.'

The room filled with thunderous laughter, only this time the sheriff let it die out naturally, himself unable to repress a smirk. 'You certainly don't sound from there.'

Katerina was not amused. 'My family didn't mingle much with the Scots when I was young.'

'I see. Now . . .' the man read the documents with a growing smile. 'Occupation?'

Katerina interlaced her hands and lifted her chin a little more. 'Trade.'

The remnant laughter morphed into booing and whistling, which Sheriff Blyth did not tolerate. After silencing the mob, he leaned slightly forwards.

'Can you be more descriptive, madam?'

Katerina glanced at me, then back at the sheriff. 'Brewer, mainly, my Lord. With a few businesses on the side.'

Blyth raised his eyebrows. 'Fortune teller, says here.'

Katerina sighed, having to swallow her temper. 'Yes . . . my Lord.'

There were whispers and muffled giggles.

'A fraudster, I see,' said Blyth, making it clear it was not a question. 'You are accused of the deaths of Mr Hector Shaw, his grandson Bertrand Shaw, Mr Peter Willberg, his niece Miss Leonora Shaw, as well as Colonel Arthur Grenville and his wife, Mrs Martha Grenville.'

Half the courtroom gasped at the very mention of the colonel. I looked back to find the Gertrude woman pressing a handkerchief against her nose – most theatrically – and Walter Fox shaking his head, a hand on his mouth.

'How do you plead?'

All the voices dwindled, people holding their breaths and straining their ears. When Katerina gathered breath, she could be heard clearly up to the last row.

'Innocent, my Lord.'

There was an instant rabble. Whistling, booing and yelling of all manner of insults – 'liar' and 'bitch' were the softest contributions. It took the sheriff a full minute to silence the crowd, after which he threatened to vacate the court and continue the hearing in private should another racket occur. I thought he would ask Katerina to describe the events, but instead he asked her to sit down and looked at our bench.

'Who took the bodies from the scene?' he demanded, and McNair raised a hand. 'Come forward.'

After taking the oath and declaring his name and rank, McNair narrated how he and another two constables had been summoned by Mr Alexander Holt, the colonel's valet. Mr Holt had identified the bodies, and this had been verified later at the morgue by Mr Walter Fox.

I was surprised that the issue of the séance had not yet been mentioned at all.

Sheriff Blyth looked through his documents. I recognised a carbon copy of Reed's preliminary report.

'Where is the forensic boy?'

I stood up and spoke before McGray had any chance to move.

'Doctor Reed is conducting further tests as we speak, my Lord.'

As I introduced myself, someone shouted something like 'sod the English rose!' and there was a ripple of laughter, but Blyth was too busy flicking impatiently through the report.

'This is really poor, inspector. Are you saying that in this day and age, Her Majesty's police forces are unable to tell what killed six fresh corpses?'

I could feel McGray's nervous glance.

'As you can see in the preliminary report,' I said, 'all routine examinations have been performed thoroughly. I myself looked at the colonel's heart and found no trace of illness.'

'Curious,' said the sheriff. 'That detail is not mentioned here. Is there any other *unofficial* matter you can tell me?'

I, of course, thought of the bloodstained knife McGray had found but saw no need to mention it until we had Reed's results.

'Nothing of consequence yet, my Lord. And since the cause, or causes, of the deaths cannot be ascertained at present' – someone shouted 'ascer-whah?' – 'I would suggest this inquest is postponed until we can offer more conclusive results.'

That caused some booing.

Sheriff Blyth read the report intently, and then looked up, analysing me.

'Are you sure there is nothing else you'd like to tell me?'

I remembered myself asking the exact same question to Katerina and felt that my eyes belied me just as much. I spoke fast.

'Only that we cannot rule this as murder if we do not know what killed those people. There is no direct evidence against Miss . . . Mrs— Madame Dragnea here. And—'

'Do sit down, inspector.'

I did so, hearing mocking giggles in the crowd and feeling terribly useless.

McGray leaned to whisper into my ear. I thought he would give me some of his best sarcasm, but I'd be surprised.

'It's all right, Frey. Ye did what ye could.'

'There is a second suspect under custody, I believe,' said Blyth. 'Bring in Alexander Holt.'

In he came, a moment later, also escorted by officers. Unlike Katerina, Holt looked ready to soil himself, crouching and hiding his face from the crowd, the jury and the sheriff.

This time it was McGray who stood up at the first chance. 'May I speak, my Lord?'

Sheriff Blyth grinned. 'Nine-Nails McGray!' and again he did not attempt to silence the laughter caused by his own words. 'Of course you can.'

I prepared myself for a scene, but McGray conducted himself with surprising composure.

'Inspector Frey 'n' me found this man at the Grenville residence. Stealing. We asked him what he was doing 'n' the lad ran for dear life. Had we decided to examine the place fifteen minutes later, this man would nae even be here.'

Blyth turned to the valet, who had taken the oath while McGray spoke. 'Is that true, Mr Holt?'

He whimpered a high-pitched 'yes'.

'He had a second set o' keys to the house,' McGray continued. 'He surrendered one to constable McNair but kept the other, 'n' he used those keys to break in. He had full access to every room in that house throughout the night.' McGray must have seen, just as I did, that the Pratt man was readying himself to speak. 'And *even* if ye rule out robbery,' he said, a touch louder, 'I can think of another thousand reasons he might want to murder his masters. I cannae think of a single one Madame Dragnea would.'

'Thank you, inspector,' said the sheriff, though from his tone he might as well have said 'shut up'.

McGray sat down and then Blyth moved on to the questioning.

Holt repeated what he'd told us the day before almost word by word – he'd fetched the guests, ignored what the family was up to, left them a little before midnight, only after ensuring no other servant remained at home, and did not return until the morning . . . to find the six dead bodies. He then pleaded innocent to the murders. Thankfully, Sheriff Blyth proceeded as swiftly as possible; towards the end, Holt's constricted voice told us he was about to pass out.

I thought the sheriff's next step would be to verify his alibis, but again I was surprised. Blyth looked at the front bench. 'I know the procurator fiscal has a few facts to share.'

He knew – so that Pratt man had talked to the sheriff before proceedings. Most irregular.

Pratt stood up and, almost preening, walked to the sheriff and offered some of his documents for inspection.

'Thank you, my Lord. Yes. I have documents here, provided by the relatives of Colonel Grenville, rest in peace. These will certainly speak in favour of Mr Holt.'

'This is the colonel's will,' said Blyth.

'Indeed. Provided by the colonel's mother-in-law, Mrs Gertrude Cobbold, who's had the courage to come here today.'

The woman was still pressing the handkerchief on her face, so hard this time I feared she'd break her nose. The act seemed to work; people around her patted her back and offered encouraging whispers.

'You will find there a list of valuables which the honourable colonel bequeathed to his valet,' said Pratt. 'The document states clearly that Mr Holt should be able to take possession of them with immediate effect. So, unless Mr Holt was—'

'Och, wait a sodding minute!' McGray cried, to the delight of the gallery. 'Does that justify him snooping around a crime—'

he corrected himself in time, 'what *might* be a crime scene? The place was cordoned off by the police! And he admitted he stole a gold pendant that belonged to Miss Leonora Shaw.'

Even from distance, I heard Mrs Cobbold gasp. Mr Fox whispered angrily at her.

Pratt smiled wide, ironically showing a horrid gold canine, whose sparkle perfectly matched his hairless head. 'Mr Holt undeniably has the poor judgement befitting of his class, but that does *not* make him ipso facto a murderer. Not only can the colonel's family vouch for him, we also have the man's own writing. In his will, Colonel Grenville refers to Mr Holt as *"more than a servant. A good, trusted old friend."* Is that what a master says about a problematic employee?'

He pointed at those lines. Blyth found them and then passed the documents to the jury. I saw several heads nod fervently, yet just as many suspicious stares.

'That means nothing!' McGray snarled, but Pratt's smile only widened. He walked so close to McGray I feared for the bald man's safety.

'Inspector McGray, correct me if I'm wrong. You are a frequent client of Madame Katerina, as the lady is best known.'

'Aye . . . Pratt.'

'How many years have you—?'

'How is that relevant, ye—?' He had to bite his lip to contain a torrent of vulgarity.

Pratt revelled in it. His golden tooth caught a glimmer from the windows. 'It would speak highly of you, as a friend of hers, to try and find other suspects so that this lady—'

'*This tarry-fingered bastard was sneaking at the crime scene!*' McGray roared, his voice resounding throughout the court-room. Pratt jumped a little step backwards. '*He stole a piece o' jewellery one o' the victims was wearing! God knows what else he could've tampered with!*'

Sheriff Blyth hammered this hand hard on the bench. '*Inspector!* Stop it. Your point has been noted. There's no need to turn this court into a fish market.'

McGray was mad with rage but had the good sense to compose himself. He sat down and did not answer.

'And I suggest the procurator fiscal also moves on,' said Blyth. 'I believe you wanted to question the accused.'

'Which one?' mocked McGray, and Blyth shot a look which silenced him.

'Miss Dragnea,' said Pratt, and Katerina was brought forward again. 'Why did you meet the six deceased on that night?' he probed, wasting no time.

'Everyone knows. They asked me to conduct a séance.'

'I see.' He turned to the jury. 'A harmless pastime, surely. Well . . . unless the wrong people are summoned to conduct it.' He lowered his voice when he turned back to face Katerina, sounding ominous. 'I heard some disturbing facts from Mrs Cobbold, which I'd like you to verify. Is it true . . . that you asked all the victims to *bleed* themselves before your . . . rite?'

There were gasps in the crowd.

Katerina stared at him right in the eye. 'It wasn't me who asked them. It was required.'

'*Required?*' repeated Pratt. 'By whom? The spirits?'

McGray made a fist and I seized his arm.

'Yes,' said Katerina.

'Which spirits?'

Katerina gulped. 'Miss Leonora told me they wanted to speak to her grandmother.'

'The late Mrs Alice Shaw. Grandmother and wife. Are you telling me this deceased woman *told* you—?'

'*She didn't tell me!*' Katerina hissed, but then composed herself.

'I am simply trying to understand,' Pratt went on with a mockingly sweet voice. 'Why would a grandmother—?'

'She hated them,' Katerina blurted out. I had to cover my brow.

Pratt spoke as if talking to a small child. 'She hated them . . . So she wanted her own kin's blood?'

'Yes,' Katerina hissed. I saw tears of anger pooling in her eyes.

Pratt finally moved away from her, but he still had one more card up his sleeve.

'Miss Leonora told her aunt, Mrs Cobbold, that in order to make this offering they were to use a very special knife . . .' I saw Katerina bring a hand to her chest as she heard that. 'A knife provided by *you*, madam. Is that true?'

Katerina's hands began shaking. I thought she was about to faint.

'Yes.'

As soon as she said it, and while the gallery exploded in surprised gasps and cries, she looked in our direction, as pale as a ghost. So *that* was what she'd not told us!

'Why did they have to use *your* knife?' Pratt asked her. 'Why not use any of theirs?'

'The— the blade had to be cleansed so the offering was pure. The spirit was angry! That's why I told them all the servants had to leave! We had to be in the house alone. I didn't want anyone else's soul to get harmed!'

My hand slid from my brow to my mouth. I pictured myself leaping towards her, pulling at her skirts, shrieking, '*please, for the love of God, stop talking!*'

Pratt came to us then. 'Inspectors, I trust you've carried out a thorough search of the site. Did you find such knife?'

McGray could have disembowelled him there and then. 'Aye.'

'Inspector Frey,' said Pratt, half smiling, 'you forgot to mention this knife a few minutes ago.'

'I did not—' I was going to say I did not know that the knife belonged to Katerina, but that would only reveal that she had lied to us earlier. Miraculously, I managed to tweak my sentence in time. 'I did not mention it because there is nothing yet to suggest it is a relevant piece of evidence. It is currently being analysed. As I said before, this audience would better serve its purpose, my Lord, once we—'

'You've made that point already, inspector,' said the sheriff. 'You too, Mr Pratt. The jury have been made aware of the existence of such knife; that is sufficient for now.' He looked pointedly at us. 'I will only remind you this once, inspectors, that it is your duty to inform the court of any findings, regardless of your own opinions . . . Unless you want to be charged with perjury and perverting the course of justice.'

Again, I had to grasp McGray by the arm, fearing he'd hurl himself onto the sheriff and bite off his radish-like nose.

Blyth then turned to Pratt. 'Anything else you want to add?'

'Only to stress the fact that this gypsy spent the entire night at the site, locked in with her six unsuspecting victims, only after making sure nobody—'

Blyth cleared his throat loudly. 'Very well, very well. I think enough has been said. We shall now let the jury go and deliberate the—'

I jumped on my feet. 'My Lord, I insist this case cannot be ruled without—'

'Sit down, inspector! You're embarrassing yourself.' Blyth looked at the jury, ignoring me even though I remained standing. 'The evidence has been presented before you. You can go and deliberate in the room provided by the court. This session is closed.'

12

McGray and I could not face waiting at the courtroom. We tried to go for a walk around Parliament House but were chased by a horde of idiots who demanded Katerina be hanged before sunset.

We went back into the building and waited at the small yard right next to the High Court chambers. I looked at that side of the building, where Katerina was now most likely to be judged. There were only a few lawyers and clerks around, all staring at us, but at least they left us be.

McGray lit a cigar with shaking hands. He grumbled, puffing smoke through mouth and nostrils like a locomotive. 'Damn idiots! And that fuckin' Pratt! Och, if I could *just*—' He encircled his hands, imagining they were around Pratt's neck. I thought it would not be a good moment to point out that Katerina had not helped herself at all.

'There is no use lamenting now. We should start thinking what—'

'There they are, laddie!'

I turned to the gate and saw it was McNair who'd spoken. Behind him came, at last, the young Dr Reed. The baby-faced man clearly had had a terrible time finding us: his hair was dishevelled and his cheeks so brightly flushed they looked as if someone had pressed perfectly round red-hot irons against them.

McGray went straight to him and grabbed him by the lapels, lifting him to his tiptoes. 'What the hell happened to ye? They're about to send Katerina to trial!'

I went to them and begged McGray to let the young man go. He tutted and clenched Reed's clothes only a little less tightly and let him stand on his soles. That was all the restraint he was capable of.

Everyone at the yard was watching us, so I lowered my voice. 'Did you carry out the tests?'

Reed looked mortified. 'Yes, sir. I finished just before the session started.'

'*And why did ye—?*' McGray went silent and fear began to creep into his face.

'I did finish the tests,' Reed went on, 'but . . . I didn't think you'd want to hear my findings here today.'

McGray and I were open-mouthed.

'What do you mean?' I asked, and Reed's voice became the softest murmur.

'I found something in their blood. In *all* of them.'

McGray's eyes could well have fallen out of their sockets. 'What?'

'I don't know the exact substance yet, but I did the Reinsch test and I can tell you there is a nasty cocktail of metals in them.'

'So they were . . . *poisoned*,' I said, though only mouthing the last word.

Reed nodded. 'And the knife gave similar results.'

McGray needed a good moment to take in the news. He finally let go of Reed's jacket, but only to spit his cigar onto the flagstones and rub his face in utter frustration.

I drew closer to Reed. 'You risked a lot concealing that from today's session.'

'I know,' he said. 'I thought it might buy you some time if the sheriff didn't hear that today. But we can't keep it secret for much longer. I need to file my report.'

I sighed. 'Yes, you are right.' I gave the young man an evaluating look. The skin around his eyes was indeed blackened. I had to pat him on the back. 'Thank you, Reed. You did very well.' I looked at McGray with the corner of my eyes. 'And I'm sure Nine-Nails will thank you as soon as he is able.'

The look in Reed's eyes told me that, despite how much he pretended to dislike me, my approval meant a good deal to him.

'I should go, inspector. If they see me, they'll want me to testify right now.'

'Indeed. Thanks again.'

Less than forty minutes passed before we were summoned back to the courtroom.

When he asked for silence, Sheriff Blyth was still wiping what looked like crumbs of meat and potato pie from his beard.

The jury's foreman, a wisp of a man, stood up to deliver their verdict from a crumpled piece of paper, which looked more like a piece of brown wrapping than a legal edict.

'We acknowledge that the cause of the deaths has not been determined,' the man read, and McGray almost sighed in relief; however, then came . . . 'but, given the circumstances in which such deaths occurred, and the fact that the six victims were of such differing health and ages, murder remains the most likely cause, and we advise that further investigations should proceed on that basis.'

Katerina lowered her head, just as the main line of the verdict was read.

'We believe Miss Ana Katerina Dragnea is the main suspect and should remain under custody.'

There were some victorious little yelps. I could almost feel McGray's hope leaving his body as he exhaled, yet all I could do was rest a hand on his shoulder.

The foreman went on. 'Even though Mr Alexander Holt appears to be an honourable man, and it is clear he was highly appreciated by his employer, his behaviour remains reprehensible and suspicious. We advise he too should remain in custody. Thank you, my Lord.'

There was a wave of applause, which would have turned tragedienne Ellen Terry green with envy. I looked around for reactions.

Mrs Cobbold still covered half her face with her handkerchief but could not repress the glee in her little blue eyes. Pratt was shaking his head, though he looked satisfied enough. Holt was on the verge of tears. Poor Katerina stared at nothing, like an empty vessel. And Sheriff Blyth seemed only too happy to finally be able to go home.

'Thanking the jury,' he said and then looked at Katerina with a rather cruel spark in his eyes. 'In light of their decision, this case now goes beyond my remit. Miss Dragnea shall be tried for murder at the next session of the High Court. Mr Holt shall also be questioned then.'

I rose to protest but would not even get a chance to open my mouth.

'Save your breath, inspector. You know how the law works, and now you will have plenty of time to investigate.' He gave me a derisive smile. 'Who knows? By the time the High Court meets again, you two might even remember all the other key elements you've withheld today.'

And he rose up amidst sardonic sniggers.

'Today's sessions are closed.'

13

'Ye never told us ye gave them the sodding knife! What were ye thinking?'

'You never asked me!'

'Och, for fuck's sake, Katerina! Are ye mad?'

'I only told Leonora. She wanted to learn the craft, so I taught her some of my methods, but I made her swear she'd never tell anyone. I never thought she would betray me like that, the little bitch!'

'Could you please calm down?' I beseeched them. It was enough with the clatter of the cab as it drove us back to Calton Hill.

Katerina sat down, her hands fidgeting with the little grey hat, her lower lip pushed out, sulking like a teenager. 'I knew if I told you about the knife, you'd take it the wrong way.'

'Do you mean like the jury did?'

'*It's like I told them!* The blade had to be—!'

'Oh, do save it, madam! This is far worse than I expected. They will try you for murder now!'

She tossed the hat to the floor and began sobbing uncontrollably, her fingers quivering around her mouth as she spoke. 'D'you think I don't know that, you prick?'

'There, there,' said McGray at once, putting an arm around her and punching me in the shoulder with his free hand. 'Aye, he's an utter English prick. Percy, how dare ye talk to her like that just now?'

'*But you were just telling her—!* Oh, never mind. We better look ahead. I do not believe the High Court will meet for at least another couple of weeks. We do have time to turn this around – but *only* if you talk openly to us.'

The poor woman was shaking from head to toe, the weight of the situation finally hitting her.

'We will not probe now,' I added. 'It has been a long day for us all. We better rest. We can plan our investigations tomorrow morning.'

McGray agreed and squeezed Katerina's shoulder affection- ately. I thought she was calming down, but then the cab crossed North Bridge, and to our right we had a gloomy view of the jail's towers – blackened bricks and sturdy walls at the very edge of the jagged cliff. Whichever spark was left in Katerina's eyes instantly faded away. She went ghastly pale and the wrinkles around her eyes and mouth seemed to grow deeper, almost as if her flesh had been suddenly drained.

'What is it?' McGray asked her.

Katerina's green eyes followed the outline of the jail, any other muscle frozen.

She whispered, 'I have seen my death . . .'

The post office buildings blocked Calton Hill from our view. Only then did she manage to move, bringing a hand to her neck.

'On that hill. I saw myself hang. I felt the—'

She ran a finger on her skin, following the line of an imagi- nary noose, and said no more. I was expecting McGray to give her some comfort, but he did not speak either. We waited in silence until we made it to the jail's fort-like gate. It took only a few minutes, but it felt like an eternity.

Just before we handed Katerina to the guards, she seized McGray's hand, patted it, and then struggled for a moment before she could talk.

'Adolphus,' she mumbled, 'promise me you'll look after him.'

McGray's shoulders dropped an inch. He looked at Katerina with terrible sadness.

'Oi, hen, don't talk of—'

'Just promise me!' she hissed, clenching his hand, her misted eyes pleading.

'Course I would, hen. *If* it came to that, and it won't.'

She took a short yet deep breath, nodded, and then turned away, saying no more.

I saw her walk off with short, heavy steps, her back slightly stooped, as if all the weight of the world had been laid on her. She could have been someone's grandmother, and I felt an inexplicable prickling on the back of my neck when I thought so.

Nine-Nails was just as affected as her, so I did not speak until we were back in the cab.

'What did she mean by that?' I asked him. 'Who does she want you to look after?'

As we rode away, McGray cast a melancholy stare at the thick stone walls. I half anticipated his answer.

'Poor woman,' he whispered. 'She has a wee son in England.'

PART 2

The Trial

14

The following morning, Katerina was crucified by the newspapers. *The Scotsman* devoted four full columns to the hearing, which included a rather grotesque profile drawing of her, captioned *Mrs Catriona Drakulea, nefarious fortune teller and* only *suspect of the Morningside murders*. The rest of the article was just as misinformed, accurate only when retelling McGray's family history, which was detailed before stating that he was a *blindly loyal disciple* of the *despicable foreigner*. So much for impartial press.

The first thing I did was check when the High Court would meet next. I was glad to hear that the court was currently sitting in Aberdeen and would not return to Edinburgh until the first week of October. That gave us exactly a fortnight to work on Katerina's case. It was still too tight, given the complexities of the case, and as usual I felt an initial wave of overwhelming despair.

My mood worsened when I walked into our office and found it empty. I had assumed Nine-Nails would have been there for hours, with a plethora of books on séances ready for me to mock on.

He would not arrive for another hour, but I wasted no time. I jotted down a list of all the people we should question and the places we should inspect – the Willbergs' home in particular.

If Leonora, for some unfathomable reason, had poisoned the knife, it was likely she had left traces.

I was about to head to the morgue when McGray burst in like a derailed train.

'*Fucking reporters, Frey!*' he roared, clasping a handful of crumpled newspapers. 'Nothing in that pile o' shite is true! *Nae a single peshin' word!*'

I waited until he was done tearing the sheets apart. 'At least they drew her nose rather truthfully.'

He growled and then punched the thin wall behind his desk, leaving a detailed impression of his knuckles on the plaster. 'I would nae even wipe my dogs' arses with that.'

Just as he said that, the huge black mastiff and the golden retriever trotted in. The nonchalant beasts laid on the floor, Tucker on top of Mackenzie, and almost immediately dozed off in a pile of fur and dribble.

'Did you say *your dogs*? Plural?'

'Aye. If the family don't reclaim him, I'm keeping the big brute. And don't ye mention him when we question them! They might've forgotten.'

I sighed. 'And you gave Holt a hard time for pilfering the Grenvilles' estate?'

'Och, how priggish ye are! Never mind. What've ye been doing? Anything useful?'

'Believe me, the fate of that animal is not my main concern right now. I was about to see Reed and check his results on the knife.'

'Ye've nae looked at that yet? Had a lie-in in yer silken sheets?'

'Oh, do shut up,' I snapped as we walked out. 'Where were you in any case?'

'Meeting Katerina. Ye saw her yesterday; she's sure she's goin' to die.'

'Let us hope her *inner eye* is wrong this time.'

We found Reed standing in front of very tidy rows of test tubes, arranged in six clusters that mimicked the six corpses on the opposite side of the room. The exhausted chap spoke before we could even utter good morning. 'Be careful, sirs. I'm working with very strong mutiatic acid.'

McGray looked intently at the labelled flasks. 'Got any more news for us, laddie?'

Reed turned off the Bunsen burner and made a few notes before answering. 'I ran the Marsh test. We can discard arsenic. I only found traces of it in Mrs Grenville, but that will most likely be from her beauty products.'

'That magnolia skin comes at a price,' I said, and then sighed. 'I was secretly hoping for arsenic.'

'Really?' asked McGray.

'Yes, me too,' said Reed. 'These people look like they died of something so poisonous it killed them even before their bodies could develop any noticeable symptoms. There are very few substances that can kill that quickly.'

'And even fewer that can be detected beyond doubt,' I added. 'McGray, do you remember those foul poisonous frogs you made me research?'

'Aye. A cherished memory.'

'There is no technique yet that can differentiate that sort of substance from those in the human body. If something like that killed these people, Katerina is as well as dead.'

McGray stared at the test tubes, not blinking, and he mumbled, 'Shite . . .'

Reed reached for six vials labelled with the names of the victims. They did not contain liquid, but thin strips of copper, all covered in dark, silvery deposits. 'As I said yesterday, there seems to be a nasty cocktail of metals in their bloods. I could perform individual tests for each element, but that would take a lot of time – and large amounts of sample.'

I looked sullenly at the six bundles of white sheets. 'We need to narrow down the list of potential poisons. The families will not be happy if we return them an ounce worth of corpses.'

'No, inspector. And they're already demanding we surrender them. One Walter Fox, Mrs Grenville's cousin, went directly to Superintendent Trevelyan. They want to embalm them as soon as possible.'

'What did Trevelyan say?' I asked.

'He told me it was *your* orders I should follow.'

I saw a fraction of a male toe sticking out of the nearest sheet. There was already a hint of blue Stilton to it.

'I'd say you take as much tissue as you think you can safely preserve and then release the bodies. I do not want another episode like the one in the Highlands.'

Only very recently we'd done our best to preserve a body for forensic inspection. Cut off from the civilised world, in mid-summer and with scant tools at hand, we had of course failed, with unspeakable consequences. McGray had at some point mocked me for my reactions, but even he seemed to retch at the memory . . . and he'd not even dealt with the thick of it.

'What about the knife?' he asked.

Reed brought it back on a little steel dish. 'Like I told you before, it has the same blend of metals.'

'Could that have come from the blood itself?' I said. 'Katerina told us the colonel was the last one to use it. He could have been already poisoned by then.'

'It is possible,' said Reed, 'but again, there's no way I can prove that. If I washed the blood away, I would also wash the poison.'

McGray stared at the little blade, still shiny underneath the clotted blood, and there was a scary sparkle in his eyes. 'Will the fiscal be aware of that?'

'Nine-Nails!' I cried. 'We are *not* lying in court!'

'The fiscal would definitely know,' Reed sentenced, putting the dish aside. 'I'm afraid that's all I can tell you right now. I know it doesn't help the lady's case. I'm sorry.'

McGray exhaled, glaring at the scientific instruments as if they were plagues from hell.

'Speaking of the procurator fiscal,' Reed continued, 'I am forced to send him my full reports as I produce them. I . . .' he lowered his voice, 'I could delay this one until tomorrow.'

I was going to object to that, but McGray pushed me just hard enough so that my elbow lightly brushed the big flask with the concentrated acid.

'Aye, do that, laddie. And, Percy, I want ye to look up in yer fancy books, or telegram any o' those Oxfordian upper-class sissies ye shared yer bathtubs with when ye were *studying*. Try to find if there's any new sodding test we've nae heard of.'

'I doubt that will—'

'Just do it,' he snapped over his shoulder as he walked out. 'Thanks, Reed.'

'Before I bury myself in books,' I said as soon as we were back in our cellar office, 'I think we should make a priority of interrogating the surviving relatives.'

McGray was looking at Mackenzie. 'Aye, yer probably right. And we have an address already.'

15

The carriage stopped in front of a rather modest house on Inverleith Row, just off the Botanical Gardens. The granite walls were eroded and covered in moss, a couple of windows were cracked, the front garden had a lawn as patchy and unkempt as McGray's stubble, and even from the road one could see how grimy the lace curtains were.

'It looks like Miss Leonora and Mr Willberg were the poorer relations,' I said.

McGray knocked at the battered door.

'Don't ye dare mention the dog,' he told me while we waited.

'Who's that?' a coarse female voice asked from within.

'CID, missus,' McGray answered. 'We're investigating the deaths of yer master 'n' mistress.'

'I know nothing.'

McGray chuckled. 'Missus, ye better open the door now or we'll open it for ye.'

'I told youse I—'

McGray began banging and kicking the door.

'*All right, all right!*'

We heard several locks and keys being turned, and the woman finally let us in.

'Yer *so* kind, hen,' McGray said as we stepped into a darkened hall. Like the façade (and the maid's face), the interior looked well past its prime: wallpaper peeling off the walls, damp stains, cracked plaster on the ceiling . . . 'What's yer name?'

The maid spoke belligerently. 'Why? Youse need to know?'

'Ye better answer me.'

The woman snorted. 'Mrs Taylor.'

'I take it ye served Mr Willberg and his niece.'

'Aye,' said the woman, who walked with a slight limp. She was fidgeting with a greasy rag and biting her already chapped lips. She was all nervousness and no sorrow.

McGray noticed it too but said nothing just then. 'Has anyone else been here since yer masters died?'

'Only Mr Fox. He's Miss Leonora's cousin.'

'What did he want?'

'Just to tell me the news.'

'Did he stay around? Did he take or move anything?'

Mrs Taylor cackled. 'What's here to take? Nae, he just told me what had happened and left. Didn't even talk of what's gonnae happen to me now.'

'Have ye moved anything?' McGray asked with as much delicacy as possible.

'What d'ye mean? That I'm stuffing my pockets with their gold? Bah! They were broke! They owed me wages!'

McGray did not hide the suspicion in his eyes. 'Very well. We're going to have a look around, and then we want to ask ye a few questions. Don't leave 'til we've spoken to ye.'

'Please yerselves. I'll be in my room. That's in the loft.'

She made her way upstairs and we heard nearly every single step creak.

'She reminds me of your old housemaid,' I told McGray.

'The one that made stews that looked like turds floating in sludge? Aye.'

The rooms told the same story: cracked furniture, faded rugs, dirty crockery strewn here and there . . . There were even a few dog droppings in a corner of the smoking room.

The first bedroom we looked at was Peter Willberg's. The bed was still unmade (most likely since the day of his death) and there were clothes scattered everywhere. There must have been at least a dozen glasses on the bedside table, all with greasy fingerprints and caked with dregs of claret and other drinks. Something sparkled at the bottom of a fat tumbler. A pair of cufflinks, carelessly thrown there, possibly by a half-drunken man. I used my handkerchief to pick them up.

'Cheap stuff?' McGray asked.

'So cheap even the bloody housemaid turns her nose up at them.' I tossed them back to where I'd found them. 'Cheap clothes as well . . . And look, this walking stick is pinewood painted black to look like ebony.'

'Trying to look the part, Mr Willberg?'

'Indeed. I can see how embarrassed he'd feel when invited to the house of his wealthier relatives.'

'Do we ken what he did for a living?'

'The documents Trevelyan gave me said that Willberg's occupation was "gentleman".'

'*Ha!* Bloody right.'

We found nothing of consequence, so we moved to Miss Leonora's bedchamber.

McGray whistled before I could speak. 'So here's where the money was going!'

This was by far the cleanest corner of the house, and the only one with some feminine touches (crocheted carpets, embroidered linen, a wilted rose still on the bedside table . . .). However, the room was also the most cluttered, crammed with books, sketches and all manner of photographic equipment.

It took a more careful look, however, to realise the eerie nature of the chamber. The ornate leather-bound books were all treatises of necromancy, conjuring and spiritualism. The hand-written sheets were filled with runes and witchcraft symbols.

McGray went through the titles and whistled.

'Do you approve?' I sneered.

'A mixed bag. Some are proper stuff; others are the sort o' quackery I saved up for the Christmas fire.'

I moved on. There were tarot cards strewn everywhere, most of them with spidery notes on the margins, along with talis-mans, strange amulets and several boxes of candles of various widths and colours. And the dozens of photographs, both pinned to the walls and spread on the furniture, were all of morbid subjects like animal skulls, bleak landscapes, dead people propped up as if still alive (a custom as eerie as it was common), and quite a few – most of those arranged neatly on the bed – were purported images of ghosts, varying from the absurd to the downright hilarious.

One showed a cloaked figure floating above the heads of a married couple – the spirit could well have been traced with charcoal, and the sitting room looked blatantly like a photog-rapher's cheap studio. Another one depicted a man looking wistfully at a piano, where a floating girl in white, perhaps his dead sweetheart, pretended to play. My favourite one, though, was the portrait of a see-through skeleton wrapped in rags, embracing a man whose attempt at a terrified pose was cringeworthy.

'Double exposure,' I said, pointing at the photo of the dead sweetheart. 'You can even see the legs of the stool on which this woman was seated.'

'I ken. People tried to sell me shite like that for small fortunes.'

I snorted. 'So she was just like you, only more gullible.'

McGray went to an old davenport desk, where a small journal lay, a dip pen keeping it open. He picked it up, leafed through it and soon enough whistled again.

'As I said, it's mixed. This missy was getting in dangerous ground; talking to the dead, banning their spirits from their former homes . . .' he turned the page and nearly gasped. '*Forcing* truths from them? This is daring stuff, Frey. I wonder if Katerina kent what the lass was up to.'

'Angering the netherworld?' I asked.

'Aye. And that reminds me . . .' He searched his pocket and produced the gold nugget pendant. 'I was sure this was a talisman. Women don't usually wear chunks of unrefined gold.'

I sighed. 'I will regret asking this – but why gold?'

'Gold is the noblest o' metals. It has affinity with the sun, so it purifies and gives strength to the body. She was protecting herself. She must have thought the spirit o' Grannie Alice might harm her. The question is—'

'How is this helping in any way?'

'Shut up! The question is, why contact an angered spirit who might hurt ye?'

I did not bother contradicting him. Instead I went to the bedside table, where I found the only sort of *normal* portrait in the entire house.

In an elaborate gilded frame, it depicted a thin man of around forty, with a thick dark moustache curled at the tips. With his bulbous nose and deep frown, he bore an uncanny resemblance to Peter Willberg. More remarkably, he was surrounded by five stern African women, all clad in intricately embroidered cloaks and sumptuous headpieces made of pleated taffeta. They all posed under the shade of an incredibly wide baobab, whose trunk took over most of the background, and there were picks and spades resting on it. Beyond the tree there seemed to be an endless grassland.

'The lass's dad?' McGray asked, looking over my shoulder.

I took off the back cover and found a brief handwritten note. '*Bill Willberg, December 1868*. Yes. No more details, though.'

'Bring that. And help me gather the rest o' the photographs. We're taking the lot with us.'

He grabbed a half-empty box of candles and in there tossed the journal, amulets, tarot cards and a stack of letters he found in the davenport desk. I added the photographs and we left the room.

'*Oi!* Come doun, missus!' McGray shouted at the stairs. 'We don't need to see yer stockings.'

She joined us, though most begrudgingly, and we went to the cleanest room we could find; a small parlour Miss Leonora probably used to embroider, for there was still some incomplete needlework forgotten on a moth-eaten sofa. I had to spread my handkerchief on it before I sat.

Mrs Taylor stood in front of us until McGray bade her sit down. She did so on an armchair, as far from us as the room allowed. She stared at the box with the photographs as I put it aside.

'How long did Miss Leonora live with her uncle?' was my first question, and the woman cackled in the same manner as before. I thought she was slightly insane, but she'd turn out to be most helpful.

'Live with him?' she echoed. 'It was *him* who lived with her. The lassie's dad – his younger brother – left her this house. Mr Willberg also came across some family money, but as far as I know he squandered it all in a few months. He got letters from debt collectors all the time and asked me to hide them from his niece. She would've been really cross had she known; he had to beg her to take him in, after all. At least that's what her auld housekeeper told me.'

'So you did not work here when that happened?'

'Och, nae, sir. They only hired me 'cause I'm cheaper than that auld snooty hag that used to serve them. The uncle didnae work and the niece spent all her gold on her spooks; of course they had to get cheaper help.'

I searched through the photographs and showed her the one I'd taken from the small frame. 'I assume this man was the father?'

'Aye, but I never met him. I only know 'cause Miss Leonora told me.'

'Do you know when he died?'

'Nae. She didnae like to talk about that. She missed him a lot. I think that's why she was so interested in all this talking to the dead shite.'

Nine-Nails grunted, and I rushed to speak before him. 'Did Mr Willberg share that interest?'

'Och, nae! He just humoured her. We both did. She was the one with the money, after all.'

'I see. What did the rest of her relatives think of her pastimes? Did they visit much?'

'Her cousin Walter – Mr Fox – came from time to time, but it was mostly her calling on him, if only to get out o' the house. The colonel, rest in peace, also visited, but much less and only when Mr Willberg wasnae around.'

'Really?' McGray asked. 'Why was that?'

Mrs Taylor sneered. 'That colonel didnae like Mr Willberg at all. I heard him say a few times the man was a parasite.'

'Did he?'

'Aye. He came several times to ask Miss Leonora to kick the lad out. The last few times he was very insistent, told her that her uncle was a drunken leech and should be in the streets, instead o' sponging from the miss's inheritance.' Mrs Taylor chuckled then.

'What's funny?' McGray asked.

'The colonel fancied himself very bloody brave 'n' manly, but he never spoke up in front o' Mr Willberg. He got all uneasy when he saw him, and they were harsh to each other, aye, but that was all. If the colonel was so worried about the lass's money, ye'd think he would've kicked the man out himself.'

Things were becoming interesting, so I produced my notebook and began scribbling. 'Why do you think that was?'

Mrs Taylor shrugged. 'Dunno. I asked Miss Leonora a couple o' times, but she never told me.' Mrs Taylor then pulled a malignant wince, as if she'd waited for years to say those words out loud. 'I think Mr Willberg knew – *stuff*, if youse take my meaning. Some dirty linen. I think Miss Leonora knew too, but o' course they never told me.'

'Do you think anyone else in the family might know?'

She nodded. 'I'd ask Mr Fox; I'm sure he will. Of all her bunch o' relatives, he was the closest to Miss Leonora.'

I remembered the thin, mercilessly tanned chap we'd seen at the Sheriff Court. He'd indeed looked angry.

'Did you notice anything strange on the days before the deaths? Miss Leonora behaving oddly, perhaps?'

Mrs Taylor shifted in the chair. 'No more than usual. Truth be told – Miss Leonora was a very strange lass. Very, very strange. The things she did 'n' said gave me the shudders sometimes. And she received some very odd visitors, most of the times to do their round tables and talk to dead folk.'

McGray leaned forwards. 'What can ye tell us about those?'

'Nae much, sir. I never lingered when they did that. I told youse, the whole business gave me goose bumps. And she knew that. Whenever she got up to those rituals with her guests I just left them a pot of tea and went upstairs.'

'Did ye ever hear her talk about *Grannie Alice*?'

Mrs Taylor went instantly tense. 'Aye. Miss Leonora and Mr Willberg were talking about her maybe a week before. He was quite upset.'

'D'ye ken why?'

'Nae. As soon as they saw I was nearby they went quiet. As youse can imagine, I didnae really care then. I had nae idea all this would happen.'

'Was the lass upset too?' McGray asked.

'Och nae, she was loonier than ever! All excitement, gathering candles and those stinking herbs she liked to burn . . . and spending all her money on new bric-a-brac for her camera.'

'And on the day o' the séance . . .'

'The colonel's footman came to pick her up very early. He ran errands for her all the time.'

'Were they nervous?' I asked. 'Did they say anything out of the ordinary?'

Mrs Taylor shook her head. 'I could nae say. That day I only saw Miss Leonora when I brought her breakfast, and then later when she walked out. But I do remember she made the poor man carry a shedload o' crap for her. Her camera and other boxes full o' trinkets.'

I looked at my notes. What she said matched Holt's statements.

'What did Mr Willberg do that day?' I asked.

'He left early, but that was very usual. He didnae spend much time here during the day. And he usually came back with too many drams in him.'

'Can you think of anyone who might want to harm them?'

'I don't know much about Mr Willberg's life, but he did look like someone who got himself in a lot o' trouble. And the colonel might've been glad to see him gone, but he's dead too, is he nae?'

'And Miss Leonora?'

'Oh, I doubt anyone would have wanted her to end like that. She was harmless. Creepy and as mad as hops, o' course, but harmless.'

I wrote her answer down and then looked at the photographs sticking out of the box. The one on top was the blood-curdling portrait of a dead baby in a coffin bursting with white flowers.

Harmless might be too rushed an assumption.

'What is to happen to this house now?' I asked Mrs Taylor as we walked out.

'I dunno, sir. Mr Willberg had no children and Miss Leonora was already on her way to becoming a mad spinster.'

'So what are ye goin' to do?' said McGray.

Mrs Taylor shrugged. 'Stay here 'til the family come round – or 'til the spuds in the pantry run out. Then I'll look for another job. If youse need a good cook . . .'

I had to bite my lip. 'We shall keep you in mind,' and I rushed away before she asked for my address.

'What d'ye think o' that?' Nine-Nails asked as the cab took us back south.

'Those were very peculiar living arrangements, though understandable.'

'I'm curious about that ill will between the two sods.'

'Yes, that was puzzling. If the colonel would not confront Willberg directly, the man indeed exerted some power over him . . . On the other hand, Willberg lived off his crazy niece's crumbs. If he knew about the colonel's "dirty linen", like that woman said, why not milk it more?'

'Maybe Willberg had dirty linen too?'

I pondered. 'Perhaps. That would have been an interesting impasse. It would explain why they abhorred each other.'

'Shall we talk to that Fox lad? He might tell us more.'

'Indeed.'

'And if he was close to Leonora he might ken why they wanted to talk to Grannie Alice. The whole bloody thing revolves around that. Katerina said so.'

I snorted, opened my mouth, but then realised I did not have the energy to contradict him yet one more time. In fact, I did not feel like talking at all – to anybody. I'd felt those irascible episodes nearly every day since Uncle's death, and though most times I managed to pull myself on like normal, today I knew I could not.

I said nothing until we arrived in our underground office. I left the box with the eerie photos, candles and talismans on McGray's desk and then walked out immediately, claiming I was off to telegram my former colleagues in Oxford and London. I did do that, but I took my time, and I also messaged a few of my former law professors in Cambridge, asking if they might recommend a Scottish lawyer who'd be interested in helping Katerina at the High Court.

After that I went to the Advocates Library, where it was fresh and quiet, and I leisurely perused the endless rows of dusty legal tomes.

It was not an entire waste of time. I did find that they kept a copy of the latest edition of Battershall's guide to legal chemistry. From the pristine pages, I could tell that hardly anybody had consulted it.

There were dozens of tests I could ask Reed to try, but all focused on detecting one single compound, and most of them required sizable samples. To have any chance of helping Katerina we'd have to narrow down the suspected poisons not to a handful, but one or two.

I spent the next few hours studying the forensic methods, the diagrams and the convoluted chemistry, distracting me from my otherwise fatalistic mood. I only registered the pass of time when the librarian came to light the gas lamps, and I also noticed my pained back and derriere. I loaned the book and rushed to the exit.

On my way out, however, I noticed a very shiny head, smoother than a billiard ball, reflecting the light of a nearby lamp. It was Fiscal Pratt, leafing through an old book. Even on a normal day I would have avoided him, so I tried to leave as quietly as possible. It was useless, for he looked up and our eyes instantly met. He nodded at me with a slight side smile, and I did not bother to nod back.

I knew that Katerina could not be the only case on his desk, and that the very thought was silly, but I could not help feeling the man had been following me.

16

The following morning I found McGray in a much brighter mood. He'd gone through Leonora's journal and correspondence with even more meticulousness than I had the chemistry books: the letters were now pinned to the walls, categorised according to senders and subjects, and McGray had done the same with pages ripped out of the journal, comparing what the young woman wrote to what had been said in her letters. If the photographs and tarot cards were mentioned, he'd also pinned them next to the relevant sheet. Quite a few photographs were still in the candle box, which lay on the floor next to the lazy dogs.

'It seems like you had a productive night,' I said.

'Aye. This lass kept correspondence with necromancers all over the land. Travelled to meet them too, and quite frequently.'

'Does she mention the séance? Her grandmother?'

'Aye, but she was very secretive about it. She even brushed off a couple o' people who wanted to assist – see this one here. A lady from Lincolnshire is begging Leonora to let her come, and in her next one she's moaning 'cause the lass told her to sod off.'

'Did Leonora at least tell them why they wanted to talk to Grannie Alice?'

'Nae. That name never appears. Not even in her private journal. Although . . .' He showed me those sheets, lined in succession. 'There were missing pages. I found entries for the ninth and the tenth of September. Then the eleventh and twelfth were clearly ripped out, and on the thirteenth – the day they died – there is only a wee note about her getting up early, to go and buy a boxful of photographic plaques.'

McGray had left empty spaces where those pages should fit.

'Do you think she tore them out herself? Realising she'd written too much?'

'Herself, somebody else . . . Who and why is impossible to tell.'

'So . . . is there anything new here?'

'Och, aye! And yer goin' to love this. A week before the séance, Leonora listed all the guests. Guess what?'

'Tell me.'

'She does nae mention her cousin Bertrand at all. Instead . . .' he pointed at the page on the wall, 'Here. Aunt Gertrude.'

'The woman at the Sheriff Court?' I mumbled, astounded. 'She was supposed to be at the séance?'

'Aye. Leonora says here she's so happy 'cause everyone had confirmed they'd be there.'

'And for some reason that woman swapped places with one of her nephews . . . Did Leonora mention why?'

'Nah.'

I nodded. 'Well, *that* is interesting. Are you thinking that—?'

'That fatty Gertrude set the whole thing up and then swapped places to save her neck? Aye, but then I remembered that Gertrude's daughter died there too. Mrs Grenville.'

'True,' I said, recalling the family tree. 'Still, we'll have to question her.'

'Aye. She'll be our very next—'

Then we heard hurried steps from the stairs.

'Inspectors,' said McNair from the door. 'There's a man at the courtyard. He insists he needs to see youse. He's making a scandal with the newspaper folk.'

'Call some other lads and kick him away,' said Nine-Nails. 'Truncheon him up the arse if ye have to. I'd help youse, but we're very busy.'

'Erm, it's the lad I saw at the Sheriff Court,' McNair added. 'That Walter Fox.'

McGray and I exchanged looks at once.

I turned to McNair. 'Let him in. This might save us some chasing.'

A moment later we were joined by the man himself, a very haughty chap in his late thirties. He was very thin, not particularly tall, and more ravaged by the sun than I'd guessed from a distance: the creases on his forehead and in-between his eyebrows in fact looked like pale streaks against his otherwise orange, leathery face.

'I hear you two were sneaking at my cousin's house,' he snapped as soon as he stepped in. 'You have no right to do that. I've just told the papers so.'

The man barely matched McGray's height with his top hat on, and his arms were like sticks of liquorice, yet he still grinned most insolently when Nine-Nails stepped towards him. I prepared myself to mop up his blood.

'Say all o' that again, laddie. All o' that. Word by word.'

The orange man was impervious. 'My cousin and uncle were the victims! It is not their house you two should be investigating.' He looked at the walls, his face contorted with indignation as he pointed at them. 'And those are my cousin's belongings!'

'We are carrying out an investigation, Mr Fox,' I grumbled, noticing the man wore a huge, most vulgar diamond ring on his right index.

'You need warrants for that! You don't just step into people's homes and help yourselves to whatever you fancy. I demand you give me a detailed list of everything you took.'

McGray looked at me, pointing at Fox and sniggering. 'Och, he's *demanding*, Frey! So sodding sweet.'

Fox raised his chin a little higher. 'If you don't, I shall tell every newspaper in Great Britain that the CID are plundering the houses of poor innocent victims.'

Nine-Nails stepped a little closer. He had the expression I tend to show when about to devour a plateful of Joan's scones. 'What else will ye tell them, laddie?'

'That you returned us six mangled bodies. I've just been at the undertaker's. They were embalming them when they saw – oh, this is so disgusting . . . They tell me their insides were a mess; missing chunks and everything. You're a bunch of savages!'

'Anything else, sir?' McGray asked.

Fox eyed Mackenzie. 'That dog was my uncle's. I'll take it right now.'

There was a moment of utter silence, like that before thunder strikes. McGray then took a hissing breath through his teeth, and I slowly brought a hand to my brow, unsure whether or not I wanted to look.

'That's too fucking much,' he said, his voice sizzling like hot oil, and in a flashing movement Nine-Nails seized Fox by the hand, doing something to his fingers that sent the man to his knees, as he let out such high-pitched wails the dogs' heads perked up at once.

'Nine-Nails, is this really—?' I waved dismissively. 'Oh, why do I even bother?'

McGray bent down, talking sweetly. 'I won't demand, laddie. I'll ask ye very nicely if ye can take yer sorry arse to our questioning room. We'd like to ask ye a few wee questions. Only if that's nae too much sodding trouble.'

'*You bast— Ahh-ha-harrghh!*'

By that point Fox had dropped his top hat, was shouting all manner of insults and kicked his legs about. He babbled something that involved McGray and hell, and I could only sigh.

'I shall wait in the questioning room,' I said, already heading there and bringing a file with my notes.

'All right, Percy. We won't be long.'

And he kept his word. I'd not been five minutes in the claustrophobic chamber when Nine-Nails and McNair came in with a bedraggled Fox. The man was pressing a chunk of ice wrapped in rags (most likely borrowed from the morgue) onto his hand, and his mourning jacket was torn at the shoulder. He and Nine-Nails sat down, and McNair carefully placed the black top hat on the table – it was now a crumpled accordion and bore a stamp the exact shape of McGray's boot.

Fox glared at me. 'The fiscal will hear of this.'

McGray shifted on his chair, making Fox jump.

'The sooner you answer our questions, the sooner you may go and talk to him,' I said. 'I assume it was your cousin's housekeeper who told you about our visit?'

'Yes. I went there to dismiss Mrs Taylor and pay her a settlement. Not that you need to know that.'

'Ye looking for anything there?' McGray probed.

'If I was, that is none of your business. I am now Leonora's closest living relative.'

'Aye. Bet ye cannae wait to put yer wee carroty hands on the house she—'

I slammed the file on the table. 'Nine-Nails, do shut up. I beg you.'

I must have uttered that really harshly, for McGray, miraculously, did shush. I looked back at Fox.

'Mrs Taylor told us you were very close to your cousin.'

'We saw each other frequently, yes.'

'Good. We are trying to find out why she organised that tragic séance. She must have told you why.'

Fox shrugged. 'Leonora was always doing that sort of thing. Ever since she was little, she fancied she had a certain gift. Some sort of clairvoyance. She said our grandmother had it too, that it ran in the family.'

'Did she tell you why she wanted to talk to your grandmother?'

Fox answered a tad too quickly to my taste. 'No. Nothing specific, I mean. I assumed she simply wanted to commune with her.'

'We are under the impression she – and all the others who attended – wanted to find something. Do you have any idea what that might have been?'

Like his now deceased uncle, Fox frowned very deeply. No wonder the sun never reached those creases. 'Find something? As in . . . an actual physical object?'

I studied his expression before answering. He seemed more curious than concerned.

'Perhaps,' I said.

'And she was asking the dead?'

'Indeed,' I answered.

He sneered. 'Good luck with that.'

'Did she tell you—?'

'No, she didn't! Are you happy? I have no idea what you mean or what she – *they* might have been looking for.'

I exhaled wearily and moved on. 'Was Miss Leonora in the habit of inviting her close relatives to that sort of evening?'

'No, not that I know of. It was usually random swindlers she kept in touch with.'

'Is there any reason you think it was different this time?'

'I couldn't tell.'

I looked at him carefully as I asked the following. 'Did she invite you to attend?'

Fox snorted. 'She brought it up a few days earlier, but I didn't even let her finish. She knew I didn't like her dealings with that nasty gypsy.'

McGray inhaled with expectation.

'You do not like her, I can tell.'

'Of course I don't! I always thought that the madwag simply humoured my cousin to squeeze as much money out of her as she could.'

'I would not blame you for thinking that,' I mumbled. 'Did you ever mention that to her?'

'Only a couple of times, a long time ago. The money itself didn't bother me that much.'

'Oh?'

Fox shrugged. 'Some people squander their earnings at the public house; some at the dressmaker. My cousin did so at a fortune teller's. At least it kept her entertained. Leonora wasn't precisely . . . gregarious.' He sighed then. 'What did worry me was that the damn gypsy knew very well how to get under Leonora's skin. Sometimes I'd visit and find her in a state because of some nonsense that woman had told her.'

'What sort of nonsense?'

He let out another snort. 'Curses running in the family, foul *humours* haunting us . . .'

'Can ye be more specific?' McGray interjected.

'Well, no! I never paid too much attention when she started gibbering about that. As I said, it was all nonsense to me, but Leonora was obsessed. She confided blindly to that woman. I'm afraid the fat harpy may have learned more about our families than she ought to.'

McGray arched an eyebrow. 'What sort o' things?'

Fox bit his lip and sat back, as if suddenly realising he'd volunteered too much.

'I wish I knew. God knows how much Leonora told her.'

'Anything yer afraid Katerina might've learned?'

Fox tilted his head slightly backwards, his eyes for a split second burning as if McGray had just made the most obscene remark. All too soon he seemed to compose himself, and the indignation became wrath.

'I hope she did.'

'Wh-what?'

'I hope your beloved fortune teller did find something scandalous. Shameful, even! And I hope – nay, I pray, she tells you before the trial, and that confirms what everybody is already thinking.'

McGray was clenching both fists. 'Which is?'

'That the gypsy ensnared them only to get rid of them; drug them or kill them and then take something from them. Perhaps that mysterious *thing* you say they were looking for.'

'Can ye prove it?' McGray hissed.

'Of course I can't, but I hope the fiscal can. I know I'll get no justice from you. Like everyone in Scotland, I know your background, and I saw how passionately you two defended that woman at the hearing.'

McGray was gnashing his teeth, one hostile remark away from tipping up the table and beating Fox to a pulp.

I changed the topic before more of Fox's limbs required ice.

'Speaking of the court, we saw you next to Mrs Gertrude Cobbold. Your step-aunt, I believe?'

Fox glared at me, and when he spoke, he showed most of his teeth. 'Yes. Why?'

'What can you tell us about her?'

'What do you want to know?'

I sighed. 'Was Mrs Cobbold close to Miss Leonora?'

'What do you mean by—?'

I slammed a hand on the table. 'Will you give me a direct answer or shall I ask my colleague here to become persuasive again?'

Fox did not seem to react, but he did tap his injured hand. The melting ice was now dripping on the table.

'Closer than me, but not overly friendly,' he said. 'Leonora called on her every now and then, but I did not mingle much with that side of the family. They always looked down on us.'

'Did they?'

'That old man, Mr Shaw, was far wealthier than my own grandfather. We on the Willbergs' side have always been the poorer relations.'

'Ye seem quite well off now,' McGray pointed out, looking at Fox's vulgar diamond.

'I made myself through hard work.'

'Have ye! A tad too quickly, it seems.'

Fox winced maliciously. 'Yes. Like I've heard your own father did.'

McGray at once raised his chin, clenching a fist. This man knew very well how to touch people's nerves.

I thought it better to move on. 'I assume you and your step-aunt have discussed the matter at length.'

Fox stared intently at me, as if trying to predict my next move. 'Y-yes.'

'Has Mrs Cobbold told you she was supposed to be at the séance?'

His eyes opened a little wider, and this time he did not attempt to conceal his surprise. 'No. How . . . how do you know that? Leonora's letters?'

'Indeed. We believe she swapped places with your step-cousin.'

'Bertrand,' Fox mumbled. He looked at us, more and more alarmed as the seconds passed. 'Did you . . . I mean . . . Have you talked to her?'

McGray half smiled. 'Why d'ye ask? Afraid yer stories won't match?'

Again Fox's eyes betrayed him for a split second, before he rapidly composed himself.

'Leonora . . . did mention her as one of the people she might invite. But no, Mrs Cobbold never told me that.'

'Do you realise that leaves her in a very uncomfortable position?' I asked, and Fox chuckled.

'More uncomfortable than your stupid gypsy? Why would my aunt want to kill her own daughter? Her father! And now she'll be looking after the three poor children.'

'Some quarrel against her son-in-law?' I ventured.

'I don't know! I told you, I didn't mingle much with them. I knew the colonel could be very difficult, but I hardly ever—'

The door slammed open then, and we all startled as we heard a shout.

'*So there you are!*'

I first saw the glimmer coming from Pratt's polished scalp. Beads of sweat made it all the shinier, glinting like his golden tooth.

McGray stood up, nearly capsizing the table. '*Get the fuck out o' here, ye Pratt!*' he roared.

Pratt hinted at a mocking smile. 'I suggest you release this man, Nine-Nails.'

'Get out!' McGray repeated, grabbing Pratt by the tie and throwing him out of the little room. He shut the door, but then we heard Pratt's voice from the other side.

'Everyone in the City Chambers is talking of how you've *persuaded* this man to talk.'

'Sod off!'

'Release him now or the jury will hear how appallingly you're treating the victims' relatives. Do you think that will help your beloved gypsy?'

McGray stared at the door, his chest swelling like bellows. I shook my head at him as a warning, just before McGray threw a few punches at the door. Fox was grinning.

'Release him now, Nine-Nails,' Pratt said, an infuriatingly cheerful note in his voice. 'Or you'll mar the validity of your entire investigation.'

McGray looked at Fox, then back at the door, snorted, and then let out a growl that grew loud and steady until he ran out of air. He punched the door one last time, so hard he nearly cracked the wood, and then opened it.

'Get yer fuckin' leather moccasins out o' here.'

Fox did not wait. He trotted his way out, pressing his injured hand against his chest and not bothering to take his ruined top hat. However, he allowed himself a sneer as soon as he was past the threshold. 'I do want that dog back.'

'*Piss off!*'

And McGray shut the door, hitting the man right on his burnt orange nose.

17

'We have to talk to Gertrude Cobbold right away,' McGray babbled, rushing to our office. 'That Fox sod might go and meddle with things.'

I checked the documents provided by Trevelyan and was happy to find all the addresses we'd need. McGray jotted one down and was calling for a cab before I could say a word.

It turned out Mrs Cobbold did not live near her father and daughter. She owned a small yet sumptuous flat in New Town, her front windows overlooking the south-west corner of St Andrew Square.

We were received by a young and fidgety scullery maid, who showed us the way to a well-appointed sitting room. Everything there spoke of wealth and comfort: sofas upholstered in mint-green damask, matching wallpapers under an exquisitely plastered ceiling, enormous china planters bursting with waxy foliage, and an ornate mantelpiece exhibiting all manner of expensive trinkets and family pictures. Those in particular caught my eye.

The girl mumbled we should wait there and scurried away. I went to look at the portraits, which were a mixture of photographs and small oils. Especially detailed, and placed prominently at the centre, was the painting of a middle-aged woman, seated on a wicker chair and wrapped in richly embroidered blankets.

'Is this Grannie Alice?' I asked, and McGray came to have a look.

The brushes were delicate and precise, clearly by a skilled artist, so I could assume it to be a reasonable likeness. The woman was very thin, with the dark, tight curls shared by her now dead granddaughters, and she was the one to blame for the family's bulbous noses. However, there was a strange beauty to her features; some sort of charm I am afraid none of her descendants had inherited. That fetching quality undoubtedly came from her eyes, painted with hair-thin traces that gave them a most vivid, entrancing effect. I felt as though a breathing person were staring back at me, with a stoic sadness that made my neck hairs stand on end.

When McGray spoke, I startled.

'Look at the hands,' he said, and I noticed that Grannie Alice was holding a dip pen and piece of paper with a half-drawn astral chart.

And then other details emerged: lurking in the dark foliage behind her were the eyes of a black cat, and the woman wore a golden talisman around her neck.

'See that?' asked McGray. 'A perfect circle with a wee dot in the centre. That's the Wiccan symbol for the sun. And the wee cat there. D'ye think she might've been a witch?'

I sighed. 'We cannot discard it, although it is far more likely that she was simply as peculiar and credulous as her silly granddau—'

'Good afternoon, gentlemen,' a sweet voice called out behind us, and I instantly blushed.

We turned on our heels and saw a young woman appear, carrying a silver tray with a tea service. She could not have been called beautiful, with a rather large mouth, freckles all over her face, and unusually wide hips, but her eyes were deep blue and welcoming – McGray's instantly sparkled.

'Och, good day!' he said, all smiles, and offered a hand to shake as soon as the girl left the tray on a nearby table. 'Inspectors Percy and McGray.'

'Ian Frey,' I grumbled, bowing at her.

'What's yer name, lassie?'

'Ethel Tomkins, sir,' she replied with a mellow, well-modulated Edinburgh accent. 'I'm Mrs Cobbold's companion. Prissy tells me you came to see my mistress.'

'Yes,' I jumped in, 'and it is rather urgent.'

'I would assume so, sir, with all this scandal around her. But I'm afraid Mrs Cobbold is out of town.'

'*Out of town!*' I squealed, at once suspecting the woman might be on the run.

McGray interjected in a much friendlier manner. 'D'ye ken where she went?'

'Of course, sir. She's just in Kirkcaldy. She has a wee summer house there. She's with the colonel's children.'

'She took them there?' McGray asked.

'Yes, the poor things. She sent them away as soon as she received the news. Only yesterday she set off to join them. I don't think she'll bring them back for as long as this horrid circus goes on.'

'Is she herself coming back at all?' I urged.

'Oh, I don't know, sir. She told me she might come for the trial, but it all depends on how the children are doing by then.'

I let out a hissing breath.

'If you really need to talk to her, I can telegram her. Prissy can run to the—'

'That will not be necessary,' I interrupted. 'We would prefer to contact her ourselves. If you please give us her Kirkcaldy address, we shall be on our way.'

'Of course, sir,' she answered. 'Do be seated. I'll fetch some paper.'

McGray lounged on one of the sofas, but I remained standing.

'Och, sit down, Percy.'

I tapped my shoe on the floor. 'McGray, the blasted woman has sailed away with the colonel's brats. Do you not find it—?'

'Here,' said Miss Tomkins, coming back with a note and, despite having caught me yet again, she kept her kind face. The girl put the note in McGray's hand, showing him a rather forward smile.

'Since we're here,' said McGray, pocketing the note, 'can we ask ye a few wee questions, lassie?'

'Oh, of course, sirs! I was about to have some tea, if you care to join me.'

'Och, aye, I love tea.'

I rolled my eyes, sighed and sat down.

I was going to refuse any nibbles, but the cucumber and roast beef finger sandwiches proved too tempting. I savoured them as McGray drank tea for the first time in months (he does not care for brews) and questioned Miss Tomkins.

Even distracted by the food, I gathered that the girl had worked there for almost ten years, hired right after the death of Mrs Cobbold's husband.

'Ye must've been a child,' said McGray, making the girl blush.

'I hope you don't expect me to confess my age.'

'I'm CID, lassie. I may have to force ye.'

I breathed out. 'I am surprised Mrs Cobbold did not live with her daughter.'

Miss Tomkins refilled McGray's cup before answering. 'She didn't like the colonel at all. I'd be more reserved about that sort of thing, but I'm sure she'll tell you the same. My mistress values frankness.'

'D'ye ken why she hated him?' McGray winked at her. 'Speak on. I won't get ye in trouble.'

Miss Tomkins twisted her mouth. 'Well, the man was impossible. Always angry and shouting at everybody. And I know he did some—'

The scullery maid came in then with a fresh pot of tea, and Miss Tomkins jumped.

'Prissy, stay in the kitchen 'til I call you.'

The young girl left and only then did Miss Tomkins continue.

'I heard the colonel did some sort of . . . murky businesses with the late Mr Shaw.'

'Grannie Alice's husband?' I asked, and Miss Tomkins nodded. 'What sort of businesses?'

'Oh, I couldn't tell you a thing about that, sir. They always spoke around it, not calling things by their name.'

'Who is "they"?'

'My mistress and her daughter, Mrs Grenville, may she rest in peace.'

I produced my pocket notebook and scribbled away, which made the girl quite nervous.

'It's fine, lassie. We won't get ye in trouble,' McGray assured her again, and for once I was thankful for their flirting.

'Do you have any hint,' I went on, 'any at all, as to what that business might have been?'

Miss Tomkins looked sideways, deep in thought.

'I know it must have happened at least twenty years ago. I heard my mistress and her daughter say once that the *troubles* – as they called them – happened just as they were planning the wedding with the colonel. Shortly before or shortly after, I can't remember.'

As I wrote that, one detail seemed to glare from the pages.

'They married twenty years ago?'

'Yes, sir.'

'But the children—'

'The eldest has just turned twelve.'

'So they were married for eight years before the first child was born?'

'Yes, sir.'

'That is very odd,' I mumbled, writing it down. 'There must have been much gossip.'

'Oh, yes. I heard that that vile Mr Willberg once even mocked the colonel at a family ball. You can imagine the sort of jokes.'

'Indeed,' I said, looking at McGray. 'I have grown very familiar with such crass vulgarity.'

'Eight years, nae issue, and then three children?' McGray asked, and Miss Tomkins looked furtively at Grannie Alice's portrait.

'The grandmother . . . I once heard that she did . . . *something* to help.'

I stopped scribbling at once. 'Something?'

'Aye – I mean, yes. She . . . well, everybody knew her interests. Apparently she brewed some . . . potions.' She grabbed McGray's hand. 'Please, do not tell my mistress you heard that from me. I mean, everybody knows, but—'

'It's all right, lassie. We'll keep ye safe.'

He smiled and went on to enquire about the day of the deaths. Miss Tomkins repeated much of what we'd already heard, and just as my attention was drifting towards the last cucumber sandwich, McGray asked her if she knew the purpose of the séance.

'I think I do, sir.'

Nine-Nails and I looked up in perfectly synchronised movements.

'You do?' I asked.

Miss Tomkins blushed again. 'Well, I – I'm not sure it will mean anything. I had it from the children, after all. I used to entertain them whenever Mrs Grenville came to visit my mistress.'

McGray and I were on the edge of the sofa.

'Tell us, lassie. I'm the last man who'd laugh at ye.'

I was going to remark that his tartan trousers were proof of that, but opted not to; the young woman already looked nervous. Again, she glanced towards the kitchen, making sure Prissy was away.

'Promise me you won't tell the family I said this,' she whispered, and we assured her we'd not betray her confidence.

She took a deep breath.

'Master Eddie, the colonel's eldest, told me this when he was just five or six. He said that Grannie Alice – they all called her that, even though she was their great-grandmother – he said that she had promised him a treasure.'

We waited in silence for a moment, and when the words finally settled in my mind I felt my shoulders dropping an inch.

'*A treasure!*' I began, but McGray silenced me with his elbow on my ribs.

'What kind of treasure?' he asked.

'I don't know. She only told him she had a treasure. Something she'd never give her children and grandchildren. Master Eddie said she was saving it for him and his siblings.'

It took me a moment to realise I'd been holding my breath, staring at the girl, with my lips slightly parted and my pencil hovering above the paper.

The statement sounded intriguing and preposterous in exactly equal measure. McGray looked at me with an expression that mirrored my own thoughts.

'Take note o' that,' he told me. 'We can ask the laddie when we see Mrs Cobbold.'

Miss Tomkins was staring at the carpet. 'I'm afraid Grannie Alice died soon after Eddie told me that, and as I said, he was very young then. He might not be able to tell you much more.'

'We'll still try, lassie. Thanks for trusting me – I mean us.'

She gave him a coquettish smile.

Right after I had the last sandwich I told her we must go. I did not tell her, however, that I intended to telegram the Kirkcaldy constables at once and ask them to make sure Mrs Cobbold did not leave town.

Nine-Nails said goodbye in a most effusive manner, and since I did not wish to witness his obtuse dallying, I walked out and went straight to the road. He joined me only a moment later.

I said, 'A little too plain for you, is she not?'

I looked up then and, to my dismay, found that Miss Tomkins had just opened the window and was waving at us. I swiftly turned on my heels and we walked away, McGray grinning.

'Aye, like ye only pick feathery angels.'

He had far too much ammunition there, so I pulled the conversation back to the case.

'We need to see Mrs Cobbold as soon as possible. Today, even.'

That deflated him at once.

'Kirkcaldy . . .' he mumbled, right before reaching for a cigar.

'Indeed.'

'That's on the other side o' the Firth o' Forth.'

I allowed myself a half-smile.

'Hardly a couple of hours away . . . That is, if we travel by ferry.'

18

Strong draughts of salty air came from the east, lashing the choppy waters and making the ferry sway violently from side to side. The sky was a blur of white and grey, but at least it was not raining. I could have almost called the trip pleasant, had it not been for McGray's guttural gagging as he leaned on the gunwale to empty his stomach into the estuary.

'Oh,' I said, feigning innocence, 'I did *not* remember at all that you get such severe bouts of seasickness . . .'

His only reply was an even stronger spurt of vomit, and I took a few steps aside to avoid the splatter.

We had only stopped briefly to telegram the Kirkcaldy constabulary, and did not even wait for a reply. We had then rushed to Leith Harbour, where we'd managed to catch the last ferry of the day. We would have to spend the night over there, since following the coastal road would take us just as long.

As I thought of that, I looked west, and amidst the morning haze I saw the milky outlines of Forth Bridge, still under construction. It looked nearly ready, and some said it might be finished before the end of the year; then again, they'd been saying that since 1885, so I had my reservations.

McGray let out a particularly loud heave, and I decided I'd take advantage of his sorry state and ask him a few uncomfortable questions.

'Do you remember what Walter Fox told us?'

McGray barely managed to give me a nod.

'I have been thinking about what he said about Leonora.'

'What d'ye— The—?'

'No, not that Katerina might know murky things about them. Although that *will* be a concern . . .'

'Then . . . whah—?'

'I mean what he said about Katerina humouring the girl, only to get money out of her.'

He glared at me from the gunwale, and I showed him a smirk.

'Do not tell me you still believe Katerina is above defrauding gullible clients.'

'Well . . . nae, but—'

'She herself admitted to deceiving people! That will not look good in court. I am fearing most of her statements will be disregarded no sooner than she speaks them.'

'Percy . . . d'ye—?'

'Do you think her above taking advantage of what people tell her?'

'I-I wouldnae—'

'Oh, would you please finish with that and answer me?'

McGray spat the last bit of bile and wiped his mouth with a rag given by one of the sailors. He looked so green it made me ill to look at him.

'Well . . . aye,' he managed after a few short breaths, 'she may take advantage here 'n' there, but it's mostly trifling stuff – the odd blackmailing of a cheating husband . . . pretending that a merchant's dead grannie is asking him to buy ale from a pious gypsy . . . Ye ken, trifles!'

'So it is not impossible that she might have wanted something from the Shaws and Willbergs; that she may have planned to swindle them in one way or another.'

McGray pinched his septum, barely keeping the nausea at bay.

'I wouldnae bet my Tucker's life on her morals, but—' He shook his head. 'Murder, Frey? Murder six people? And if she was able to plot a murder that had us all scratching our heads, why then frame herself in such a clumsy way?'

'What would strike you the most? The murders themselves, or the clumsiness?'

He could not answer, turning back to the sea and readying himself to spit out another batch.

'McGray, could she . . . could she have thought you'd be able to get her out of it?'

But he only answered me with spew.

He looked so frail and miserable, I spoke with unprecedented frankness.

'Could she have believed she was untouchable, having such close connections with the police? Could that have made her overconfident? Emboldened her to commit such a horrible act?'

McGray could only give me a fleeting look, and in his sickness he betrayed himself; I saw a hint of doubt in him as well.

Just as the wind began to dwindle, we docked at the surprisingly busy piers of Kirkcaldy.

The smell of the town's whale oil factory was unbearable, and it did not do much to ease McGray's queasiness.

As soon as we alighted he went to a merchant lady, snatched a piece of raw ginger from her stall and began gnawing on it. I gave him some time to recover, staring at my pocket watch the entire time and trying not to look too amused by his disgrace. We then called a two-seater cab that took us south.

Besides whale oil, the town also had the dusty smells of industry, filled with wood yards, mills and warehouses all clustered along the seafront, but the farther we rode, the quieter things became. Within a few minutes endless grassland opened up to our right, and to the left we had the grey waters of the River Forth, the southern shore but a dark strip on the horizon.

We approached a group of leafy oaks, until I saw that they surrounded the lawns of a small granite house, situated a hundred yards or so from the riverbank. There was no sound other than the river and the breeze, and I envied the peace of that little plot of land.

As the cab turned around the trees, I saw a thin constable with a preposterous moustache dismounting from a rather measly horse.

'Wait for us,' McGray told the driver, and we stepped down. 'Got our message, laddie?'

'Aye, sir,' said the constable, 'but we had a wee bit of a squabble at The Turf Tavern. I came as soon as I could.'

'What's yer name?'

'Constable Talbot, sir. Is it true this has to do with the scandal of that gypsy—?'

'Follow us,' McGray rasped, and then zigzagged towards the house, his legs still somewhat flimsy from seasickness.

We knocked at the door and I took a deep breath. 'We should be cautious. We will either find that Mrs Cobbold has packed and fled with her grandchildren – and you might want that, McGray, for then she'd become the main suspect – or we will find her utterly distraught. Both her father and her daughter died that night.'

A wide woman opened the door. She was quite old, stumpy, lacked two front teeth, and wore her white hair in two coarse braids. She cast Constable Talbot a suspicious look.

'What youse want?'

I let McGray do the talking. He is better than me amongst rustic Scots.

'Is Mrs Cobbold home, missus?'

'Why?'

'We need to see her. It's about the—'

'I can see what it's about. Come in if youse must.'

Right then the wind brought us the voices of children playing somewhere behind the house, and I let out a sigh of relief.

'You better wait outside,' I whispered to the constable. 'It looks like the woman has not fled. We do not want to upset her too much. Not yet, at least.'

Talbot looked rather disappointed but did step back.

The housekeeper took us to a very nice sitting room, as cosy and neat as the one we'd seen at St Andrew Square. Mrs Cobbold's expensive taste was evident, with the nice upholstery and the enormous planters. The room's best asset, however, was its wide south windows, looking over the field that separated the house from the river. On a very clear night, I thought, all the lights of Edinburgh could be seen from there.

'Wait here,' the woman rather commanded, and left at once.

I caught McGray smiling.

'Are you going to make love to this one too?' I asked.

He chuckled. 'She looks a lot like Betsy, my dad's housekeeper. She still lives in the farmhouse where . . . it all happened.' He nodded at his missing finger, no further explanation required. 'I should visit her one o' these days. She's nae getting any younger.'

I checked to make sure we were alone, and then whispered in McGray's ear. 'I do not think we should mention the . . . treasure. We should ask the child first.'

'Indeedy. I'll do that, yer terrible with children.'

'I will not deny that,' I said and, feeling restless, went to the window. After a moment, I caught a glimpse of a very young girl running amidst grass as tall as her. She was gone within a blink, but it was enough to realise how carefree and happy she looked. 'McGray,' I muttered, 'I do not think they have been—'

'The missus will see youse in the study,' the housekeeper barked then, and led us to the adjacent room, which also overlooked the bay.

We found Gertrude Cobbold bent over her desk and scribbling frantically, half buried in the centre of a pile of paperwork. She still wore mourning clothes, but that was the only hint at her losses. Her face was composed, her writing neat and straight. In fact, the only signs of strain were her tense lips and the many pen nibs, some bent and some broken, scattered all over the desk.

She looked up, but only to examine us, and then went back to her writing. 'I hear you came with a police officer.'

'Normal procedure,' I lied. Her smirk told me she knew. 'We need to ask you a few questions, ma'am.'

'I am very busy, as you can see. I need to liaise with the executors, arrange the funerals, see what is to happen with Grenville's house . . . look after the poor children . . .'

'It will only take a moment,' I said. 'This is part of our ongoing investigation.'

She laughed scornfully. 'Nothing I can say will help you save that damn gypsy. I'm sorry to disappoint you.'

'Ma'am, we have travelled all this way to—'

She banged the pen on the desk, the nib piercing paper and polished mahogany. Her eyes were all fury. 'And I just lost my father and my daughter. And then I went to court, only to see you two defending that filthy cow as if she were your mother.'

So Mrs Cobbold was raging instead of mourning. I understood. Sometimes hatred is more bearable than pain.

'We are carrying out an impartial investigation, ma'am.' But even I knew I sounded as silly as the Prime Minister promising higher interest rates on government bonds.

Mrs Cobbold merely laughed and then reached for a new nib for her pen.

I changed my approach. 'You may refuse to talk to us, but your silence will not help your family's case.'

She looked at me, laughed with utmost mockery, and then threw the pen aside and lounged on her chair. 'Very well, sit down. I can spare a moment to tell you a thing or two; do what I can to help the court pass sentence on that murderer.'

McGray was keeping his temper under control, but only just. He got straight to the point.

'We ken ye were supposed to attend the séance.'

The woman's jaw dropped ever so slightly, but her skin blanched instantly. Her pupils flickered between McGray and me, her frosty façade all but fallen.

'Who told you that?' she whispered.

'Doesnae matter, missus. I can tell it's true. Ye were meant to be there, but ye sent yer nephew Bertrand in yer place.'

Mrs Cobbold shifted as if suddenly realising she'd been sitting on nails. 'I did not "send" him. I changed my mind about taking part. I don't know who fetched Bertrand to take my place.'

'So you *did* know about the session,' I intervened, and her lips went tense.

'I did.'

'Ma'am, so far nobody has been able to tell us the purpose of that meeting.'

Mrs Cobbold let out a high-pitched *ha!* 'Not even the damn gypsy?'

'She only kens youse wanted to talk to Grannie Alice. Yer mum. *Youse* didnae tell her more.'

That took Mrs Cobbold by surprise. I was expecting her to throw a tantrum. Instead, she remained silent.

'Why did youse want to talk to her?' McGray asked.

'Why does that matter?' she spat. 'That doesn't change the fact that they all died and your treasured cow survived.'

'Then you should have no problem telling us,' I added. 'You were summoned. You *must* have known.'

Her eyes flashed in a gesture that much reminded me of Walter Fox, as if quickly weighing her chances.

'*They*,' she said, rather too intensely, '*they* wanted to talk to her. I did not. Even if I believed in those damn tricksters and their ploys, I have no need. I told my mother everything she needed to know when she was alive. I'm the one who saw her die; I was holding her hand. She and I parted in peace.'

McGray tilted his head. 'But the others didnae?'

She laughed. 'Why don't you go to your gypsy and ask the dead yourself?'

'That's actually a very good idea. Frey, write that down.' I could not possibly tell if that was a joke or not. He looked at Mrs Cobbold. 'And ye, missus, stop being so cryptic. Did they tell ye what they needed from Alice?'

Mrs Cobbold gulped as if she'd swallowed a conker. 'No.'

She was lying, it was obvious, and McGray lost his temper.

'We're trying to find out what killed yer daughter, for fuck's sake!'

The woman let out a sharp breath. 'I've told you all I know, you twisted little man! I only agreed to attend that silly session because my daughter Martha insisted. And she herself just wanted to humour her stupid cousin Leonora.'

'And that's all they told ye,' McGray probed.

'Yes!'

That last yelp was almost feral.

I moved the questioning on before McGray further antagonised her.

'In the end you did not attend, ma'am. Why did you change your mind?'

She inhaled deeply to calm herself. 'I was going to host the séance in my flat – again, only because Martha nagged so much about it. Then the old gypsy said it must be done in Grenville's house, where my mother had spent the last years of her life. Something to do with her . . . *essence*, or that sort of stupid thing, so I refused.'

'Can you tell us why?'

'I didn't get along with my son-in-law. I swore I'd never set foot in his dwellings. Besides, I did not want the children to get scared with all that nonsense. I told Martha to send them to me for the night. Just as well – the gypsy didn't want any witnesses.'

'Speaking of the colonel,' I said, 'we know that . . . we know how he treated his wife – your daughter.'

Again, the woman's hard shell appeared to crack. Her chest swelled a little, she looked sideways with a quick movement of the neck, and then bit her lip as her eyes misted up.

She cleared her throat. 'You'd have seen her body, I suppose.'

'Indeed,' I said, more gravely. 'A post-mortem was unavoidable. I am sorry.'

I was going to ask her to tell us more, but the woman did so spontaneously, as if she'd been yearning to speak up for a very long time.

'I instigated that marriage. There is nothing I regret more in my entire life. Grenville was my mother's second cousin, or so I was told – it was a convoluted connection, apparently. He was very gallant back then and my Martha was besotted.

'My mother overheard when he came to me and my husband, asking for Martha's hand. She told us once and again we should not allow the union. She told us Martha would be miserable.' She had to force a deep breath to keep tears at bay. 'She . . . she told us she'd read it all "in the cards", so of course we ignored her!'

McGray was going to intervene, surely to ask more about 'the cards', but I raised a hand, begging him to let her continue. He acceded.

'My mother also told us about their . . . barrenness. She said the marriage would be cursed. We laughed at her then, as you can imagine . . . We were not laughing seven years later, when there was still no hint of a child.

'Poor Martha came to me many times, telling me that Grenville blamed her. That he called her a dry—' She gulped then, and it was as though she'd awoken from a trance. 'You don't need to know more of that. It has nothing to do with . . . your investigations.'

'Did yer mum help them?' McGray asked.

Mrs Cobbold looked surprised. 'Did someone tell you?'

McGray kept his word and lied. 'I've heard plenty about yer mum's skills. Nae hard to guess.'

'She . . . she did help Martha. I don't know how; it had to do with herbal teas she bought on the black market and keeping odd talismans under the bed. I still don't know if all that worked; all I know is Eddie was born soon after. We were all overjoyed. Martha especially. When she was pregnant, Grenville left her alone. He even became kind.' She smiled wryly. 'As kind as that pig could be.'

I asked the next question with as much tact as possible.

'Ma'am, could your daughter . . . perhaps . . . might she have wanted to do something against the colonel?'

I was expecting another burst of rage, but instead her sardonic smile widened. 'Before the children came . . . yes, maybe . . . But not now,' she rushed on, seeing our astonishment. 'Martha had her little ones to think about.' She cast me a piercing stare. 'You are not suggesting my daughter did something that night, are you? Her father was there. *I* was meant to be there.'

'No, of course not,' I said, again lying. I'd seen more illogical behaviour before.

'I hope that's all,' she said, back to her initial curtness. 'I told you, I'm very busy.'

I looked at the window. 'We would like to talk to the children.'

'Absolutely not. That is out of the question. The children had nothing to do with this matter.'

'We know that, but—'

'And I don't want them to hear the news from two odd strangers.'

'Odd?' I repeated.

'*Ye've nae told them yet?*' McGray cried.

'I know what's best for them,' she snapped. 'They're my responsibility now. The poor creatures are nearly destitute.'

She leaned back then, most likely thinking she'd said too much.

'Destitute?' I echoed. 'But the Morningside mansion . . .?'

'Never fully paid. It will have to be sold to settle their parents' debts.'

I remembered Mrs Grenville's perfectly groomed skin and Reed mentioning that she'd been found wearing very expensive jewellery. I imagined them spending lavishly, borrowing money without restraint; and now their children were out there in the grassland, playing, oblivious to their parents' deaths and their own future tribulations.

'Which reminds me,' Mrs Cobbold added, 'you have kept all the jewellery my daughter was wearing on that evening, and also my father's watch and wedding band. I want everything back. I know how things tend to disappear when under police *custody*.'

'I will personally see that those belongings are sent back to you,' I said, as a sort of peace offering. 'But we do need to talk to the children. We can assure you we will not tell them what has happened.'

Mrs Cobbold twisted her mouth at the suggestion. It took so much persuasion I could fill several pages with the tug of war, but the woman finally gave in, under the condition that she and her housekeeper were present at all times. They were in their rights, so we agreed and followed them outside.

The well-kept lawns that surrounded the house gradually gave way to the wild grassland, where only the heads of the boys stuck out as they sprinted joyously from here to there.

The housekeeper called them with a commanding yelp and the two boys came at once. Their trousers were covered in mud, their jackets peppered with hay and their faces red.

'Where's Alice?' the housekeeper demanded.

'She keeps hiding there,' said the younger boy, pointing at the grass.

The woman stomped ahead like an angry heifer, but McGray moved faster.

'Don't worry, hen. I'll take care o' this.' He went deep into the grass, which soon covered him up to his waist, and from a distance, it looked as though he was wading in a swamp. 'Hey, look who's here!' He then plunged his hand in the grass and lifted a young creature by the bow of a now muddy dress.

The child kicked about and laughed with sheer delight.

'*Ahhh!* You're so ugly!'

'Och nae, are ye mad? I'm really handsome. Come on, madam.'

The child, thrilled to be carried around like a sack of potatoes, continued to laugh long after Nine-Nails put her back on the ground, next to her brothers. All three looked at McGray with giggles, and me as if I were a sour headmaster.

Seeing them there, lined up before us, still grinning from their games, made me feel terribly sad. Their innocent, carefree days were just about to end, the injustice of life about to hit them with all its might. No wonder Mrs Cobbold was delaying the news as much as she could.

'These gentlemen want to know a few things,' she said, and then added, with a rather threatening note, 'Answer truthfully.'

'Nothing to be worried about,' McGray told them. He patted the muddy trousers of Daniel, the middle boy, with the edge of his boot. 'I'll let youse go to yer office soon enough. Which one o' youse was the last one to talk to Grannie Alice?'

The children looked at each other, rather baffled, and Mrs Cobbold seemed to fluff up like an infuriated turkey.

'Why do you need to know—?'

McGray silenced her with a murderous glare, but just as quickly smiled at the children.

'Well?'

'I hadn't been born when she went to heaven,' said the young girl, and then added with authority, 'She was my *great*-grandmother.'

'You were already on your way, darling,' said Mrs Cobbold, her attempt at a sweet tone quite stiff.

Then the eldest boy raised a bashful hand, the blush on his face increasing.

McGray went to him. 'What's yer name, laddie?'

'Edward,' he mumbled.

'Are ye twelve?'

'Twelve and a half, sir.'

'Good. When was the last time ye talked to her?'

Young Edward counted with his fingers. 'Six . . . Seven years ago, sir. I was five.'

'D'ye remember it well?'

The boy nodded. 'She told me she was going away but that I would see her again.'

Clearly a bitter memory, for the boy tensed his lips and clenched his fists, in a patent attempt to repress tears. The colonel surely had told him a thousand times that little men did not cry.

McGray rested a hand on the boy's shoulder. 'There, there. Ye *will* see her again, one day. What else did she say?' Young Edward did not answer, and Nine-Nails bent down to whisper. 'She told ye something ye were supposed to keep secret, right?'

After a seemingly endless moment, Edward nodded, and Mrs Cobbold's eyes opened wide.

McGray spoke softly. 'I think she'd understand if ye told me now. Please, what was it?'

Young Edward looked doubtfully at Mrs Cobbold. She hesitated as well, but in the end assented.

His voice sounded constricted, as if saying those words took all his energy.

'Grannie Alice said I had a gift.'

McGray nearly gasped. 'A gift?'

'She said I had it – and that she had it, but nobody else. She said one day I'd find— I'd find out what she meant.'

Nine-Nails looked at him with eerie intensity. 'And have ye?'

For a while the boy looked deep into McGray's eyes. He had the dark pupils of his family, which looked like bottomless wells. His lips parted, but then he said nothing. He shook his head in a rather scared gesture.

'Did she tell ye anything about . . .' McGray looked at Mrs Cobbold with the corner of his eyes, and whispered, 'a treasure?'

The boy shook his head one more time, taking a step back and freeing himself from McGray's hand, which still rested on his shoulder.

'Ye sure?' McGray insisted. I could see his hand, the one with the missing finger, trembling, perhaps keen to seize the child and shake some answers out of him.

Young Edward did not even move. He simply stared at his murky shoes, everyone around him in deep silence. His brother and sister suddenly looked just as tense. Could they perhaps know as well?

Edward looked at Mrs Cobbold. 'May we go, now?'

She gave him a curt nod and the children ran back to the fields, as quick as gazelles frightened by a gunshot.

I did not know then, but I'd see those children again. Soon. And it would not be pleasant.

19

Kirkcaldy at least had a very decent inn right in front of the harbour, surely where the wealthy factory owners spent their nights on business trips. We were served a surprisingly delectable dinner, and after that, just before the last rays of daylight faded away, I decided to go for a walk around the wharfs. McGray joined me, offered me a cigar, and we marched in silence for a while, simply taking in the tranquillity of the place. All the merchants and fishermen had gone home, so all we could hear were the sounds of the sea, the occasional draught and the calls of seagulls as they glided over the swaying boats.

'That boy was lying,' I said at some point. 'He clearly knows something.'

'Aye, and now his fat grandma is aware o' that. I'm worried she'll besiege the laddie 'til she finds out.'

'Perhaps it is the same secret she is trying to protect. Did you see her face? She is also hiding something.'

'Och, aye, blatantly! And it has to be something only *the six* kent about. She trusts they'll keep quiet now, dead and buried. Only Kat—' McGray halted and his eyes brightened, just as he puffed at his cigar and held the smoke.

'Nine-Nails . . . are you, *again*, thinking what I think you—'

'Aye. Why bother talking to the living when we've someone who can talk to the dead?'

I breathed out. 'And how is Katerina going to—?'

'That Cobbold woman reminded me. We still have their possessions at the morgue. Katerina can read from those, especially if there's at least some metal in the objects. We'll do that tomorrow.'

'McGray, we have no time for those idiotic games! We still have one more branch of the family to question.' I looked at the small copy of the family tree I'd drawn in my notebook. 'Bertrand Shaw's mother and brother. They might—'

'Make us waste even more time,' he interrupted, gave a last puff of his cigar and then threw it to the waters. 'It's decided. We'll see Katerina tomorrow.'

And he rushed to the inn at once, escaping from my *very* reasonable objections.

Due to previous traumas, I refused to share a room with Nine-Nails, and despite my now usual nightmares and struggles to sleep, I could almost have called that a pleasant night.

The following morning, however, the weather changed for the worse, and the trip back was excruciating for McGray. He ended up regurgitating his dinner and breakfast over the gunwale whilst lashed by icy rain, which provided more amusement for me.

We went to our respective homes to freshen – McGray certainly needed a change of clothes – and agreed to meet back at the City Chambers.

I barely set foot in the office, for McGray was already there when I arrived, and still in a foul mood. He grunted as he tied up a leather pouch.

'What took ye so bloody long? Ye were s'posed to change clothes, nae bathe in ass's milk 'n' honey.'

He had a point. I was in no rush to witness another display of Katerina's alleged 'skills', so I had taken my time. I still protested though.

'What do you mean? I barely stopped to wash—'

'Och, never mind. I don't need to hear what ye do and don't scrub. Let's go. I've got everything here.' He jerked the jingling pouch and we set off.

As the cab took us to Calton Hill Jail, McGray listed the items.

'A pair o' spectacles from auld Mr Shaw, a pearl choker with a golden clasp from Martha Grenville, a signet ring from the colonel . . .'

'The one he used to beat his wife with?'

'Aye. Then the gold nugget from Miss Leonora, a very nasty and cheap pocket watch from Mr Willberg . . .'

'And if you say so, it must be truly ghastly. And for young Bertrand?'

'He didnae carry anything. Nae watch, rings; nothing. Reed just found a few shillings in his pocket.'

'Will that do?'

'At least for a dram or two on the way back, worst case.'

'I thought you got everything for free at the Ensign.'

'Nah. I have to pay from time to time. Else Mary'll start thinking I only romance her for the free drink.'

'How coarse,' I let out in a sigh.

The rain had become thunderous by the time we made it to the jail. We had to trot across the esplanade and the guards even had to lend us some towels. We were wiping our faces at the questioning room when they let Katerina in.

Only three days had passed since the hearing, but she looked a year older to me, somewhat thinner, and all the wrinkles on her face a little deeper. At least she seemed to be making an effort to keep her spirits up; she was wearing her usual clumps of mascara and the bright purple eyeshadow she was so fond of. On top of the murky grey jail dress, she wore one of her shawls, blindingly orange and trimmed with cheap glass beads.

'Ye look well, hen,' McGray told her as soon as the guards left us.

'I do what I can, my boy. I'd like to wear my pendants,' and she patted the empty piercings on her earlobes, 'but they must think I'll stab the guards to death with those.'

McGray winked at her. 'Well, yer a fearsome lady.'

Katerina attempted a smile, and then eyed the pouch on the table. 'You brought me something to read?'

'Aye. We thought ye might be able to tell us more about these folk. We believe they're all hiding something.' McGray began to display the articles on the table, but Katerina looked sombre. 'What is it, hen?'

She moved her fingers as though they were the legs of a spider – a gesture far less dramatic without her two-and-a-half-inch nails.

'My . . . My eye might not help this time.'

'What d'ye mean?'

Katerina was now staring at her fingertips, as if looking at a dead pet. 'The jail's doing something to me, Adolphus. I can't reach out like I used to.'

Nine-Nails leaned closer to her. 'The isolation? The strain? Is that it?'

'Not only that . . .' she said. 'I see a shadow, Adolphus. It's cast everywhere. It's like a – shroud . . . like a hand clutching around me . . . smothering me little by little.' She reached for her neck but could not bring herself to touch her own skin. 'I can feel it grow stronger and darker. More and more every morning.' She looked up, her pleading eyes fixed on McGray.

'We're doing everything we can,' he assured her. 'But we need ye to try and help us. Here, concentrate on these. Pretend it's the good auld times 'n' I brought ye something for a random case.'

As he said that, he laid one of Bertrand's shillings on the table. All six objects were now lined in a perfect row.

Katerina bit her lip, took a few deep breaths and moved her fingers in an insect-like manner. Hesitantly, like a girl who is afraid of the dark, she closed her eyes, and very slowly brought her hands to the items. She did not touch them at first, her palms simply hovering a few inches above them. Her eyelids, shivering and not fully shut, showed us the veiny whites of her eyes.

I always feel a little shiver when she does that, and usually remind myself she might simply be very good at her act. Right then, however, it was her own life that was at stake.

Her fingers glided from side to side, gradually getting closer to the shiny objects. I pictured them as red-hot irons, and Katerina was preparing her hands for the blistering heat before daring to seize them.

Her fingers accidentally rubbed the top of Mr Shaw's old spectacles, and Katerina jumped in the chair, muttering.

'It's that shadow again,' she grunted, clenching her fist as if she'd truly burned herself.

She tried again, tapping the items with various degrees of confidence. The choker's clasp seemed almost harmless, and so did the shilling. Mr Willberg's nasty watch was far more unpleasant, just like the colonel's signet ring. However, Leonora's gold nugget and the spectacles were like blazing fire.

'Take those away,' Katerina mumbled.

McGray did so, though barely taking his eyes from her.

Katerina tried to touch the ring, even held it up for an instant, but then winced as though in terrible pain, and dropped it. The same happened with the watch.

'Sorry, I can't do those either.'

I heard the desperation in her voice. Could it all be pretence? Could it just be that her trick no longer worked? That she could not send a discreet spy to watch over her 'clients' whilst in jail?

McGray left out only the choker and the shilling.

Katerina stretched her hands, cracking her knuckles and each joint in her fingers, and then went for the choker. She held it by the pearls, gently caressing the golden clasp, each time touching it for a little longer.

'It's her,' she whispered.

McGray was not blinking. 'Who? Martha?'

Katerina tilted her head, then shook it. 'No . . . Alice.'

We both gasped. I found that even *I* was on the edge of my seat.

Katerina then picked up the shilling with the other hand, rubbing it between her index and thumb. She nodded.

'Yes . . . Alice . . . left her mark everywhere. She's like a stain. Pure hatred.'

'Is she the shadow ye've been feeling?' McGray asked.

Katerina opened her eyes suddenly and inhaled with a hiss. 'Yes! She could well be.'

'So . . .' I said, 'the dead spirit that killed those six people is *also* preventing you from seeing anything?'

Against my best efforts, my tone oozed sarcasm, but those two nodded vehemently, thinking it made perfect sense.

Katerina shut her eyes hard, now gripping the choker and coin. She tilted her head as if trying to make out the faintest of noises.

'There is a . . . there is a sound . . . It's like she's whispering. Just one word, over and over . . . But I can't . . .' Her chest swelled in agitated breaths. 'Meh— meh . . .' And she opened her eyes. '*Mary?*'

'Mary!' McGray repeated, and Katerina again nodded.

185

I passed the pages of my little notebook and looked at the family tree. 'Nobody in the family has that name.'

'Write it down anyway, Percy,' said McGray.

Katerina had gone perfectly still, looking sideways, again as if trying to hear more. Only after a very long time did she give up and returned the choker to the table. The shilling, however, she held high.

'There is a stronger imprint from this. I don't know why. It might be just that Alice's shadow is not so strong here.'

'That belonged to young Bertrand,' McGray said.

Katerina raised an eyebrow. 'It makes sense. I only met him briefly, but this *feels* like him. Alice's hatred still clouds it all, but at least I can look into it. He stands apart. You should talk to those who knew him best.'

I could not repress a snort. 'I did say we still had that branch of the family to question. And I did not need to rub trinkets to know that.'

McGray was too deep in thought to mind my cynicism. He sat back, stroking his beard.

'This hatred o' hers . . . focused on her own folk . . .' he groaned. 'We should've asked Mrs Cobbold how Grannie Alice died.'

'Should we?' I jumped in. 'Why? Do you think one of her relatives killed her and she came back for revenge?'

Again, I'd said it with utmost derision, but Katerina and Nine-Nails could not have looked more serious.

McGray picked up the shilling. 'Her hatred is nae so strong here, in Bertrand's stuff. He was also the only one who was nae intended to go to the séance.' He tapped his lip with the coin. 'We need to find out how she died. That may explain many things. There might've been a Mary involved.'

'I am not sure which *things* you hope that will explain,' I mumbled as I scribbled. 'Or how that might help us get this woman out of jail.'

'I wish I could see more,' Katerina lamented. 'These trinkets would usually help me . . . *But this shadow—!*'

She put her elbows on the table and pulled at her hair, growling again, only this time from the depths of her throat. It was a horrible sound.

McGray stood up, patted her shoulder and whispered something I did not catch. Katerina took deep breaths, and when she looked up again, I saw she'd barely managed to repress her tears.

'There's one last thing I want to ask ye,' McGray said. 'D'ye think Grannie Alice really had *the eye?*'

'I couldn't be sure, but it wouldn't surprise me. She's a very strong spirit; leaves her mark everywhere. And Leonora had some talents too. Why?'

'Nae long before she snuffed it, Alice told her great-grandson he had the eye too.'

'The eldest boy?' Katerina said.

I was going to ask how she knew about him, but she'd surely tell me she 'could feel it'.

'Aye,' McGray answered. 'We think she also told him about – whatever it was the family was looking for.'

Katerina's full expression shifted, her eyes suddenly gleaming with a hint of hope.

'If the boy has the eye,' she said, 'he might be able to help us.'

'D'ye think he might see through the shadows? With his blood connection and all?'

'Yes. It's not certain, but at least possible.' She shook her head. 'Although I'd need to work directly with him. He will not be trained in this at all; I would have to show him the path.'

I laughed, closing and pocketing my notebook. 'This is ridiculous! You cannot subject that poor boy to this.'

'Why nae?'

'First, the grandmother will never allow it. And second, it is stupid.'

Katerina was far too tense to respond with wit.

McGray simply sighed. 'Percy, would ye prefer to wait outside? With a bleeding nose?'

'I think the best we can do now is go and question those people, or do anything in the realms of reality that might help the case. The clock is ticking and we appear to be exactly where we started.' McGray opened his mouth, but I raised my voice, '*Even* if you managed to traumatise that poor child, and he does commune with his dead great-grandmother, and she does admit she killed *the six* because they wronged her in life – how is that going to help you in court?' And I stared directly at Katerina as I said the latter.

A very uncomfortable silence followed, and Katerina's little hint of hope soon vanished.

McGray glared at me as if to say 'well done'. He squeezed Katerina's hand and gave her some reassurance.

'Adolphus, could you please do me another favour?' she said beseechingly just before we left.

'Sure, hen.'

She bit her lip. 'Please, could you have a look at my business? The brewery. Fat Johnnie has come almost every day to show me the books, but he's always been terrible at charging and collecting debts. I wouldn't dare ask you, Adolphus, but I need to look after my finances . . . now that my boy might—'

'Stop sayin' that! We'll get ye out o' this. I swear.'

He smiled at her, but Katerina barely managed to slightly twitch the corners of her mouth.

I did not know what to tell her. Things did not look any more promising. In the end, I simply shrugged at her and left the room.

'She can help everyone else but herself?' I said as we walked to the exit.

We stopped by the main entrance, for outside it was still raining with a vengeance.

'Ye heard her,' said McGray, relighting a half-smoked cigar. 'Alice left her shadow on everything.'

'That just seems too convenient.'

'Convenient?'

'How much did she charge you for her "consulting services"?'

He winced. 'What are ye suggesting?'

'What if her "eye" is but a network of dubious contacts who find things out for her? People who follow all her gullible clients, including you. She'd be unable to communicate with her minions from prison, so she—'

But McGray tossed the cigar stub and stormed away. I felt a pang of guilt as I saw his slouched shoulders being lashed by the rain. What horrible doubts must be assaulting him . . . For years Katerina had fed his outlandish beliefs, but also his last shreds of hope for his sister. Unmasking the gypsy as a fraud would also mean that a cure for Pansy had always been a false promise.

I had never truly believed the girl could be brought back to sanity, less and less the more I learned about her condition, but I also knew that my former self would not have spoken quite so bluntly. My temper was getting the better of me, my patience thinner and thinner as the days passed.

I massaged my brow, once more feeling that horrid wave of gloom that did not seem to let me go.

Before I dove into the rain I looked back, and caught a glimpse of Katerina being escorted back to her cell. Our eyes met but an instant, before the guards shut the door.

I thought I'd better talk to her again. Alone, for there were things she'd never confess in front of McGray.

As I trotted across the esplanade, a dark thought began to creep into my mind, uncalled yet unstoppable.

That she might well be guilty after all.

20

Not much could be achieved the next day, it being Sunday, so I indulged in a lazy festival of cigars, brandy, overeating and reading cheap novels. Neither McGray nor the pressures of the case interrupted that bliss, yet I must admit that by the early evening I was already beginning to feel some boredom. On Monday, however, I would regret asking for excitement.

The morning papers already announced, front page, the date for the trial: second of October, and reading the number made me feel prickles in my hands. We only had nine days left to prepare. Nine!

Regretting my day of laziness I ran to the City Chambers, where I found McGray pacing like a lion.

I attempted a 'good morning', but Nine-Nails brandished the official notice from the courts, already quite crumpled.

'They're fuckingly well connected, those bastards from *The Scotsman*. They must've been told even before our own notice was written.'

'Proba—'

'And ye have a few telegrams.' He pointed at the envelopes strewn on my desk. All of them open.

'*Did you read—?*'

'Aye, I did.'

'That is my correspondence!'

'Och, nothing private, Percy. They're from yer sissy law colleagues in Oxford.'

'Cambridge.'

'Aye. That's what I said.'

'No. You said Oxf—'

'Och, what's the sodding difference?'

'Do not ever say that if you end up down there. They'd castrate you and exhibit one of your testicles in each university.'

I picked up the messages and began reading, whilst McGray gave me a florid briefing.

'They think I'm mad, they think Katerina's mad *and* guilty, and they suggest we find her a damn good lawyer.'

I sat down, overwhelmed, and scanned the final telegrams. 'It is what I suspected. They say we should focus on getting her life imprisonment, rather than hang.'

'Read on.'

'Unless . . . we find enough evidence against Holt, the valet. If he is pronounced innocent, the best verdict we can hope for Katerina is *Not Proven*.' I nodded. 'Oh, that is right. I'd forgotten you can do that in Scottish law. But they admit it is very unlikely.'

'How can it be unlikely?' McGray snapped. 'There's nae way to prove Katerina murdered the six.'

'I know how things work at juries, Nine-Nails. They tend to gather in a rush, most of them looking forward to their evening beers, and pass sentence based on who spoke louder. Why do you think I quit the law?'

'Because yer an—'

'*The fact*,' I interjected, 'that there were poisonous metals in the six bodies will be proof enough for them; and her providing the knife they used to bleed themselves will seal the deal. The only actual missing piece there is a motive, and I bet Pratt must be doing everything he can to find one.'

'Aye, that bastard's goin' to be trouble. I went to check on Katerina's brewery. Her lad, Fat Johnnie, told me that some fancy court's sod, as bald as a boiled egg, had already been there asking questions. On Saturday evening, when most of the clients were already half blootered and their tongues were very loose.'

I raised a brow. 'And you fear Katerina's reputation may not be totally unblemished?'

He snorted. 'Aye. But she had nae reason to kill those six sods. Five o' them were nae even clients!'

I sighed and looked at the last telegram.

'One more suggestion of theirs – which is rather a preparation for the guilty verdict – is to find people who can vouch for . . .' I had to repress a smirk; these were serious matters, 'who can vouch for Katerina's *good* character. We should definitely do that. If all else fails, that may at least save her from the gallows. All in all, it will take a superb lawyer to influence the jury and judge.'

McGray sat on his desk, arms crossed, and looked at me with cheeky eyes. 'Aye. I . . . I wanted to talk to ye about that.'

I held my breath for a second. 'W-why?'

Nine-Nails stroked his beard. 'I've heard yer dad was the best lawyer in Chancery Lane.'

Silence.

Then I threw my head back and cackled so hard I nearly fell off the chair. I looked at him, cackled again, this time for longer. I looked at him one more time. His expression had not changed.

'I am *not* going to do that,' I said, my hilarity slowly receding.

He raised his eyebrows and his forehead furrowed.

'*I am not!*' I repeated.

He was not blinking now, and I grunted.

'Nine-Nails, I can assure you, for everything that I hold most dear – I will *not* ask my retired, obnoxious, elitist lump of a father to travel all the way here to defend a clairvoyant with a reputation.'

McGray was beginning to smile.

'It is absolutely and categorically out of the question!'

I handed the telegram over and walked away before I changed my mind, but I still ruminated furiously as we crossed High Street on the way back.

'He hates Scotland, he hates foreigners, he hates women *and* he hates the poor. There is not a chance he will agree.'

'Och, stop moaning. Ye always drown in a thimble. At least we have to try.'

'I can picture him and my bitch of a stepmother reading my message, roaring in laughter until their sides split.'

'I thought they did that with yer letters anyway.'

I scowled at him, and McGray put his palms in the air.

'All right, all right, Frey! Actually I have to thank ye. Katerina will appreciate ye doing this for her.'

But that did not improve my mood. 'Even if he agrees, he will have to come in a rush and will barely have time to go through the evidence and—'

'What's that?' said McGray.

He was looking at the cluster of reporters who had become a fixture of the City Chambers, ever more specimens from other cities joining into the blasted scrum – curse their notebooks and pencils and damn their tasteless bowler hats and baggy raincoats. Right then they were gathered around a woman with a toddler in her arms. The lady was shouting in utter abandon, her face red and soaked in tears, and the toddler's sobs could be heard all across the street.

Constable McNair was begging her to go away, but each time he tapped at her shoulder, the woman jerked away and shouted with renewed energy.

'What's the matter?' McGray asked as we drew closer.

'They're the ones defending the gypsy!' one of the reporters cried for the benefit of the woman.

She immediately ran to us and pulled at McGray's coat. Her shouting, the reporters and the cries of the child became an unintelligible cacophony drilling my ears.

McGray took a deep breath and then howled from the bottom of his stomach, his lips vibrating like a sousaphone, the echoes bouncing all across the street. His call for quiet prolonged itself until everyone along the Royal Mile had turned their necks toward us, either daunted or baffled. The toddler, far from scared, simply stared at Nine-Nails with her mouth open and embellished with a trickle of dribble.

'Who are ye?' McGray asked the woman, who raised her chin and spoke truculently.

'Mrs Holt.'

'Ohhh, I see.'

'My husband didnae kill anybody. Youse know that! Yer going to send him to the gallows only to save a scheming gypsy killer!'

'Madam—'

'And without him they'll evict us! We have nowhere else to go!'

'Who's they? Yer landlord?'

'Aye!'

All the reporters around us were scribbling at unthinkable speed. McGray knocked a bowler hat off the nearest head.

'Oi, the spectacle's over! Get yer sorry arses out o' here!'

'We are only reporting a matter of public—'

McGray took a sharp step forwards and the men instantly backed off, one of them nearly falling on his back.

'Come in, missus,' he told Mrs Holt. 'Now that yer here, we'll ask ye two-three questions. McNair, look after the wee lassie.'

He'd not finished the sentence when the woman dropped the child in McNair's arms. The toddler immediately went for his bright ginger hair, which she pulled as she let out the most delighted of giggles.

We led Mrs Holt to one of the questioning rooms and offered her some tea to calm her down. She demanded milk and two sugars.

'My husband didnae kill anybody,' she reiterated as soon as the cup was placed before her. 'The colonel adored him.'

McGray's retort did not help. 'Mrs Holt, we found yer husband stealing from a crime scene.'

'*He wisnae!* He was taking what's ours.'

'Oh, here we go again,' I muttered, and while they argued the same point over and over, I went through my notes and the existing files. I heard McGray asking her the same questions we'd asked her husband, and though everything she told him matched, in my opinion that proved nothing (the jury would most likely disagree with me, especially if the woman showed up carrying her doe-eyed daughter). As I pondered, something in the records caught my eye.

I banged the papers on the table as loudly as possible.

'Mrs Holt, we would like to search your . . . residence.'

I discreetly pointed at a line in Reed's report, and McGray understood at once.

'Aye!'

As soon as she heard that, Mrs Holt tensed every single muscle on her neck.

'Why?'

'And we would like to go there immediately,' I added.

She lost all colour. 'Youse are nae going to nose around my home!'

Had McGray smiled wider, he would have dislocated his jaw.

'D'ye have something to hide, missus?'

Mrs Holt's chest swelled, her hands shaking around the cup of tea.

And she would not meet our gazes.

21

The reason for her apprehension became evident as soon as we opened the door to the tenement.

We were instantly hit by a smell that was a mixture of stale ale, flatulence, orange peel and meat gone bad. The table was crammed with dozens of dirty dishes, fish bones, congealed gravy stains, greasy tankards and bowls with dregs of three-day-old broths. A nearby chair was piled with a mountain of dirty linen and clothes, and I will not even attempt to describe the kitchen.

McGray whistled. 'My, oh my! The Holts really are a pair o' pigs!'

'And they keep a child in here!' I said, putting the key back in my pocket. We'd purposely asked Mrs Holt to wait for us at the City Chambers, for neither of us wanted her looking over our shoulders as we searched the place. 'Where to begin?' I sighed, tempted to use my own socks as gloves. McGray, on the other hand, was almost diving into the rubbish with enviable confidence.

'Ye can look at the bedroom.'

'Urgh . . .'

'Or ye can sort out all that rotten crap on the table.'

Instead of answering, I produced my handkerchief, covered my nose and made my sorry way to the adjacent room.

The bed was a tangle of grimy sheets and there were countless clothes and undergarments scattered on every surface. It struck me why Mr Holt would own quite so many union suits. At least the chamber pot had been emptied and washed – even Mrs Holt had her limits.

Whenever possible, I kicked about the clothes, especially the undergarments, but more than once I had to lift them with my bare fingers, especially those under the bed, which were also embedded with fluff made entirely out of dust.

I was about to call the search fruitless, but then I heard McGray's eager voice.

'Oi, look at that!'

I found him in the kitchen, looking into a cupboard, from where he drew out two amber bottles.

'Bedbug killer and rat poison,' he read. 'Is this what ye had in mind?'

'Indeed,' I said, recalling the line I'd signalled at the questioning room.

Reed had made a very long list of candidate poisons, highlighting that many of them, like mercury, could be extracted from normal household items. If those bottles contained the same substances found in the bodies, we'd have a good case against Mr Holt.

'Though now that I see this pigsty,' I added, looking at the surrounding mess, 'I would not raise my expectations too high. It looks like they do have a lot of creepy-crawlies to kill here.'

We searched for a good while further but found nothing more. Just as we walked out of the medieval building, rejoicing in the fresh air, a middle-aged man with a grey beard and an impeccable tweed jacket approached us.

'Good day, gentlemen! Are youse the inspectors? Here to talk to Mrs Holt?'

The man looked jovial enough, but we still regarded him with suspicion.

'What are ye to them?'

The man swiftly removed a leather glove and offered a hand to shake. 'Their landlord. Nick Saunders. Pleased to meet you.'

'Ye own this dump?'

'I wouldn't call it a dump, sir, but yes.'

'Did ye come to evict the missus and the child, now that Holt's in jail?'

Mr Saunders stroked his beard, visibly uncomfortable.

'Inspectors, I would have to evict them even if Holt was free. I was going to do so on the thirteenth. I've only allowed Mrs Holt to stay for a little longer precisely because her husband is awaiting trial.'

'And it does nae make ye feel bad?'

'Why, of course it does! Especially with the wee child, but I'm not a rich man, inspector. I don't rent out mansions, like that Lady Glass. I barely make a living out o' my tenements.'

'What can you tell us about Mr Holt?' I asked, for nothing would come out of chiding the man. 'Did you ever notice he might be . . . up to something?'

Mr Saunders shook his head. 'I wouldn't say so. The first few months he lived here – that is, before he began hiding from me to avoid paying rent – he spent almost all his free time at home or at the pub around the corner. Not that it was often. I believe the colonel, rest in peace, kept him very busy most of the time.'

'Would you say they had a friendly relationship?'

Mr Saunders frowned. 'I – I've answered these same questions already. To a fiscal, I believe.'

McGray laughed bitterly. 'Don't tell me. Bald, snooty, with a golden tooth and a face like he's smelling shite?'

Mr Saunders chuckled. 'That's a very accurate description.'

'Humour us, please,' I asked him.

'Well . . . I never met the colonel in person, but I can tell you they were on good terms. The colonel sent me a couple of payments when Mr Holt was falling behind with the rent. You wouldn't do that if you disliked your valet.'

McGray seemed quite disgruntled.

'Could ye do us a favour?' McGray asked the landlord.

'If it's in my hands, of course.'

'Don't kick 'em out before the trial.'

'I was not intending to do so, inspector. As I said, I feel sorry for the child.'

'Thanks. I can tell ye Mr Holt has come across some money. If he goes free, I'll make sure that goes to ye instead o' the pub.'

'That sounds like a fair deal.'

Mr Saunders and McGray shook hands on that, and then the man bowed and went away.

Nine-Nails would not stop grunting as we strode across the pebbled streets of the Old Town.

'What is it?' I asked him, but we walked a full street before he answered.

'He's innocent, Frey.'

'What do you mean?'

'Holt's innocent. I ken. I've felt it ever since we caught him.'

'You do not know that yet,' I said, and then brandished the bottles. 'We still have these to analyse.'

But I had precisely the same feeling. Mr Saunders's statement, however brief, was perhaps the most telling. Why would any man want to kill a generous employer who even took care of his debts? And Holt, as much of a rogue as he might be, did not strike me as a murderer. One learns to foresee these things. Guilt almost always reeks. And that was precisely what made my suspicions on Katerina all the more worrying.

*

Back at the City Chambers we immediately stumbled across McNair, who was chasing Holt's daughter across the corridors.

'Looks like she's winning,' Nine-Nails mocked.

'Youse better go see the mother!' McNair retorted, his temples covered in sweat. 'She's nae alone.'

We went directly to the questioning room, and when McGray opened the door, the first thing that caught my eye was the world's most lustrous scalp.

Pratt was leaning over the table, just as Mrs Holt signed what looked like a very lengthy declaration.

'Oi, Pratt!' McGray roared. 'What the fuck are ye doing here?'

The man rose with a pompous grin, only exceeded by the downright joy in Mrs Holt's eyes.

'I am making sure this lady makes a formal statement. Something we can present at court. We do need to bring some formality to your clearly biased investigation.'

'Biased!' we cried in unison.

'And you two were wrong to search her house without a warrant. There are laws in this country, inspectors. They won't always bend in your favour.'

'*Why, ye son of a—!*'

McGray pounced on Pratt, nearly tipping the table, then seized the man's collar and smacked him against the wall. Mrs Holt yelped, jumped to her feet and cowered in a corner, while I ran to Nine-Nails and did my best to pull him away.

'This won't help anyone!' I shouted, nearly dropping the bottles of poison.

Pratt was smiling with a sly twinkle in his eyes. 'Oh, do beat me, Nine-Nails! Do! I beg you. It will look so good on the records for the trial.'

It was I who threw him a slap. '*Oh, shut up, Pratt!* You don't want me to set this brute on you. McGray, let the egghead go.'

He did not, still breathing wildly, but apparently I'd taken the edge off his wrath.

I turned to Mrs Holt. 'And you have given your statement now, so go! Here is the key to your putrid den.'

'Those bottles are my—'

'*Go!* Bloody hell!'

She sneered, snatched the key and then preened on her way to the door. 'As you wish, sirs. I still need to talk to the press. They're waiting for me.'

Nine-Nails raised a hand, mentally strangling that blasted woman. At least that gave me a chance to prise Pratt from his grip.

'What a sorry spectacle,' he said, smoothing his jacket.

'I'll make ye a sorry spectacle if ye don't fuck off right this instant!'

Pratt was surely going to say something very smug, so I interjected.

'And *I* will encourage that.'

Pratt grabbed the papers from the table with a flounce, and finally left.

'I'm his sodding challenge!' McGray snapped as we walked into the office. He kicked a tower of old witchcraft books that flew everywhere. One landed on the lounging dogs, who did not seem disturbed by it. 'He couldnae get my sister, so now he's set on ruining Katerina like a bitch on a marrow-dripping bone.'

McGray lounged on his chair, banging his boots on the desk, and just as he was about to burst again, there was a mousy knock on the door.

'*What!*

A lanky young man walked in with hesitation, and I instantly felt sorry for him – tiny round spectacles, laughably fleshy lips and a soft chin that very much reminded me of the almost non-existent mandible of Queen Victoria. And his eyes had a dreamy expression, as if the cogwheels in his brain did not quite fit each other.

McGray looked at him with unmitigated wariness. 'And you are . . .?'

The chap straightened his tie. 'Elmer Sperry, sir. Since Miss Dragnea has no counsel, I've been assigned her defence.'

'Och, for fuck's sake!'

Sperry moistened his disturbingly thick lips. 'I was wondering, if it is not too much trouble, that you might allow me to—'

'Piss off.'

Sperry looked back, blinking as if he'd just heard another language. 'Erm . . . e-excuse me?'

'I said piss— Are ye *deaf*?'

'Erm, no, no, sir. But I do need the files in preparation for—'

McGray made to stand up . . .

'Come back later, come back later!' I gabbled as I ushered him out.

As soon as the sorry chap was gone, McGray settled in his chair, put his soiled boots on the desk, and stroked his stubble as he exhaled like a locomotive's whistle.

I knew I should not even attempt to talk to him, so I went to the morgue and gave Reed the poisons to analyse. Unprecedently, he offered me a cup of tea – a ghastly brew, but I had to gulp it down as a token of camaraderie. I left, making a mental note to buy him some decent leaves.

When I returned to the office, McGray was still breathing sharply, but at least he was now standing in front of the wall lined with evidence, pondering. I thought it better not to disturb him, so I began sorting out some paperwork, until—

'*Of course!*'

His yelp made me jump and drop a stack of documents, and I saw him poking a sheet on the wall, so hard he nearly pierced the paper. I went closer and saw it was a page from Leonora's journal.

'Grab yer coat, Percy. Quickly.'

'Why? Where are we going?'

'To the crime scene. I think we missed something.'

22

I have been poisoned whilst on a moving train, I have ridden open carts at night while beaten by a witch, I have rowed across Scottish lochs with certain death right behind my back – yet none of those trips was as convulsive and scary as that short ride to Morningside.

McGray paid the cab driver a ludicrously handsome amount, and the reckless young man took us there in an impossibly short time, ignoring bumps, potholes, sharp corners and panicked pedestrians.

I stepped down rather shaken and ran after Nine-Nails. He unlocked the house and rushed to the upper floor.

When I walked into the parlour, I noticed quite a few differences. In his search, McGray had pulled furniture, carpets, and moved the camera aside. I saw he'd dragged it, leaving a trail of smashed glass.

'Is that the spot where you found the knife?' I asked as we both knelt down.

'Indeedy, but that's nae what I want ye to see.'

'Then what?'

'Look at the shards. How many plaques d'ye think got smashed here?'

'I . . . I could not tell. One? Two?'

I felt silly, but McGray grinned. 'Just what I thought!'

And he then went to the wooden box, the one with the new plaques and the chemicals, which still sat against the panelled wall.

'D'ye remember the note in Leonora's journal? The one she made on the day of the séance?'

'Vaguely. You did not give me time to—'

'She wrote she woke up early to buy a boxful of new plaques. A *boxful*, Frey.'

And to illustrate his point, he opened the box. I saw the green velvet lining, which still bore the marks of withdrawn glass, and then understood.

'This is half empty,' I mumbled, leaning closer to the fabric, and counted the marks.

'At least eight are missing,' McGray concluded, and then pointed at the pile of shards. 'And that does nae look like the wreckage of eight sheets o' glass.'

Indeed it did not.

'Katerina also said Miss Leonora had taken several photographs,' I said, and then I raised my chin. 'Holt? Could he have taken them too?'

McGray nodded. 'Either that, or they're still in this room somewhere.'

I looked around, my mind working at full speed. I saw the broken camera and pictured the scene in my head: Miss Leonora, excited beyond words, taking photographs at full speed.

'She'd have to store them in the dark,' I said, 'and it would have been somewhere handy, so she could work at speed . . . She must have had another box at hand, which is now gone. Holt *must* have—'

McGray raised a finger. 'Leonora sat by the window . . .'

'Yes,' I said. 'Opposite Katerina. Surely to get the best angles.'

'Aye, but . . . Was that arrangement fortuitous or premeditated?'

'Three words of more than two syllables in a row! That has to be a milestone.'

McGray did not pay attention. He leaned over the wall, and began tapping the oak panelling with his knuckles.

'My auld man used to hide his whisky from my mother. He had a—'

The sound shifted from dull to hollow. McGray knocked again, now with his fist. The sound was unmistakable.

I held my breath as he studied the edges of the panel. There were no hinges or keyholes, but the inlaying was carved so that one could pull it out with the nails. And McGray did so as he let out a victorious cheer.

And there they were: a neat stack of plaques, wrapped in a black cloth.

'Leonora's photographs!' I gasped, while McGray picked them up as gingerly as he would have done a newborn. 'Everything that happened at the séance is recorded there. The ritual, the deaths . . .'

'The spirits.'

23

'Of course!' McGray said, hugging it in his lap as the mad driver took us back to the City Chambers. 'Leonora had to keep the exposed plaques safe from the light, but she must've been laden with all the equipment, so instead of carrying another box she improvised. She stored the plaques in that compartment as she went on, so she could keep pulling new ones out o' the box freely. That's why she had to sit there! It was all—'

He did not finish because the entire cab bounced, we both banged our heads against the roof and the precious box nearly slipped off his lap.

We made it to the headquarters and stormed into the photographer's office. The little plaque on the door, which read 'R. Wedgewood' and 'NO ENTRY' almost fell off when McGray slammed it open.

'*Shut that door, you cretin!*' the man cried, guarding his trays of half-developed images from the daylight. 'You'll ruin my work!'

I had to oblige, for McGray would not listen. Once closed, we were lit only by a dim light, turned red by the coloured glass of the oil lamp's chimney. The pasty Wedgewood, who seldom ventured out of his little workshop, and reeked of the chemicals he spent his life with, was glowing with fury.

'I'm busy, get out!'

'Nae. We need ye to develop these,' Nine-Nails said, placing the box on the nearest workbench and nearly knocking over a few jars of chemicals. Wedgewood leapt to catch them just in time. 'Right now.'

'Leave them there. I'll get to them.'

'Are ye deaf too? We need them *now!*'

'Now?' Wedgewood cackled. 'They'll be ready when they're bleeding re—! Wait, what are you doing?'

McGray was rummaging through the drawers, tossing files and old photographs until he pulled out a bundle of very poor-quality portraits – toddlers, newly-weds and the sort.

'I ken just for how long ye've been doing this.'

Wedgewood gulped.

'With police resources?' I asked.

'Aye. This bastard's been milking the place to keep his own business.' McGray rolled up the photos, used them to hit the man on the head and then to poke him in the chest. 'Ye better work on our evidence right now. And I mean *right* sodding now!' He waved the roll of pictures before Wedgewood's eyes. 'In the meantime, we'll keep these for ye.'

And we walked out of the tiny room, this time not bothering to close the door behind us.

'McGray, do you have dirt on everyone in the police force?'

'Aye. Be careful what ye say in front of me.'

The next hours were an agonising wait, McGray smoking and pacing across our office like a husband waiting for his wife to give birth. Once more, I envied the lazy dogs, piled up on each other and dozing in a comfortable corner.

Sperry, the sorry lawyer, came by at some point. I rushed him out before McGray decided to skin him alive, and decided I could use the time to brief him as best as I could. We sat in one of the questioning rooms, and I gave him all the documents I could spare.

I was hoping his idiotic demeanour might conceal a hidden genius, but sadly it was not so. The poor chap was as slow and dim-witted as his exterior suggested, and I could soon picture Pratt flogging him at the High Court. I would have found some humour in that, had there not been a human life at stake. And since the best I expected from my father was a succinct 'ARE. YOU. MAD,' things looked bleak indeed.

When I walked back into the office, McGray's nerves were on edge. We still had to wait for a while, but before long we heard the rushed, erratic steps of the photographer coming down the stairs. It was dark by then, the cellar lit by an oil lamp and the amber glow from the street lights, coming through the barred windows. In the dim light, Wedgewood's pale face almost seemed to glow. His eyes were bulging like those of a frog, his grey hair was now a matted mess, and his hand quivered as he raised a file.

'You must look at this,' he whispered, his mouth dry.

We jumped to our feet, and McGray snatched the photographs so swiftly he nearly tore them.

I came closer, bringing the lamp, and we leaned over as McGray opened the file.

The picture on top, still somewhat damp and stinking of ammonia and sulphur, sent instant shivers down our necks.

24

It was a blurry photograph of the round table. Though positioned to have Katerina at the centre, she was almost completely obscured by the glare of many candles. Only the bases of the candlesticks could be seen, for they faded as the light of the flames became a pure white stain that dominated the image. At its core, however, lay the shock.

A human hand. Apparently floating in the air.

It was a blood-curdling sight: dark and apparently charred, with twisted, spidery fingers, finished in sharp tips and set like a menacing claw. The skin was coarse and cracked, like the bark of an ancient tree, and the wrist looked like a tangle of exposed nerves and tendons.

More striking still was that the arm also became diffuse as it approached the flames – or rather, the spot where we could tell the flames would have been, for the overexposed plate had rendered a bright white blur there.

The hand appeared to be materialising from the fire itself, propelled upwards as if to catch something in the air.

It was exactly what Katerina had described: 'a shadow taking shape in-between the candles; something solid sprouting from thin air'.

The hand of Satan, she'd said, and the memory of her tale made me shiver.

'Evidence enough?' McGray asked.

'This cannot be,' I muttered. 'It has to be some trick with the light. Some—'

But I could not deny what my eyes saw. There it was, as sharp and clear as the horrified faces of Colonel Grenville and Mr Willberg on the margins of the picture.

McGray took the file and spread the pictures on his desk. Neither Wedgewood nor I spoke; we examined the photographs in stunned silence.

There was an image of the group, Leonora included, clearly taken before the ritual began. All the men were standing behind three chairs, reserved for Katerina, Mrs Grenville and Miss Leonora.

Though nothing compared to 'the hand of Satan', the image was still grim. Katerina was again the focal point, but her face could barely be made out, concealed under her black veil. Her cheekbones and nose, projected on the material, were the only clear features, and they rather made her look like a living skull. How fitting.

In the hand of Miss Leonora, I recognised the fob and wire to activate the camera's switch, which she pressed as she stared into the lens with eerie intensity. Mrs Grenville had attempted a smile, but it made her look manic instead. Bertrand seemed about to wet himself, while Mr Willberg and the colonel looked decidedly put out. The old Mr Shaw, who Bertrand held by the arm, had been wearing his spectacles, which reflected the light and made it impossible to read his expression.

'They all look fine there,' I said. 'That is – unharmed.'

The next image was of everyone gathered at the table. Katerina was flanked by Mr Willberg on her right and the colonel on her left – the latter looking at her with blatant disgust. Mrs Grenville sat next to her husband, and by her side was her father. Bertrand was on the opposite side of the table, next to Mr Willberg, and he would have been holding Leonora's hand during the session. She did not appear, busy behind the camera.

The rest of the photos were from the séance itself. They had been taken in quick succession and with completely the wrong light. Lit from below, everyone's faces looked spectral: sunken eye sockets nestled in brightly white brows, cheeks and chins, which seemed to float in an almost uniform blackness.

At the centre of all those photographs was the glare of the candles, becoming brighter and brighter from one exposition to the next, and just as the light increased, the faces went from agitated to distorted. And then the ghastly hand finally appeared.

'Is this the last image?' I asked.

'Yes,' said Wedgewood. 'All the plates you brought were numbered. Though there was an empty slot in the case.'

'That would've been the one that smashed to smithereens when the camera fell,' said McGray. 'The picture taken after this. What I'd give to see it . . .'

This time I shared his curiosity. I looked at the photographs over and over before I spoke again.

'Do you think they died very soon after this was taken?'

'Aye. Look at where they're sat. That's exactly where they found them. My guess is they dropped dead just minutes later.'

I shook my head. 'Unfortunately we've discarded heart attacks. These photographs would have persuaded the jury they were all scared to death.'

'*I* was nearly scared to death when I first saw them,' Wedgewood admitted, mopping sweat from his brow with a rag that stank of sulphur. He scurried off then, eager to escape those ghastly images from hell.

'*One word o' this to anyone and yer dead!*' McGray roared at him.

I cannot tell for how long we stood there, scrutinising each image, but particularly the one with the blood-curdling hand.

Ironically, it was the silence that brought us back to our senses. The City Chambers were now deserted, and all we could hear were the dogs' occasional snores.

McGray straightened his back, though keeping his eyes fixed on the pictures.

'Go home, Frey. I'll probably need ye fresh in the morning.'

I took a few short steps away, still mesmerised. 'You should rest too.'

'Nah,' he said, rummaging through a drawer, from which he produced a chunky magnifying glass. 'I'm goin' to look at these very carefully . . .'

Nothing would have moved him from that spot, maybe not even the City Chambers catching fire, so there I left him, bent over the desk, his nose an inch from the photographs.

I walked the empty corridors, my steps echoing all around. When I stepped into the frosty night, my nerves were still altered, making me see that horrid hand in every shadow of the streets, every time I blinked.

Of one thing I was sure – I would not manage to sleep at all.

25

By the next day, everyone in Edinburgh talked of nothing but the trial.

Mrs Holt had given venomous statements to the press, detailing her miserable dwellings, how her poor little child would die of hunger, and how callously she'd been treated by a police inspector whose name she did not wish to recall, but who happened to have nine fingers. The article was illustrated with a drawing of the woman carrying her child, which made her look like a grieving Madonna.

The papers also announced that Colonel Grenville would receive a military funeral, scheduled for Friday. He and his wife would be buried in the grounds of St Cuthbert's Church, in his family crypt, while the other four would go to Grange Cemetery, closer to Morningside. All the bodies, however, would be present during the larger-than-life service at St Giles' Cathedral, followed by a solemn procession. In the last lines, the newspaper exhorted the public to stay away and respect the grief of the few surviving relatives. I could only laugh at the irony. The article was more like an open invitation, designed to exacerbate the public resentment.

As expected, when I made it to the City Chambers there was a small crowd gathered at the entrance, calling for justice for the good colonel and demanding Mr Holt be allowed 'to return to his sweet wife'.

I lowered my head, trying to conceal my face with my hat, and managed to scuttle through without being seen. I was not surprised to walk into the office and find McGray still bent over the photographs, with the magnifying glass and wearing the same clothes.

'Is it morning already?' he said when he saw me come in. I pointed at the dull light coming through the barred windows. 'Och, right!'

He blew out the oil lamp on the desk and rubbed his eyes.

'Did you find anything?' I asked him.

'Only one thing, but it just confused me even more.'

He showed me the photograph that directly preceded the one with the dark hand. There was something on the table-cloth, right on the edge of the photograph, which had not appeared in any of the previous images. It looked like a dark pebble.

'Is that the gold nugget?' I asked.

'Aye. She took it off. That would explain how Holt "found it" on the floor; it most likely fell during the commotion and rolled close to the door. So Holt was telling the truth.'

I frowned. 'Why would she do that? If I saw a twisted hand floating in mid-air, the last thing I'd worry about is removing my cufflinks.'

'Nae only that. The nugget was a protection charm. It'd be like a nun seeing the devil and deciding to drop her rosary.'

I sighed. 'One more bloody thing to consider. And you say you found nothing else?'

He let out a long sigh. 'Nothing, and I better stop looking. These are driving me mad.'

I checked the time. 'Shall we go and question the surviving Shaws? They are the only relatives we have yet to question.'

'Aye, but I need to go 'n' get some breakfast first, I'm starving.' He whistled at the dogs, who sprinted up as if already knowing there was food to be had.

Walking next to McGray's tartan trousers it was impossible not to be spotted by the nosy crowd. Luckily, we had giant Mackenzie, who growled and barked like a devilish beast as soon as anyone hostile approached. Some of the things people shouted at us, however, were so crass and vulgar they made me shudder. Still, none of that was even nearly as off-putting as watching McGray devour six fried eggs with a side of sausages and some ghastly-looking meat stuff he called 'fruit loaf'.

The coquettish Mary came by, and as she served McGray yet another helping of food, I recalled Katerina's words, uttered when she touched the victims' trinkets.

There is a sound . . . It's like she's whispering. Just one word, over and over . . .

Mary . . .

I shook my head. Mary was a very common name, and there was no chance this young woman could have been involved.

She and McGray chatted on merrily, and as soon as he finished his meal, we set off to New Town.

Bertrand, we were not surprised to learn, had lived with his mother all his life, just like his younger brother Harvey. They'd all shared a townhouse in Albany Street, and I must admit I was impressed when I saw the wide, well-appointed façade.

When a housemaid let us in, however, it was obvious that their wealth had been steadily fading away too. The wallpaper was peeling off in places, the ornate rugs had patches, and the varnish of the stairs' banisters was almost gone at the edges. On the other hand, everything was clean and tidy; the faded upholstery immaculate, the worn china proudly displayed on the cabinets. It was as if the objects themselves clung to their dignity in the face of hardship.

We were asked to wait in a modest parlour, where they kept a small altar for Bertrand. His rather unflattering portrait was on the mantelpiece, wrapped in a black bow and surrounded by evergreens and white lilies.

It struck me then that we had seen none such display in Mrs Cobbold's properties; neither at her flat in St Andrew Square nor at her summer house in Kirkcaldy. I dismissed the thought, remembering she'd wanted to keep the news from the young children.

'Remind me how these people fit in the family,' McGray said.

'Bertrand was Mr Shaw's grandson. His father was Grannie Alice's youngest son, Richard.'

'He's dead, I suppose.'

'Yes.'

'That means Mrs Cobbold is Alice's only surviving child?'

'I . . . suppose so,' and I checked in my notebook. 'Indeed, with Mr Willberg now dead, she is the last one.' I raised my eyebrows. 'Curiously, on the Willbergs' side there is only one survivor: Walter Fox.'

McGray raised his chin a smidgen. 'And those two were together at court. D'ye think it might mean something?'

I pondered for a moment but did not have a chance to answer, for we heard a rhythmic sound, a metallic squeak, coming from the corridor.

We turned our heads just as Harvey Shaw made his way in, propelling his own wheelchair.

'Good day, inspectors,' he said with a very soft voice and offering a hand to shake. He was the only family member who did not share the dark curly hair. His was a dull blonde, and his rather plump cheeks and pallid skin spoke of someone who very rarely ventured outside. 'You've come to enquire about my brother's death, I suppose.'

'Indeed,' I said. 'We are very sorry for your loss.'

'Thank you,' he answered, staring at his late brother's portrait. 'It's not sunk in yet, I'm afraid. I'm still surprised every morning when I see my brother's empty spot at the breakfast table.'

'Were you very close?' I asked, but Harvey could only look down and nod.

'I'm afraid we need to talk to yer mother too,' McGray added.

Harvey rubbed his hands nervously. 'My mother's been bedridden since we heard the news. But I can answer anything you might ask.'

'Sorry to hear that, lad,' McGray said, 'but it's important we question everyone directly.'

Harvey looked at us in complete silence, as if for a moment he'd forgotten we were there. He then twitched.

'Oh, do sit down, please. May I offer you anything? Tea?'

'No, thank you,' I said.

McGray and I sat, and Harvey placed his chair facing us. The old thing squeaked not only when he moved it around, but whenever he gestured or shifted his weight, no matter how slightly. It soon got on my nerves, but the man did not seem to notice.

After a few preamble questions, I got to the point. 'What did you know about the séance?'

Again he rubbed his hands, and they would not be still for the rest of our conversation.

'Nothing at all, sir. I didn't even know it would take place.'

McGray leaned forwards. 'Ye sure?'

'Yes, sir. We only heard of it on the same day, when the colonel's valet came to fetch my brother. I understand it was my step-cousin who organised the whole thing, but the Willbergs and I have never talked much. Leonora visited once in a blue moon, but she always talked about really strange things; spirits, talismans, souls in purgatory – and séances, precisely. I never liked her much, I must admit. She scared me, so I avoided her whenever I could. She'd talk much more to Bert and Mum.'

'When was the last time she visited?' I asked.

'Quite a few months ago. It must have been January or February. I remember it was still snowing.'

'What about the late Peter Willberg?' McGray asked. 'Or that other lad, Walter Fox? When did ye last see them?'

'Oh, it's been years.' Harvey counted with his fidgety fingers. 'Five – no, six years ago. They came to the baptism of Cousin Martha's child, little Alice. But we didn't even talk; they and Leonora left very early.'

'How so?'

'I think they weren't invited. The colonel didn't like them at all.'

'We know that,' I said. 'Do you have any idea why?'

'No, sir. I think it was a business matter, from many years ago, but the family never talk to me about such things.'

'And I assume you did not know the purpose of the séance either.'

'Sorry, sir. No. As I told you, that valet came asking if Bert could help them. Our cousin Martha sent a note begging him to. She said the colonel would be most displeased if he refused. She was afraid he—'

Harvey bit his lip.

'We are aware of the colonel's temper,' I said sombrely.

'My poor cousin,' Harvey mumbled. 'She never talked about it, but we all knew the colonel mistreated her. Aunt Gertrude never forgave herself for instigating their marriage.'

'She told us so herself,' I said. 'Do you know why she did so?'

Harvey rubbed his hands hard as he looked at the entrance, perhaps to make sure nobody heard.

'I believe the colonel helped my grandfather get into some business or other. Nobody ever told me this, of course, but

I believe Aunt Gertrude wanted to keep the wealth in the family.'

'Do you know what kind of business?' I asked.

'No, sir. I was only a child when they married. My cousin herself was in her teens.'

I took note of everything, feeling things were very slowly beginning to coalesce. 'Can you think of anyone who might have wanted to harm them?'

Harvey looked at the blanket on his legs, thinking hard. It took him a while to answer.

'Well . . . I know Mr Willberg had a reputation. He had so many drinking and gambling debts all across the city, nobody would sell him liquor anymore. Rumour has it he even hired thugs to act as "servants" of fictitious patrons.

'The colonel himself was a very scary man . . . but everyone seemed to admire him, as if he were some sort of messianic war hero. More based on his height and good looks than anything else.'

There was clear bitterness in those words.

'Then again,' Harvey continued after a sigh, 'Martha, my grandfather . . .' he gulped. 'And Bert . . . I cannot think of anyone who'd want to harm *all* of them at once. It simply makes no sense.'

'Was Bertrand a good brother?' I asked him.

'Oh, yes. People always mocked him for his timid manner, but he effectively ran things here.'

'Did he?'

'Yes. Mother has always been of a delicate disposition, much worse after my father died. And with my paraplegia I'm of no use. Bert looked after us both for years.'

McGray looked extremely frustrated, and some of the sentiment began to creep into me. He stroked his beard and gave Harvey a scrutinising look.

'Have ye read the papers?'

'I have, sir. As you can imagine, I don't get out much.'

'So ye've read all that's being said about the deaths.'

That made Harvey visibly uncomfortable. He kept rubbing his hands together and said nothing.

McGray spoke again. 'Madame Katerina, the clairvoyant, believes Grannie Alice had some grudge against them.'

Harvey became very tense. He parted his lips and was about to speak, but then there came a cry from the corridor—

'And do you believe that?'

We saw a very thin, middle-aged woman in her nightdress. Her bony face was lined with sharp wrinkles, and her hair, once blonde but now almost completely white, swung in a very long plait.

'Mrs Shaw?' I said, even though I recalled everyone in the family called her Mrs Eliza.

'Mother!' cried Harvey. Seeing them together it was clear they were mother and son, sharing no features with the rest of the Shaw family.

'Do you believe a word of what that woman says?' she repeated, taking faltering steps into the parlour. The house-maid had to hold her by the arm, and only let go of her when Mrs Shaw was settled in a nearby armchair. The woman must have been in her fifties, but looked at least a decade older; even her blotched hands trembled like those of a very old person.

She seemed mortified – quite understandably – but McGray had the good sense to offer our condolences first. That settled her just enough to have a conversation.

'We've been told yer relatives wanted to talk to the late Alice Shaw. That they—'

'Nonsense,' Mrs Shaw snapped. 'Worse than nonsense. Blasphemy.'

McGray, rather than looking offended, spoke soothingly. 'Ye don't believe ye can talk to the dead?'

'I believe what the scriptures say,' she replied quickly. 'The dead are resting; awaiting resurrection.' She produced a crumpled handkerchief and pressed it against her face. She took a few deep breaths, and then looked wistfully at the portrait of her dead son. 'I know I will see my Bertrand, but it will be in Heaven, at the end of times. Not before. Not as an apparition floating in my parlour.' She seemed on the verge of tears, but managed to compose herself. 'So-called spirits or ghosts or visions are just abominations. The hand of the devil.'

Both McGray and I looked up so swiftly our necks could have snapped.

'Why—' I said before McGray had a chance to spit out some gibberish. I softened my tone too. 'Why did you . . . choose that word?'

'He's crafty, the devil,' said Mrs Shaw. 'He promises us the same things the Lord gives us for free, and we still manage to fall into his snares.'

There was an eerie quality to her voice, her eyes apparently lost in the void. She almost resembled Katerina when delivering one of her omens. It seemed to disturb Harvey, who rolled his squeaky chair across to reach one of his mother's hands.

They were a very sorry picture, sitting there together and attempting to give each other comfort, when it was clear they were both distraught for their loss . . . and just as fearful for their future.

McGray pressed his fingertips together (one as usual left without a partner) and mulled for a moment. He was choosing his words.

'Missus,' he said, 'Grannie Alice, we've heard, thought she had *gifts*.'

Mrs Shaw looked up, her eyes twinkling.

'Yes,' she said soon enough. 'I knew of my mother-in-law's eccentricities. Why are you asking?'

'Did she ever tell you anything about it?'

Mrs Shaw shook her head, looking confused. 'Well . . . yes. But she talked about it all the time. She always told me to burn lavender and keep talismans and that kind of thing.'

'And I feel ye didnae like that.'

'Of course not.'

'Did youse ever have arguments?' McGray offered a gentle smile, seeing that the woman hesitated. 'She was yer mother-in-law. Youse must have at some point.'

Mrs Shaw nodded coyly. 'I tolerated her. She was my son's grandmother and she was always very polite. It was only once that I had to ask her to leave this house.'

'Did ye?'

'Yes, but only because the things she said were getting sacrilegious.'

'Sacrilegious? How?'

Mrs Shaw gulped. 'I've told you already. All her witchcraft rituals.'

'Aye but . . . d'ye remember the particulars?'

She shook her head. 'No, not at all. I never paid much attention to her gibberish. And that one time was seven or eight years ago.'

I took a short breath. 'Was that shortly before her passing, by any chance?' I knew it must have been, but I was still interested in her reply.

Mrs Shaw looked down. 'Y-yes. Just a few months. In fact, that was the last time we spoke.'

I took note of that, and noticed that Harvey stared intently at my little notebook. Our eyes met briefly, but he immediately looked away.

McGray, in fact, was staring at Mrs Shaw just as intensely.

'Did anyone else in the family claim to have those gifts?'

She smiled bitterly. 'On the Willberg side, yes. Miss Leonora, as everybody knows now.'

'Indeed,' I said. I was going to ask something else, but Mrs Shaw had not finished.

'And Alice's eldest daughter too. Her name was Prudence.'

I looked again at the family tree. 'Walter Fox's mother?'

'Yes, sir.'

I arched an eyebrow, as I underlined her name. 'How . . . did Prudence pass away?'

'A very sad affair, sir. She became pregnant at an old age. She must have been forty or forty-one. She longed for more children after she had Walter, but the years went by and it did not happen. Grannie Alice . . . *helped* her with one remedy or another. Her doctors told her it was very dangerous, but she wanted to keep the child. Her husband had just died, you see. But she had a miscarriage and bled to death.'

'Very sad indeed,' I mumbled. 'How old was Walter Fox back then?'

'Oh, already a man. Eighteen or nineteen.'

'He must have been devastated,' I said. 'What did he do?'

'He went abroad for years,' said Harvey. 'For a while nobody knew where or what for. We even suspected he was dead, but one day Leonora and her uncle heard from him. He'd become a gems dealer.'

'Did he?' I asked, recalling his vulgar diamond ring. Something began to brew in my mind. 'Do you . . . do you know where he lived all those years?'

'Everywhere,' said Harvey, 'but mostly in Africa. For the diamond trade.'

I recalled the photograph of Leonora's father, surrounded by African women. And also the children talking of treasures. I had to conceal my anticipation.

'Did his business have anything to do with his uncle? Leonora's father, I mean.'

Harvey arched an eyebrow. 'I don't know . . . Do you, Mother?'

Mrs Shaw shook her head.

'I told you, I didn't know them that well. Leonora's father – what was his name?'

'William,' I read from my notes.

'Yes, true. I know he had some businesses abroad at some point, but where and what . . . I . . . I don't know.'

I wrote that down, though a little more slowly. There were fragments there, and they all seemed about to coalesce.

'When did he come back?' McGray asked.

'He bought a house in Edinburgh a couple of years ago,' said Mrs Shaw, 'but I wouldn't say he's ever been *back*. He still travels a good deal, and not only for business. He likes to flaunt that he's a wealthy man now, especially . . . in front of us.'

They fell into an uncomfortable silence, until the maid came back with a cup of herbal tea for her mistress. She stood by her like a Roman guard, watching us with a defiant face.

We decided it was time to leave, but before I stood up, I underlined the name Walter Fox.

26

'He leaves the country,' I said, dunking a biscuit in my cup of tea, as McGray and I stared at the enormous family tree we'd pinned to the office wall. 'Obviously shattered by his family tragedy – father, mother and unborn sibling dead almost all at once . . . Possibly feeling undervalued by his richer relatives . . . Makes his way in the world, and then, relatively soon after he settles back, all this happens.'

'Revenge?' McGray ventured, carelessly scratching Tucker's ear.

'Against whom? The mother died of a miscarriage.'

'It does look very iffy.'

'Indeed.'

'And I'm starting to believe he might have the eye too.'

I had to laugh at that, spilling some of the Earl Grey. 'Are you indeed?'

'His mother had it; his grandmother too.'

'Nine-Nails, even if I believed anybody had the bloody *eye*, Alice told Eddie, her little great-grandson, he was the only other one with it. And I would have assumed that another grandson with the *eye* is one of the things you'd be able to *see* with the bloody *eye*.'

'Frey, say *bloody eye* like that again and I'll shower ye with yer sodding tea.'

I savoured the buttery biscuits. 'Tell Joan how thankful I am for these, by the way. Do you want to go and question Fox now?'

McGray stretched his back, stood up and stared at the names, the photographs and the pages from Leonora's journal.

'What is it?' I asked, and he rubbed his stubble as if trying to set it on fire.

'I'm just afraid it might be another sodding dead end and we'll waste yet another damn day, like chasing Mrs Cobbold all the way to Kirkcaldy.'

I looked at her name on the wall. 'That was not an entire waste of time. She did look like she was hiding something. And it appears she has developed some close connection with Walter Fox.'

'And she only escaped the séance at the last minute, I remember. But it makes nae sense. Why murder her own daughter?'

My eyes moved across the wall. 'Mrs Grenville's death makes little sense indeed. So do Leonora's and Bertrand's.'

'Or the auld Mr Shaw. He was ten minutes from snuffing it anyway.'

'Crude but, let us face it, accurate. I shall be pleased if by sixty-five I am still able to get out of the bath unaided.'

'Nae if ye keep stuffing yer face with shortbread, ye won't.'

'Says the man who gobbles up a dozen fried eggs on a regular— Oh, never mind. Back to the case.' I pointed at the centre of the family tree. 'The colonel and Mr Willberg, I have to say, do look like people who might have made some enemies. It would not surprise me if there was someone who hated them so much they did not care who else died on the evening. Remember the wounds on Grenville's hands? He may even have come from a skirmish that day.'

McGray nodded. 'Aye, yer right. But that means we'll have to question absolutely everyone who met them. And we're running out of time. *And* if we don't have a case against anyone, we only have that sodding halfwit assigned to defend Katerina . . .' He turned to face me. 'Nae word from yer dad yet?'

'No. Although it is likely my telegram is sitting on a little silver tray, with another twenty unopened messages, while he sips cognac a mere couple of feet away.'

That did not improve McGray's mood. Then, as if the universe were set on bringing him down, Dr Reed came by, looking extremely tired. His workload must be crushing him again.

'Inspectors,' he said after a yawn, 'I've finished the tests on those bottles from Mr Holt's dwellings. I ran them twice, just to be sure.'

'And?' McGray urged.

Reed bit his lower lip. 'Both the rat poison and the bedbug killer were rich in the same element.' Our faces brightened, but then Reed struck the blow. 'Arsenic.'

'Arsenic?' we cried in unison.

He nodded, barely keeping himself awake. 'Yes, inspectors. The one poisonous metal I had discarded with enough certainty.'

'Blast!' McGray cried, even if the result corroborated our suspicions.

I sighed. 'It looks like Holt did not do it after all . . . Unless, of course, he used a very sophisticated poisoning method – which, quite frankly, strikes me as beyond the man's capacity.' I looked at Reed. 'Do you still have the samples of tissue?'

'Yes, sir. I'm keeping them in ice and I replenish it every morning. Do you want me to run any test on those?'

'No, not yet. But do keep them well stored. Thanks, Reed.'

He left, mumbling something in-between yawns.

McGray and I remained silent for a good while, as befuddled as we'd been throughout the investigation.

I stared at the family tree. With its tangled connections and the sea of documents and evidence, it resembled an enormous spider ready to strike. And the name of Grannie Alice, circled and underlined, was like the tiny body from where all the spindly legs emerged.

27

The next few days were an absolute blur.

McGray and I separated to cover more ground, and we talked to every neighbour, friend, acquaintance, dealer and trader even slightly connected to the Willbergs and the Shaws. I'd wake up first thing in the morning, go through my list of leads over breakfast, and then cross the length and breadth of an increasingly rainy Edinburgh. I'd only return home well into the night with a pile of useless notes, sore feet and a shattered brain.

Time was slipping through our fingers like running water, yet neither of us had found anything of consequence. We learned about Mr Willberg's gambling and unpaid taps, and how Colonel Grenville appeared to have made most of his money outstandingly quickly. I had the feeling there might be something else there, but nothing seemed gargantuan enough as to spur a sextuple murder.

We had only four days left by then, so we had to start entertaining the possibility that Katerina might be sentenced. McGray nearly punched me in the face when I suggested it, but we had to be prepared for every eventuality. Word from my Oxford contacts arrived that day, none of them able to provide more help with regards to the chemical tests.

After reading that, McGray finally agreed we begin looking for people who might speak in Katerina's favour, like my Cambridge colleagues had advised.

She made us a lengthy list of her regular clients, who spanned all the ranks of society. Even Edinburgh's Lord Provost, like McGray had once guessed, had consulted her a couple of times. And, to our utter shock, my landlady, the mighty Lady Anne Ardglass.

McGray and I shared the legwork. He would visit all the clients that lived south of Princes Street (Old Town and similar slums), whilst I would go to New Town and also the few wealthy estates south of The Moors.

He had tremendous success. Nearly everyone he spoke to agreed to vouch for Katerina, but I was not too sure how useful that would be. They were all working people; butchers, horseshoers, seamstresses . . . Mary from the Ensign of course. I was afraid a contemptuous jury would laugh.

I, on the other hand, had a terrible time. As soon as I mentioned the word 'gypsy' in the better-to-do neighbourhoods, they all slammed their doors on my face, denying any connection with Katerina. Word about my enquiries circulated at staggering speed, and by the end of the day everyone in New Town was crossing the street at the sight of me.

It did not help at all that a dubious newspaper devoted three full pages to detail Katerina's life and dealings, in an infamous article entitled *The Mystery of the Gypsy Seer. Assassin Ghost or Silent Murderess??*

I did not bother calling at Lady Anne's, even if I walked past her gigantic townhouse and, being one of her tenants, I had a perfect excuse. Her hatred towards McGray had only worsened after the dreadful Lancashire affair, in which she was deeply involved, and my refusing her granddaughter's hand (long story . . .) would not help our case at all.

Most of my Thursday was spent briefing that idiot Sperry, and by the time I returned home I had a splitting headache. The man was so useless we might as well dress up a baboon on the day: he kept asking me the same questions over and over, and he could not even memorise the names of the family members, always referring to the dead Bertrand as Walter Fox. And when I handed him the photographs – the *hand of Satan* on top – he let out the most childish high-pitched moan. He then told me, in the same pitiful tone, that Pratt had been pressing and bullying him. '*Of course he will!*' I had roared.

After that, it took three large brandies to dull my head enough to fall asleep.

Layton had to stir me the next day. The sky was so darkened with stormy clouds, it made very little difference when he opened the curtains.

My mood, if anything, had worsened.

'Would you like to see today's papers?' he asked me as I ruminated dry toast, eating on my feet.

'No, thanks. In the past few days I have scribbled and read the equivalent of the complete works of Madeleine de Scudéry.'

I made my way to the door, but Layton followed me with the rolled newspaper.

'Sir, I must insist you do.'

'Will it ruin my day?'

'Erm . . . inescapably, sir.'

'Then I am in no rush to see it.'

I grabbed my coat and rushed onto the street, where the clouds looked like a turbulent dome of thick, black vapours, swirling about like the spurts of milk in my tea. In fact, the air above the entire city felt oppressive, invading the lungs and spreading despair. I lifted my fur-trimmed collar and moved on, but I would not forget that sky for quite a while.

I found another shouting rabble gathered around the arches of the City Chambers – more numerous and far more indignant than in previous days.

I was in no mood to confront an illiterate mob, so I walked stealthily to the Advocates Library, just across the road, and as I settled in a secluded corner, I asked a clerk to tell McGray where he could find me. The same clerk brought me a gaslight, for the entire library was shrouded in semi-darkness, hardly any daylight getting through the windows.

I felt my eyes heavy after going through my notes for a while, and upon stretching my neck, I spotted a silent figure on the other side of the chamber. That glossy scalp again.

Pratt met my eye and almost twitched, immediately burying his face in his book. A rather pathetic move, for the reflection of my lamp made his sweaty head gleam like a street light.

'For goodness' sake,' I hissed, standing up and approaching him with long strides. I would not let this go on. 'Have you been following me, Pratt?' and my voice echoed throughout the library.

His chest swelled. 'What? Don't be ridiculous! I have more than one assignment to look after.'

'You do seem to be devoting considerable time to this case in particular.'

'I'm simply doing my job. Unlike others, I do happen to have a serious post. But do not worry, inspector; that woman will be sentenced very soon and you'll be able to go back to your kelpie and will-o'-the-wisp hunting.'

I took a step forwards, the purest rage burning in my chest. I wanted to strangle him on the spot. I even raised my hands, my fingers ready to wrap his wobbly neck. And then, as if awoken from a dream, I realised what I was about to do.

These outbursts were like my nightmares; like those nasty memories of the loch on fire, coming back to me at will, and I could do nothing about them. I saw the torches again, flashing before my eyes, and then the face of my dead uncle also appeared. That startled me, and it was like a second awakening.

Pratt was staring at my trembling hands. He let out a muffled chuckle, his golden tooth catching a gleam from the lamp.

I turned on my heels at once, saying nothing, for I feared I might lose control, and went back to pick up my papers. I heard Pratt's footsteps right behind me.

'I see that Nine-Nails has passed some of his charm onto you.'

I did not reply, gathering the documents as swiftly as I could. Pratt, however, saw the three files I had entitled *Walter Fox*, *Peter Willberg* and *Col Arthur Grenville*.

'You believe there is something untoward there,' he said, his mocking tone fuelling the fire in my stomach. 'You can feel it with your guts, can you not? Something lurking just underneath the surface, yet you cannot grasp what it is.'

I pretended to ignore him, but then he delivered a punchline he'd clearly longed to spit out for a long time.

'That's what I always felt about the McGrays.'

I nearly dropped the stack of files.

Pratt began to whisper, his voice all too polite; however, there was poison in his eyes.

'I don't know what stories of family bliss Nine-Nails may have told you, but I know one thing: healthy young ladies do not simply lose their minds whilst on a laid-back summer holiday in the countryside. Something happened there, Mr Frey. I know it.'

I made to leave, but he grasped my arm.

'The late Mr McGray was an irascible rogue, and many people seemed to know things about him they would not repeat. The man built his fortune from scratch, yes, but his ways were not always . . . honourable. He made many powerful enemies. Quite deservedly.'

I pulled away and used my free hand to shove him at the chest. Pratt staggered and nearly dropped backwards, but his smile never faded.

'*If I catch you following me again—*'

I did not bother saying more. I simply walked away before my temper got the better of me. I heard his voice fading in the distance.

'I'll hardly have much more time to follow you. You only have three days left!'

I took all my notes and documents to the New Club, hoping to find some peace and quiet, but the place was racketing like a parrot-packed aviary. There were no free tables in the first-floor dining hall, and even the corridors were busy with chatting gentlemen.

My favourite spot at the main smoking room was taken by a rather large old man; however, as soon as he saw me, he coughed as if about to spit his lungs out, stood up as quickly as his chubby legs allowed, and stomped out, making some of the glassware clatter. I realised he'd been one of Katerina's clients: he had been snooping over his butler's shoulder as the servant refused to let me in to make my enquiries.

At least I had my favourite armchair and table, just by one of the many windows that overlooked Princes Street.

The waiter came by. 'Anything to drink, sir?'

'Yes. Brandy – no, claret. I'll start with the claret, I need my mind sharp.'

As I settled and displayed my work, I peered at the people around me.

On the other side of the room there was a group of middle-aged men; all grey-haired, big-bellied and either holding cigars or swirling glasses of liquor. They were gathered around a newspaper, whispering in each other's ears, at times gasping and covering their mouths most comically. Here's a token of wisdom: upper-class gentlemen at clubs are far worse gossips than washerwomen.

I had taken but a few sips of claret when a skinny man burst in and ran straight to the windows, shouting with uninhibited excitement. 'They're coming!'

Every soul in the room stood up as if thrust by springs and squeezed together by the windows, their hands and noses pressed against the glass. With their black jackets and stretched necks, they reminded me of vultures peering on a dying beast.

Another three men came from the corridor and very ungentlemanly pushed themselves around my table, nearly knocking my glass over.

I had to look out, and immediately saw the cause of such havoc.

Six dark percherons came into view from the western side of the road, their heads decked with black feathers. They were slowly pulling a gilded hearse, as ornate as a small cathedral, bursting with white flowers and mourning shrouds. Nestled in them were the coffins of the colonel and his wife; his was draped with the British flag and his military decorations.

I then heard the laments from the bagpipers, the music rising as the men in kilts marched behind the hearse.

'What are they doing?' I blurted out, recalling the funeral arrangements I'd read in *The Scotsman*. 'I thought the service would be at St Giles' Cathedral.'

'But they'll bury them in St Cuthbert's graveyard,' said a nearby gentleman, and I cursed my poor foresight. Of course they had to take the procession along Princes Street; there was simply no other route from the cathedral. And that took the funeral to the city's widest road, turning the gloomy affair into a public carnival.

The pipers were followed closely by a black landau with the roof drawn back. I instantly recognised Mrs Cobbold, seated very straight and sporting a flamboyant mourning hat with ostrich feathers that rivalled the horses'.

I then had to rub my eyes to believe what I saw.

The children were with her!

Edward, the eldest, was looking around with a distorted face, at once angry, confused and grief-stricken. The younger ones, Daniel and little Alice, were simply frozen still.

'What a hypocrite!' I muttered. So much talk about shielding her grandchildren, and yet here she was, parading their teary eyes along the busiest street in Edinburgh, in a carriage followed by a morbid crowd.

A random woman approached their carriage to put a flower in the little girl's hand, and everyone around applauded. I even spotted several bystanders crying – people who probably had not even heard the name Grenville before the colonel's death.

Mrs Cobbold looked up, casting an arrogant stare at the crowds, the long funeral cortège that followed her and then the buildings on the northern side of the road. All windows must be crammed with curious faces. For a moment I thought she stared directly into my eyes, and saw what looked like the hint of a scorning smile.

I could stand it no more. For the second time, I gathered my documents and stood up swiftly, leaving two young men to fight over my spot by the window.

As I rushed out, I saw the newspaper the gossipmongers had been reading. They'd tossed it carelessly on one of the armchairs, and it was that front page that caught my eye. From a distance, it looked like a solid black square, as if the press had broken and flooded the entire sheet with ink. I picked it up, already fearing what it might show, but the headline still made me gasp.

THE MORNINGSIDE MURDERS:
HORRID NEW EVIDENCE.

Below it, the front page showed a ghastly engraving, printed across eight columns, which reproduced in utmost detail the photograph of the hand of Satan.

Not only that. The paper implied, quite shamelessly, that Katerina had used her demonic arts to kill the six – the same paper that a few days ago had mocked the very idea.

I felt my blood boil.

And then, amidst my anger, I realised that the news had been circulating since the morning.

McGray would already know.

28

'Do not break any bones! McGray, *do not*—!'

He was already storming into the Advocates Library, clenching the newspaper in his hand; Tucker and Mackenzie ran behind him, barking wildly.

Officers and clerks moved aside as if Nine-Nails were an expansive wave, tripping and dropping their books.

We found Sperry at one of the furthest tables, surrounded by documents. He saw us coming and jumped up, tipping his chair over and babbling.

'I didn't! I didn't—'

He tripped and fell backwards, but as soon as he touched the floor, McGray grabbed him by the collar with one hand, lifted him and slammed him against the bookshelves. Tomes of law fell all around.

'Ye leaked this!' Nine-Nails shouted, waving *The Scotsman* right in front of Sperry's face. Tucker barked and Mackenzie showed his fangs.

'It wasn't me!' Sperry cried, his legs flailing desperately.

'*Don't lie to me, ye little shit!* Or I'll punch yer gob 'til yer face looks even more like a baboon's arse!'

'You will only make matters worse!' I warned, but again he ignored me.

I saw three officers coming in with truncheons, McNair amongst them, looking terribly worried.

Sperry whimpered miserably until something behind McGray's back caught his eye. He raised a quivering hand. '*It was him!* He came to me last night and snatched all the files!'

All our heads turned in that direction to find Pratt's shining scalp.

McGray dropped Sperry, who fell as limply as a poorly-stuffed scarecrow, and hurled himself at Pratt, ready to rip him apart.

The three officers, two very brave clerks and I managed to seize Nine-Nails just in time, I do not know quite how, but there were files and sheets of paper fluttering in the air.

'That would have been said in court anyway,' Pratt said coldly, as we all struggled to keep Nine-Nails at bay. The bead of sweat on his bald head betrayed his smug demeanour.

'Ye calculated it so fucking well!' McGray snarled. 'Get that shite on the front page just on the day of the sodding funerals. Fuel people's resentment. Make sure the jury will be nicely prejudiced!'

Pratt was about to smile, but then the enormous Mackenzie pounced at him. Constable McNair managed to seize the dog's collar and, after much jerking, subdued the animal.

Still struggling with the dog, his ginger freckles flushed, McNair came closer to Nine-Nails. His eyes were pleading.

'I . . . I must ask you to leave, sir,' he whispered. 'We'll get in trouble if you don't.'

Pratt had the good sense to go, and only when he was out of sight did we release McGray.

He said nothing. He simply looked around. All the faces around him were scared or baffled or reproaching.

When he left, slouching and dragging his feet, with the dogs whimpering as they followed, I felt terribly sorry for him.

*

Layton nudged me the following morning, and I found I'd spent the night on my armchair, my back and neck cracking with every move.

As I rubbed my eyes, preparing myself for the herculean task of standing up, Layton opened the curtains.

'You have a visitor, sir,' he said, and just then I heard a racket coming from the corridor.

'This early?'

'It is ten o'clock, sir.'

'*What?*' I cried as I jumped on my feet, so quickly I saw stars. 'Why did you let me sleep for so long? I have work to do!'

Before Layton answered, there was a loud thud resounding from the ground floor.

I rushed downstairs, rubbing my sore neck and perfectly aware of my dismal appearance. I found several trunks piled up at the entrance hall, the main door wide open, and a muscly loader bringing even more luggage. I was going to ask him what he was doing, but then something enormous blocked the scant morning light from the entrance.

The first thing I saw was a wide, distended belly, tightly constricted by a black overcoat whose brass buttons were about to burst out like bullets.

'*Father!*'

The old Mr Frey stepped in, his confident stomps like those of a proud rhinoceros, a hand resting on his ermine lapel and the other grasping his ebony walking cane.

'Is it you?' I squealed.

'Oh, Ian, what a stupid question. You sent for me, did you not? By the way, you look ghastly.'

'I . . . I did, but—' I shook my head, struggling to reawaken my brain. 'I never – *ever* thought you'd come! Did you . . . did you perhaps misread my telegram?'

He chuckled as he paid the loader. 'Gypsy, six deaths, your unhinged boss thinks a ghost did it. Even with your atrocious grammar, I could not have possibly misunderstood; it is in every paper in London.'

'*Is it?*'

'Yes. This is precisely the type of alarmist silliness they always use to fill up the back page. Your stepmother actually fainted when she spotted your name.'

'*Actually fainted*, you say?'

'Oh, you know the act. She dropped dramatically on her chaise longue and did not move until the maid brought her some smelling salts.' He then looked at Layton and barked, 'When the devil are you going to take my coat, you bloody overgrown poker?'

Layton had just arrived and closed the door, and I saw a slight smile on his face as he received my father's hefty garment – as if being shouted at was the right order of things in the world.

'By all means, do not show me the way,' Father snapped sarcastically, heading to the stairs. 'I still remember where everything is. But do bring me a cigar before you sort my luggage. And see that that bloody mare gets fed.'

'Mare?' I repeated, rushing to the open door.

Knowing my misogynist father as I did, I half expected to see my stepmother come in. The reality, however, was infinitely more pleasant. There, standing proud, her pristine white coat gleaming against the dull greys of the street, was my Bavarian warmblood.

'Why, you brought Philippa!'

'Yes. Elgie insisted – that is why it took me so bloody long to arrive. I had her sent from Gloucestershire, and I will tell you one thing – she is one nasty, sulky mare, just like your ex-fiancée.' And as Father went upstairs, he grumbled something about how only barbarians can survive with just the one servant and no horse.

I could not help myself and went to pat my precious Philippa. She was indeed in a mood, but I knew she'd be restored after a wholesome meal and a long rest.

'Give her a few carrots,' I told Layton, aware of my sudden glee, and then went after the old Mr Frey.

He was already lounging in my favourite chair and looking at my disarray of paperwork with dubious eyes.

'I thought you did not like Scotland,' I said.

'Oh, I abhor the damn country, but Edin-bloody-burgh will be a thousand times preferable than hearing Catherine and that blasted trollop Eugenia prattle about the wedding plans. It is nauseating, Ian.'

I slightly winced at how casually he'd uttered the name Eugenia – my former fiancée, whom he'd also just compared to a sulking horse. I could not say much in her favour, for Eugenia broke our engagement last year to go and marry my eldest brother.

Father was shaking his head, oblivious to my clear discomfort. 'Do you know how many yards of white ribbon it takes to deck the pews of St Mary Abbots Church? Do you know the meaning of the bloody species of white flowers that must go on a wedding bouquet? Do you know the minimum length an organdie train should be, so society does not whisper the bride's family is scrimping?'

'No.'

'Well, I *do* now, and I wish I could scrape it off by sand-papering my brain.'

'I know a forensic man who could do that for you.'

'Ahh, but you should have seen Catherine's face when I told her I was leaving. I did not mention a word until my trunks were being carried away. Oh, the laughter!'

'Did you . . . tell her the reason? That you came here to defend a gypsy clairvoyant at Scotland's High Court?' I only asked that question out of my own disbelief.

Father let out his booming laughter. 'But of course I did! That was the cherry on my bloody cake! She will probably despise you until the day she dies.'

'Not much of a change there.'

Layton walked in then, proudly bringing the box with the good cigars. Father grabbed one, barely glancing at the man.

'Bring me brandy – no, claret. I'll start with the claret, I need my mind sharp. And get me whichever meat or cheese or food you have around, provided that it is fatty and not Scotch.'

And as he said so, he leaned closer to the files.

'Father, I must tell you something before you begin.' I sat nearby so I could lower my voice. 'I . . . I am not entirely sure this gypsy woman is innocent. She—'

'Oh, Ian, you always make me laugh! Do you think I made my name by defending only the right and just?'

'I . . . suppose not. But—'

'A successful lawyer does not give a damn about those petty details. A lawyer's job is to get his client free.' He bit the cigar and snapped his fingers at Layton. '*Fire!*'

The reader may have noticed it is quite impossible to speak over the old Mr Frey, so I said as much as I could whilst his mouth was busy lighting his Cuban.

'We have no idea yet as to how *the six* died. There is the possibility of a poisoned knife, but we have no clues as to the motive. Not even a faint lead to suggest—'

'Not important.'

'*Not important!*'

Father chuckled as he savoured the tobacco. 'Oh, Ian, I am so glad you dropped out of Cambridge. You would have been a lousy lawyer; the laughing stock of Chancery Lane. I am only here to try and get that woman out of jail. Who did what is utterly irrelevant to my work.'

'What about justice, or—?' I held my tongue, knowing I was only inviting more abuse.

'Justice, you said?' Father asked. 'Justice is very, very rarely delivered at court.'

I stared at him, indignant. 'Then where?'

Father was already immersed in the files. He did not even look up when he answered.

'I wish I knew.'

29

Father spent the entire day reading the statements, my notes, the relevant newspapers, and from time to time asking me to clarify what my 'sloppy sentences' meant.

At some point I had to go to McGray's house to retrieve the documents he kept, and also the statements he had collected from Katerina's less affluent clients. When I arrived, I found Joan, George and the servant boy Larry furiously scrubbing the portico, dotted with splatters of unidentifiable filth. I noticed a young but intimidating constable now guarding the property.

Joan jumped up as quickly as her knees allowed and, as rubicund as ever, greeted me with her thick Lancashire accent.

'Master, so good to see you! Did you get my butter biscuits? I sent 'em with Mr McGray, so I wasn't sure they'd get to you!'

'Yes, Joan. Delicious. But – what happened here?'

'People have been throwing shite at us!' Larry shouted, scrubbing with the skill only a former chimney sweep can have.

'Don't swear to the masters!' old George snapped, pinching the boy's shoulder.

Joan had gone sombre. 'He's right. The moment that nasty picture appeared in the papers, people came here like vermin. Thank God they sent us this peeler, but who's got to clean? Us, poor devils!'

I shook my head, thinking of the hordes of idle people who took the trouble of carrying rotten things to soil a neighbour's home.

'I hope this ends soon,' I told her reassuringly as I stepped in. 'At least today I have good news.'

When I told Nine-Nails my father was taking charge of the defence he gave me a rib-cracking embrace, lifting me several inches from the floor, and I became intimately acquainted with the true scent of his ragged overcoat.

'This does not guarantee she will go free,' I said as soon as I found myself back on my feet, but McGray's eyes were already glowing with renewed hope.

'Och, I ken. But at least she has better chances. I'll have to thank yer dad!'

I tittered. 'Oh, believe me, the less he sees of you, the better the outcome.' I went to his library, which was as messy as ever, and began collecting the scattered statements. 'I assume the missing ones are at the office?'

'Aye.'

'Very well, I will fetch them. And I will dismiss Sperry while I am there.'

Nine-Nails was pouring himself a celebratory whisky, but he spilled half the measure as he shook with laughter.

'Ohh-ho-ho-ho . . . neh! Wait here, I'll do that myself.'

And sadly he left the house before I could beg him not to break any bones this time.

I was back home an hour or so later and, feeling reduced to a petty clerk, I left the pile of documents on Father's table. Instead of thanking me or even greeting me, he passed me an envelope without taking his eyes from the page.

'Make sure this reaches Lady Anne.'

I nearly stumbled when I heard the name. 'Anne . . . Ardglass?'

'Yes! I addressed it clearly enough.'

'Are you asking her to—?'

'Oh, Ian, do you want me to work on your case or answer your silly questions? Yes! I am asking her to vouch for the gypsy.'

I could not contain a hearty laugh. 'I must tell you that the old woman despises McGray. *And* me. She will never testify.'

Father finally looked away from the work, if only to pour himself more claret.

'I still hold some of her conveyancing documents. The old crone owns a very pretty townhouse in London, just off Hanover Square, and she did not acquire it through strictly lawful means.'

'She will rather lose a property than help us.'

'Why do you think so? I understand why she might despise that Nine-Stubs Malone, but why would she despise *you*?'

I let out a sigh. I would not mention the fact that Lady Anne had unceremoniously offered me the hand of her grand-daughter and I had refused – now that I came to think about it, perhaps she'd only done so to ensure my father would never use her dirty linen against her. It was much preferable to tell Father about the deathly Lancashire affair. 'Do you remember that her only son died?'

'I . . . vaguely recall reading it in the obituaries, yes.'

'He did not die. Well . . . he *is* dead now, but for years he was locked in the lunatic asylum here in Edinburgh. His early death was a sham. Lady Anne was embarrassed of his condition.'

Father finally looked at me with undivided attention. 'And how come you know all this?'

'Last January the man murdered a nurse, and then a few other people. *Nine-Stubs* and I were in charge of chasing him.' Father began chuckling. 'E-excuse me, Father, did you find that story in any way funny?'

'Why, no! I find it juicy.' He snatched the envelope back. 'I shall include all that in my threats.'

I watched indignantly as he penned the dreadful addendum. 'Not only will you force an elderly woman to testify at the High Court – which will be most scandalous and humiliating for a lady of her rank – but you will also threaten to reveal her darkest family secrets? That would ruin her reputation for the rest of her life.'

'Bah! How long might that be?'

'McGray thinks forever. He even mentioned she might have done a pact with the devil.'

'Well, in that case she will have to spend eternity in shame.'

I shook my head. 'Father, you do scare me sometimes.'

He laughed, raising his glass in a toast to himself. 'Are you not happy I am on your side this time?'

30

The city air felt increasingly oppressive as the time passed. I thought it was simply my own anxieties, but the autumn weather held its share of blame; the clouds grew thicker and darker until they looked like a solid roof, yet remained reluctant to pour any rain.

The sky finally broke on the morning of the trial, lashing the streets like an Amazonian downpour. I heard the relentless drumming on the window as I adjusted one of my better ties, and then peered out into the street, where gusts of brown water flowed and splashed around the overwhelmed sewers.

The Scotsman (which Layton had to iron, for it had arrived dripping wet) mentioned the trial on the front page with, if possible, even more alarming language. The horrendous image of the hand of Satan featured again, though thankfully much smaller than the previous Friday – this I can only attribute to the newspaper trying to save on ink.

Father and I set off very early, and I had to endure his endless complaints about the weather.

'What a glorified slum,' he said as we approached the castle-like towers of Calton Hill Jail. 'The Scotch really like to overcompensate.'

Thankfully the tempest had discouraged onlookers, and our way in was relatively painless – though we both moaned in the exact same manner as our shoes plunged into the muddy yard.

McGray's cab arrived just a moment later. To my astonishment, he was cleanly shaven and wore a perfectly fit black suit.

'My, oh my, you dressed decently!'

He shrugged. 'It's Bram Stoker's. He never asked for it back. Bit tight round the crotch, mind.'

We went to the questioning room, where Katerina was already waiting for us.

Mary from the Ensign pub was with her, giving her some last touches of make-up. Her flare of ginger curls obscured Katerina's face, but I could see they were both wearing their Sunday best – demure grey dresses, plain shawls and discreet, yet clearly new hats.

Mary moved aside to greet us, and when I saw Katerina's face, I could hardly repress a squint.

Though her make-up was fit for a court, the woman looked yet another decade older. Thinner, paler, and the bags under her eyes hung like dry, empty folds of skin. There was still some fire in her green eyes, albeit much diminished. She was like the flame on a candle wick, slowly yet consistently fading away.

The necessary introductions were made, though Father, as is his custom, never offered a hand to shake. He nodded at Mary, though not looking at her. 'Get rid of the washerwoman.'

She gasped and raised a fist, but McGray held her by the shoulders and whispered something into her ear. Mary could only scoff and mumble between her teeth as she walked out.

Father installed himself at the table, staring at Katerina with as much scrutiny as she did him. She raised her chin proudly and he winced as he bit his cigar – which he'd keep between his teeth throughout the meeting. Their stance made me think of two ancient titans, measuring each other's strength before delving into an Olympian skirmish.

'Madam,' Father said at last, 'I have heard that you can be reticent to taking advice. I will only tell you this: Do as I say and you might, just *might*, walk out of this alive. Ignore me and you will be doomed for certain. Either way, at the end of the day I walk out happily to a large glass of brandy. Do we understand each other?'

Instead of looking at Father, Katerina turned to McGray. 'How much am I going to have to pay for this?'

'Och, just listen to the haughty sod!'

Katerina grumbled and looked back at Father, which to him was agreement enough.

'Very well, madam, this is how we shall proceed: As much as possible, I will steer the questioning away from the . . . erm, *particulars* of your profession.'

'The brewery?' Katerina said, her eyebrow so high I thought it would touch her hairline.

'Of course!' Father answered, spilling ashes over the files as he turned the pages. 'When you narrate the events of the thirteenth, stick to what you said at the Sheriff Court. Can you still remember that?'

'I'm not an idiot.'

'Add no embellishments or details. Do not volunteer information. Do *not* defend your "dark arts", or whatever the devil you call them. And that goes for you too,' he used the cigar to point at McGray. 'The last thing we need is your idiotic opinions in the air.'

'Och, *who the fuck d'ye*—?'

'*Do* save your foul breath,' Father interjected, his voice bouncing in the little room. 'Even if I gave a damn, I do not speak your Scotch patois.'

'*What*—?'

'Yelp like that again and I shall walk out and leave you to fix this petty mess on your bloody stupid own! Do we understand each other?'

Nine-Nails clenched his fists. He had to force three deep breaths before he managed a hiss.

'Aye.'

'Excuse me, *what*?'

McGray went red as a piece of iron in a kiln.

'Yes . . .'

Father gave him a fulminant eye, as if to leave clear who was in charge, before resuming.

'Now, about judges: they are peculiar creatures. They know your life is in their hands and they adore that, so we want to keep him happy. If he says you speak, you speak; if he says you dance, you ask to which tune. Like in every court session there will be the issue of time; the court is likely to hear half a dozen cases today – none as eagerly awaited as yours, of course. Be succinct and do not repeat yourself, else the judge will become impatient. Thankfully, your case will be the first one to be heard, so it is less likely he will send you to the gallows because he wants to rush for his luncheon.

'One more thing. I have managed one outwardly respectable person to vouch for you. The old woman you all call Lady Glass.'

'You what?' cried Katerina.

Nine-Nails was astounded. He stammered before managing any discernible words. 'How . . . how's that possible?'

'Father did some conveyancing for her in London,' I said.

'Oh,' said McGray with instant understanding.

Father went on. 'My – let us call it *agreement* with the lady includes divulging nothing about her businesses and her lunatic son in exchange for her help. I shall word my questions so that the issue does not come up, but be aware of that. Do you have any questions, madam?'

'Yes. What about the twat?'

'*What?*

'She means Pratt,' said McGray. 'The fiscal.'

'Oh, I see.' Father closed the file. 'Be prepared. From what Ian tells me, I gather he might have something up his sleeve. Now, madam . . .' He interlaced his fingers, lowered his chin and cast Katerina the same piercing stare I'd learned to fear as a child; that which in a flash could make me confess murder. 'Is there anything else we should know? If so, this is the time to speak.'

Katerina, however, remained silent, with the same uncomfortable grimace we'd seen before the session at the Sheriff Court.

'Whatever you might tell us, I will still defend you,' Father insisted, but Katerina tensed her lips further, as if attempting to seal them by sheer pressure. 'Very well. Now, I suggest we get on our way. You do not want to be late for your own trial.'

31

The cabs had to negotiate puddled roads, stubborn horses and pedestrians running recklessly across the streets to escape from the storm. I know Edinburgh has never been a sunny idyll, but that morning, with the entire panorama blurred and darkened, the city felt like an unwelcoming stranger; the buildings grittier, the air stale and the people threatening.

It took us nearly forty minutes to cover the one mile to Parliament House, and when I finally saw the blackened spire of St Giles' Cathedral, only just outlined in the blustery sky, I had to sigh in relief.

Unsurprisingly, we were recognised at once. There was no gathering crowd, but the passers-by still yelled curses as the drivers took us around the building. When they halted, by the back entrance, I had to take a deep breath before opening the door. As soon as I did so the lashes of rain came in, my umbrella and overcoat useless under the elements.

McGray covered Katerina with his own overcoat as we darted to the door. We were less than a yard away when a couple of mindless thugs ran to us and deliberately kicked the mud around us. Mary took the worst of it, her dress soaked all the way to her knees.

'*Blast*, this is why I hate the Scotch!' Father roared as we all made our sorry way through the corridors, leaving a trail of water and dirt on the marble floors.

Two very tall constables were waiting for Katerina, ready to handcuff her.

'We'll be there, hen,' McGray told her, affectionately squeezing her hand right after the constables had fastened it. 'First row.'

For an instant Katerina's eyes misted up. She blinked tears away, raised her chin and pulled back her shoulders.

'Thank you, Adolphus.'

And there we left her, walking briskly to the courtroom. We could hear the murmur of the crowd well before we got there, as though we were approaching a colossal beehive.

The stumpy officer opened the door for us and I had to force a deep breath.

The High Court of Justiciary was an imposing chamber, everything in it designed to intimidate: its vaulted ceiling, that carried echoes throughout the space, the gilded plastering, the sober wood panelling, and especially the judges' bench, raised high enough to leave no doubt as to their authority.

When we stepped in, the place became a bedlam. The ascending rows for the public were a solid mass of chattering humanity, and as soon as they saw us – rather, as soon as they recognised Nine-Nails – we were pelted with boos and unrelenting vulgarity.

The front row was the only one that did not attack us. It was occupied almost entirely by women in their finery, some entertaining themselves with needlework while the session began. To them this was akin to an evening at the theatre, only free and far more exciting.

Shoving his way through the seats, I saw Katerina's servant, Johnnie, again with a large tray of pork pies he was selling for a sixpence. I was not shocked by his presence but by people paying such a ludicrous amount.

An usher showed us the way to the seats reserved for the advocates and witnesses, right behind the dock. The young Dr Reed was already there, looking as tired as he always did these days. He greeted us with a silent nod.

I saw that all fifteen members of the jury were already seated on the side gallery, some staring at the crowd with stiff lips, others whispering into their neighbour's ear. They all struck me as grumpy, sallow and not particularly brilliant middle-aged men; one was even picking his nose without shame.

Father must have read my anxiety, for he came to me and said, 'They always look like that, Ian. I've seen worse.'

I sat there, feeling like a useless piece of scenery in the drama that was about to unfold, and waited.

A moment later I saw Pratt, preening towards his bench and bringing a hefty stack of documents under his arm. I had to blink twice before I fully recognised him, for his bright scalp was covered with a white bench wig. He nodded at us, though with a sardonic smile, and then waved at some point in the rows. McGray and I looked in that direction, and very quickly found Mrs Cobbold and Walter Fox amongst the crowd. Just like at the previous session, they sat together. Her sideways smile was a bad portent.

'The auld bitch did come,' McGray told me. I thought he was also looking at Mrs Cobbold, but then he pointed at the furthest corner on the last row of seats. Surrounded by two officers, her stiff butler and a broad-shouldered manservant sat Lady Anne. She still wore mourning clothes and a hat almost as wide as an umbrella. 'Och, the cow looks dreadful . . .'

I noticed her paleness, but I did not have time to examine her face carefully. Right then the name Judge Norvel was announced, and I felt a pang of anxiety as we all rose to our feet.

'So it begins,' McGray mumbled.

Judge Norvel carried himself with an enviable self-confidence, only possible in those who have exerted power for so long they no longer notice. He was a very lean man, with sharp chin and cheekbones, a pointy aquiline nose and bushy white eyebrows as angular as his jaw. Today he was clad in the heavy ceremonial robes reserved for the most serious criminal cases: a red gown with a white jabot around the neck, spread over a jacket faced with red ribbon crosses on the chest. The full-bottom wig, with its white curls, rolled down all the way to his chest (in McGray's later words, 'like the dusty corpse of a scruffy French poodle').

The hubbub had completely died out to a tense silence, as the man scrutinised his court with menacing beady eyes. The occasional ruffle of clothes and a single cough were the only sounds until Judge Norvel sat down and invited the audience to do the same. He picked up the agenda laid before him, his long, knotty fingers like the twigs of an elder tree.

'Today's first session is for the six Morningside deaths,' he said with a thick Edinburgh accent that particularly emphasised the R's, his voice a rich baritone that effortlessly traversed the courtroom. 'Summon the accused; Mr Alexander Holt, and Miss . . . Ana Katerina Dragnea.'

Two pairs of officers brought them in, Holt marching first, crouching like he'd done at the Sheriff Court. He too looked pale and poorly, but nothing like Katerina.

As soon as she walked in, all manner of insults and jeers rained down on her. Again she kept herself firm, her back straightened and dignified, as Judge Norvel bellowed furiously. His cry for order was deafening – even Father's head jerked a little – and by the time Katerina and Holt were standing in the dock, the chamber was again in complete silence.

'I know this case has received particular public attention,' he said, 'but I will not have this institution become a boisterous pen of baboons. Another outcry like this and this session will continue privately.' Norvel then read the indictment, the selection of the jury and the names of the barristers. 'Procurator Fiscal George Pratt—' a soft trickle of puerile laughter. 'And . . .' the judge's bristly eyebrows raised, 'William Otto Frey Esquire, acting as counsel for the prisoner.'

He tilted his head as he stared at my father, who in turn raised his chin, proud of still being recognised at courts.

'Proceed with the oaths,' said Norvel, and one of the clerks did so.

Holt's trembling voice was only just intelligible, whilst Katerina's sliced the air like a knife.

'How do you plead?' Norvel asked.

Again Holt stammered his 'not guilty', and Katerina took a deep breath and said the same with conviction. Though nobody spoke, the audience's disagreement could be felt like a monster swelling behind our backs.

Norvel cleared his throat, pleased by the unbroken order.

'Gentlemen of the jury,' he began, 'this case, as you all might know already, has been particularly distressing to our entire city, and even the nation. I suspect that much of what happened on the night of the thirteenth of September will remain shrouded in mystery forever; nevertheless, the most prominent facts shall be exposed here today, in hopes that the truth transpires and justice may be administered.

'Hear the statements *without* prejudice. And I cannot stress this enough: what the press has been so kind as to expose so far,' he cast an accusing glance at the bench of reporters and sketchers, 'must not, *must not*, influence your judgement. All that matters is what is heard at this session today.'

He paused for a moment, allowing the words to sink in.

'The events, as we understand them so far, are that, on the night in question, the six deceased,' he listed all the names and occupations, 'attended what is colloquially known as a séance, in the hopes of . . .' he cleared his throat, visibly uncomfortable by having to read such facts, 'in the hopes of contacting a deceased relative, Alice Shaw, nicknamed Grannie Alice. The session was hosted at the residence of the late Colonel Grenville, and was facilitated by Miss Dragnea, present. By the first defendant's wishes, all servants and other family members were told to vacate the dwelling for the night. Then . . .' he sighed, 'by means which remain as yet unknown, the six attendees perished during the night. Miss Dragnea was the only survivor and was found, surrounded by the six deceased, the following morning by Mr Holt. As Colonel Grenville's valet, Mr Holt was the last person – other than Miss Dragnea – to see the victims alive.

'Our head of forensics, Dr Wesley Aaron Reed, summoned here for cross-examination, has not been able to determine the cause of the deaths beyond doubt; however, the lead theory is that some sort of undetectable poison was embedded in a ritualistic knife, provided by Miss Dragnea and used by the six victims to – ahem – make blood offerings.'

The more he spoke the more anxious I felt. To a fresh listener, the facts would sound simple and incriminating enough.

Judge Norvel put the summaries aside. 'I shall now let the prosecution call their first witness.'

'My Lord,' Father prompted as he jumped to his feet, his voice as commanding as the judge's – he'd told me many times it is not the smartest man who wins at court, but he who speaks the loudest – 'before we proceed I would like to remind the honourable jury that the focus of this trial is *not* to elucidate what happened in that parlour, nor to give in to drama or speculation. Neither of the accused can be sentenced unless their culpability is demonstrated beyond any reasonable doubt by rational, cold, undeniable facts.'

Norvel did not look amused. 'Thank you, Mr Frey. We'd all be lost without the timely aid of the English.'

There were some loud guffaws, which Norvel was happy to oversee.

Pratt stood up then with a proud air and put a noticeable emphasis on his Scottish inflections; much more than in the pre-trial inquiry. 'My Lord, I would like to question Mr Holt first.'

When he heard his name, the man startled. He then went to the witness box with trembling legs, and Pratt asked him to retell his version of the facts. Despite his nervousness, Holt managed to give a brief account that matched all previous statements. Pratt listened as he studied some papers.

'I see here,' he said, 'that you were caught at the crime scene some time later. Retrieving a few items from the house. Is that correct?'

Holt began to sweat profusely; so much so, one of the officers had to offer him a handkerchief. 'Y-yes. But it was an inheritance!'

Pratt went on to recite in detail the items we'd seized.

'Is this relevant?' Norvel said.

'I beg for your patience, my Lord,' said Pratt. 'I must offer further light on the matter of that petty inheritance.'

Norvel twisted his mouth. 'Go on.'

Pratt picked up a bundle of sheets and went back to the witness box. 'Mr Holt, I have to ask you a rather personal question. How much did the colonel pay for your services?'

Holt almost choked, his face going red as he said the number. 'Fifty-five pounds a year, sir.'

There was a general gasp at the audience.

'Extremely generous for a valet,' said Pratt.

Holt again wiped some sweat. 'I . . . I served the good colonel for many years, sir. He valued loyalty.'

'And so I see. He also included you in his inheritance, which I happen to have here,' he raised the legal document for everyone to see and offered it to the judge for inspection. 'I also took the liberty of taking Colonel Grenville's will to a reputable merchant on St Julia's Close to give me an estimate of the value of said inheritance. Just under forty pounds.' And he offered the last sheet to the judge, who nodded after a quick scan.

'Even if we ignore the good relationship that existed between Mr Holt and his master,' said Pratt, '*even* if we look at this from the most cynical and utilitarian point of view, why would this man want to murder an employer who paid him a salary no master in this city would be willing to match?' He looked at me as he stepped in my direction. 'Inspector Frey, a gentleman like you must have a valet. How much do you pay him?'

I cleared my throat. 'Under . . . A smidgeon under thirty pounds.'

While people laughed, McGray whispered into my ear, '*Thirty!* I pay George eighteen . . .'

'Very well,' said Norvel, 'you have made your point.' He turned to Father with contempt. 'Would you care to question the accused?'

'*Oh, indeed I would!*' Father replied, smiling and rubbing his hands as he took the floor.

Holt gulped, and I even saw a fleeting spark of fear in Pratt's eyes.

'Mr Holt, you found the six victims. Dead. Am I correct?'

'Y-yes . . .'

'You knew the police would need to investigate.'

'Yes.'

'They asked you to give them the keys to the house.' Holt could not answer; he simply nodded, knowing where that was going. 'Now, when the police asked for your keys, I assume you understood they needed *all* the keys. I assume you, despite your clearly poor judgement, understood the seriousness of the situation: that the house must be locked, that nobody should trespass and interfere with the evidence.' There was no answer, so Father leaned closer. 'Did you understand that, yes or no?'

Holt nodded, his lower lip protruding in misery.

'And yet you lied. You kept a key and you made your way into the house. Whether you were entitled to the items or not is irrelevant.' He looked at the jury. '*Irrelevant.*'

It was then that McGray, for the first time in days, smiled.

Father went back to Holt. 'Now, there is one more thing. You initially told the inspectors you had taken nothing from the parlour. Is that correct?' Holt turned purple – actually purple. 'I need you to say yes or no.' There was still no reply, so Father appealed to us. 'Inspectors, is that correct?'

'Indeedy,' said McGray.

'*And yet,*' Father went on, 'you were in possession of a neck-lace . . .' As he spoke, he retrieved the file with the photo-graphs. 'A rather distinctive one; a raw gold nugget set on a chain.' He purposely sneered at Holt before turning to me. 'Is that correct?'

'Yes.'

'Now, the preposterous photograph that the alarmist press reproduced recently,' he cast Pratt a cruel look, 'and which was, of course, leaked through the fiscal here . . .'

Pratt jumped to his feet, but the way Norvel and Father stared at him made him desist.

'As I was saying, that photograph has clearly stolen the limelight, but there is a crucial one nobody cared about . . .' He pulled one from the file and raised it as he walked slowly in front of the jury. 'You can see here, clear as day, the said necklace lying on the table. Two of the victims appear there, at the very spot where they were found the day after. This is irrefutable. That necklace was on the table around which the six victims died, merely moments before the tragedy took place. This proves that Mr Holt broke into the house, then into the very crime scene, and helped himself to this!'

He paused, gave time for the jury to look at the picture, and then presented it to Judge Norvel. He then went back to Mr Holt.

'So you lied not once, but *twice*?'

The man was about to cry, and Father did not wait for his reply.

'This sorry man cannot be trusted. Everything, *everything*, that comes out of his mouth should be considered a lie.'

He made another pause for the sake of drama, and then concluded in a much softer tone, bowing to Norvel.

'That is all, my Lord.'

Pratt then summoned Mrs Holt, who wore a brand new hat trimmed with an extravagant tangle of ribbons, most likely purchased to honour the occasion. The woman gave the most affected account of her husband's character, how much he loved his baby daughter, and how much the colonel appreciated him. Her eyes were always on the reporters' bench, blatantly posing for them to sketch her.

Holt's landlord, Mr Saunders, gave a more temperate statement, as did the keeper of his local pub. They confirmed Holt's whereabouts on the night of the murders and in the preceding weeks. They'd noticed nothing odd in him at all and, like Mr Saunders had told us days before, Holt spent almost all his spare time at the public house. That was clearly not the behaviour of a man concocting a plot for murder.

Pratt offered to summon Mrs Cobbold, who, as the colonel's mother-in-law, had known of his appreciation for Holt, but Judge Norvel deemed it unnecessary. Instead he summoned Reed.

The young man, sunken on the low seat and with his rouged cheeks, had never looked more like a child.

Judge Norvel looked at the jury. 'I would like to remind you that Dr Reed, despite his youthful looks, is a most professional man. His investigations and statements have shed invaluable light on the recent murder at the Deaf and Dumb Institution, which you may also have seen in the papers. Listen to him with due respect.'

The praise only managed to make him redder, and I feared Pratt would stalk him like he would a wounded deer.

Thankfully, Father asked to speak first. 'Dr Reed, I have studied your reports most carefully. Outstanding work, if I may say.'

'Thank you, sir.' Reed eyed me when he said that, as if telling me 'this is how you address people'.

'I see you only did two chemical tests on the victims' remains. The Marsh and the . . .'

'The Marsh and the Reinsch tests, sir. The latter suggested there was a complex cocktail of metals in their bloodstreams.'

'Could you identify the substances in particular?'

'No, sir. That would have required many more tests.'

'Why were you unable to perform them? Was it merely time constraints? Were you at any point pressured to release the bodies?'

'The family did put pressure on us, especially since the colonel was to receive a military funeral, but the more important issue was the amount of sample required. Most of our tests are destructive in nature, and given the number of possible substances, we could have ended up with very little left to bury.'

'So we remain none the wiser.'

'Precisely.'

'Can you conclude that those metals were the cause of death?'

'Again, it is difficult to say. It *is* very striking that all the six blood samples yielded the same preliminary result, but without knowing the exact culprit chemical, I could not possibly tell.'

McGray allowed himself another little smile. Things seemed to be improving.

'Let us talk about the infamous knife,' said Father then. 'For reasons I cannot fathom, this object has received unmerited attention as a piece of evidence. Dr Reed, as you state in your report, you were *not* able to carry out any additional tests on that blade.'

'That is correct, sir.'

'Enlighten us, please.'

'The knife was embedded with the victims' blood. If I'd found any poison there it would be impossible to tell whether it came from the knife or was already present in their bodies.'

Father asked him to repeat that statement for the benefit of the jury.

'Let us for one moment concede,' he went on then, '*hypothetically* of course, that the knife was indeed poisoned. You have other reservations as to that theory, do you not?'

'Yes. For instance, the only poisons I know that can cause such sudden deaths are of biological nature. Things like the venom of snakes.'

'And, as your report states, those substances are difficult to detect in a human body.'

'Impossible, sir.'

'*Impossible!*' Father cried, feigning delighted surprise. 'Impossible . . .' he repeated, as if to himself. 'Pray, tell us why.'

'The more similar the substances are, the more difficult it is to separate them and tell them apart. Metals are easy to spot; we wash away the tissue with acid or caustic solutions and are left with a residue. We cannot yet do that with poisons of a biological origin; they are made of the same compounds as our own bodies. We cannot wash away human tissue with an acid or an alkali without also destroying any toxins secreted by a living form.'

'What you are saying is that it is *impossible* to confirm whether or not the knife was poisoned, regardless of the nature of the substance.'

'It would be extremely difficult with our available techniques, sir.'

'In which case you'd place this theory of the knife in the realms of speculation.'

'Indeed.'

Father sighed, visibly content. 'In your very professional opinion, what would you say might have killed those six unfortunate people?'

Reed shook his head. 'I examined the bodies and performed all those tests with my own hands, and I'm still as baffled as everyone else in this chamber.'

Father grinned. 'Thank you, Dr Reed. You have been most helpful.'

It is customary to ask whether the prosecution has anything to add, but Father simply went back to his seat, as if implying there was nothing further to say.

Pratt, undeterred, approached Reed. 'My Lord, if you allow, I would like to stress a few points.'

'Go on,' said Norvel, his eyes now clearly on the chamber's clock.

'Dr Reed, indulge me in my ignorance. You just said you were not able to perform any further tests on the knife?'

Reed looked rather puzzled. 'Yes. For the reasons I—'

'Oh yes, you made a very good case for what modern science can and cannot do, but the fact that no tests were made—'

'They could *not* be made.'

'Could not? I do not think that is the most accurate way to put it.'

Reed moistened his lips. 'What I mean to say is that if they *had* been made they would have rendered very uncertain results.'

'So you cannot categorically rule out that the knife was poisoned?'

'*Oh, what a stupid question!*' Father cried from his seat, startling everyone, and then spoke at full speed before anyone could silence him. 'He already made it clear he can neither confirm nor deny that! You cannot sentence anyone on that basis; that is why you Scots created the not proven verdict!'

Norvel banged a fist on his bench. '*Mr Frey*, another outburst like this and I will have you removed from this chamber!'

Father crossed his arms, though rather smiling.

Pratt cleared his throat, feigning a humble expression. 'I was simply pointing out the obvious. This excellent doctor's techniques cannot discard Miss Dragnea's involvement. However, the fact remains that the knife was hers! She instructed the victims to bleed themselves using that instrument and specifically told them they should use no other.'

'That hardly—'

'Dr Reed, if we found that Miss Dragnea had a clear motive to murder all – or, for that matter, *any* one of the deceased, would you not suspect such a knife to be the sole possible vehicle to administer a poison that would result in the deaths we've seen?'

There was a deep silence. I could almost feel the hundreds of craning necks behind me.

Reed bit his lip so hard I thought he'd make himself bleed, and his cheeks were turning a very strange shade of green. 'I . . . I am here in my capacity as a forensic man. That sort of speculation is beyond me.'

Pratt nodded, but with a disturbing air of victory.

'Thank you, doctor. That's all. Believe it or not, you have been very helpful to me.'

And he returned quietly to the bench, leaving the entire courtroom as silent as a grave.

'What did he mean by that?' McGray murmured.

'I have no idea,' I said, 'but I do not like it at all.'

32

Judge Norvel called for a brief recess. The session had already lasted much longer than usual and the jury were growing restless.

We initially retreated to one of the waiting rooms, but the air felt just as stifling as in the courtroom, so we went to the small central yard. It still rained hard, but at least the air was fresh. Clustered miserably under our umbrellas, we shared fire for our cigars.

'He definitely has another card to play,' said Father. 'He must know something we do not.'

'Could he nae be acting the doaty?' McGray asked, and I was shocked Father understood his common parlance.

'No. I would be deeply surprised if there is nothing behind it.'

Reed joined us then, trotting to reach our umbrellas. His face looked like parchment.

'Och, laddie, are ye all right?'

Reed swallowed painfully, a fist pressed against his mouth. 'I threw up.'

McGray whistled. 'Dear, oh dear! How d'ye feel now?'

'Very good, in fact.'

McGray patted him on the back, offering his cigar. 'Here, have a wee smoke. Ye did brilliant.'

At the first puff, Reed began coughing uncontrollably. Father and I took a small step back, fearing there was still some bile in the poor chap's stomach.

We were summoned a few minutes later, everyone already feeling the strain of the trial – even the gossipmongers at the front row, now drawing sandwiches from their wicker baskets.

The interest was renewed when Father summoned Lady Anne.

Every single neck craned in her direction, for she'd been spotted from the very start. Pulling a pained grimace, Lady Anne stood up, her jaw parallel to the ground, and with trembling hands she beseeched the help of an officer, her butler and her manservant.

I knew her far too well not to see this was all an act, but I had to admit she played it remarkably, descending at glacial speed, squinting at every step and stomping her cane to make sure people saw it.

'*Och, it's Lady Glass!*' someone shouted from the crowd, and the old woman simply clutched a hand at her chest, looking quite the martyr. She then pretended to stagger, all three men rushing to hold her, the entire courtroom gasping. The women at the front were shaking their heads.

Lady Anne finally took her seat at the witness box, grunting with every move, and as she took the oath, I could examine her more carefully. Her cheeks were sunken like never before, as were her eyes, the outlines of a sharp skull perfectly delineated. She still wore mourning clothes, which contrasted starkly with her pale, almost grey skin. The woman indeed had had a most difficult year; everyone knew about the scandalous death of her nephew last November, but only a handful of people knew the rest of her tragic family history.

'Mr Frey,' said Norvel, addressing my father but staring at the seemingly frail old woman, 'I fail to understand why you need this honourable lady to testify. You better convince us.'

'Thank you, my Lord. I shall. I simply mean to demonstrate that the accused, despite the unorthodox line of her *side* business – which is by no means her main source of income – and . . . well, the obvious fact of her being foreign, is still a decent person.'

There were several chuckles in the background, some even from the jury.

Not intimidated at all, Father picked up the thickest of his files. 'We have collected a considerable amount of statements from people who have turned to Miss Dragnea for advice. People from all walks of life, who have nothing but good words for the accused.' He offered the file to Norvel. 'The gentlemen of the jury are welcome to scrutinise these statements, but for the sake of brevity I will only bring forward two of them.'

Norvel leafed through while Father talked to Lady Glass.

'My lady,' he said after thanking her for her endurance and patience, 'I understand you are familiar with Miss Dragnea's services.'

Lady Anne coughed and replied with her deep, authoritative voice. 'Yes.'

'I shall not bother you for too long, my lady, but surely you understand the weight of your statement, given your rank and your . . . *unblemished* reputation.'

She could have skinned him alive, and this time she did not hide it, her veiny eyes burning with rage.

'Yes,' she snapped. 'I understand.'

Father allowed himself the briefest of smiles.

'I truly appreciate it, my lady. It is not necessary for us to go into the details of Miss Dragnea's *several* visits to your home.' Indeed it was not; the fact itself was shocking enough, as proven by the wave of gasps and murmuring that ensued. 'I am sure the gentlemen of the jury will be content to know your opinion of the lady's character.'

Lady Anne tensed her lips, the tendons on her neck popping out like the ribs of a corset. Her image of a fragile grandmother was evaporating fast.

'Madame Katerina is a good businesswoman,' she blurted out as if reciting a memorised verse. 'She has never attempted to trick me and I find it extremely hard to believe she would mean harm to anybody.' She and Katerina exchanged piercing stares. Lady Anne squinted a little, displaying utter malice for a split second. 'She is also . . . a good *mother*.' There was another general gasp as Lady Anne pretended to cough, if only to cover her mouth and conceal her sardonic smile. 'Very good mother, in fact; she has managed to secure education for her boy in England. *Even* without the help of a husband.'

And thus she injected her poison – pretending to deliver a compliment, yet with the sole intention of ventilating another shocking aspect of Katerina's life. The women at the front row looked aghast.

'*Incapable* of murder,' Father interjected, his harsh voice startling many. He mellowed his tone then. 'A very good mother, *incapable* of murder, would you say?'

Lady Anne smiled, as if to appear endearing, her eyes fixed on Katerina.

'As far as I can tell.'

Father nodded, appearing jovial, but I knew him better. He must be cursing the woman's ancestry.

'That will be all, my lady. Unless the procurator fiscal has any further questions.'

'Not at all,' said Pratt at once, dedicating Lady Glass a deep bow. 'I would abhor myself for exposing the honourable lady to more of this gruelling process.'

Lady Anne gave him an affectionate nod and began her sorry way back to her seat. As she walked past us, aided by the same three men, she cast McGray and me the vilest, most venomous stare. I could almost hear her hiss *you shall pay for this.*

'My last witness, before I summon the accused,' said Father, 'is Miss Mary Maclean, of the Ensign Ewart public house.'

Mary gave a lengthy, heartfelt account of everything Katerina had done for her. She was far more loquacious and articulate than I had expected, narrating the death of her father, the burglaries and her many hardships while trying to keep the pub open. By the time she was done, the entire row of ladies was a sea of tears.

Father went back to his bench looking quite proud of himself. Even Judge Norvel's frown had softened a little.

And then there came Pratt.

He walked to Mary with a friendly countenance, but instead of stopping by her, he came closer to us and pointed at McGray.

'Miss Maclean, do you know this man?'

Mary looked as puzzled as everyone else. 'Aye.'

'What is your relation to him?'

I had to do my best not to let out a painful growl. It was clear where he was heading.

'He's a regular at my pub,' said Mary.

Pratt laughed openly. The contrast between his treatment of Mary and Lady Anne could not have been greater.

'A regular! And does Mr McGray visit your premises *only* to consume food and drink?'

The freckles across her face went redder. 'What d'ye mean?'

Pratt passed a stack of signed statements to Norvel. 'Quite a few of your other *regulars* have declared that you and Inspector McGray have had an intermittent – what should I call it not to offend the more respectable ladies in this chamber?'

Norvel cleared his throat loudly, just as some giggles were heard. 'The fiscal shall make his point clear or move on.'

Pratt grinned. 'Of course, my Lord. Given Inspector McGray's well-known friendship with the accused, I think this detail is most relevant. You see, this is all a very nice chain of influence: Miss Maclean is a . . . *liaison* of Inspector McGray, who has been in charge of this case's investigations. He has been seconded throughout by Deputy Inspector Ian Frey here' – I nearly cried *I am not a deputy!* – 'who in turn happens to be the son of the honourable barrister Mr Frey, who has travelled all the way from London, interrupting his well-earned retirement, only to defend this woman, a very unlikely client for a man of his stature. And only God knows how this Mr Frey managed to coerce a statement from such a respectable character as Lady Anne.'

'Refrain from speculating,' Norvel interrupted, and I allowed myself a smile. He was clearly on nobody's side.

'Sorry, my Lord. That last sentence may well be speculation, but the greater truth remains: Miss Dragnea clearly has played her cards well. She knows perfectly where and how to place her influence. She—'

'I believe you have no further questions for Miss Maclean?' Norvel interrupted again.

'No, my Lord.'

'Well. We shall now conclude by hearing the statement from the accused herself.'

33

As advised, Katerina retold the events without sentiment and adding nothing to the common knowledge. However, she still kept the entire chamber hanging on her every word. Father did not ask anything regarding the spirit of Grannie Alice, and did not mention the photograph of the hand of Satan again. Katerina concluded by telling the court how she'd felt stifled and then had passed out. Just like she'd told us, the last thing she remembered was Colonel Grenville and Mr Willberg steadily gripping her hands, and the last burst of flash from the camera.

'I understand that Miss Leonora Shaw was a good client of yours,' said Father.

'Yes.'

'Did she pay well?'

'Yes, sir. Very well. Always promptly. And she tipped me all the time too.'

'So her death is in fact a great loss to your business?'

Katerina's face went sombre. 'Not only for the money. She was a fine young lady. People thought she was a little strange, but I liked her. She was a kind soul.'

I was not sure whether that was true or just some embellishment.

'And you had no relation with any other of the victims?' Father asked.

'None. I had only heard about the colonel, but I'd never seen him in the flesh. I knew nothing about the others. I met them all for the first time that night.'

'And you are absolutely sure of that?'

'Yes, I'm under oath,' she grumbled.

Father smiled. 'Of course you are, madam.' He turned to face the jury and judge. 'So there you have it. This woman had no connection with the deceased, no grudge and no business other than the occasional custom of Miss Leonora Willberg. Why murder six individuals about whom she knew next to nothing?' he went on with grandiloquence. 'Where is the motive? Where is the benefit? Where is the *logic*?' A few men from the jury nodded or whispered into each other's ears. Father looked at them with satisfaction. 'You can tell there is none.'

Katerina almost managed to smile at him, but then Father gave her a most condescending look.

'How could *this woman* possibly have known more about such honourable people? How could she have a grudge against a colonel? A war hero? She? A woman of such decidedly inferior origins? Uneducated, vulgar – foreign!'

Katerina was grinding her teeth, glaring at Father with so much wrath I feared she was jinxing him there and then.

'The lack of forensic evidence,' Father went on, none the wiser, 'has been well established. There is neither evidence to incriminate this lady, nor to prove what killed those most unfortunate people. *So . . .*' he then counted theatrically with his fingers, 'no motive, no means and no murder weapon.'

Norvel feigned a yawn, despite the jury's evident attention, and Father took the hint.

'In conclusion, this miserable wretch is but a victim of shameful prejudice against her outlandish looks, her preposterous line of business, her ghastly intonations and her inferior blood. I am in fact surprised that this judiciary has kept her imprisoned for this long without a shred of solid evidence.'

Katerina was not the only one offended by the statement.

'Are you done making a mockery of the Scottish law, Mr Frey?' asked Norvel.

Father faced the crowd most eloquently – he and my eldest brother always revelled in doing so – and delivered his conclusion with a powerful tone. 'I am done stating what is fair and just. Thank you, my Lord.'

And then he sat down.

'Will the prosecution wish to question the accused?' asked Norvel, with a clear note of impatience.

Pratt stood up somewhat sluggishly, but the look on his face was of pure joy. It seemed he'd been waiting for this moment all along, and was now dragging it out as much as he could.

'Indeed, my Lord, and I am glad that the counsel's questioning has brought up Miss Dragnea's connections with the victims.'

I felt a horrid discomfort creeping up my chest. I saw Father shifting in his seat.

Pratt picked up a thin file and raised it like a trophy. 'I have two pieces of new evidence, which Inspector McGray was too busy to find himself,' he cast us a derisive look. 'I must add that his entire investigation has been clearly biased in favour of this . . . woman, and my findings, which were not difficult at all to obtain, will demonstrate that.'

'What the bloody hell . . .?' McGray whispered.

Pratt heard him, and his smile widened as he addressed Katerina. 'Madam, selling watered-down ale is your main business, is it not?'

She went red with fury. 'I have never watered down my ales!'

'Oh, of course not. It must be the work of evil spirits.' He leisurely opened the file. 'And you also loan money, do you not?

At extortionate interest rates.' Katerina barely nodded before Pratt bombarded her again. '*And* you also charge interest on your clients' taps, I understand.'

'None of that's illegal,' she spluttered. 'Every pub keeper does it when monies are not paid for a while.'

'Not illegal, indeed.' Pratt laughed, and then paused for an unnervingly long time. 'Madam,' he said at last, reading from the file, 'does the name Mackenzie sound familiar at all?'

'Mackenzie?' McGray mumbled, his frown deeper than ever. 'Willberg's dog?'

Katerina had gone ghostly pale. Her voice came out as a mere whisper.

'Yes.'

Pratt grinned. 'Please, enlighten the jury.'

Katerina gulped, her well-restrained bosom starting to heave, her skin slowly turning paler. 'That's . . . one of my debtors.'

'Your greatest debtor, I have heard. I believe he owed you nearly eight hundred pounds, both from drink and from arrears on personal loans. Is that correct?'

'Y-yes . . .'

'Oh God,' I whispered, beginning to see where this was going.

'And have you met this man?' asked Pratt.

'No. He sent servants to collect the barrels . . . They paid well at first but . . . then the servants vanished. I never saw the master himself.'

Pratt had never resembled a vulture as much as he did then.

'Of course you have not!' he exclaimed. 'Because he does not exist.'

There was a general outcry, which Norvel had to appease, and Pratt enjoyed every instant before resuming.

'Several of your regular clients – of your ale business, that is – heard that you repeatedly sent out threats to this debtor.'

Katerina attempted to speak but Pratt again raised his voice, pulling three sheets from the file and brandishing them for all to see.

'I happen to have the most recent ones here! Sent to a residence on Inverleith Row, by the Botanical Gardens. Do you know who really lives there?'

'God . . .' McGray and I whispered in unison.

'I see the inspectors *do* know,' Pratt said. 'That is the address of the late Leonora Willberg, who shared her residence with her uncle, and the *real* debtor, Peter Willberg.'

Katerina jumped to her feet and roared, '*I didn't know that was a fake name!*'

Some people giggled, others gasped. Father covered his face and McGray clenched his fists.

'A woman like you?' asked Pratt. 'Whose job entails *knowing* things? I find that hard to believe.'

'I am under oath. I've told you—!'

'It would have been very simple,' Pratt interjected, 'to send one of your brutes, like the one who's been selling pies here today, to enquire who lived in that address. You would have soon pieced the clues together. Mr Willberg's was indeed a poor deception.' He went on spluttering as he approached Katerina, the poor woman sinking in her seat as if the words were bullets. 'This she-wolf had a clear motive. She found out the identity of the defaulter, she saw there was no hope of getting her money back, so she planned a swift revenge.'

'*I didn't know—!*'

'*She had but to seize a knife*, rub it in something she knew for sure a forensic man could not detect – she'd know well where to source such things, of course – and pass the poisoned blade on to her victim to do the job himself.

'Her sickening disregard for the rest of the attendants' lives simply speaks of her abominable nature. She is a most *dangerous* woman; the spawn of dubious nomads who only disembarked in our country to pollute Her Majesty's lands.' He glared at Katerina, whose wrathful tears now rolled copiously down her cheeks, and then he hissed, 'I have nothing further to say.'

There was a moment of befuddled silence, everyone struggling to take in all that. Then, rising gradually, there came an outburst of thunderous applause.

For once, Norvel could not silence the crowd.

34

We retreated to the waiting room while the jury deliberated. The entire building seemed to have gone colder and darker, my father's cigar shining like a glow-worm as we waited for Katerina.

The constables brought her, and as soon as she stepped in she thrust herself into McGray's arms. She clasped his lapels, letting out tearing cries.

'I didn't know, Adolphus! *I swear!* I swear on my life!' Now, in utter distress, her accent sounded Scottish enough to believe she indeed hailed from Dumfries.

McGray embraced her like he would have an old aunt. She buried her face in his chest and wept uncontrollably.

'Yes,' she said after a while, her voice muffled, 'from time to time I've had to bully my debtors. But everybody does! I might send a thug or two to collect my monies, or a wee letter telling them I'd have to break their legs if they didn't pay – but I've never carried out the threats! *Never!* They almost always pay at the first warning!'

'There, there,' said Nine-Nails. 'Ye couldnae have suspected this.'

Father puffed at his cigar, staring sombrely at the distraught gypsy. He cast me a quick glance and shook his head. There was nothing further to say.

I offered Katerina my handkerchief, but she barely had time to mop her tears. McNair came in right then.

'The jury's ready.'

'So soon!' McGray cried.

'I am surprised they even bothered moving to the jury's room,' said Father, extinguishing his cigar with utter displeasure. 'I am surprised *I* bothered lighting this again.'

We marched back to the courtroom in silence. Hardly anyone else had left the room, surely predicting the swift outcome.

The jury were filing back in and taking their seats, their faces ominous. I recognised the foreman, a full-bellied man who walked in last, holding a piece of paper with a very short statement. As soon as the courtroom settled down, he addressed Norvel with a shaking voice.

'My Lord, we have arrived at a verdict for both of the accused.'

Norvel had sat down as confidently as before, his arms resting comfortably on the sides of his chair as if it were a throne.

'Proceed,' he said.

My eyes went to the dock. Red-eyed as she was, her make-up smeared across her face, Katerina still looked far more dignified than Holt, whose legs trembled like jellied eels.

The foreman raised the document, his hands stiff on the paper, and he read.

'We find Mr Alexander Holt . . . *not guilty* of any of the six Morningside deaths.'

Mrs Holt jumped to her feet and thanked God with raucous cries, only to be pushed back to her seat by a nearby officer. Holt himself seemed to be deflating like a punctured bagpipe, letting out the longest sigh of relief I'd ever seen. I even thought he'd pass out, but then the foreman spoke again.

'*We do*, however, find him guilty of breaking into premises clearly demarcated by the police, deviating the course of the inspectors' investigations with his mere presence. We recommend a fine, as well as imprisonment.'

At this Mrs Holt shouted all manner of protests. Norvel, with just a nod of his pointy chin, commanded an officer to take her away. The poor constable had to lift the woman by the waist and carry her out of the courtroom as she thrust and kicked about, her two petticoats flapping in the air for all to see. Holt, on the other hand, looked pleased enough with the verdict – if anything, he seemed more concerned by his wife's behaviour.

When the hustle and bustle died out, the foreman cleared his throat. He was holding the statement so tightly he was about to tear it in two.

'With regards to the second accused . . .' the courtroom went deathly quiet at this, 'in light of the evidence here presented, Miss Ana Katerina Dragnea –' the man drew in a short breath, barely a second, but that tiny pause felt like an eternity to us all, 'has been found guilty of all the murders.'

The echo of the man's voice faded, and the icy silence lingered for a moment. It was like that pause between lightning and thunder, and then the court exploded in cheering, mocking and a shower of the most debased insults. Norvel, to my astonishment, did nothing to contain the people's wrath. He lounged back, interlacing his bony fingers, as if feeding from the clamour.

I could only wince at what I heard, appalled by the harsh, unforgiving verdict.

What was this dark, hideous monster that lurked inside humanity – this thirst for blood and shame that only rose from the mob but never from the individual – cruel, merciless, almost animalistic?

McGray, next to me, was so livid he could not even move, every single tendon on his neck and jaw protruding. I wanted to pat his shoulder, but I feared the slightest touch might make him burst like gunpowder.

At last Norvel howled for quiet, his booming voice even more effective than earlier. The silence, however, was not the still, icy shush of a moment ago, but an agitated one, people fidgeting and murmuring in expectation.

'I thank the jury for their swift decision,' said Norvel. 'Is this a unanimous verdict?'

'It is, sir.'

'Very well, I shall reciprocate with an equally swift sentence.'

Everyone stood up automatically to hear him. I felt my blood rushing up my temples, almost buoying at my ears.

'Miss Dragnea, your crime has shocked an entire nation. You have ravaged families, orphaned three young children of the most reputable background, and murdered one of the most illustrious military men that Scotland has begot in recent history.

'It remains for me to pass the rightful punishment.' He leaned forwards, placing a hand on the edge of the bench, like the talon of a bird of prey. 'Miss Ana Katerina Dragnea is hereby pronounced for doom; to be taken back to Calton Hill Jail, where, at a time appointed as per procedure, she shall be hanged by the neck, by the hands of the common executioner, upon a gibbet, until she be dead.

'God have mercy on your soul.'

Katerina stood almost perfectly still as she heard it all. From where I stood I could only see a fraction of her face, but that was enough to assess her desolation. Her shoulders had slouched a little further, the corners of her mouth had pulled down into a dejected grimace, and she stared ahead without blinking, devoid of any hope.

And yet, there was no shock in her gestures. She was facing her destiny with gloomy, stoic resignation.

As if she had always known.

PART 3

The Punishments

35

FATE OF CLAIRVOYANT SEALED

That was the front-page story in all the newspapers the following morning, and in some of the afternoon editions on the same day. I refused to read them, and only saw the massive headline when Father extended *The Scotsman* over his breakfast, shaking his head and still grumbling things he might have said.

The date of the execution was named shortly after, and as soon as we were informed, McGray and I decided to pay Katerina a visit and tell her in person.

She'd be the first female to be executed in years, so she was allowed certain perks. She had been transferred to a wider cell, with a barred window overlooking the jagged slopes of Arthur's Seat, still lush with purple heathers. Farther away was the imposing outline of Castle Rock, the foot of the hill surrounded by morning haze, as if floating above a sea of clouds. Even the most expensive hotels on London's Park Lane did not have such privileged views.

Katerina was also allowed to receive visitors there, and when we arrived, Mary was helping her braid her hair. The young woman was smiling as she worked white ribbons into the plaits, but her lips quivered and her eyes were glazy, as if just about to burst in tears.

The air was so peaceful I almost envied Katerina, sat on the edge of the bed, evaluating Mary's work with a hand mirror. When she saw us enter, she even smiled.

'She's very good, isn't she? I wish she'd told me sooner!'

Mary could not contain herself anymore. She hunkered, covered her mouth and sank onto the bed, sobbing miserably.

Katerina surrounded her with an arm. 'There, there, my lass. We talked about this.'

It was astonishing to see the sentenced woman so tenderly consoling the visitor.

McGray cleared his throat. 'We . . . we have some news.'

Katerina nodded, and then whispered into Mary's ear, 'Would you bring me some tea, dear? That would help me.'

Mary wiped her tears, her freckles redder than usual, and sniffed loudly as she stood up. 'Aye, of course. I'll finish yer hair when I come back.'

'Ask Malcolm, the guard with the long scar. He's a good lad.'

Mary attempted a smile as she walked past us. McGray patted her on the shoulder with affection. He did not look much better himself, so I took the bullet for him.

'The . . . the date has been set.'

She was trying hard, but Katerina could not fully repress a gasp. She raised her chin, fixing her gaze on me.

'Tell me.'

I gulped. One never gets used to delivering that sort of news.

'The law requires to wait three Sundays after sentencing, so . . .'

I could not go on, her green eyes staring intently into mine. She then looked down, began counting with her fingers, and only then did I manage to say: 'Twenty-first of October, at eight o'clock in the morning.'

There was a moment of silence, Katerina still counting. I was going to repeat the date, thinking she'd not heard, but then she looked up. To our astonishment, there was a content look on her face.

'I will go on a waning moon,' she said, now looking wistfully out the window. 'The perfect time to detach from this world and meet rest.'

Katerina said nothing for a while, as if she'd forgotten we were present. When she looked at us, it was with a quiet smile, the kind of gesture mothers reserve for their young children when they set off to build forts with broomsticks and tablecloths.

'I don't want you two to feel guilty,' she said. 'I've seen what awaits.'

McGray took a short step back.

'Ye must be wrong,' he spluttered, as stubborn as ever. 'Ye said yer eye was all out of joint.'

Katerina took a deep breath. 'The first time I saw it was when you were bringing me back from the Sheriff's. Remember?'

I did. Her face had been frozen still, her green eyes fixed on the outlines of Calton Hill as the carriage drove us across the bridge. *I have seen my death*, she'd whispered.

'I just didn't like what I saw,' Katerina went on. Like she'd done upon her vision, she ran a finger on the skin of her neck, following the line of an imaginary noose. 'I've had time to take it in. It's all right. It's all part of the greater—'

'Oi, shut it right there! I won't sit around and let ye go to the gallows. Even if ye *had* done it!' McGray sat next to her, that persistent spark burning in his eyes again.

Katerina nodded and reached for his hand. 'I know you won't. You'll be with me 'til the very end. I've seen it.'

McGray gulped. His eyes were starting to pool tears, which he hastily blinked away.

'It's all right, my boy,' Katerina assured, squeezing his hand. 'I'm at peace. I'm settling my businesses. Johnnie will sell the divination room and there should be plenty to keep my son in school until he's of age.' She winked at me, half smiling. 'I'm good with numbers. I've always been. I've been muddling clients with them for twenty years!'

I nodded, unconsciously smiling back at her. I secretly wished that, when my time came, I could accept it with half her equanimity.

McGray was everything but resigned. He wanted to submit an immediate appeal, but Father advised him otherwise; an appeal unsupported by new evidence was most likely to be dismissed. Father recommended we investigated further for another fortnight, and only appeal if all else had failed by then.

I did not hear much from Nine-Nails for the next few days. He took all the files home and worked from there. Joan, who called frequently to bring me roasts and pastries, told me that McGray spent every waking hour locked in his library, reading, drinking and mumbling to himself, with only the dogs to keep him company.

I would have visited, but I would not have been pleasant company for anyone. My mood was just as grim, and without the pressure of the trial, I was soon drifting back to the nightmares, the gloomy memories and the unexpected surges of anxiety.

Father, who'd been as irascible as a bear with a splinter, did not help my spirits. He had not lost a case in almost thirty years (the last a lawsuit against a merchant from 'Aber-bloody-deen'), and he moaned on and on about the nasty gossip that would circulate in London – the ageing Mr Frey, decaying barrister, utterly humiliated – *by the Scots! Again!*

Fortunately, his hatred for Scotland was far greater than his fear of ill-intentioned upper-class natter, and he packed his trunks soon enough.

On the morning he left I retreated to my study and attempted to read, but it turned out impossible. Father kept shouting orders at the loaders as they took his luggage out, and poor Layton ran up and down to meet his last-minute demands.

Just as the racket subsided a little, the old Mr Frey came by, flustered and wrapped in his thickest, hairiest overcoat. As he sat in front of me, I heard Layton approaching.

'Do you expect me to jump on a train without having had a drink?' Father snapped. 'Bring me a brandy. *Now!* And a flask for the trip.'

Layton was back within the minute, bringing a tray with a decanter, two tumblers and a small silver hip flask. Father grabbed the latter.

'Oh, you blithering idiot. It is a sodding eight-hour trip! Do you think this will do?'

'Sir, I – I am afraid we do not have a larger—'

'Then how come you are not rushing to the shop as we speak? I leave in fifteen minutes, you thoughtless fool!'

He still shoved the hip flask into his breast pocket, watching how Layton dashed away.

'Ahh, I do like to see them run. It is almost as amusing as torturing Catherine.' He winked at me as he said that, and then poured two drinks – both unusually kind gestures.

He lounged back, savouring his drink, and I pretended to read on. I could tell he was about to give a monologue which I did not have the energy to face. After a while I looked at him, and found him staring at the window. Outside it was drizzling, the sky dull and grey.

'I am sorry, Ian,' he said. 'I failed you.'

I closed my book and let out an impatient sigh. 'You did what you could. The case was a lost cause.'

Father shook his head. 'Lost causes used to be my speciality . . . Maybe that is why I was so keen to help you. I mean, I truly wanted to escape London and the wedding psychosis, but I also wanted to help you.'

I chuckled. 'I am your new lost cause.'

'Well, of course you are! It is like you made everything in your power to become one. All these hopeless trifles, all these assignments of yours . . . They will never bring you fortune, and only very, very rarely will they bring you glory. In fact, they will only make you more and more miserable if things continue like this. Unless, of course, you meet an untimely end like that poor frog Maurice.'

'Father, do you have a point?'

'Laurence and I only joined the bar for the money and the prestige. Elgie is also after the applause; he would have abandoned his music already if that Stoker fellow had not hired him at the Lyceum. Oliver – *pff*! He just sits around and eats. But you, Ian . . .' He had to take a long swig of alcohol to go on. 'You have this . . . reckless drive. Your inspector job means everything to you. It always has. You have always given it your very best; you always dive straight into these silly inconsequential cases, even if it breaks your back or gives you very little in return – which is not something I can say about any of your brothers. Or myself. I do wonder what it might be like to feel such hunger in life. Sometimes . . .' He needed another swig. 'Sometimes I envy you.'

He could not look me in the eye when he said that, and I must admit I felt just as uncomfortable, so I decided to go for the liquor too. As I leaned over the tray, I saw myself reflected on the polished silver – bleary-eyed, pale, my septum still slightly bent where it had once snapped, and when I picked up my drink I saw the scars where my hand had been burned . . . twice.

I smiled bitterly. 'You are only looking at the glamour of it.'

Father began to chuckle, and it soon morphed into an

unrestrained cackle, too infectious to resist. I had to smirk as we clinked our glasses and drank to my dishonour.

'I am really sorry about your Uncle Maurice,' Father said then. 'He was an irresponsible wreck, but I know how much he meant to you.'

I sighed, and for some strange reason, the words rolled uncontrollably out of my mouth: 'I still dream about that night.'

Father said nothing, and I fixed my eyes on the golden brandy. When I looked up, Father was again staring out the window, though looking at nothing.

'I still dream about your mother,' he whispered. 'She opened my Great Parade.'

'Your what?'

Father smiled. 'Did you never hear your grandfather say that? When his old friends started to die, he called it The Great Parade. He said you never want to be first – or last.'

I chuckled, recalling my late grandfather's humour. As dry as bones.

Father sighed. 'Oh yes, Cecilia died far too soon. I thought we still had so much ahead. We—' he shook his head. 'I married again, but if I could still be with her . . .' He finished his drink and stood up swiftly. 'Don't tell Catherine. If she ever has to hear it, I want it to be from me!'

We both laughed earnestly and clinked our glasses, perhaps for only the third time in our lives.

Only a moment later we heard Layton coming back from the shop and saw him come in covered in perspiration.

'What took you so bloody long?' Father shouted, snatching the new flask as he made his way to the door.

Before he crossed the threshold, he hesitated, a hand on his waistcoat pocket, patting his rounded belly. I could tell he was about to say something, but in the end he simply winked at me and rushed downstairs, where I heard him shout more orders.

I looked through the window and saw him get into the loaded carriage, still reprimanding poor Layton. He waved his cane at me as the driver spurred the horses, and a moment later Father disappeared around the corner.

That was the last time I saw him alive.

36

We were well past the end of summer, with nothing but increasing desolation ahead of us. The days grew darker and shorter, the leaves began to wither and the air became damp and colder. And on those evenings I would sit there in my parlour, alone with my nightmares and my fears and my sad memories.

I heard nothing from McGray and entertained myself sorting out petty paperwork at the office, until that dreadful Monday afternoon when Mrs Holt burst into my office.

'There you are!' she cried, carrying her sobbing child in her arms.

McNair came running behind her.

'Sorry, sir! I couldnae stop her!'

'I need to talk to you,' she pleaded as McNair tried to pull her away. 'My husband needs you!'

McNair was going to lift her up like they'd done at court, but she kicked about again, and the little girl cried hysterically, balancing precariously in her mother's arms.

'*Oh, stop it you both!*' I roared, standing up and banging my fists on the desk. 'McNair, take that child away while I dispatch this . . . lady.'

McNair did obey, though carrying the girl at arm's length.

'Now, madam,' I said as soon as the drilling cries could not be heard anymore, 'I do not care what your husband has to say. He should have spoken before the trial.'

'He says he can help your gypsy.'

'She is not my—' I rubbed my face. 'How could he possibly help her?'

Mrs Holt came closer. 'He says he can tell you something about the colonel. Something nobody else knows.'

'What is that?'

'He wouldnae tell me. He wants to talk to you. I know my husband; I can tell it's very important.' I took a deep breath, far too tempted to tell her to go to Halifax. 'He won't play games with you. I swear it on my child's life.'

I could feel the despair in her voice, tears welling in her eyes.

She came closer still, seeing my reticence. 'He said something about the colonel . . . having a fight on the day he died.'

The man's grazed knuckles instantly came to mind. Those wounds that had looked so fresh in the morgue.

'And what did he—?'

'That's all he said,' she prompted. 'Please, sir, please! It will only take you an hour. That's all I ask of you.'

I grumbled, thinking she was right. Unlike Katerina, time was something I had in ample supply. Saying nothing, I reached for my coat and hat, Mrs Holt prattling how thankful she was.

'Look after the girl,' I told an overwhelmed McNair as we stepped out. 'We shan't be long.'

'*But I'm nae wet nurse!*' I heard him scream, fighting to get the child's hands off his ginger hair.

I was tempted to check if McGray was at home, but I imagined he'd be in a sorry state, so I decided to conduct this questioning on my own terms.

We reached Calton Hill soon enough, which I found gloomier and colder than ever before. That place must be hideous in the middle of winter.

The guards took me to a questioning room, and before walking in I asked them to take Mrs Holt away. The woman protested with her usual vulgarity, and I was only too glad when the door was shut and her voice could be heard no more. A few minutes later they brought Holt, manacled and wearing the inmates' uniform.

The man looked ghastly. He'd been transferred to jail some ten days ago, but with saggy bags under his eyes and a patchy stubble, it seemed he'd been ravaged by famine and disease for months. He was vigorously scratching his head, most likely infested with colonies of nits or fleas. I instinctively pushed my chair back.

'I suppose incarceration is not as comfortable as you expected.'

'Don't mock me, sir,' he whimpered. 'I've never been so miserable in my life. They gave me three years. *Three years!* For breaking into a house where I stole nothing from!'

I did feel a pang of compassion for him, but feigned some indifference.

'What is it you need to tell me? I am fiendishly busy at the City Chambers.' He did not need to know I was as idle as an upper-class spinster. 'I know Colonel Grenville had a fight. Your wife said—'

'Oh, but there's something else, sir!' he nearly squealed, and then lowered his voice. 'She's not around, is she? My wifey.'

'No. In fact I asked the guards to keep her as far away as possible.'

Holt rubbed his dry, prickly chin. 'You . . . you must swear she won't hear any of this.'

I sighed impatiently. 'Yes, yes. Confidentiality. Gentleman to gentleman. Go on.'

'Sir, I *must* hear you swear—' I made to stand up and Holt cried at once, 'I was having a hanky-panky!'

The words bounced in the little room, and as I sat down, Holt covered his mouth.

'I see,' I said. 'With whom?'

Holt covered his mouth; his voice came out muffled. 'Miss Leonora.'

I winced. 'She? With *you?*' I looked sideways and shrugged. 'Then again, she *was* pretty strange . . .' Holt was on the verge of tears. Shame, guilt, heartbreak, all converged in his distorted face. I softened my tone. 'For how long?'

'A few months. Six, or a wee more. The colonel sent me to do chores for her. We talked . . . one thing led to . . .' he saw my reproving stare and snorted. 'You're a man, you must understand me. With my girl being born I couldn't— you know . . .'

I sighed and nearly uttered 'how disgusting'.

'But Miss Leonora was so special,' Holt said. 'Everyone misunderstood her. Her relatives mocked her; her uncle was a drunken idiot always getting her and himself in trouble; ladies her age didn't want anything to do with her . . . The poor creature felt so lonely. One day she just burst into tears in my arms.' He began whimpering like a child, mopping tears with his mucky sleeves. 'That day – the day she died, that is – I picked her up early. You might remember I told you so. We pretended she needed something for the camera. The truth is we went elsewhere. We— Oh, she loved Arthur's Seat . . .'

'That is fine,' I said. 'I do not need to know the details.'

He began whimpering, so I gave him a moment. I felt little compassion for a chap who frolics around just after his wife gave him a child, but I needed him to talk, so I played the compassionate man. I told the gaolers to bring us two cups of tea – a ghastly brew that tasted of cinders – and when we

Hyb Cymunedol Grangetown / Grangetown Community Hub

Customer name:
RUPALIA, Rupesh (Mr)
Customer ID: ****4609

Items that you have checked out

Title: The darker arts
ID: 05146813
Due: 08 September 2023 23:59

Total items: 1
Account balance: £0.00
17 April 2015
Checked out: 6
Overdue: 0
Hold requests: 5
Ready for collection: 0

Telephone : 02920 780 966

were alone again, I asked, 'Is that why you took her necklace? The gold nugget?'

Holt nodded, sipping his tea as if it were the most delicious nectar and warming his hands with the cup. 'I never wanted to sell it. It was going to be a memento; something to think about—'

'So you went into the parlour to retrieve it,' I blurted out. 'And then lied to us.'

'I'm telling the truth now! And you saw the photograph, so you know it's true!'

I massaged my brow. 'Go on. I shall decide if I believe you or not.'

'Leonora . . .' Holt had to put the cup down, but he would not let go of it. 'Leonora told me things about her family. Things about the colonel. She made me swear I wouldn't tell, and even if I wanted –' he gulped '– I couldn't mention a word to my wife, of course . . . And if the colonel ever found out I was aware of his dirty secrets, he—'

'What did she tell you?' I prompted.

Holt took a deep breath. 'Leonora told me her poor dad died of some disease he caught in Africa . . . wherever that is.'

'What was he doing there?' I asked, my mind going through the collected pieces. 'Gold mining, I assume? Were they part of the African gold rush?'

'Yes, sir. Leonora's father and uncle worked there for some time, but I believe the actual mine belonged to the Shaws.'

'The richer side of the family,' I mumbled. 'Sending their poor relations out there to do the dirty work . . .'

'Leonora said almost the exact same words.'

'Do you know what killed her father?'

'I don't know, sir. She wouldn't tell me. It might have been some – you know – man's problem. He barely made his way back. His brother-in-law died in the mine, and I think this other lad, one of the Shaws, died on the trip too.'

'Wait, wait,' I said, pulling out my little notebook. I looked again at my tiny copy of the family tree. 'So, Alice's son-in-law, married to her eldest daughter, Prudence, died in the mine.'

'Yes.'

'And her second eldest, William, according to my notes, managed to travel all the way back, if only to die with his daughter, Miss Leonora.'

'Yes.'

'And who was the man you said died on the trip?'

'The old woman's youngest son.'

I looked at the far left of the tree. 'That would have been Richard Shaw, Bertrand's father.'

'Right, sir.'

I wrote all that down as speedily as my hand allowed. 'And you say you don't know which disease killed Miss Leonora's father.'

'No, sir. She didn't like to talk about it. Whatever it was, the poor wretch died in her arms. That gold nugget was the last thing he ever gave her. That's why she always wore it.'

I grunted, still scribbling. 'How come nobody talked of this during the investigations? They never even—'

I looked up then, recalling our encounter with the children at Kirkcaldy, and young Eddie's words.

'A treasure!' I let out in a whisper.

'Sorry, sir?'

'Never mind.'

Holt began fidgeting with the teacup. 'Sir . . . Leonora told me that the family didn't get the mine through very honest ways, if you take my meaning.'

I frowned. 'Did she tell you the particulars?'

'No, sir. She only said it had been a disgraceful thing. That no one had been out of guilt. It got her very upset, so I didn't press for more.'

I stared at the family tree, running my fingertips along it, and then mumbled, 'Everyone involved in some sort of fraud . . . Even Mrs Cobbold and the colonel and all the Shaws . . . Yes, that would have kept them quiet.' I began drumming my fingers on the table, a thousand possibilities all swarming through my head. 'What else do you know? You *did* mention that Colonel Grenville had a fight that day. Did it have anything to do with this?'

'Maybe, sir. I wasn't with him when it happened, fetching the guests and all, but I know he was supposed to meet this lad in the afternoon.'

'Who?' I urged, and Holt for the first time showed a hint of a smile.

'Will you speak in my behalf? Will you see they take me out of this shithole?'

I grunted, my patience wearing thin. 'I can only do my very best. And I cannot guarantee you will be released immediately, or at all.'

Holt sneered. 'Well, with such thin promises I don't think I'll—'

'*Dammit! I'm so sick of being polite!* I cannot guarantee you'll be released, but if you do not talk right now, I swear on my mother's grave, Nine-Nails and I will make sure that every single blasted second you spend here will be a bleeding fucking hell!'

Holt seemed to have sunk several inches down his chair. His little eyes were burning with indignation, but he knew his only hope was to talk.

'He went to meet that orange idiot. Walter Fox.'

37

I made my way back to the City Chambers so quickly I even forgot to bring Mrs Holt with me. I only remembered her when I saw McNair, still carrying the woman's child. The naughty girl was about to make him cry.

'Oh, sorry, McNair,' I said as I rushed past him. 'The mother is still in jail.'

'*What!* But sir—!'

I did not hear his protests – and I can only assume he did reunite mother and child at some point – for I dashed straight to our darkened basement. I ignited the gaslight and brought it to the little box with Miss Leonora's possessions. I knelt down and began rummaging through the items. I tossed aside the bunch of candles, still wrapped in a very old receipt, and pulled out the photographs, the letters and the journal.

I picked up the photograph of her father, still in its gilded frame. I saw the man, his resemblance to his now dead daughter, and the African women around him. I studied the background much more carefully this time. There was a thick baobab tree behind them, with picks and spades leaning onto the massive trunk. I now recognised they were all encrusted with dirt. The entrance to the mine might well have been behind the photographer's back, and they might have been staring at it as they posed.

The lamp shook a little in my hand, and something in the depths of the box caught a glint of light. The gold nugget; not a talisman after all.

When I picked it up it somehow felt heavier than before, and I could swear I felt pinpricks on my fingertips. For a reckless instant, I almost believed in Katerina's gifts.

Without thinking of it I put the pendant in my breast pocket, and then went back to Leonora's journal. McGray had folded the corner of a page, and underlined the phrases '*To ban spirits from their former homes . . .*' and '*Forcing truths out of them . . .*'

I felt a shiver that made me stand up, and went to the wall lined with photographs, notes and evidence. I stood there for a long while, passing the light over the sea of names and documents. I scribbled 'treasure' next to the children's names, and then followed the curved lines of the family tree.

According to Holt, Grannie Alice would have lost two of her five children to the enterprise. Could William Willberg, Leonora's father, have brought back not only a gold nugget, but piles of the stuff, and given them to his mother to hide? It made sense.

'They wanted to find it,' I speculated out loud. 'And Grannie Alice was the only one who knew, so they . . .' And then it hit me. 'Maybe someone wanted it all for themselves!'

I went through the names of all the surviving relatives, my hands running on the twisted bloodlines.

Mrs Cobbold had lost her father, daughter and son-in-law. I could not picture her scheming such a terrible crime.

Eliza and Harvey Shaw lost Bertrand, their only support. They claimed they had not been aware of the séance, and that rang true; if they'd been up to something they would not have allowed Bertrand to attend.

That left me with only one candidate. A little separate from everyone else, almost lost in a corner, was the name of Walter Fox.

I took a deep breath and read the nearby notes. Eliza Shaw had told us a good deal about him. Walter had moved to Africa soon after his father's death. And his mother had died too around that time, after miscarrying Walter's unborn sibling.

'And he lost no close connection at the séance,' I mumbled. Mr Willberg and Leonora were his uncle and cousin, yes, but the man had lived abroad for years. From his own words, he did not like Mr Willberg very much, and even though he visited Leonora rather frequently—

'Perhaps it was *him* who suggested the séance.'

I shed light on the family tree again. Walter was now the last survivor of the Willberg offspring.

'Inheritance?' I mumbled, sitting on the edge of McGray's desk. I put the lamp down and covered my face, at once invaded by excitement and relief. Katerina may still have some hope.

I'd need to act quickly: comb Leonora's journal for any mention of Walter's influence, question the man himself, detain him if needed. And I'd also have to search for any documents related to the mine.

However, I'd not get a chance to do much that night.

I had barely begun collecting the documents in Leonora's box, when I heard some female cries coming from the ground floor. The voice and the accent were unmistakable, and a moment later I saw the distraught face of my former housekeeper.

'Joan!' I cried. 'What are you doing—? What happened?'

The poor woman was as pale as a ghost, her eyes reddened with tears of desperation. She was still clenching a kitchen rag in her trembling hands, and her hair and clothes were dripping rain.

'Sir, you have to help us! Please, come quick!'

'What is it?'

She tried to speak but the sobs did not let her.

I grabbed her by the shoulders and shook her. 'Please, Joan, what is it?'

She took a couple of deep breaths, wringing the filthy rag. 'Mr McGray, sir . . .'

'What with him?'

'Oh, sir, he's gone crazy! He . . . he brought home a boy . . . The poor creature was screaming!'

'A boy! What b—?' I gasped. 'Ohhh . . . please, please do not tell me—'

Joan nodded fretfully, wiping her nose with the cloth. 'Yes, sir. The colonel's son. The master snatched him.'

38

'*I knew it!*' I said again and again as the cab took us in a frantic race to McGray's home. 'I knew I could not leave the bloody fool alone!'

'I'm so sorry, sir,' Joan moaned by my side. 'I didn't know who else to go to.'

'You did well, Joan. And do not worry, we shall fix this.'

'The poor child looked so scared, sir! You should've seen him cry . . .'

I said nothing else, for I was as concerned as her.

We made it to Moray Place just as the sun was setting. We ran to the entrance hall, where George, McGray's ageing butler (and Joan's current lover), met us. The old man trembled from head to toes, his weak knees shaking as his joints were about to give in.

'They're gone!'

'What d'you mean they're gone?' Joan shrieked.

Poor old George put up his hands, staring at his empty palms. 'I'm so sorry, sir . . . I tried to detain him for as long as possible.'

'Where's Larry?' Joan asked, referring to the young boy who helped them with the house chores.

'He went with them,' George said, barely managing to enunciate. 'The master asked him to fetch candles and other trinkets, and they left with the wee lad.'

'Where?' I urged.

George's chest heaved. He looked at me with hopeless eyes. 'The Morningside house. Where they all died before.'

Joan instantly covered her mouth, muffling a deep gasp.

I closed my eyes for a second, doing my best to keep myself calm; a distraught trio would not help anyone right now.

'We must go there now,' I told Joan. 'I might still persuade Nine-Nails to return the child before it is too late. Could you come and take the boy with you, if the situation turns . . . difficult?'

'Yes, sir. Of course!'

I rushed back to the entrance steps, but before I reached them, George pulled my forearm.

'Sir, take me with youse, please.'

I looked at the frail servant, unsure as to how he might be able to help, but I saw the desperation in his eyes and I could not refuse.

We squeezed uncomfortably in the cab – it was designed as a two-seater, and Joan was not what you would call *slim* – and the driver took us south as fast as his measly horse could manage.

Nobody said a word. We simply sat and watched the streets running past us at what felt a glacial speed. By the time we made it to Morningside the sky was pitch-black, the silver moon sending only a weak gleam through the clouds.

We alighted at the gates of the gardens and I dispatched the cab driver – the fewer witnesses, the better. The wrought-iron gate was in fact unlocked, perhaps left open by Nine-Nails, so we stepped in without problem.

I felt as if I were in one of my dreams, escorted by a couple of elderly servants as we approached the ominous house where *the six* had died. There was a single light coming through one of the windows. *That* window. The rest of the house looked like a black, menacing monolith. Unsurprisingly, the main door was ajar, and we found the staircase lit by the faint glimmer from the first floor.

Just as I climbed the first step, I heard the whimper of a child.

'*McGray!*' I shouted, darting upstairs as fast as I could.

The door to the parlour was wide open, McGray's dogs posted on each side like Phobos and Deimos. They growled at me, baring their fangs, but I stepped in nonetheless.

I first saw a dozen burning candles on the central table, shining like the entrance to a dark tunnel. The candlesticks stood on the same white tablecloth used on the night of the deaths, still smeared with wax and black ashes. McGray was lighting the last wick, his back turned to me. When he moved I saw an ornately carved chair beyond: with its dark mahogany and auburn upholstery, it looked like a portentous throne, oversized for the slender creature who sat there.

I gasped when I saw him.

Poor Eddie Grenville was so pale, his face glowed in the half-light, the red rims around his eyes like open wounds. He was wearing a grey woollen jacket, matching trousers and a tiny ascot tie, like a miniature gentleman. And just like such, his hands grasped the carved ends of the chair's arms.

'Is he all right?' I demanded, advancing in huge strides.

'Course he's all right!' McGray snapped. 'D'ye think I'm a monster?'

I growled, ready to strangle him. 'Monsters would spit in my face if I called you that! You kidna—' I pressed my eyelids, my voice going high-pitched, 'you kidnapped a child, McGray! *You kidnapped a child!*'

I felt I was sinking, and I believe it was Joan who dragged a chair so I could sit.

'And not just any child,' I went on, 'but a child who just lost his parents! You have *excelled* yourself, Nine-Nails! Look at the poor thing! This will be the end of you!'

'Och, stop whingeing, I'm goin' to take 'im back! And if the laddie looks scared it's 'cause—'

'You will be prosecuted for this even if you do take him back!' I jumped to my feet as I howled, spitting with every consonant.

Eddie startled, apparently more scared by my rant than by his situation.

Larry, Joan's servant boy, emerged from the shadows. He brought a large glass of milk, and he helped Eddie drink from it.

'It's all good, master,' he told me. 'We're good friends. I told him Master Nine-Nails won't hurt him.'

They were around the same age, yet Larry could not have looked more different in his third-hand clothes, his weathered face and his hands still scarred from his chimney-sweep days. And he must be at least three inches shorter than Eddie, who had clearly never suffered hunger. However, there was an air of complicity between the two boys, a glint of mischief in their eyes, as one offered drink to the other. It was that instant, unprejudiced friendship that can only occur in childhood.

And that made me all the more indignant.

'I am taking him back right now,' I said, rushing towards the boy.

I had barely touched his wrist when McGray pushed me back and planted himself between us.

'Ye'll have to get past me for that, Frey.'

He stared at me as menacing as his dogs, and I felt outrage consuming me from within.

'Oh, you blithering idiot! We must act quickly if we want to mitigate the consequences of your mammoth imbecility. Who did you have to beat when you kidnapped him?'

'Och, d'ye think I'm that stupid? Why beat someone when ye can just lift a child in the park when the nanny isnae watching?'

'How can you talk so calmly? If they saw you take him—'

'I didnae snatch him myself. We sent one o' Katerina's men.'

I covered my brow. 'We? Oh, good Lord . . . Let me guess. This is all her idea.'

McGray made a so-so gesture with his hand. 'Half hers, half mine. We were discussing our options for days. Couldnae really tell who came up with it first.'

I sighed, and foolishly attempted to reason with him. 'McGray, listen to me. I found new evidence. Katerina may still be proven innocent, but you will shatter all her chances if you keep—'

'Och, shut it, Percy! I tried to follow yer soddin' advice and see where that took us. I'm doing things my way now.'

'At least listen to what I have to—!'

'We're wasting time! The séance has to be tonight. The moon is almost at the same phase it was on the thirteenth. Ideally it should've been yesterday, but the rascal I hired—'

'*Oh, Jesus bloody Christ, listen to yourself!* You want to force a child to talk to the dead! This is why the entire world thinks you are as mad as a bag of ferrets!'

He grabbed me by the collar, ready to punch me in the face, and Joan and George rushed to him with pleading cries. Tucker and Mackenzie came in then, encircling us and barking like demons.

Amidst the mayhem there came a small voice, shouting once, twice, becoming louder until we heard the words.

'*I want to do it!*'

All our eyes went to Eddie, the dogs suddenly silent. His lips trembled and there was a twinkle of tears pooling in his eyes, but the boy stared at us with a determination beyond his years.

I took the chance to pull away from McGray.

'You, little man,' I said, 'are still too young to—'

'*Let me do it!*' he screamed, and his tone surprised me. It was a firm, commanding voice, yet melded perfectly with the insistence of a capricious child. 'Let me do it and I won't tell anyone who brought me here.'

McGray arched an eyebrow. 'This might work even better than I thought . . .'

'This is ridiculous,' I insisted, and with my quickest movement I seized Eddie, but the boy writhed and kicked about as if I were about to dip him in hot oil.

'*No! No!*' he roared, crying and clinging to the chair with a desperation I have seldom seen. '*Leave me alone! I want to talk to mother!*'

I had to carry him by the waist as if he were a small barrel. His shouting echoed throughout the house.

'Who's torturing the laddie now?' McGray said.

'Do you think this is a joke, Nine-Nails?' I growled, walking to the door and receiving the best beating the boy could give me. 'See what you have done! You should be ashamed of yourself, making this child believe he can see his mother here!'

'*But I'm the only one who can!*' Eddie screeched. He sank his teeth in my forearm, and I could not help dropping him onto the floor. Eddie glared at me with a wrath unimaginable in a creature his age and pointed at me with a trembling hand. 'Take me away and I'll tell grandma it was *you* who snatched me!'

His words hung in the air for an instant, until McGray cackled. 'Aye! Let's do that instead!'

'*Why, you little—!*'

I do not know how I managed to compose myself, for I was ready to bend Eddie over my knee and give him a good smack. When my homicidal urges had subsided a little, I squatted down next to the boy. He recoiled like a cornered kitten, but I seized his wrist again.

'Edward,' I said, as tenderly as possible, 'I know what you feel right now.' He struggled but I held firmly. 'I lost my mother when I was even younger than you are now. I must have been your brother's age. I . . .'

I felt a painful gulp forming in my throat. These were things I had never said out loud.

'I hid under the tables. I kicked and thrashed and hated everyone for not letting me see her. I felt that burning yearn as well; the *need* to see her. The need to see those who have left us. And she is not the only one I have lost along the years.' I gulped, took another deep breath and then pointed at my chest. 'You feel it right here, do you not? As if something is truly tearing you inside?'

Eddie's tears rolled fast and copious, and he nodded. I squeezed his very thin shoulder.

'It is cruel. Unfair. I know. It is the most devastating feeling, but it is precisely that despair that fuels all this spiritualist nonsense. Some people will see your pain and will try to take advantage of it.' I looked at McGray with the corner of my eye as I said so, thinking of his sister. 'Sometimes I even wish it were all true. That would mean I could really see them again.'

For a moment nobody spoke. Poor Eddie sobbed on, wiping tears with his sleeves. I offered him a handkerchief and he blew his nose mightily. Then I helped him to his feet. Despite being drenched in tears, he seemed a little more composed. However, when I tried to pull him to the door, he again resisted.

He looked at me and sniffed. 'I still want to do it.'

'*What?*'

'I have to try.'

'Oh, you cannot be serious. Did you not—?'

'Ye heard the laddie,' said McGray, taking the boy back to the chair. 'I'm nae forcing anyone.'

I shook my head, glaring at him. 'You know perfectly well what you are doing. You always do. And you never give a damn who you drag to hell with you.'

McGray looked up, his chest swelling. 'I ken ye miss yer uncle, but if there ever was one person I didnae wish any harm—'

'*Oh, sod off!* Do as you wish. Traumatise this child. Get yourself imprisoned. Dig a tunnel out of Calton Jail with a spoon! But I will not take part in this anymore.'

'In fact,' said McGray, 'ye sort of have to. I need seven people at the table.'

I must have let out the most mocking cackle of my life, but as I did so, I looked at the dour faces around me.

Joan began to wriggle her shawl, and George rested a hand on her shoulder. I knew them far too well; they were entirely loyal to McGray and would help him no matter what.

'Stay with us, sir,' said Joan. 'Please. What if the spirits arrive and we're all alone with two boys?'

'Oh, Joan, this is absurd!' I looked at them all, everyone as determined as the next. I turned to McGray. 'Even if I agree, you have two boys, two elderly servants' – Joan tried to protest – 'and you and I. Who is the seventh?'

'Reed's on his way,' said McGray, 'although he thinks I want him to collect some evidence . . . Which is nae really a lie, if ye think about it.'

Whilst I pondered, we heard the sound of hooves crossing the garden.

'It's him,' said Larry, peeping through the window.

'Reed will not agree to this,' I said.

'Och, I hope he does. I'd hate to bring up his body-snatching days again.'

'Body snatching?' Joan repeated, the gossipmonger at the ready.

Reed appeared at the threshold a moment later. He halted mid-step, staring at the candles and the table, and McGray pulling crystals and a bottle of whisky from a sack. The doctor's face was initially paralysed, his features only a little less childish than Eddie's. He barely managed to draw in some air.

'Oh no . . . Oh, no-no-no-no! I'm not even—'

He did not finish the sentence, but sprinted backwards and we heard him run down the stairs.

'Och,' McGray grunted impatiently, going after him with huge strides, 'if youse excuse me . . .'

I was going to take the chance to sneak away, but George came to me and again grasped my arm pleadingly.

'Sir, ye ken my master. He won't let the boy go until he's through with this.'

'I know you are doing this for him, but—'

'Please, sir! And then ye can take the laddie right away. It won't take an hour.'

Joan came closer, also giving me a supplicant look, and the boys were on the edge of their seats. In the distance I heard Reed's squeals, surely as McGray dragged him back.

I sighed, begrudgingly walking to the table. 'Oh, dear Lord. Let's make haste. Mrs Cobbold must have gone to the police already.'

McGray brought Reed then, pulling him by the back of the collar as if the young chap were a fidgety cocker spaniel. He screeched when he saw me. 'Inspector Frey! Don't tell me you agree with all this!'

I interlaced my fingers, all my will gone. 'I never do. As usual, I was also dragged into it.'

Larry, grinning rather cruelly, pulled a chair for the doctor.

'Come on, sir. It's a lovely night to talk to the dead.'

39

We all took our seats and McGray passed a round of drinks for the grown-ups. Reed pushed his glass away, looking deathly pale.

'Wet yer whistle, laddie,' McGray told him. 'It'll calm you down.'

'I'd rather not,' Reed grumbled, but McGray pushed the glass back to him.

'Don't tell me yer afraid Grannie Alice might come 'n' kill everyone in the room like she did before.'

Reed's eyes opened wider. 'I . . . I had *not* thought of that. Thank you for planting the notion in my head!' He then downed the whisky in one go. McGray was going to pour him another measure, but Reed snatched the bottle and took three anxious gulps directly from it.

I preferred to savour mine, enjoying the fire in my throat as I scrutinised the six faces around me. How similar it must have felt to be in this very room a month ago. I tried to imagine the scene, placing the faces of *the six* on the seats we now occupied.

Eddie, next to me, sat facing the window, on the chair Katerina would have taken. I felt a pang of sorrow as I looked at his rounded cheeks, his skin still as smooth as a baby's. Such an innocent, tender mind. Death should not be of his concern. Not so soon.

'Do not be too upset if nothing happens,' I whispered at his ear.

McGray, who also sat next to Eddie, passed around five silky stones, brown and ochre, hastily tied to strings.

'Tiger eyes,' he explained. 'Katerina said we should all wear them around our necks. They'll protect us and anchor us to the world o' the living, in case the spirits . . . well, youse ken, get unfriendly.'

Reed had another swig, longer this time.

I picked mine up, wrinkling my nose. 'Do I have to?'

McGray made a fist. 'I'll crush yer nethers if ye don't.'

'No protection for the boys?' asked Joan.

'Nae, they're pure souls. The dead won't mess with them.'

George coughed. 'Larry? Pure?' And Joan playfully slapped his hand.

I sighed in resignation as I tied my own amulet, feeling the weight of the stone against my chest. It did feel like an anchor, somehow.

McGray produced a sheet of paper from his breast pocket, unfolded it and placed it before Eddie.

'Read this, laddie. And then just let things unwind. Yer in charge now. The rest of us just have to hold hands . . .' he glared at me, 'and keep from being a soddin' nuisance.'

I inhaled deeply (most of us did) as I took Joan's cold hand. She began praying under her breath, her eyes shut tightly, and McGray did not stop her. In the cold darkness, we all seemed to find her litany somewhat soothing.

Eddie leaned closer to the sheet, the candlelight casting sharp shadows on his rounded features. As he read, his eyes looked like the empty sockets of a china doll.

'We mean no harm to you.'

His voice was shaky, and I felt his little hand trembling in mine.

'We seek only wisdom.'

Joan prayed a little faster, the words melding together until I hardly understood them.

Eddie took a deep breath, leaning on the last line and reading it in a whisper.

'Commune with us. We seek justice.'

I must have imagined it, I know, but as soon as he uttered those words the entire room felt even colder, as if struck by a wave of icy air that came from nowhere in particular.

I tried to shut my eyes like the others, but as soon as I did so, I felt an inexplicable, irrational fear build up inside me. It was like an invisible hand, icy and bony, creeping up my spine. And thus we waited, in complete silence. There were a few cracks and bumps, those which always come at night after one has put all the lights off.

I was telling myself so, but then I thought I heard whispers.

They were not Joan's. These sounded completely different – in the distance, but at the same time as if spoken right into my ears. They were throaty, whistling voices, uttering indistinct words.

Suddenly Eddie stirred, and I was glad everyone else had their eyes shut, for I jumped in my seat.

'Offering . . .' he hissed, his words making my heart beat faster. The boy frowned. 'Want . . . Offering?'

McGray knew at once.

He produced a small scalpel, which I recognised as an instrument from the morgue. I wanted to ask if Katerina had 'blessed' that blade too, but before I could speak McGray had already pricked his thumb and was squeezing drops of his own blood onto the nearest flame.

The candle scintillated, the blood singed in the fire and the vapours ascended in reeling shapes. My heart raced and my eyes flickered from swirl to swirl, expecting to see a twisted hand materialise in the air, ready to take hold of us.

And that cold – that ghastly cold – clutched around my neck.

I felt queasy. The candles went blurry and everything around them seemed to fade into the blackness, like when you stare at something so hard it becomes diffuse. To my eyes the flames turned into floating balls of light, dancing in the air – like torches above tranquil waters.

I felt a sting of fear in my chest and pinpricks in my fingertips, just like I had that night in the Highlands. The fear returned to me, not like in my nightmares, but fresh and renewed. I could almost smell the woodlands and the burning bodies. I was there again. The only reminders of where I truly sat were the weight of the stone on my chest and my hands being clasped by Eddie and Joan.

I thought I saw something taking shape amidst the flames, their glares moving and solidifying into something that soon looked like a familiar brow.

And eyes.

I shook my head, forcing myself back to reality. *It is only you, Ian*, I told myself.

Of course this would affect me; the darkness of my own bedroom did. And yet here I was, in the same room where those people had died inexplicably, playing the exact same game.

Then, for an instant, a face flashed before me. His face. It was like one of my previous visions, only far sharper and clearer. It was like staring right into Uncle Maurice's face, far closer than I'd ever done in life, his skin grey and silvery, his pupils glowing from within. I threw my head backwards and shut my eyes, my heart pounding.

Go, I thought, a drop of cold sweat rolling down my temple. *I don't want to see you like this.*

I forced in deep breaths, just as a tremor began to take hold of my body. And the words escaped from my mouth. '*Go and rest . . .*'

'It's thin,' someone said at the exact same time.

It was a throaty, unrecognisable voice. I thought it had come from my own head, but then Reed let out a gasp.

Eddie had said it, and at once I heard the dogs whimper.

I opened my eyes again, back to the here and now, and saw McGray leaning slightly towards the boy.

'Thank them for coming,' he said, but Eddie only nodded.

'It's thin,' he said again, never opening his eyes and only barely moving his lips.

'What is thin?' McGray asked. I could see the spark of the candles reflected in his eyes, every muscle on his face rigid.

'It's thin like paper,' Eddie answered.

There was a flicker in the light, most likely caused by Reed's breath, but it made Joan startle. The dogs began to howl then, like wolves crying to the moon.

McGray bit his lips, impatience bubbling under.

'What is thin like paper?' he asked again, only just managing a gentle tone.

Eddie balanced his head from side to side. The movement did not seem natural; it was more like looking at a ghastly puppet being dragged by invisible strings.

'The wall,' he muttered.

Then he tilted his head at an odd angle, and again the light made him look like a carved doll whose eyes had been ripped out.

'The wall to the underworld.'

It was as if that sentence spread a deathly chill that made us all shiver. Joan let out a soft whimper, and then resumed her prayers, faster and faster as she went on. The dogs began trotting around us, letting out erratic howls and barks.

'It's paper-thin,' Eddie said again, and then his hissing tone mellowed. 'Cross.'

A nasty tingle ran along my spine; I heard Reed whimper and Larry breathe agitatedly. I imagined an invisible, intangible mass swelling in the room and enveloping us all. As cold as death. The only one who appeared composed enough was old George.

Eddie began panting, and I thought I could see condensation coming out of his mouth.

'Be not afraid,' he said, and then a wicked smile appeared on his face. 'Cross.'

He began trembling. Slowly at first, but soon I felt the tremors spreading along my own arm.

'Cross!' he insisted, his head and limbs jerking more and more.

'Is he all right?' I asked. The whites of his eyes glimmered between half-shut lids.

As if to silence me, Eddie squeezed my hand with unexpected strength, digging his nails into my skin, and then his face contorted as if stricken by searing pain. His voice, impervious, did not match the grimace.

'*Cross!*' he hissed, his spine bending forwards as if something tried to burst from his chest. I thought I heard his ribs crack, just as Eddie forced in a throttling breath.

'*McGray, we have to stop!*' But my voice seemed to worsen it all, sending the boy into an uncontrollable fit. His head began flailing about so violently I thought his neck would rip out. The dogs barked madly.

'Break the circle!' McGray said at once, and we all did so.

Eddie would not let go of my hand, his tiny nails digging into my skin.

'Blow out the candles!' McGray shouted.

Joan jumped up, but almost instantly fell back on her chair as if her legs no longer worked.

Eddie banged his own head against the table, leaving a red stain on the cloth, and McGray and I instantly lifted him and took him away. The boy thrashed and kicked as he'd done before, screaming with a booming voice.

As we tried to restrain him, I caught a glimpse of George and Reed blowing and snuffing the candles with their bare fingers. Some fell on the table and there was a brief fire, which Larry attempted to smother with his flap cap.

I thought I saw the smoke ascend and swell to form clutching fingers, but then George extinguished the last flame, and the entire world became dark and quiet.

40

The white, milky glow of the clouds was far too intense, almost blinding, and I had to blink hard as I faced the sky. Nevertheless, I gazed on. That slight discomfort was far better than the damning stares the superintendent had been casting at me.

He was leafing through my statement, drumming his long fingers on the desk.

'And the boy simply decided to run to Inspector McGray's house?'

'Yes, sir. The child said so himself.'

I could not avoid him any longer. My eyes went from the window to him, and his expression was everything I expected and more – Trevelyan's lips were so tight they'd effectively disappeared, and his auburn eyes quivered with wrath. He believed nothing in our report, and I had become far too cynical to pretend I cared. I simply endured his glares and said nothing.

'You look rather haggard, inspector,' he said after a moment of scrutiny.

'You do not expect me to look fresh after last night's ordeal,' I said. 'As Inspector McGray detailed in his own statement, we spent the best part of the night following the track of the boy's kidnapper. That, of course, after running to Doctor Reed's home to ensure the boy received proper treatment for that bump to his head. That is why McGray sends his apologies.'

In reality I had persuaded him to stay away. He did not handle figures of authority terribly well.

'I see,' said Trevelyan. 'How commendable. Shall I start proceedings to get medals for the two of you?'

'Oh, no, sir. That would be pushing a little too far.'

Trevelyan did not even blink. 'You don't say.'

He closed the file abruptly, perhaps pretending it was my face he was slapping.

'I am a reasonable man, inspector, but I will not tolerate a farce like this again. Do you understand me?'

I lounged back in my chair and made the slightest movement that could be reasonably recognised as a nod.

'Now leave,' Trevelyan concluded, but his lips never popped back out.

I left his office still staggered by how well things had worked out. Eddie had kept his word, telling everyone he'd been abducted from St Andrew Square by a gigantic ruffian (which was not really a lie), that he'd hit his head while escaping, and that the nearest residence he was familiar with was McGray's, since he'd read it in the papers.

Mrs Cobbold, who had indeed called the police as soon as she noticed the boy was gone, had already been notified, and we were simply waiting for her to come and pick up the child.

I found Eddie waiting patiently on a bench nearby the main entrance. The constables had given him one of their jackets, which on him looked more like a poncho, and Reed had applied a bulky bandaging that resembled a mismatching turban.

'Feeling better?' I asked him, sitting by his side, and Eddie nodded. 'Your grandmother should be here in no time.'

He nodded again and murmured a shy thank you. He'd been awfully quiet since we managed to calm him down, which happened almost as soon as George extinguished the last candle. The boy's body had gone lax in our arms and for a dreadful moment I'd feared he might be dead.

'Mr McGray says the spirits did come,' he mumbled.

I sighed, now feeling terribly guilty I had allowed all that to happen. I was sure we'd simply sit there in the semi-darkness, feeling silly, until either Larry or Eddie became utterly bored. If I'd known . . .

'What did you see?' I asked him.

Eddie looked at me, his wide eyes full of hope. 'Mum came to me. I heard her. I saw her eyes.'

I sighed. I wanted to tell him it had all been in his head, but he looked so hopeful and reassured, I did not have the heart.

'She said I shouldn't be afraid,' he muttered.

'Did you say something back?'

'No. I tried, but I couldn't. And she knew. She said it was fine.'

'Do you . . . do you remember saying anything to us? Speaking out loud?'

The boy frowned, looking side to side, and then shook his head. 'I only heard Mum.'

I felt so sorry for him. Those visions might be with him for the rest of his life. At least he might find some comfort in them.

I tousled his hair and we waited in silence.

Mrs Cobbold finally arrived, swathed in showy mourning clothes that made her look like a neckless ostrich. She ran to her grandson, lifted him in the air and hugged him so tightly I feared he'd asphyxiate. All the while she glared at me. By now she must have been told our made-up story and, like Trevelyan, she would not swallow a word of it.

She put the boy down and pushed him in my direction.

'Say *goodbye* to the inspector, Edward,' the woman commanded, emphasising the word.

Eddie offered me a coy hand.

'Be good,' I told him, but I hardly shook his hand by a second, for his grandmother pulled him away and they swiftly disappeared through the City Chambers' gate.

I sighed then, thinking I had another child to worry about.

McGray sat pensively by his desk, his muddy boots on top of a tower of old witchcraft tomes.

'How did it go?'

'I averted most of the damage,' I said. 'Trevelyan will never forgive this, though. And the chubby old hag is clearly suspicious.'

Nine-Nails shrugged, which exasperated me.

'Is everything a triviality to you? You kidnapped a little boy! You risked so much to achieve – well, nothing at all.'

There was a moment of complete silence. I even doubted McGray had heard me, until he kicked the tower of books with all his might, sending crumbling pages and ancient leather flying all across the basement.

'Did ye nae hear the laddie? He says he saw his mother.'

I had no energy left to contradict him, but neither was I willing to accept his idiocy. I went to my desk and sat on the very uncomfortable chair.

'I believe the boy is convinced he saw and heard something, which was only to be expected in a troubled child. Even *I* thought I saw and heard things.'

Nine-Nails shook his head. 'Yer impossible, Percy.'

I preferred not to remark on the irony.

'Even if we assume that all that you claim was real,' I said instead, 'the late Mrs Grenville coming back from the realm of the dead to bid farewell to her son . . . she did not tell us anything that might help Katerina.'

McGray stared at the notes he'd pinned to the wall. 'The wall is paper-thin. Cross it.' He exhaled. 'It was like she was inviting us . . . inviting the laddie to join her. What if the same thing happened that night? What if—?'

He halted there, pulling his hair as desperation took hold of him. He knew I was right, and there was little I could say. We only had six days before the execution, and our options were slipping away with every tick of the clocks.

'I think it is time to submit the appeal,' I said. 'Father drafted it before he left.'

McGray lounged back, but did not look at me. He stared ahead as he stroked the stub of his missing finger.

'He said the appeal is most likely to fail without new evidence, right?'

I sighed. 'We must at least try. They might agree to delay the execution, which would give us more time to investigate.'

'Investigate what?'

At last I had a chance to tell him, as concisely as possible, about Holt's confession the day before – the deaths related to the gold mining business; how Leonora's gold nugget was not a talisman but a memento of her dead father; how Walter Fox might be the ultimate beneficiary now that everyone on his side of the family was dead.

McGray's eyes opened wider and wider as I went on, and when I was finished he stood up and threw a bundle of documents at me.

'*And ye said nothing last night? Are ye mad?*'

'I bloody tried! But you were far too busy scarring a child for life.'

He was already grabbing his overcoat. 'Och, never mind. Come on, I need ye to help me beat the truth out o' the orange bastard.'

'*No-no-no!*' I shouted. 'We cannot confront him until we have at least some evidence to throw at him.'

'Och, Percy, what the fuck?'

I put my palms up. 'You are getting desperate, and I do not blame you. But we must be cautious precisely because we have very little time left. If we go to Walter Fox right now, we'd just be giving him a chance to destroy evidence or run away to his dear Africa.'

McGray was writhing his coat just like Joan had done her apron. He tossed it back onto the rack, growling.

'Shite, I hate it when yer right! So what does her ladyship suggest?'

I sighed. 'We submit the appeal right now, if only to try to buy us some time. Then we look for evidence. This gold mine affair will have left a trail easy enough to follow – conveyancing, import statements, deeds.'

McGray growled louder.

'We do not need the full story,' I added. 'Just enough evidence to open a case against him.'

'Assuming yer right, we'll still need to find out how he might've done it.'

I allowed myself a side smile. 'Not necessarily. If we play our cards wisely, he might even tell us himself.'

41

We submitted the appeal right away and then paid Katerina a brief visit.

By then she'd made the cell a second home. Next to her bed she had now a little table, covered with half-written letters I recognised as farewell notes. There was also a vase with fresh flowers, filling the room with a soft perfume, combined with the scent of soap and clean cotton sheets.

McGray whistled.

'Aye,' said Katerina, wrapping herself more tightly in her bright green shawl. Only then did I notice she was once more wearing her offensively low cleavages, her bulging bosom free to rock at will. 'They treat you like an empress here. All you have to do is die for it.'

McGray bit his lip. Katerina's nonchalance before death made us uneasy.

She raised her chin. '*So* – I can tell you learned nothing at the séance, am I right?'

We both stood there rather nervously, like children before the schoolmistress.

'I knew it would be a waste of time,' she said, and then gave me a look of complicity. 'I tried to convince this lad, but you know what he is like.'

McGray looked so upset I preferred to save my comments. Instead I said, 'The boy claims he saw his mother.'

Katerina nodded. 'Aye, that's what I expected. The mother wouldn't have let any other spirit through. Not so soon, at least.' She shook her head, her mouth twisted in a bitter smirk. 'I supposed it is sealed now. Then again, I already—'

'We still have an ace up our sleeves,' McGray interjected. 'There's still hope. We just learned—'

Katerina raised a hand. 'Don't. Don't tell me more. Go and do your thing if that makes you feel better, but I have more important things to worry about.'

'But—'

'I want to see my son!' she snapped, for the first time since the trial showing real concern in her eyes. Then she turned, entreating. 'Could you arrange that? I haven't seen him in eight years. He won't even recognise me . . .' A shadow set on her face, far darker than the certainty of death. 'He will be ashamed of me . . .'

We wanted to offer her some comfort but did not know how. The boy had grown in a boarding school, ignorant of his origins. He would certainly be astonished to find his mother in jail, pronounced guilty of six murders. And he would not be the first young man to look down at his humble past.

Katerina shut her eyes and sighed. 'Also, *please*, can you find me a priest?'

McGray's jaw was tense. I could tell he was doing his best to compose himself, so I spoke for him. 'Have they not offered you one already?'

'Aye, son, but I want an Orthodox one. Eastern Orthodox. My parents' faith.'

'Of course,' I said. 'We will send out requests. My father might be able to locate one in London.'

Katerina whispered a clumsy thank you. She stretched her free hand to hold mine, but as soon as she touched me, the woman twitched. Her eyes even cleared, momentarily oblivious of her situation.

'Oh, son,' she cried, 'your uncle had a message for you!'

It was my turn to take a step back. That was the last thing I would have expected to hear.

'But you refused to hear him,' she added, a shade of sorrow in her tone. 'You told him to go away . . .'

My mind went blank. How could she possibly know? It was not the first time she surprised me in that manner, but it had never struck so deep into my chest.

She, on the other hand, smiled. 'My eye is coming back. I can feel his soul's at peace. He probably wanted to tell you so. You've been seeing him a lot, haven't you?'

It was my turn to gulp, and for one selfish moment all my sympathy for her vanished. There she was, uttering a seemingly harmless sentence, yet managing to hit my most vulnerable nerves.

'You have to let him rest,' she said, but I just sneered. 'I know, I know. It all sounds hollow when you hear it from someone else. But I've had my losses too. Parents, brothers, sisters . . .' she hesitated, her voice for once quivering. 'Babies . . .'

She looked sideways, and her green eyes danced as if following imaginary shadows.

'It's harder on the living than it is on the dead,' she said. She took a deep breath, and then gave me a firm look. 'But listen to me carefully – I usually charge a fortune for this sort of advice – let him go.

'Remember him, yes. Remember all the dead. Celebrate that you met them and that you shared some of your life with them. But also let them go. Life is change. Move on. Let *them* move on. You won't find peace until you do. And they won't either.'

She looked alternately at us when she said that, but neither of us managed an answer. We simply lingered there, looking at our own feet like scolded children.

Nine-Nails sniffed, his back bent miserably. Then, all of a sudden, he cleared his throat stridently and jumped to his feet, almost banging his head on the ceiling.

'That's bollocks.'

'W-what?' Katerina turned to him so fast I feared her breasts would overbrim.

'I don't care what ye say, hen. I'm getting ye out o' here.'

'I—'

'And ye'll give me free divinations 'n' free ale – *good* ale – for as long as ye live. And that will be so fucking long even yer child will regret the deal. Ye understand?'

Katerina shook her head. 'Adolphus, boy, can't you—?'

'Save it, we're in a hurry. And we need ye to give us some names for the investigation. That is, if ye have any soddin' interest in staying alive.'

42

Katerina's murky network of contacts finally paid off. She knew people in the customs office who owed her favours and who gave us full access to any import and export records we wished to see. We decided McGray was the natural choice to deal with them. In the meantime I would consult land registries, the newspaper archives, and recruit Joan to hunt for more family gossip.

Before any of that, however, I volunteered to take care of Katerina's requests. I telegrammed my father and a few other acquaintances in London, asking if anyone could contact an Eastern Orthodox priest. I also sent a message to Johnnie, telling him Katerina's son must be sent for as soon as possible. As soon as I got his reply assuring he'd look at that, I began the hard work.

Three days later – a blur of rushed meals, sleepless nights and endless rounds of coffee and claret – I met McGray at his cluttered library to discuss our findings.

We were both exhausted, our bodies strewn on the sofas like rags, with just enough energy to swirl our whisky tumblers.

'I found gold,' said Nine-Nails. 'Mind the pun.' And he tossed a bundle of documents onto the coffee table.

'Imports records?' I said, leafing through them.

'Aye. Turns out that Colonel Grenville and his father-in-law, that auld Hector Shaw, imported eye-watering piles of gold.'

I read for a moment. 'Wait. I do not see their names here. Only—'

'Peter Willberg.'

I raised an eyebrow. 'Did they do everything under his name?'

'Indeedy. If the mine was a dodgy business, it was only natural they'd look for a scapegoat. Willberg took care of all the imports and the sales. I bet ye didnae find any deeds or transactions linking the colonel and the auld Shaw with African mines.'

'Indeed I did not.'

McGray stretched an arm, patting Tucker's head, and pulled a hefty stack of documents from underneath the dog's muzzle. 'Look at these.'

They were covered in dribble, so I only handled them after wrapping my hand with a handkerchief.

'Bank statements!' I cried. 'How did you get—? In fact, do not tell me.'

'Peter Willberg paid a lot o' cash into five accounts. Three belonged to the fathers of Bertrand, Leonora and Walter Fox. However—'

'Dear Lord,' I said. 'What he gave them is nothing compared to what the colonel and the old Mr Shaw hoarded.'

I pondered for a moment, enjoying the excellent bouquet of McGray's single malt.

'Leonora's father,' I recounted, 'and Walter's and Bertrand's . . . They were all dispatched to Africa to extract the gold.' I took note of that, encircling their names. '*The three diggers . . .*'

'And yet they got tuppence compared to the other two. Even Willberg, who sat very comfy in a warm office, got more than the poor devils digging the ground on the other end o' the world.'

I nodded. 'That would have caused . . . bitterness, to say the least.' We both had the same name in mind. 'Walter was in his teens back then,' I said. 'He would not have liked this at all.'

'And the colonel went to meet that sod right before the séance,' McGray added. 'We still have nae idea what for.'

'If Walter instigated the séance and then somehow tampered with the knife . . .'

'Which Katerina gave to Leonora.'

'And Walter visited her frequently . . .'

The names and the facts remained floating in the air for a while, until McGray snapped his fingers. 'What if we send him one o' Katerina's men to squeeze some information out o' him?'

I lifted my head lazily, giving Nine-Nails a quizzical brow.

'Och, don't look at me like that, Percy. Nothing drastic – just a wee scare to make him talk. A burst lip . . . a broken knee . . . that sort o—'

'*No,*' I said firmly. 'Do nothing of the kind. Walter is a blasted rogue. He'd use any kind of coercion against us. And he has Pratt in his pocket. It would not surprise me if he gave him that blasted golden tooth.'

'Och, we have to rush things somehow. We're running out o' time!'

I sighed. 'We will have a verdict on the appeal tomorrow.'

'Aye, and they hang Katerina two days after that.'

Aware as I was of the fact, I still felt a pang of fear when he said it. How could time have passed so quickly? It was as if some terrifying magic had compressed the past six weeks into a blink.

I realised it was well past midnight, so I downed my drink and stood up, my legs numb and my back sore.

'Time to rest,' I groaned. 'Tomorrow will be anything but quiet. Shall we meet directly at the court?'

'Neh. If they reject the appeal I'll probably strangle someone with my belt.'

'True.'

'And I can spend the time looking for more evidence. I'll never forgive myself if we find the last piece o' the soddin' puzzle after Katerina—' He stopped then, snorted and leaned over a mountain of old ledgers. 'They should give the sentenced more time. Three Sundays to save someone's life . . . It's ridiculous.'

'It is the law,' I reminded him. 'Flawed as it may be . . .'

I left then, dodging the drooling Mackenzie and Tucker. I cast a last glimpse at McGray, bent over the table and absorbed in the documents.

At least the work kept him from going mad.

That was how he'd dealt with his parents' death. That was how he still dealt with his sister's incurable madness – the one useful trick I could learn from him.

43

The appeal, unsurprisingly, was dismissed by the courts.

An independent judge had studied evidence, files and statements, and concluded there was no reason the case should be reassessed.

This coincided with a series of three sordid articles in *The Scotsman*, which retold the details of the crime, the court proceedings, and also gave a meticulous account of Katerina's murky side businesses. Now that she had a foot on the gibbet, more and more of her old 'clients' had come to the fore, revealing ever more embellished tales of corruption, fraud and seductions.

Trevelyan happened to be reading those very articles when I stepped into his office – and it was no coincidence.

'No,' he mumbled.

'S-sir?'

'The answer is no.'

'May I at least be allowed to expl—'

'You are here to request I delay the hanging, are you not?'

'Yes, sir, but—'

'I can't do that.' He lifted the newspaper. 'Have you read this?'

'I only had time to skim through the first pages.'

'Did you know that the Lord Provost has on occasion consulted that blasted gypsy?'

I swallowed. 'The – the fact may have been brought to my attention.'

'An "anonymous source" has declared so. Not so anonymous since the Lord Provost dismissed his valet only last month, and the man was spotted at the Caledonian Station purchasing a first-class ticket to London. These newspapers must have paid him well.'

I sighed. 'Is this the reason our appeal has been dismissed? The most powerful man in Edinburgh lobbying the courts?'

'I cannot tell. Possibly.'

I felt exasperated. I nearly turned on my heels and left, but that would have equated to signing Katerina's death sentence myself.

'Sir, may I at least sit down and explain?'

Trevelyan sensed my concern. 'You may, but unless you offer me some outstanding piece of information, I am afraid this will be a complete waste of our time.'

I did sit down, and explained the situation as carefully and briefly as possible: we had a good lead to follow, and the execution might take place merely hours before we secured enough evidence to reopen the case.

Trevelyan did listen, and when I was done he lounged back, interlacing his fingers and looking at me with the most conflicted gesture.

'I am under strict orders to carry out the hanging as planned.'

'Orders? The Lord Provost has no authority on the judiciary.'

Trevelyan simply sighed at this. We both knew how the world worked.

'So he will let an innocent woman die in order to keep his name clean?' I blurted out.

Trevelyan tensed his lips, the tendons around his mouth sticking out. 'The woman has been tried and sentenced.'

'And I just told you it may be the wrong verdict!'

Trevelyan stared at me without blinking. I could see the battle in his auburn eyes, the man trapped between his own morals and orders from high above.

He leant slightly forwards. 'Go find some evidence. If you do, bring it directly to me, whatever the time, and I will speed up things. That is all I can do for you.' He glanced at the newspapers. 'And if this gypsy does get out of this, it would be best for her to deny publicly all these stories.'

Still utterly frustrated, I nodded and left.

On my way to the office I was intercepted by Constable McNair – who had still not forgiven me for leaving him with Mrs Holt's child. With him came a rather old, haggard-looking man, so thin I feared his wrists would snap if we shook hands.

'Inspector, this lad's looking for ye,' said McNair, and before I could give him another abnormal assignment, he turned on his heels and left.

The grey man bowed at me. 'Mr Reynolds, sir. Undertaker. I have been hired by Miss Dragnea.' And he offered me a small letter. I recognised the handwriting. 'The lady wants me to take care of her funeral arrangements. Her man servant has covered all expenses.'

'What do you want with me?'

'The lady mentions your name in the letter, sir. Says I'll need a special permit to get into the jail to retrieve her remains, and that you may be able to help me.'

As I held the letter and read Katerina's requests for her own funeral, something clicked in my mind. Whatever the outcome, there would still be a world after Monday. The sun would rise, people would go to work, I'd drink my morning coffee and do my ascot tie, and all the practicalities of life, like interring a body and paying the men who did it, would have to be dealt with. The fact that Katerina herself was taking care of those particulars – the acceptance, the resignation that it implied – made my heart ache.

'She wants her remains to be treated with dignity,' Mr Reynolds added, after I'd been silent for a while.

'Of course,' I mumbled, folding the letter. 'Wait here. I will see you have a permit issued right away.'

And I went right back to Trevelyan's office, before his guilt waned.

Also, I was in no rush to give McGray the news.

He was nowhere to be found.

I first went to his house, but only saw Joan and George. They told me Nine-Nails had sent Larry to enquire at the courts, and when he heard the outcome he'd sunk into a chilling silence. He had then left the house, telling no one where he headed – in fact, only opening his mouth to tell the dogs to stay. Joan had never seen him so pale. George said he had, and I did not need to ask him when.

Joan offered me a whisky, but I refused and went back to the office. I was sick of facing doom and misery, and the familiar solitude of the crammed basement, with its damp walls and dusty piles of witchcraft books, ironically, offered some comfort.

I spent the rest of the day and most of the day after investigating Walter's gem trade, yet finding very little. I did manage to locate a couple of his dealers – dodgy men who were less than co-operative and who barked at me that Nine-Nails McGray had already knocked at their doors.

By the end of the second evening I left the office feeling that now familiar oppression in my chest, which had been growing in me steadily from the very start. I felt as if we had upturned every stone except those nearest to us – the most noticeable, the most obvious one.

And now we had so little time I could not even think straight.

The City Chambers was desolate by then, so it surprised me to see a lonely, dark figure walk along the shadowy courtyard. Something caught the glimmer of the street lamps.

A shiny, smooth scalp.

'*You?*' I cried, for Pratt was staring directly at me.

He smiled with obvious malice, his teeth more yellowy under the gaslight.

'Working late, inspector? Still hoping for the best?'

I said nothing. I simply walked away, describing a wide circle around him, as if avoiding a Biblical leper.

The evening was surprisingly mild and I yearned for some fresh air, so I headed home by foot. I might even take Philippa out for a late ride.

I took the long route, walking towards the brooding Edinburgh Castle. I passed by the bustling Ensign Ewart pub, and was tempted to check if McGray was there, but I did not have the energy to face him. I told myself I'd do so very soon, though.

I went down the steep steps of Castle Rock, which took me into the gloomy Princes Street Gardens. The trees' foliage had already turned brown and yellow, and I meandered over a crushing carpet of dead leaves.

Somehow I wandered westwards, and I found myself facing the dark tombstones surrounding St Cuthbert's Church. Colonel Grenville and his wife rested there.

I cannot tell what, but something pulled me in that direction, and I walked in-between the graves as the last gleams of sunlight died in the sky. It was not difficult to find the Grenvilles' crypt, still decked with garlands of evergreens and white flowers, now mostly withered.

I stood there for a moment, not moving or thinking. The sounds of the city were barely audible in those sunken gardens, and the fresh breeze heightened the sense of absolute, undisturbed peace.

As I stared at the dying petals I wondered if Grannie Alice also lay there. Perhaps it was she who had drawn me there, to confide in me the ultimate secret we'd been searching all along. I also wondered if Martha Grenville could have really visited her son. I wondered if my own uncle had indeed shown his face to me. Was it possible that I had ousted him as he attempted to speak to me one last time?

The alternative was hardly a consolation: that this was all there was to see. A cold grave. Boxes with bones slowly crumbling into dust. And when the city eventually met her end and the ages eroded this land, that dust would be carried away and become lost in an undistinguishable mass of sediments.

I nearly gasped at the thought, but then I heard something. It was a faint ruffle, impossible to identify, closely followed by the crunch of leaves on the ground. I looked back, my eyes squinting in the dim light, and almost immediately I saw the outline of a heavy-built man.

Tall and broad-shouldered, he stood some twenty yards away, but approaching at a steady pace. I heard another sound from the opposite direction. I looked back to the crypt, and nearly gasped when I saw a second man emerge from between the graves.

Him I could see more clearly. The street lights projected the shadows of naked branches on his features. His skin was pasty and scarred, and he chewed on a toothpick.

I felt my empty breast pockets. I had not carried a gun for weeks.

'Good evening,' he said with a rasping voice.

I gave him a nod and walked away, only to find that a third man had appeared out of nowhere. He and the first figure, now alarmingly near, stood motionless in my path.

'Ye have a light, boss?' the pasty man asked.

'At home,' I said.

The man spat the toothpick and took a few steps in my direction. There was no trace of emotion in his face.

'Pity,' he said. For a moment we simply stood there, frozen still, and then all hell broke loose.

The three men fell on me like a pack of wolves. I tried to run, but before I could take a single stride they'd already seized me. They pulled my shoulders down, bringing me to the ground as if I were made of rags. And just as I fell on my back, the first man came to me, lifted his muddy boot and stamped it right on my crotch.

Needless to tell my male readers how much that hurt (and a good portion of my female readers will tell me they've had far worse), so I will simply say that I recoiled, seeing stars and letting out a squeal so high-pitched I must have awoken half the dogs in the city.

So painful it was that I barely felt the man grabbing my collar, lifting me and thrusting a punch to my stomach. Depleted of air, I fell slack on the ground. I felt their grubby hands picking me up, I smelled their breaths and sweaty bodies, and prepared myself for a good thrashing.

The second blow to my stomach lifted me cleanly in the air, and this time I swirled and fell face down, tasting soil and leaves as I struggled to breathe again.

I saw their boots, ready to kick me to a pulp, and I shut my eyes and covered my face as best as I could.

Then there was a gunshot.

To me it sounded muffled, as if travelling through a mass of water, and I thought I heard a horde of feet trampling all around me. For a horrifying instant I thought they were crushing me, but then I realised they were in fact running away.

There was a second gunshot, only this time I heard it clearly. I desperately tried to move, but all I could do was jerk my legs and spit on the ground.

A cold hand pulled my shoulder and helped me roll onto my back. The figure leaning over was blurred, my eyes misted by the pain. I only managed to see something white, silvery, glinting in the dark.

'Inspector, are you all right?'

The voice sounded familiar enough, but the pain I still felt in my torso and nether regions left little room for rational thought.

'I'll call us a cab.'

I was lifted and dragged across the graveyard, and only when we reached the bustling Princes Street did I manage to plant my feet on the ground.

At once I retched, bending forwards and emptying my stomach on the kerb. I felt a hand patting me on the back, and the next thing I saw was a two-seater cab halting before me. The driver jumped down and helped me in.

'Where to, sir?' he asked as soon as I was secured on the seat.

'Great King Street,' I said automatically. In hindsight, I should have gone back to the City Chambers, but I was still too stunned to think.

The dark figure sat next to me and the cab set in motion. I focused on the rhythmic sound of the hooves, breathing deeply and clutching my sore gut.

'Take us through Leith Street,' the voice said, and then, just as I realised that would take us through the longest possible route, I recognised him.

I looked up, momentarily forgetting all pain. The street lamps lit only half the face, but that was enough. I saw the glimmer of white teeth framed by leathery, orange flesh, and the glint of the vulgarly oversized diamond ring.

'*You!*'

His face was distorted with worry. So much so I almost believed his good intentions.

'It was so fortunate I happened to be strolling down there,' he said. 'And with this.' He opened his jacket to show the derringer attached to the lining. 'Imagine what could have happened otherwise.'

'*Stop!*' I yelled to the driver, banging on the cab's ceiling. I was so shaken Fox easily pulled me back to the seat.

'Please, inspector, let me take you to your home. You are in no condition to—'

'*You arranged this!*' I growled, kicking about in a paroxysm of rage. 'You slimy, seared, rotten shred of baboon's buttocks! You—' I gasped. 'You and Pratt . . . He *has* been following me!'

'Inspector! Do you have no faith in humanity anymore?'

'No.'

'Why, I do not feel I deserve—'

'*Stop the damn cab, you blithering idiot!*' I howled from the bottom of my stomach, seeing that the driver was turning into the narrower, darker side streets.

The man did halt, but only when we were a good distance from the main road.

I kicked the door open and jumped off. As soon as my feet splashed on the ground I heard Fox's voice right behind my back.

'If you need to know something about me, why don't you ask me directly?'

I turned very slowly to face him. It was beginning to rain, and I was so furious I expected the drops to boil as soon as they touched my skin.

'Very well. Why did you send your damn bullies to scare me?'

Fox hinted a smile, but the wretch was too clever to admit anything out loud.

'A few of my contacts and patrons told me that this nine-fingered man appeared asking, quite specifically, if they had any dirt on me. You seem a sharp man, inspector; you surely understand that's not good for my business. It scares the clients away.'

I was furious. Livid. I felt my heart throbbing with rage and my tensed muscles, ready to hurl myself at the bastard and beat his ghastly leathery face until it resembled a plateful of fried haggis. I still do not know how, but I managed to turn on my heels and walk away.

'What did you want to know?' he repeated. 'Something about the gold mine?'

I stopped. I was tempted to turn, but the rain strengthened and I walked on.

'Or was it about my last quarrel with the colonel?'

I stopped again. I could not ignore that. When I looked back Fox was already next to me.

'There *was* a gold mine,' he said in a murmur. 'Grenville and his father-in-law acquired it through tricks and fraud. They forged some deeds to support a supposed claim to those lands; however, they lost those documents.' He laughed scornfully. 'Or rather, Grannie Alice took them.'

I said nothing. I simply stood there, looking suspiciously at him.

'The mine was always under her name. The false claims on the mine relied on her having ancestors who lived very briefly in Africa. Alice had no trouble going to the bank, accessing the family safe and retrieving the deeds. She did so right after my uncle, my half-uncle and my own father died. The poor sods got really ill while smelting gold, working themselves like dogs in the mines. And they were not the only ones; their workers fell like flies, like they always do in gold mines.

'Grannie Alice was distraught, as you can imagine. She despised the colonel, her husband, her own son and daughter for taking part; for championing the scheme and then spending lavishly on the profits. And I think she must have despised herself even more for allowing it all to happen, so she hid the documents from them.

345

'Years later she attempted to gather them all, I assume to surrender the documents or reveal where she'd hidden them. Sadly, my great-grandmother died just the evening before. Poor thing. She collapsed in the middle of the street.'

I remained as expressionless as before, wincing only when the ever-thicker raindrops lashed my face.

'I travelled to the mine recently,' Fox added, 'only to find that a local company had taken possession of it. Illegally, of course. They'd bribed the land registry, but we could only prove it by showing our deeds. That mine must have been active almost uninterruptedly for the past fifteen to twenty years. Can you imagine how much they'd owe us? That was when the search began. The Grenvilles stripped their house, as you might have noticed during your investigations.'

I finally nodded, recalling the stripped floorboards and plaster.

'As to my quarrel with the colonel . . .' Fox sneered. 'I summoned him. I knew that the séance was taking place, and I also knew how naïve my cousin Leonora and my uncle Peter could be. I knew the Shaws might want to trick them, so I warned the colonel that I would defend what rightfully belonged to our side of the family. He lost his temper, like he always did when someone challenged his almighty word, and he tried to punch me. Fortunately, in my profession I have learned very well how to dodge blows.'

I stared at him for a moment, taking in all that he'd said.

'How to dodge blows,' I echoed. 'Indeed you have. You wanted to defend your family's rights – yet you refused to take part in the séance.'

Fox looked down, unable to repress a smile.

Suddenly I felt the full weight of the rain and its coldness.

'You did it,' I hissed. 'You killed them all! Somehow you tampered with Katerina's knife! Was that why you always visited Miss Leonora? Or did you swap it when the colonel went to see you?'

It was his turn to remain silent.

'You know where those deeds are! And now you are just waiting for the waters to calm down before you retrieve them!'

'Can you prove any of that, inspector? Here I am, helping you escape some lowlifes who nearly—'

I could not repress myself anymore. I grabbed him by the collar, my hands shaking in wrath. 'You murdered six people! *And an innocent woman will be executed because of you!*'

Fox flinched at first, but then his cynical smile crept back.

'Be careful, inspector. Unlike you, I do have a witness.' And he pointed at the cab driver, who'd been watching intently.

I pushed him away, at least getting some satisfaction as I saw him stumble backwards.

Fox smoothed his clothes as he jumped into the cab. He grinned at me as soon as he closed the door.

'Even if all the gibberish you've said was true, you'd not expect a magician to reveal his secrets, would you?'

I clenched my fists, but all I could do was watch him go.

'Good evening, inspector. And – take care of yourself. You have no idea how many scoundrels are at large in this city.'

44

I was not able to sleep until the small hours, and then I spent most of the Sunday pondering my options.

That damn Walter was right. I had no way to prove he'd arranged the assault, and given my connections to Katerina and McGray, everyone would laugh at my claims.

I also thought it best not to tell Nine-Nails, at least for the time being. He and Katerina knew far too many people who might break Walter's legs, and as much as I would have approved, that would not help anyone at the moment.

Whenever I thought of it my guts went on fire. The bastard would walk away, Katerina would die, and there was nothing we could do about it.

I had a much-needed bath, haircut and shave, but I still looked terrible, my eyes framed by dark circles, my frown deeper than ever, and the skin sticking to my cheekbones as if I'd starved for days. Layton seemed worried, for he kept offering me biscuits, cognacs and fruit.

And then a note arrived.

It came from McNair, telling me there was an odd-looking 'giant' at the City Chambers, who could barely make himself understood but apparently claimed to be some sort of religious person.

I attempted to explain in a note that the man must be the East Orthodox priest Katerina had asked for. Halfway through the page I realised I was writing pure and laughable prattle, so I went to meet the man in person. I asked Layton to find me the best bottle of Bordeaux from the cellar, and I set off.

No wonder McNair had messaged me. The priest was imposing; as tall as McGray but twice as wide around the waist, and he had a curly beard, grey only at the middle, which cascaded all the way to his wide belly. He spoke in grunts too, even if his eyes were as gentle as Tucker's. He rummaged through a carpet bag even wider than him, and handed me a note from a former colleague in Scotland Yard. The giant – called Athanasios Something-topoulos – had just emigrated from Greece and spoke no English at all, but he was the only Orthodox priest they'd been able to locate in London. More importantly, he was happy to impart Katerina the last rites.

McNair also gave me a note from Katerina's servant. That one, unfortunately, bore very sad news. I could only fold it and put it in my pocket.

I then led the priest to Calton Hill Jail. The poor man gasped as we walked along the esplanade; there were men already working there, hammering wooden beams and iron rivets to assemble the gallows.

We found Katerina feasting on roast pork, rye bread, gravy, mashed potatoes and some slimy, yellowish mass I could only assume was pickled cabbage. Katerina clearly adored the latter, smacking her lips and grinning as she looked up at me.

'Last supper, son. What a pity you can only die once!'

Her hair was braided differently, now with white and violet ribbons, so I assumed Mary had also been around today.

When Katerina saw the priest her eyes brightened as if suddenly lit by the sun. She went to the man, knelt and kissed his hand. The man patted her head very gently, talking to her in warm mumbles nobody except him could understand. He helped Katerina rise, steered her back to her chair and made signs for her to resume her meal. He then sat on the bed and began mumbling prayers, as he opened his carpet bag and pulled out a Bible, incense and a heavy stole.

I put the wine on the table and the spark in Katerina's eyes was comparable to that ignited by the prospect of eternal salvation.

'Tell me you brought the good one this time.'

I could not help but smile. 'The best one in my cellar, madam. I even kept this one from my father.'

Katerina snorted. 'Is that supposed to be a compliment?' She reached for my hand then, so suddenly I almost twitched. 'Come, drink with me, my boy,' and she shouted at the grumpy guard. 'Oi! Fetch us three glasses!'

He brought three scratched tumblers soon enough, while I opened the bottle. Katerina snatched the cork and sniffed it whilst I poured the drink, moaning in ecstasy as she exhaled.

'Ahh! Beautiful! Not like the stinking, watered-down shite I sell.'

Again, I had to smile. 'You said, *under oath*, you never do that.'

She eyed the priest. 'Aye, and I'm so glad he won't understand me. He'll just have to absolve me.'

I offered a glass to the priest, who accepted it without fuss, and we three clinked our glasses in the strangest toast of my life.

Katerina savoured the wine, swirling it in her mouth like the expert I knew her to be. 'If someone told me I'd have my last drink with the likes of you!'

I let her drink and eat for a little longer, before I had to go to the bad news.

'Katerina,' I said, after emptying my glass. 'There is something I need to tell you. I just had a note from Johnnie.'

'Aye. The bastard's not come to see me. Is he well?'

'I suppose he is, but he tells us – well . . .' I took a deep breath and delivered it as fast as possible. There was no way I could soften it. 'Your son will not make it in time.'

Katerina's face froze for a moment, her lips still relaxed in a smile, but all the spark had gone. She blinked as if I'd spoken in dialect.

'W-what?'

'I am so sorry,' I added, the words sounding terribly silly.

Katerina opened her mouth, but nothing came out. She reached for her glass, but she could not even bring herself to touch it. Her eyes flickered as if lost in the dark.

'Johnnie received a telegram from the boarding school,' I said, unable to stand her agonising silence. 'They could not apologise enough.'

She swallowed painfully. 'But . . . But we sent for him with plenty of time!'

'I know,' I said. 'According to the headmaster there was some issue with the stagecoaches. The earliest he could arrive is Tuesday.' I instantly regretted giving her the vexing detail. Her eyes opened wider, and I could not face them. 'I am so sorry. I have nothing else to tell you . . . I am very, *very* sorry.'

It was the first time she truly crumbled. Very slowly she brought her hands to her face, and then broke into the most distraught, most tearing wails. The laments bounced between the walls, at once angry and desolate, making her entire body shake.

The priest prattled at me, obviously wanting to know what was wrong, and the scant Latin I learned in Cambridge came in handy for the first time.

'*Filius* . . . erm . . . *non venit.*'

The man nodded immediately. He went to Katerina and placed his enormous, hairy hand on her head, whispering ever so tenderly. His voice was deep and soothing, with a gentle warmth that made words unnecessary.

It took her a while to calm down, and I waited patiently in my seat.

I suspected the headmaster had consciously chosen not to send the boy. The news – and Katerina's reputation – had travelled fast. He'd probably thought it was best that the child did not get to see his cunning, murderous mother as she was about to be executed.

Katerina finally uncovered her face, mumbling miserably.

'I made my hair for him. And my make-up. I wanted him to see I wasn't the witch everybody thinks I am.'

Ironically, her face was now a mess, her rouge and mascara smudged all over. I offered her my handkerchief and she took it with utmost gratitude.

What a simple, universal gesture of compassion. It made me feel slightly better too; able to offer at least a drop of comfort. I pity a world where handkerchiefs are no longer in fashion.

'I always thought one day I'd meet him . . . I would explain everything. I'd tell him how sorry I was, but that I had to let him go! I was waiting for him to get a wee bit older, so he might understand . . . But now . . .'

She pressed the cloth against her face, in a renewed wave of tears.

'How old is he?' I asked, attempting to take the edge off her grief.

'Eleven,' she whispered. 'My Michael. He must be so handsome already. At least he'll have an education . . . More than I ever had.' She then took her glass, and I poured her some more. 'Thank you for bringing me this, son. It was very nice of you.'

I took the hint. She clearly wanted to deal with the news on her own. And she also needed some privacy to . . . ready herself. I stood up, but she spoke before I could utter any farewells.

'Tomorrow . . . *Please*, don't come.'

'E-excuse me?'

She rose too, and held both my hands. 'The fewer who see me, the better.' And even then she managed a playful smile. 'I prefer you remember me looking pretty like this.'

I stammered, not knowing what to say.

'Adolphus will be here,' she added. 'I told him not to, but you know what he's like.'

'Yes . . .' I mumbled. 'Yes, I do.'

She then raised a hand and patted me gently on the cheek. Her smile widened.

'You *will* be happy, my son. You may not believe it now, but trust me. I can see it in your future.'

I could not believe my eyes were pooling tears.

'I . . . thought foresight was considered blasphemy, madam.'

She winked at me. 'I know you won't tell him.'

And then she kissed my hand and said nothing more. She turned away and knelt by the priest, who was already burning incense and chanting in Latin from a prayer book.

I stepped out, but before I left I took a good look at her; her hands pressed together, her finest purple shawl, her intricate hairdo, her lips moving slightly as she prayed.

And then the guard closed the cell door.

45

I felt as if I walked into a cavern.

The Ensign pub was lit only by a couple of gas lamps, which cast sharp shadows on an assembly of sagging faces. They were all inebriated enough, but instead of the usual racket and dances, they sat around the fire. Most of the men were chanting a slow Scottish lament, swaying dreamily with their tumblers and pints in their hands, their glasses occasionally catching the glow from the flames. Those who did not chant were humming the deep, dark melody, and the few women around simply drank in silence. At least the place was much warmer than the damp streets.

Nine-Nails was at his usual table, his feet up and nursing a generous measure of whisky. The bottle – from his late father's distillery – was already half empty, and Tucker and Mackenzie dozed underneath the table, lulled by the gloomy song.

He only saw me when I blocked one of the gaslights, and gazed languidly at me. At first I could not tell whether he was depressed or irreparably drunk. I then remembered how much alcohol it took to knock him out.

His look went from lazy to bewildered. 'Och, what happened? Ye look like someone squashed yer crotch.'

My innards heaved at the mere memory, but I forced myself to feign a smile.

'I ran out of lavender for my baths.'

'Aye, that explains.'

'May I join you?'

Nine-Nails did not answer. He simply groaned and kicked a nearby chair in my direction, which to him was the equivalent of a red carpet. He offered me his own glass, poured more whisky in it, and then went on drinking from the bottle.

We drank in silence for a while, listening to the men's chants (I would have wiped the tumbler's rim, but I'd given my last handkerchief to Katerina). McGray spoke when the laments reached a particularly low passage.

'I went to see Doctor Clouston.'

The sentence took me by surprise. I asked the first question that came to my mind.

'Did he give you any news on your sister?'

McGray shrugged. 'He said the new medicine didnae work.'

Tears had built up in his eyes, reflecting the erratic twinkle of the hearth, but somehow he managed to keep himself from shedding them.

'But that's nae why I went to see him.'

Right then my attention was caught by Mary, who emerged from the backrooms, carrying a tall tankard of ale. She nodded at me respectfully, and then installed herself in one of the benches closest to the fire. Men made room for her, and then the humming shifted, spontaneously following the rhythm at which the young woman swayed. She began singing with a sweet, tremulous voice:

I've seen the smiling
o' fortune beguiling,
I've tasted her pleasures
and felt her decay.
Sweet is her blessing

and kind her caressing,
but now they are fled
and fled far away.'

McGray spoke on only when Mary began repeating the verses.

'I begged Clouston he signed a certificate of insanity for Katerina.'

'What?!'

I regretted the hysterical pitch of my question. Fortunately, Mary's singing had obscured it.

'What . . . what did he say?'

I knew it was a pointless question.

'Refused, o' course,' McGray grunted. 'I kent he would, but I still had to try. He said—' Nine-Nails had to take a long swig, letting the fire of the spirit overpower his pain. 'He said he'd never done that while consciously knowing it was a lie . . . And I—'

He said nothing more, his eyes fixed on Mary as she delivered her tragic song, allowing tears to roll freely down her freckly cheeks.

'Did you say something you should not have?'

Again, a silly question.

McGray drank without answering, but I could picture the scene: Nine-Nails knocking over furniture, punching walls and throwing files in the air, while the good doctor stood stoically, letting him release all his frustration. I pitied Cassandra Smith and the other orderlies who'd have to clean up the mess.

'Doctor Clouston is a reasonable man,' I said. 'I am sure he will understand.'

Nine-Nails nodded, though not looking terribly convinced. After a few songs and many swigs, he said, 'See ye at Calton Hill tomorrow?'

I exhaled and stared at my drink, feeling both guilty and relieved. Mostly guilty. 'Katerina asked me not to be there. She said—'

'I believe ye,' he interrupted, reading my discomfort. 'Sounds like her. She tried to convince me too.'

Tucker emerged from under the table and lay his dribbling muzzle on McGray's knee. His whimpers were strangely in tune with the sad singing.

'I failed her,' McGray sighed, scratching the dog's ears.

'Excuse me?'

He was misery itself. No wonder the dog had felt it.

'I failed Katerina. Just like I failed my parents. Just like I keep failing my sister.' As he kneaded Tucker's neck, I caught a glimpse of the stump on his right hand. 'The more I care about someone, the more shambolic the way I fail them.' He gave me a wry smile. 'Ye should still be fine, Percy.'

'Thank goodness,' I mumbled after a chuckle, and then raised my glass, suddenly feeling as dejected as Nine-Nails. 'Cheers to the Great Parade.'

'Whah?'

I shook my head. 'Never mind.'

And we drank on in silence, listening to the slow ballads until there were just a few drops left in the bottle.

There are times when words are pointless.

46

I lay in bed for hours. Tossing, turning, throwing the sheets aside only to pull them back a moment later, my mind besieged by the myriad of possibilities I should have considered, people I should have interrogated, questions I should have asked, documents I should have consulted . . .

And that torrent of thoughts paralysed me.

I imagined Katerina at her cell, perhaps on her knees and praying, perhaps writing one last farewell letter to her son, perhaps drinking the last drops of the Bordeaux I'd given her. I was sure she was not sleeping; in a few hours she'd have an eternity of that.

That thought made me jump off the bed. I wrapped up in my dressing gown and went to my parlour. After opening the curtains, I sat down on my favourite armchair and stared at the droplets that peppered the window, looking like golden stars under the glow of the street lamps.

They made me think of a gold-rich ore, the night behind them the dull gravel from which the metal had to be extracted. I pictured the three diggers and their African workers, sweaty, diseased and covered in soot, as they leant over the melting—

Something happened.

As the droplets fused and rolled down the window, I evoked

a forge: the shining metals emerging from crushed rock, pooling at the bottom of a crucible as they went from solid to liquid . . . and then becoming . . .

My entire body went cold, my hands grasped the cushioned arms of the chair, and as if pushed by an invisible force, I jumped on my feet.

'*Of course!*' I shouted, and with the image still vivid in my mind I ran to the downstairs parlour – the one I never used and whose walls were lined with Lady Anne's books.

My hands trembling, my heart pounding, I went desperately through the shelves.

There was no rhyme or reason in their display. They were all second-hand and most likely bought by weight, just for decoration.

'There must be a bloody encyclopaedia here . . .' I grumbled, and I began throwing tome after tome onto the floor.

Layton came soon enough, bringing a candlestick with five lights.

'Sir, are you all right?'

'Have you seen an encyclopaedia?'

Bedazzled and still half asleep, he pointed at the top shelf. I saw the twelve matching volumes, bound in green leather, faded and crumbling at the edges.

I had to pull one of the armchairs over and jumped on it. Layton brought the light closer and I picked the fifth tome, marked *FEL – GRI*. Still standing on the chair I turned the pages frantically, tearing a few, until I found the entry for gold.

My eyes flickered through the lines and I became conscious of my loud breathing. If I did not find what I was looking for, I'd need to break into the Advocates Library, or any—

'*Gold extraction!*' I read out loud, but with the excitement I lost my balance and nearly fell on my back. I dropped the book and Layton miraculously managed to hold me in place.

I jumped down, picked up the tome and read the now creased page.

My eyes opened so wide they could have fallen onto the open book, and then I let out one of the most despicable syllables in the English language.

'*Shit!*'

47

'What time is it?' I spluttered.

Layton shed light on the pendulum clock. 'Just before five, sir.'

'*Damn!*' I yelled, running to my room.

I had exactly three hours to prove my theory right, gather the evidence and take it to Calton Hill. One minute too late and Katerina would be dead.

My heart skipped a beat at the thought. I donned a pair of trousers, did not bother putting a shirt over my union suit, and only put on a jacket because Layton ran to me with one.

Philippa would not thank me.

I woke the moody mare with hysterical cries, and soon enough we were galloping towards Albany Street. We reached the Shaws' house within minutes, and as I jumped off the mount I thanked God they lived so close to me.

I banged their door, my frantic voice echoing across the still darkened street. There were only a couple lights at the neighbours' windows; servants readying their masters' fires and breakfasts, probably.

The Shaws' house, however, appeared deserted.

I felt a cold fear, thinking they might have left town. I had no time to go anywhere else. I would never make it to—

The door finally opened, the terrified maid struggling to put on a brave face.

'I'm from the police,' I snapped before she could utter a word, and made my way in despite her protests. 'I must talk to your master or mistress right now. It is urgent.'

'Sir, they're asleep!'

'Then wake them! Someone is going to die!'

The poor woman tried to pull me by the arm, but I walked undeterred towards the staircase.

'*Mrs Shaw!* I shouted. '*Harvey?*'

The maid pulled desperately, begging me to leave. I did my best to calm her down, until I heard a cry.

'*What is it?*'

It was Eliza Shaw, rushing downstairs in her nightdress and wrapped in a ragged blanket.

'Ma'am, I need to ask you some questions. It is about—'

'*Get out!* she snarled, rushing in my direction to push me to the door. 'I know what it is about and I don't care. I've answered all your questions already!'

I held my ground despite their pushing and shoving. 'Ma'am, I must—!'

A throaty, blood-curdling growl interrupted me.

'*She said get out!*'

It was poor Harvey Shaw, coming from a downstairs bedroom. His legs useless, he dragged himself across the floor, grasping a handgun.

I put my palms up. 'Harvey, I mean no harm!'

'*Get out! This is my home!*'

'Put that down, I'm only here to ask a few questions.'

He kept aiming at me, but with a flimsy, quivering hand, his eyes about to burst in tears.

I took my chances, leapt in his direction as the women behind me screamed, and snatched the gun from his hand. I shoved it in my pocket and then lifted the poor man.

Harvey was as light as a feather, his legs mere bone and sinew. He did not even struggle as I carried him to the nearest parlour. I deposited him carefully on a sofa, seeing the anger and humiliation on his face.

I spoke as soothingly as I could. 'It is all right. I need your help.'

He covered his brow, suddenly crying like a little child. 'I'm no man!' he spat. 'I can't even protect my own home . . .'

His mother came in and sat next to him, casting me a murderous look.

'I am so sorry I had to barge in like this. You are the only relatives of Alice I can still talk to.'

That much was right. Mrs Cobbold would never receive me after the episode with her grandson. And Walter – well . . .

'I was hoping the gypsy would be dead now,' said Mrs Shaw.

'In a matter of hours, but—' there was no time for explanations. 'Harvey, I need to know how your father died.'

The young man cried on and on, and I felt desperate. I wanted to shake him until he spoke, but I had to restrain myself.

I appealed at Eliza. 'He got poisoned in the mines, did he not?'

She nodded, still glaring at me.

'He was weakened?' I asked. 'Felt pins and needles in his limbs? Found it more and more difficult to breathe? Trembled and twitched all the time?' The poor woman looked down and covered her mouth. 'I am sorry. I did not mean to—'

'Yes, all that,' she blurted out through her hand. 'From working in the mines.'

Harvey uncovered his face, taking in sharp, deep breaths, his face terribly flushed.

I placed a hand on his shoulder. 'Now, tell me, how did your grandmother die?'

'Grannie Alice?' he asked, looking confused, and I nodded. 'She . . . she just collapsed.'

'Was anybody with her?'

'No . . . no. She . . . she had just gone for a walk.'

'The doctors said it was natural causes,' Eliza intervened. 'Why? Do you think—?'

'Did she want to gather the family to conduct a séance?'

They lifted their faces in utter shock. Neither said a word.

'I know Alice wanted to see the family together just before she died,' I added. 'But the meeting never took place. Did she intend to hold a séance?'

Eliza Shaw did not even blink. She stammered before saying, 'How on Earth could you know that?'

I did not. It was my best guess, but I did not tell her that. 'So it is true,' I pressed.

Eliza barely managed to mumble. 'Yes. To talk to her dead children. She wanted all those who had something to do with their deaths to be around. She said they owed an apology.'

I rose then, my chest swelling in agitated breaths.

'It is true . . .' I whispered. 'Dear lord . . .'

Eliza was on the edge of the sofa. 'But as you said, it never took place. My mother-in-law died the day before.'

I nodded, the entire picture finally taking shape in my head.

'I will need you to sign that in an official statement,' I said. 'The apology part in particular. You two may be the last living people who can testify to that.'

'What do you mean? Why is that so—?'

But I did not hear the rest of her sentence. I was already running to the door, which the maid had left open.

Philippa twitched when I touched her, and then stepped sideways when I attempted to mount.

'Oh, Father is right,' I shouted, 'you are as stubborn as me!'

I pulled the reins firmly and jumped up with one swift impulse. Philippa neighed and jerked, refusing to go where I wanted.

'Oh move, you silly thing! You're not the bloody queen of the Alps!'

She did move, though very slowly at first, as if doing me the world's greatest favour, and only after much spurring did she speed up into a nice gallop.

It was already six when I darted into the Royal Mile, the street already abuzz with workers and carts. I imagined one of them might be the undertaker's, on its way to Calton Hill, carrying Katerina's coffin.

As I tethered Philippa I pictured the poor gypsy. By this time she'd be getting dressed, perhaps helped by Mary, while the Greek priest chanted unintelligible prayers just outside her cell. And McGray must be there already, dejected and kicking the dust.

I ran to our office, feeling breathless and making a mighty racket. Just as I went past the door to the morgue, a puzzled Doctor Reed peered out.

'Inspector? What are you doing here? I thought—'

'*Oh, you're here!*' I cried, elated, and grabbed the young man to plant a noisy smooch on his forehead.

'What? Are you drunk or—?'

'Follow me,' I spluttered, though not giving him much of a choice. I pushed him into the cellar and the poor doctor nearly tripped on a ghastly Peruvian idol as tall as him.

'Inspector, I'm running some urgent tests for—'

'*Shut up and listen!* We have a chance to save Katerina!'

Reed snorted. 'Really, are you drunk? They'll execute her in less than two hours.'

'*I know how bloody long we have!*'

I went to the box with all the evidence from Miss Leonora's house and emptied the contents on the floor. The two items I was looking for rolled away and I chased them. One was Leonora's journal. The other was a little bundle of brown paper.

'What's in there?' Reed asked, rather perplexed by the care with which I unwrapped the items.

I pulled out one of the candles. 'I need you to test this for mercury. You will find the protocol there.' And I pointed at Battershall's guide of legal chemistry, which still sat on my desk.

Reed stumbled, and for a moment I thought he'd faint. I had to hold him by the arm.

'The can— the candles . . .' he stammered. '*Of course!* Mercuric fumes would kill instantly! Before even causing any anomalies we could detect! But how can you be sure that—?'

'Use as little sample as you can. I will need the candles as evidence. And if you have time, test the bodies' samples for mercury residue as well.'

'I . . . I . . .'

'Oh, don't tell me you got rid of them!'

'No, no. Inspector McGray told me—'

'*Then go!*' and I pushed the book against his chest, steering him towards the stairs.

It would be foolish to expect he'd have the tests ready in time for me to rush to Calton Hill. Even at full gallop it would take me nearly half an hour to get there and then make my way through the morbid crowd.

I could imagine the crass, illiterate mass of onlookers, gathering at the gates of the jail, some even installing picnics at the higher points of Calton Hill, all eager to see the wicked gypsy dead. They must be there already, jubilant, as if it were a midsummer holiday.

I tossed the candles and the journal on my desk and sat down, forcing myself to take deep breaths. I would have to piece the full story together, prevent the execution, and only show the forensic results later. But for that I needed to think clearly. I had to focus.

The journal first.

I went to the entries preceding the séance, recognising the paragraphs I'd read a dozen times. McGray had added quite a few notes in pencil, especially when the late girl's handwriting was not particularly clear. I thought he'd be holding Katerina's hand right now, as she knelt down and let the priest pray for her.

I was thankful for his notes, for they saved me precious time. I went through the pages, my pulse raising as I got closer to what I looked for . . .

Madame Katerina is a very patient tutor. She told me Grannie Alice's spirit is very elusive and angry. It will take especial offerings and rituals to summon her . . .
   We'll need to cleanse the rooms somehow . . .

Another entry, from a few days later, made my heart jump. It read;

I found Grannie's old candles in the cellar. The receipt was still in the wrappings. <u>It told me all I needed.</u> Grannie Alice blessed the sticks herself.
   I mentioned them to Madame Katerina and asked if we could use them to cleanse the room.
   She said they'd do.
   To think they sat there, forgotten, all these years! What better way to link us to dear Grandmamma!

I turned the pages, scanning at full speed, but found nothing else. '*What better way to link us to dear Grandmamma!*' That was the last mention of the candles.

'Suspicious but not conclusive enough,' I grunted. 'Not without the forensics . . .'

I picked up the candles and pulled them from the wrapping. There I found the yellowed, faded receipt. I remembered seeing it weeks ago – it felt like years – and very carefully I brought it to the light; I did not want to scorch what might be the most crucial piece of evidence.

Some of it was written with ink, but mostly pencil, barely visible, and penned by a very shaky hand. To make matters worse, the writing was tiny.

I jumped to McGray's desk, rummaged through his drawers and pulled out his thick magnifying glass. I looked again, squinting, and after a seemingly never-ending time I managed to decipher a handful of words:

36 blessed candles . . .
Mrs Alice Shaw
£15.00 . . .

'*Fifteen pounds for candles!*' I cried.

I read on. On the very edge of the sheet, in even smaller writing, there was a signature I could not read, but also . . .

31b, Mary King's Close

I looked up, gasping.

'Mary King's Close!'

It all came back to me in a rush. I instinctively reached for my breast pocket, looking for my little notebook, before realising I was still wearing my nightclothes. I'd left the tiny booklet at home. I could even picture it on my bedside table. Fortunately, I remembered those lines well; Katerina's words when she'd touched Martha's pearl choker and Bertrand's shilling.

There is a sound . . . It's like she's whispering. Just one word,
over and over . . .

Mary . . .

And then I looked at the family tree, at the dates when the Grenville children had been born. I remembered Martha

Grenville, unable to conceive for eight years, had turned to her grandmother for help. Grannie Alice giving her remedies . . . Herbal teas 'from the black market', as Eliza Shaw had told me. What better a place to conceal a witchcraft shop than the depths of Mary King's Close!

I glanced at the other side of the family tree. Alice's eldest daughter, Prudence, had had the same troubles. She'd given birth to seared-skin Walter in 1851 and would not become pregnant for the next eighteen years, just before her death. With the aid of her mother's remedies.

'Alice knew her occult arts very well,' I mumbled.

I stood up, ready to make my way to Calton Hill, but then hesitated.

I looked at the evidence at hand: a few cryptic entries in Leonora's journal, some candles, and a faded receipt from an establishment that now was most likely rubble buried underneath Edinburgh's High Street. The executioners would laugh at me if I showed up at the foot of the gallows with that.

'Think, Ian, think!'

I massaged my temples, but for a moment all I could see were the gaolers already bringing out the noose and testing the platform's trapdoor. I'd seen on many an occasion people begging for mercy, for more time.

You've had plenty of time, they'd tell me.

I needed something else – a more conclusive document. Perhaps a proper description of the candles . . . Or . . .

'Dammit!' I groaned. It was the same predicament we'd had for six weeks. How on earth would I find something else now? It was not as if the answer were standing right in front of my—

And then I remembered young Eddie's voice, hissing and unnerving, his childish features lit by candles that had made him look like a ghoul.

It's thin like paper . . .

I looked at the wall behind McGray's desk, and recalled the many times I'd caught him pressing a stethoscope against it, listening for ghosts. I'd never done so myself, but . . .

It's thin like paper . . . The wall to the underworld.

Cross.

Be not afraid . . .

My entire body shivered.

I went to McGray's desk, picked up the old stethoscope and listened through the wall. I had to hold my breath, for my panting was obscuring the faint noises.

It was like pressing my ear against a conch shell; rushes of air whistling through what must be a cavernous void, only they came and went at erratic intervals. I could tell the wall was very thin, the whistles sometimes sounding eerily clear, like actual human laments. No wonder Nine-Nails spent hours there, imagining they were the breaths of spirits trapped underground.

I tapped at the wall with my knuckles, paying attention to the hollow sound. The damp plaster was flaky, and I began scratching it with my fingers. Then I looked at the room behind me, and wondered if this very office had been part of the convoluted lattice of streets, now buried under the City Chambers building.

'It might well be,' I mumbled, 'added to the complex as an afterthought . . .'

I stared at the wall and its spots of mould, indecision corroding me. I'd need tools . . .

Just as I thought that I took a step backwards, ready to run across the building to fetch a bludgeon, but then I tripped on something – the ugly Peruvian idol, still on the floor after Reed's stumble.

'May the Inca gods forgive me,' I muttered, grabbing the heavy carving and charging against the wall.

The plaster came down immediately, revealing the old frame of timber filled up with rubble. I growled and snorted, letting out all my frustration against that blasted chunk of shabby wall. I threw blow after blow, more and more furiously, until a small hole opened through. I leaned closer, bringing the gaslight.

The gap was barely the size of my head, and the darkness beyond was impenetrable, but I instantly felt a cold draught on my face, stinking of damp and decades of stagnation.

'God,' I groaned, the foul odour making me jump backwards.

I resumed the thrashing, hammering the edges until the gap was just wide enough to let me through. By then the basement was full of suspended dust that made my eyes tear.

I raised the desk lamp, fanning the dust away, but its pathetic light was barely enough to show me more than a couple of yards ahead. I ran upstairs, grabbed the first bull's-eye lantern I could find and ignited it as I darted back.

The beam travelled much farther, but all I could see was a distant wall of crumbling brick. That space was enormous. I could spend days wandering there and still find nothing.

Another wave of despair was coming. I attempted a deep breath, but with the floating dust I only managed to give myself a fit of coughing.

Should I dive in there blindly? Hoping for good luck, or a miracle or—

The stethoscope, still around my neck, finally slid off and hit the floor, and I pictured, as clearly as if I'd seen it yesterday, the antique map on McGray's desk.

He had a map of the old Close!

Only . . .

I looked at the mess around me: piles upon piles of documents and notes we had collected, inspected, and either catalogued or tossed aside for the past . . . I'd last seen that map nearly five weeks ago!

371

I rested my back on the crumbling wall.

'Think like Nine-Nails,' I mumbled, acting out his movements. 'I pick something . . . I leave it here . . . I get a greasy giblets sandwich . . . I pick something else . . . Never clean . . .'

I went to the messy desk and began flinging things. Like geological sediments, I could almost tell the dates in reverse as I cleared the layers of paper, files and old napkins.

I threw aside the last yellowy page and found the desk itself, dotted with stains and crumbs whose age and nature I did not dare guess.

'*Damn!*' Another deep breath. 'Think like Nine—' But at once I pictured him putting his muddy boots up, regardless of what lay on his desk. Behind it there were a few mounds of debris and books. I rummaged through them desperately, past caring what I broke or tore.

And there it was! A map from more than seventy years ago, all creased and stained with fat.

It looked just like a modern map of Old Town, the streets following the same line of the current road, but the labyrinthine closes around it were completely alien to me.

And it had numbers! The numbers of the land plots. Mercat Cross, right across the road from us, had stood since medieval times, so it was my point of reference. As soon as I spotted it I picked up the lantern and moved on. I fastened the lantern's leather straps around my shoulders and pushed myself through the hole. The beams' splinters caught my sleeves, and for a moment I thought I'd be stuck there like a hopeless moth on a cobweb. I groaned and pulled, tearing my jacket and falling forwards on my hands and knees, the lantern sticking painfully against my stomach.

My hands rested on soggy soil, and I retched at the thought of all the festering matter that would have settled there through the years.

I stood up clumsily and straightened my back to shed light around. I held my breath as I took in what lay before me.

An entire road.

It was an underground street, half the width of the Royal Mile itself and descending northwards in a steep slope. I saw door frames and windows, boarded-up many years ago, stone walls stained in saltpetre, trickles of water percolating from the surface, and the once pebbled road now entirely covered in rubble, stones and rotting joists.

I moved the beam from side to side and then onto the cavernous ceiling. Then I turned back to the hole I'd just opened and looked at the comparatively newer wall. According to the map, our basement had once been the narrow gap between two buildings, giving way to one of the many side streets all along the close. The place was like an entire little town on its own!

'Thirty-one B . . .' I mumbled, looking for the receipt's address on the map. I found it somewhere to the north-west, towards what was not Princes Street Gardens and the Bank of Scotland. The tiny plot was almost at the end of one of the wider closes.

I strode there immediately, but found no side street. I retraced my step and lighted the old archways, foolishly hoping to find a number. Of course there was nothing. Any paint, sign or embellishment had faded long ago. Some of those dwellings had been abandoned for more than a century, and like most of the Royal Mile they were much older than that. After a distressing moment, I convinced myself I was at the right spot, only the side street I needed had been bricked up. Perhaps as those roads were being closed.

I tried to calm myself, which is no mean feat when one cannot breathe.

'You still have a few moments to spare,' I whispered, and on I walked, thinking I would do a quick search. If I'd found nothing after a few minutes I'd rush back and take my chances with whatever evidence I already had. 'I hope I've not just sealed Katerina's fate,' I told myself as I weaved through rocks and bricks and piles of debris.

Right then I saw a fleeting figure lurking between the wreckage. A white, ghostly glimmer before the light, which vanished before I could even blink.

And I went after it.

48

I moved quickly, shedding light on every threshold and window around me. I reached a half-buried door, its upper half opening into sheer blackness, and I thought I glimpsed that ghostly shape again. I was not sure, but I had no time to think. I climbed on the rubble, dragged myself through the opening and then rolled down an unexpected drop.

As I stood up, my knees sore, I tried to find my location on the map. But then I heard a distinct clatter. Stone hitting stone. And then a soft, high-pitched child's giggle. It made me shudder.

'Hello?' I shouted, my voice echoing.

I was in a narrow gallery, barely six feet wide, lined with regular stone shelves. I thought of ancient crypts, and feared I'd see decayed bones resting all around me.

The air was fouler there, and as the stench hit me I also saw flickers of light right before my eyes. I recognised the vision at once; the torches that had been haunting me ever since Uncle Maurice had died.

I felt a wave of anxiety, reliving that irrational fear that took hold of me at night.

'Not now,' I said, covering my mouth and nose. I tried to breathe, but that pungent air only made me feel worse.

Katerina's words resonated in my head. *Your uncle had a message for you . . . You told him to go away . . .*

'*Not now!*' I howled, crouching. I nearly fell on my knees, pressing a hand against the cold, grimy stone for balance. It was that damp, disgusting touch that brought me back to where I was.

I reached the other end of the gallery, cut off by tonnes of rubble, turned back, and there I saw it again: a white rag disappearing quickly through one of those crypts.

'*What are you?*' I shouted.

I had no time to think. I clambered onto the small vault and pushed myself through. The gap led to another chamber, slightly larger, which opened up into a winding corridor. I trotted ahead, realising I was going deeper and deeper into the ground. I thought I must be stepping into what had been someone's cellar, but then I tripped on a large stone, and again I rolled until my shoulder crashed against a solid wall.

The stench there was unbearable. Fresh urine and human faeces.

And the lantern had cracked and gone out.

I could not see a thing. I only knew I lay on my back, against a curved nook, many feet underneath the streets of Edinburgh.

Then the entire earth shook.

It was gentle, and I thought I'd imagined it, but then I felt it again. I pressed a hand against the rock and felt the vibration. It came and went rhythmically, every few seconds, like clockwork. And with every tremor also came a distant, muffled echo. I realised I was hearing the bells of St Giles' Cathedral, summoning people for the seven o'clock mass. Katerina would hang in exactly an hour, and here I was, lost in an underground labyrinth with nothing but a broken lantern.

Right then, with a pang in the chest, I realised that my hands were empty. *I had dropped the map!* Perhaps as I'd fallen on my knees.

I searched my pockets frantically. I still had the box of matches I'd used to ignite the lantern. I sighed in relief as I lighted one, but as soon as the tiny flame lit up the void, my heart stopped.

Scant inches from my own face, something sparkled.

A pair of glimmering eyes.

I yelped and instantly dropped the match, which went out as soon as it hit the damp soil.

The bells stopped, and then I heard it clearly . . . Rasping breathing . . .

Something stood next to me, so close I could feel the waves of moist, fetid breath. I could hear it move, slithering around like a watchful snake.

Fear invaded my body, freezing my chest. I did not want to look. I did not even want to move, lest I touched that creature panting in the darkness.

I shut my eyes and groaned. I was sick of seeing lights and faces; of hearing noises in the night and telling myself, over and over, that they were not real.

I clenched the matches, pressed my lips together and forced myself to pull one out. I opened my eyes as wide as I could, took in a lungful of that foul air, and struck the match, ready for whatever that cavern had in store.

The tip caught fire, and when the light filled the cavern, my fear materialised as a wave of icy pins and needles.

There they were, the glinting eyes, staring straight into mine with reckless bravery, and underneath them a set of bent, stained teeth, bared and ready to strike. Matted hair and layer upon layer of caked dirt obscured the actual features of that being.

It was a child – a feral child – bent on all fours like a crawling beast, and wrapped in murky rags tied together. I could not even tell whether the sad wretch was a boy or a girl.

The child hissed at me but would not come closer. It was like standing before a small predator, measuring each other's strength.

I held my ground, but I still raised my hands and spoke slowly.

'I don't want to hurt you.'

The child hissed again, leapt in my direction and pretended to swipe at me, only to retreat immediately, retaking its previous spot.

I had a good look at the ground. Bones, rags, rotten vegetables and excrement. I felt so sorry for the poor creature I nearly wept. That child must have been left in a gutter at a very early age, perhaps by a shamed mother or a father who could no longer feed any more offspring.

'I need to leave,' I said after a gulp.

The child hissed again.

'I need to leave,' I repeated, signalling upwards.

The child stared at me suspiciously. Surely I was not the first grown-up to meander down here, and this child had clearly learned to fear us. When I thought of the vulgar crowd now gathered at Calton Hill, eager to watch a woman die, themselves only a shade removed from the beasts of the field, I could not help but despise the world above us.

Cautiously, I leaned towards the lantern.

The child hissed.

'I just need this to leave,' I said, moving ever so slowly. Fortunately, the child did not attempt to strike me. I picked up the lamp and inspected it. The front glass was shattered, but I could still use it. As soon as I lit it, the child growled and recoiled in a corner of the small cavern.

I kept my eyes on the poor creature as I withdrew. I'd come back with help, but right now I must find my way out.

However, as soon as I set foot on the ascending rubble, I had another stupid idea. Stupid indeed, but it would not hurt to try. I turned back gingerly, being careful not to shed the light straight into the child's eyes. They were still fixed on me.

The words sounded silly in my mind, even sillier when I said them.

'Have you ever . . . met a witch?'

The creature looked up and hissed again. For a moment nothing happened, and I was about to leave when something came out of the child's mouth.

'Witch . . .'

The syllable was perfectly clear.

'Yes, a witch!' I said. 'Did one ever live here?'

'Witch . . .'

I waited, beginning to fear the child was just repeating my word, but then the little, soiled hands began to crawl in my direction, and then past me. The child's eyes remained on me, watchful, still not trusting me.

And then the child sprinted away, so fast I startled, and then I pursued.

I heard the throaty groans, echoing along the passages and tunnels as I ran. I could not see the child anymore; I had only my ears to guide me in that maze. I lost track of the turns, my full attention set on not losing the poor creature. Soon I was well and truly lost, the child's voice fading in the distance.

'Damn!' I cried, cursing myself. I tripped and nearly fell on my face. I would never get out of there in time; I would not even get a chance to show the evidence. Scarce as it was, it might have made a difference!

'Witch . . .'

I lifted my chin. The voice had come from above. I raised the lantern and saw, level with my forehead, what must have been a window frame before the floor underneath had sunken. I rested the lantern up on that sill, and just as I pulled myself upwards, a pair of tiny, grubby hands snatched the light away.

'Oh, Lord!'

Clumsily, I managed to climb up the window and roll through it. I fell four feet down, my battered shoulder again hitting first, and panting and snorting I brought myself to my feet.

There was the child, clutching the lantern, and leaning over something obscured behind a pile of rubbish.

I gasped at the contents of that small chamber. It looked like an abandoned storeroom, with broken shelves, piles of smashed crates, and jars and demijohns of all shapes and sizes, many still intact. I had seen similar storerooms before.

'Witch . . .' the child murmured with a playful, yet terribly eerie smile.

I approached, already fearing what I'd find behind that debris.

'Oh, God!' I let out, covering my mouth.

The child had knelt down by a skeleton, caressing the brown skull as if it were a beloved pet. The bones lay amongst a bed of rags, as if that person had died in a bed made of straw which had rotted away a long time ago. Ghastly rags, torn and riddled with holes, still stuck to the bones. I could not help imagining what that bed must have looked like as it decomposed along with its owner.

This was the place; the shop from which Grannie Alice had obtained her supplies.

Those murky bones most likely had belonged to a witch.

A million questions came to my head: Had the child met that woman when she was alive? How had she died? Had someone missed her at all? Had people forgotten her when they boarded up this section of the close? Would people even know this was her dwelling? Perhaps she'd kept it secret, the better to run her dubious witchcraft business.

'Bible . . .'

The child startled me.

'Excuse me?'

The child kept petting the skull, but then put the lantern down and pointed at a corner of the chamber.

'Bible . . .'

And on top of a soiled crate I saw a small bundle of old books. I picked one up with utmost care. It was falling apart, the bindings crumbling in my fingers and the pages curled after years in the damp. I brought it close to the lantern and saw that the small tome was packed with handwriting and diagrams of plants I had never seen. It was a witchcraft book.

The one underneath had star maps. The next one was written in crude symbols that reminded me of ancient runes. I did recognise numbers, however, and what looked like lists of ingredients in a recipe book.

'These are no Bibles . . .' I mumbled.

'Bibles . . .' the child repeated.

The last book was the widest and thickest. Also the one that appeared to be the newest.

'Accounts!' I cried, and in my excitement I nearly ripped the first pages off. 'This is a ledger!'

I looked for the dates that would match Alice's receipt, and for a moment I lost track of the precious time I had left.

'Here it is,' I said, the child smiling at my contagious excitement. 'Mrs Alice Shaw . . . fifteen pounds . . .' and I panted before I could read the entry out loud. *'Pharaoh's serpent!'*

I leant against the wall, everything finally making sense.

'This also explains the photographs! The hand of Satan! Leonora did not fake it! It did happen!' I closed the ledger carefully. 'Candles! Are there any candles here?'

The child stared blankly at me.

I pointed at the lantern.

'Light. Fire. Things to make fire.'

The child did not move, and I began rummaging through the crates and shelves, desperately looking for the last piece of evidence.

I did find them, at the bottom of a crate that fell apart as soon as I touched it – a bunch of candles I instantly recognised. I snapped one in half and found exactly what I expected. I would have yelled in triumph, but then St Giles's bells chimed again, sounding louder and clearer than before. The walls vibrated once more, dust falling from the shelves I'd disturbed.

And my heart jumped.

It was seven thirty.

I had half an hour left.

49

Katerina heard the bells too, just as the priest placed a small Orthodox cross around her neck. It was a humble pendant made of brass, but she thanked him as if it were the most precious gift.

Streaks of incense floated around the cell as the towering Greek man prayed for her. His chanting, low and soothing, was the one thing that kept Nine-Nails from thrashing everything in the room.

He stood by the door, finding it difficult to breathe, and not because of the dense air. Each inhalation threatened to become a sob, so he clenched his fists and bit his lips. He had to stay firm; he had to do it for Katerina. There would be plenty of time to lament.

Someone rapped gently at the door and they all startled.

It was time to go.

'*Do you have them?*' I spluttered as I stormed into the morgue. 'Any results?'

Reed gasped when he saw me completely caked in dust, my sleeves torn and my shoes smeared with mud and other filth.

'No, but— Oh, inspector, where have you—?'

'Never mind!'

And I ran back to the office, Reed right behind me.

'But the hue of all the samples is looking promising. I can scribble you a note. The hangman might— Oh dear Lord! What happened here?'

He was staring at the hole in the wall, the piles of brick and rubble, and the coy child peeping from the shadows.

'Write me the damn note!' I snapped. 'But quickly!'

I saw a jute sack on McGray's desk and dropped the contents on the floor – rotten leftovers of one of his lunches. I shoved in the crumbling ledger, all the candles, the receipt and Leonora's journal. I felt my movements had never been so slow or clumsy, my pounding heart reverberating throughout my body. I climbed the stairs two at a time, crashing into a couple of officers, but I had no time to stop.

Reed chased me along the corridors, paper in hand, writing the note as he moved. He managed to sign it just as I reached the front courtyard.

'Here,' he said, handing me the paper, and I shoved it into the sack without even glancing at it.

I ran towards Philippa and jumped on the mount before she had a chance to react.

'*If you make but the slightest fuss—!*'

Reed untied her with shaking hands and I spurred her at once, darting into the Royal Mile still dragging the tether.

'Good luck!' Reed shouted, his voice already faint in the distance.

The gallows awaited under the light rain, the hangman and a couple of assistants ready at their posts. Around it there was only a small retinue of guards, advocates and selected witnesses, all dressed in black. The jail's physician was amongst them, present to certify that the sentence was carried out fully. He stood next to Mr Reynolds, the undertaker, who had the coffin ready to receive Katerina – if possible, he'd do so within minutes of her being pronounced dead. Last in the line was George Pratt, who had managed to attend as a representative of the prosecutor's office. He smiled scornfully, as if intent on showing off his gold tooth.

Despite the few attendants, there was an unexpected uproar when the first guards stepped out of the main building. Those were the voices of the other prisoners, crammed against their barred windows, and the crowd that watched from the hill. They all burst in savage cries, as if about to witness an illegal dog fight. And their shouting roused the voices of all the people gathered on the other side of the jail's gates.

Their screaming went wild when Katerina emerged, manacled and sporting her finest dress and lace veil, both dyed in black. She walked impassively, her chin slightly raised, her chest rising and falling as she took long, deep breaths. To the disappointment of the crowd, she looked composed and dignified.

Behind her came the Greek priest, tall and imposing, swinging a censer and chanting prayers. His vestments, bright purple and embroidered in gold with byzantine motifs, caught everybody's eye and received the roughest abuse. Some of the prisoners even spat at him, as though he were a strange demon from a faraway land, living proof of Katerina's wickedness.

Nine-Nails and Mary came last, she clung onto his arm, her eyes red, and tears flowing down her cheeks.

They stopped a few yards from the gibbet, and Katerina stared at the swaying noose, which moved gently under the cold wind.

The jail's warden, a flabby middle-aged man, began reading the sentence. He spoke in a hurry, for the rain was starting to drip down his forehead.

*

Philippa galloped frantically across the Royal Mile, dodging carts and pedestrians. A barrow emerged from one of the side streets, right in front of us, and the driver hollered as we dived in his direction.

Philippa rose on her hind legs, neighing wildly, and I had to cling to her neck not to slide off the saddle. She fell back on all fours, only just avoiding the other horses, and even as she stumbled I had to spur her again.

We turned left on North Bridge, so fast I felt the jute sack swinging in an arc and slipping from my grip.

I clenched it as we crossed the bridge, galloping above the noisy railways. A train moved right underneath the road, and when its columns of black smoke dissipated, the towers of Calton Hill Jail emerged in the distance. They had never looked so unreachable.

Katerina squeezed McGray's hands in hers and gave them one last motherly kiss. He could not contain his tears anymore but rushed to wipe them with his sleeve. Pratt's smile widened a little.

'I'm so sorry,' McGray mumbled.

Katerina took a little step closer and stood on tiptoes. It looked as though she was going to kiss him on the cheek, but instead she whispered.

'Your sister . . . she still loves you.'

McGray startled at that, and Katerina smiled.

'There is a little corner, deep, deep in her mind, where she loves you so.'

At this point the hangman came to her, with the key to her manacles, and gently pulled her towards the platform.

Katerina gave one last squeeze to McGray, all too brief, and then walked away. She kept her misty eyes on him. 'She'll always love you. Remember that.'

She looked alternately at him and Mary as she climbed the wooden steps. She even smiled at George Pratt when the hangman unlocked the handcuffs.

'When the platform drops,' he told her in whispers, 'don't just let yourself go. Pull your weight down. That will help the fall break your neck. You'll die with very little pain. Otherwise you might hang there for a very long time.'

Katerina bowed her head. That was the one time she trembled.

The drizzle hit my eyes and face like tiny, icy needles, as Philippa crossed the sumptuous Waterloo Place at full speed.

Even from there I could see the people gathered on Calton Hill. I could see them wave in excitement, and the wind brought the sound of their heartless cheering. I felt a pang of fear, thinking I was too late. Right then, from behind me, the bells of St Giles' Cathedral chimed eight o'clock.

'Damn!' I grunted, just as Philippa followed the curve of the hill and I saw the jail's walls emerge before us.

But that was no relief. There was a thick crowd gathered by the gates, blocking the entire road, already crammed with carriages and carts attempting to pass.

I pulled the reins, jumped down and darted ahead as fast as I could.

'Let me through!' I shouted as soon as I reached the edge of the mob.

The bells went on, unforgiving.

The hangman withdrew Katerina's veil with utmost delicacy, almost as if she were a bride, and lay it on her shoulders, making sure it would not crease.

'Here, madam, please,' he said, showing the centre of the trapdoor and moving the noose aside so that Katerina could move into place.

She took a deep breath, stared at the sky and stepped ahead. She felt the hands of the hangman, surprisingly warm, as he took off the chain and crucifix.

'Would you prefer to keep it in your pocket?' he asked, folding the chain carefully.

She nodded, and as he inserted the crucifix into her sleeve, the hangman adjusted the noose around her neck.

'Move! Get out of the way!'

I shoved through the people around me, my body shaking with impotence. The gates were less than eight yards ahead, but in-between stood an indistinct mass of bodies crushed together like fish in a can. People could not have moved even if they'd wanted.

The hangman took a step back and made a respectful bow.

'Madam, forgive me for my sad duty.'

Katerina breathed long, deep and slow, as if feeling air through her lungs had become a sudden pleasure.

'Forgive me . . .' she stammered, 'for not tipping you . . .'

The man bowed and stepped back, just as the sound of the last chime faded away.

'*Let me through, dammit!*' I howled, tearing my throat. '*I have evidence!*'

I raised the sack above my head. A grubby hand grasped it and tried to snatch it, and I threw maddened punches in every direction.

A guard saw me then. I recognised the long scar on his face. Malcolm was his name. He too recognised me from the countless visits, and immediately tried to move in my direction, having to fight over every inch.

I pushed and kicked, past caring whom I hit.

Then I noticed the sudden silence. The bells had stopped. The cheering of the crowd rose steadily.

Katerina looked at Mary and McGray one last time, made a little nod, and then, gently, closed her eyes.

The noose was not even itchy.

People had lost all restraint. The crowd on the hill roared, demanding blood, and the sound of their clapping reverberated in my chest like a roll of drums.

I could see the guard in front of me, his freckles, even the beads of sweat on his upper lip. He stretched his arm in my direction. We were inches away, yet people would not move. They *couldn't* move.

I growled, brought a hand to my pocket, reaching for my gun. I went cold as I remembered I'd not carried a weapon. I had not carried one since—

I felt something; cold metal against my hand.

The butt of Harvey's derringer. The one I'd snatched from his trembling hand as he threatened me lying on the floor. I pulled it out in one desperate yank, praying it was loaded.

The gibbet's platform dropped. A split second before the shot.

Katerina heard it just as her feet slid down the wooden boards. She gasped, opened her eyes and looked up, finding nothing but the grey sky.

And then she fell into the void.

50

The crowd parted in front of me, as if the shot had been an invisible shockwave. I ran forwards, hearing their panicked cries but also the commotion that came from within the jail and the hill behind me.

A male, drunken voice boomed around, brought by the wind seemingly from all directions.

'*She's dead!*'

There were cheers all around me. People clapped and whistled.

My entire body went numb, as if my blood had instantly drained from my limbs, and I nearly stumbled, but then Malcolm grabbed me by the arm and pulled me forwards.

Another guard opened a side door, just enough to let us in, and I ran into the esplanade, where I wailed in horror.

Katerina was hanging by the neck, squirming like a worm on a hook, gagging in agony and grasping the rope around her neck. Her skin was turning purple.

'*Stop!*' I hollered, dashing in her direction.

A guard blocked my way, grabbed me by the waist and pulled me backwards. I jerked desperately, my eyes fixed on the dying woman, not even hearing the shouts from the crowd. I saw her tender neck, the skin beginning to tear, and suddenly my entire body shook.

I was in the Highlands again, witnessing someone's death whilst being pulled backwards by unyielding hands.

'*I have evidence!*' I screamed. '*I have—!*'

Someone pulled me from the guard and I had a fleeting glance of McGray hitting him with the butt of his gun.

I had no time to think or look. I hurled myself in Katerina's direction. In her despair she kicked me, and I had to drop the bag and clasp her legs with all my might. She gagged and retched as I struggled to place her calves on my shoulder. Mary ran to me and helped me push upwards.

Only then did I see McGray embroiled in a fist fight with the two nearest guards. Another two men came to us and tried to pull Mary away.

'*She's innocent!*' I growled, my voice even louder than Mary's shrieks. 'I can prove it!'

A giant hand threw a blow on the guards' arms, freeing Mary, and then the poor gaolers flew backwards, pulled by the back of their collars by the world's strongest arms.

'*You?*' I panted.

It had been the priest.

The man planted himself in front of us, arms outstretched, and we finally managed to get a proper hold of Katerina.

There was a gunshot then, and I heard McGray's voice.

'*Och, stop it, youse idiots!* Ye, pick that up!'

Katerina stopped jerking. I looked up, fearing the worst, but then I heard her cough and gulp.

I barely managed a deep breath, and then peeped over the priest's shoulder.

McGray was pointing at the guards and witnesses with his gun. The man I recognised as the hangman had just picked up the jute sack. Behind them stood . . .

'This is outrageous!' Pratt shouted. 'Move away! You're just prolonging that whore's agony!'

'Whore yer mother!' McGray snapped. 'The dandy says he has evidence.'

'The jury have spoken! *She has been sentenced!*'

I felt my knees trembling. 'I can explain!' I groaned. 'There's evidence in that bag!'

'A few candles?' the hangman asked, rummaging through the contents.

'I can ex—' I faltered, nearly falling on my knees, and McGray had to rush and help me.

'Ye took yer fucking time!' he hissed.

'Why, you are welcome!'

'I'll take it from here, ye try and reason with those sods.'

In one swift movement he pulled Katerina's feet, and immediately supported them on his very broad shoulder, all the while pointing his gun at the guards.

I rubbed and patted my face, trying to catch my breath as swiftly as possible. The rain was falling harder, but it helped me reawaken. I heard the booing from the hill and the jail, and the scornful screams demanding death.

'Let go of that woman!' Pratt spat. 'She has been tried!'

'This proves she is innocent!' I cried, snatching the bag from the hangman's hands.

'Does it?' said a fat man, whom I recognised as the jail's warden.

The hangman, whose voice was surprisingly civilised given his profession, came closer. 'If that is true, I cannot proceed with the execution. However . . .' he glanced at Katerina, still suspended in the air and coughing from the depths of her throat, 'I doubt you can convince us with candles.'

'Step back and I will show you,' I said.

Pratt shook his head, splattering rain like a bulldog. '*I refuse to*—!'

'*Do what he says, ye Pratt!*' McGray cried and shot at the skies.

The sound silenced the crowds, and the hangman took the chance to push Pratt and the jail's warden away.

'We'll give them a chance,' he concluded.

I pulled out one of the candles I'd snapped in half, its wick surrounded by a thin layer of powder much whiter than the wax itself. I stuck the stub in-between a crack on the flagstones, so that it stood upright.

'Lord, I hope this damn thing works,' I mumbled. I searched frantically in my pockets, but found nothing. I looked up, feeling flustered. 'Does . . . sorry, does anybody have a match?'

'Jesus!' McGray snapped.

Malcolm threw me a box.

I struck the match, protecting it from the rain with my hand, and drew it closer to the candle stub. I had to wait until some of the wax melted, before the actual wick caught fire. All the while I stretched my arms, holding my breath and praying for the damn thing to ignite.

It finally did and I jumped backwards.

We all stared at the tiny flame, watching it grow and flicker in the soft wind. We waited in absolute silence. Even the crowd had quietened.

Nothing was happening.

I gulped, and a moment later saw Pratt striding towards the gibbet.

'Very well, you had your—'

'Look, look!' the warden shouted.

There was a spark, and then something moved.

It was a tiny shape beginning to protrude from the wick. At first it looked like an earthworm emerging from disturbed soil, the same slithering, unsettling movements. And then it grew and ascended, as people around gasped.

The shape became thicker; a repulsive form that swirled and twisted. It was as if the dry skin shed by a serpent had been suddenly awakened by a fakir and it now moved upwards in some sort of enchantment.

A second snake emerged, much thinner and swirling in faster movements, coiling around the first one. The mass became too heavy; it broke and fell on the ground, where it went on growing, swelling and twirling, moving like a living thing that crawled towards our feet.

'Look!' someone else shouted, and our eyes went back to the candle.

More and more worm-like masses kept erupting from it, twisting like a mass of tangled snakes materialising from the bluish fire. The tip of a serpent caught fire, and side-snakes grew from the spot like ghastly tentacles. I pictured the same things sprouting at the séance, looking like a hand from a certain angle.

We all watched the spectacle unfurl, mesmerised, until . . .

'*Put that out!*' the warden screeched.

A moment later, just as the second knot of serpents broke and fell, one of the guards came with a bucket and threw water on the candle.

As the ghastly residue cooled down, white vapours hissed and ascended lazily to the sky, people instinctively stepping backwards.

All faces were pale, all mouths open, and for an eerie moment nobody could utter a word, until the warden rose a trembling finger, pointing at Katerina.

'She's a witch!'

I slapped my forehead. 'Are you really so stupid? It was the fumes! The fumes these candles release that killed those people!'

The hangman was the first one to come forwards. He knelt down to inspect the now crumbling snakes. They were as delicate as tobacco ashes; no wonder we'd found nothing at the Grenvilles' table, where the candles' wax had smothered them.

'I would not touch them if I were you,' I said. 'They are as poisonous as the fumes. They are lethal in a confined space.'

'Like the séance room,' the hangman said. 'And these look like—'

'The fingers on the photograph that leaked to the newspapers,' McGray said. Even then, Katerina holding on for dear life, there was a slight note of disappointment in his voice.

'And these documents,' I said, brandishing the bag, 'demonstrate that Madame Katerina did not supply these candles.'

'Let me see that nonsense!' Pratt demanded, but I pulled the bag away.

'We should do that inside. The rain will spoil what little is left of these papers. In the meantime, I suggest you release that poor woman.'

I looked at her then. She was just regaining colour, and her green eyes, misted with tears, watched me with unspeakable gratitude.

McGray came to me, squeezed my shoulder and got close to whisper something in my ear. I was expecting an uncomfortable display of emotion, but instead—

'Have ye noticed yer still in yer nighties?'

51

I sighed, lounging in the armchair as the rain battered the window at Trevelyan's office.

He'd made me wait for a while already, but I was in no rush; my only other engagement was a much-needed visit to the tailor – the jacket Layton had hurriedly passed me had turned out to be my best merino wool one, and Katerina had very kindly offered to replace it.

When Trevelyan walked in, I made to stand up.

'At ease, inspector,' he said, taking his own chair. He saw the thin file I'd lay there. 'Is this your report?'

'Indeed, sir.'

'Good. I managed to fix an emergency appointment with the Court of Appeals. I am afraid it is in twenty minutes, so you will have to brief me.'

'Oh, of course, but I will need to go back to the very start.'

'Go on,' he prompted, interlacing hands and looking at me with undivided attention.

'It all began in the sixties. Colonel Grenville, back then a captain, was posted in Southern Africa. He did a decent job there, but nothing as grand as he'd have people believe. Right before he was dispatched back to Britain, the gold rush of Bakalanga began.'

'Baka—?'

'It is now the Bechuanaland Protectorate.' I'd rehearsed the name in my head all morning.

Trevelyan lifted his eyebrows. I might as well have said Brobdingnag. 'Go on.'

'The price of the mining land had naturally gone sky high and was increasing by the day. Still a young man, the then captain did not have the capital to buy a plot himself, so he resorted to his distant cousin, Alice.'

'The now infamous Grannie Alice?'

'Yes, sir. One of her ancestors had lived in Africa very briefly, and the colonel wanted to use that to forge claim on a very convenient plot. I gather Alice initially refused his proposals, but the scheme must have been championed by her second husband, Mr Hector Shaw.

'The man agreed to invest substantial amounts of money on the enterprise. He might have been influenced by the still fresh news of men becoming instant millionaires in California and British Columbia. Mr Shaw provided not only the capital, but also forced his son Richard to travel there, as well as his stepson William Willberg, and his stepdaughter's husband, one John Fox.'

'Walter Fox's father?' Trevelyan asked. I did not like the way his eyebrow was pulling upwards.

'Yes, sir.'

'We'll come back to him in a moment. Go on.'

'It is not difficult to imagine Alice's dismay. Two of her sons and her son-in-law dispatched to the furthest end of the African continent to dig gold. And all this happened whilst her eldest daughter, Prudence, was with child. Alice herself had helped her become pregnant . . . aided with – well, she fancied it was witchcraft. She sourced all her materials from a hidden shop in the depths of Mary King's Close.'

Trevelyan was leafing through the report. 'You say here that sections of the close have been sealed off along the decades.'

'Indeed, sir. I finally have had time to look into it. At some point the place was well-known as a black market hub; it was an ideal lair. There are a few working shops there even today, but as the years passed the supports have weakened. Entire sections have collapsed; some others have been closed off.'

Trevelyan nodded. 'So, Alice's daughter was pregnant, while effectively all her sons but one went away to dig gold. What about the other one? Peter Willberg.'

'The late Mr Willberg remained in Britain to manage the gold sales and the legal matters. All transactions were made under his name, in case the fraudulent means Mr Shaw used to seize the mine were ever discovered.

'Colonel Grenville perhaps did not trust that the Shaws and Willbergs would share the profits with him. He felt entitled to it; after all, the mining business had been his idea. He secured this by marrying Alice's granddaughter, even though Martha was only sixteen back then. He was thirty-one.'

'When did things begin to go off track?'

'Within a few months, so shortly after their wedding. Mining conditions were gruelling. Workers were not as cheap and as readily available as the family had taken for granted, and the ones they could afford began to die like flies. Richard, William and John ended up doing much of the work themselves. *Real* mining work.'

'You devote an entire page to the gold extraction process. Summarise it to me in a way that will not try the judges' patience.'

I sighed. 'First, the raw gold ore is finely crushed and passed over mercury. Only the gold attaches to it, so the sand and rock can be easily washed away. You end up with an amalgam of mercury and gold. The mercury is then boiled away, as it vaporises at much lower temperatures than gold. This leaves a residue that is almost pure gold . . . And, of course, a cloud of one of the most poisonous vapours known to man.'

Trevelyan annotated this in the margin. 'Go on.'

'The original plan was to reinvest all initial profits; hire more workers and so on. Instead, the family spent the money in trivialities, such as Martha's engagement receptions and Peter Willberg's drinking.

'After extracting and shipping a very respectable amount of gold, the *three diggers* – as Inspector McGray and I nicknamed them – telegrammed the family, threatening to return unless they were sent money, workers and supplies.

'I believe the old Mr Shaw was about to give in, but the colonel, his wife Martha, her mother Gertrude and Peter Willberg were appalled. They already had ambitious plans for their futures, all fuelled with African gold. They insisted the scheme went on. Grannie Alice apparently objected, not only thinking of the welfare of her sons but also of the workers they were sending to their early graves. In the end, however, she did nothing to stop the operation. And she could have, since the mine was under her name.

'Soon after, John Fox was killed in the mine. Prudence, his wife, was heavily pregnant by this point. The news caused a miscarriage and she did not survive for long. At the same time Alice's two sons became seriously ill, so they attempted to return to Britain. Apparently, they left everything behind; gold nuggets, tools, clothing, everything. Sadly, only William survived the journey. Richard, Alice's youngest son and apparently her pride and joy, died on the way. William himself would not survive much longer. He barely managed to meet his mother and give her a letter from her poor Richard.'

'And their illness was related to their work on the mines, I imagine.'

'Indeed. They probably took some measures, but they were gradually poisoned from the mercury they used to process the family gold.'

'Mercury . . .' Trevelyan mused. 'This begins to fit in nicely. Continue.'

'Exactly thirteen years after the deaths, Grannie Alice decided to host a séance, allegedly to try to commune with her dead children.'

'Thirteen years later? Does that have some mystic meaning?'

'Inspector McGray says it is very likely. *The six* also died on the thirteenth of September, which happened to be a Friday.'

'Don't jump ahead. Go back to that séance. Was it . . .' he quoted my report, 'in 1882?'

'Yes. With the exception of Bertrand and Leonora, Alice invited the very same people who died six weeks ago.'

Trevelyan looked up, astounded. 'Did she? To . . . impart justice?'

'There is no other explanation. Those were the people she held responsible for the deaths of the three diggers, and also countless African workers. Throughout those thirteen years she withheld the deeds to the mine, so she lured her relatives to the séance, telling them she'd finally surrender the documents, perhaps after communing with the dead diggers.

'She bought the "special" candles from her usual witch at Mary King's Close.'

'The stubs you burned in front of the executioners?'

'Indeed.'

'Now, this is what the judges will be keenest to know. What was that?'

I sighed, for my little act at the jail's esplanade had given me a reputation. Many prisoners still believed I had performed witchcraft, and the rumours had travelled swiftly.

'In the black market it is known as *Pharaoh's Serpent*. It is a mercury and cyanide compound.'

Trevelyan whistled. 'Mercury *and* cyanide?'

'Indeed; not something your regular beeswax dealer would supply, but something that has been known for centuries. Rumour has it the French monarchs used it as their poison of choice in the middle ages.

'On closer inspection, only a section of the candles contained Pharaoh's Serpent. The rest of the wick was simply daubed with other mercuric salts. I believe it might have been some sort of . . . very well-designed timer.'

'Timer?'

'Yes. The candles had to burn for a while before the fire ignited the Pharaoh's Serpent powder, all the while poisoning the surrounding air. It is as if the purpose was to have the serpents – later mistaken for the "hand of Satan" – appear just as the victims expired.'

'Yet the one you burned at the esplanade . . .?'

'I had snapped it in half, so the Pharaoh's Serpent was instantly exposed.'

'I see. So, Alice planned to murder her guilty kinfolks with the very substance that had killed her two sons and caused the demise of her daughter.'

'Precisely. I cannot tell whether she planned to die along with them, but it is very likely. As I said, she must have been riddled with remorse.'

'But that séance never took place?'

'No. Alice, it turned out, would die the day before.'

'How?'

'The family say she went for a walk and simply collapsed on the street.'

Trevelyan raised his chin. 'That sounds . . . suspicious to say the least.'

'Indeed, sir, but that happened seven years ago and most of the people who could have been involved are now dead. Besides, Alice was already seventy-six; a ripe old age, even in our times of laudanum and advanced medicine. Perhaps the strain of her plan proved too much for her.'

Trevelyan let out a tired breath. 'We'll have to leave that mystery for another time. Now tell me about the last séance. How did it come to happen?'

'It was unwittingly triggered by . . . ehem . . . Walter Fox.'

Trevelyan's lips tensed like never before. 'Speaking of him . . . He is making quite a bit of a fuss.'

'*Is he?*' I asked, my tone a little too high-pitched. I'd been expecting to hear that sort of news at some point.

'He came to us this morning. He was assailed last night. The thugs, however, took nothing.'

'Nothing? How very odd.'

'Indeed. They did, on the other hand . . . break both his knees.'

'*Did they?* How uncivilised.'

'Inspector Frey, your name was mentioned.'

I chose my words very carefully.

'I can assure you, even under oath, that *I* had nothing to do with it.' I leaned forwards, before Trevelyan could enquire further. 'And those who might have, as you can imagine, would have ensured I knew nothing about it beforehand.'

Strictly speaking I was not lying. When explaining to Nine-Nails and Katerina how I'd unravelled the truth about the poisoning, I'd also told them about Walter's assault. They said nothing then, but exchanged conspiratorial looks. Now I saw the results.

Trevelyan only sighed, his lips tense, and moved on. 'How did Walter trigger the séance?'

'He built up a thriving business as a middle-man in the jewellery and precious metals market. Last year he travelled to

Francistown, where the family's mine was located. The place has grown exponentially in the past few years, as you can imagine. It is now at the core of that line of business.

'Walter, of course, visited the mine, expecting to see an abandoned facility to which he could lay claim. Instead, he found that another Scottish company had already settled there, with forged deeds and documents too, and was making eye-watering profits. That company, I should add, had the good sense to use decent equipment and hire more skilled workers; not out of the goodness of their hearts, but to ensure the life of their business.

'Fox, as you can imagine, was incensed. The only way to prove that the mine had belonged to them was to find the old deeds and take the case to the local courts.'

'And they thought Grannie Alice would rise from the grave to tell them?'

'Yes. That only shows how desperate they were. Alice's house had been stripped and searched. The séance was their last hope, all instigated by Miss Leonora Shaw, who had an unhealthy interest in necromancy. She believed she and Grannie Alice had . . . *special* faculties.'

'And that is why she was an assiduous client of Katerina Dragnea?'

'Yes.'

Trevelyan went to the last page of the report. 'I am satisfied that the gypsy didn't supply or even come to touch the poisoned candles . . . Those documents you found are clear enough. But the question remains. How did she survive?'

'Two reasons, from what I can gather now. Firstly, she was not exposed to the vapours for as long as the others. She told Miss Leonora to "cleanse" the parlour with those candles for a few hours before the session.'

'And the second?'

I sighed. That was a tad more difficult to explain. 'Katerina claims she could . . .' I cleared my throat, '*feel* late Alice's anger, so she carried out some rituals to protect herself. Those included covering her face with a veil dampened in herbs and oils. That probably gave her some additional protection.'

'So. . . her rituals did save her?'

I grunted. 'Fortuitously, yes. Although Inspector McGray has other ideas.'

'Which are?'

I shifted in my seat. 'Sir, you can imagine them.'

'Indulge me, inspector.'

I sighed. 'He claims that Grannie Alice *did* rise from the grave. That this series of coincidences are in fact the result of her invisible hand. That the six deaths are her revenge from the other world.

'McGray even claims that Mrs Cobbold was not harmed because she and Alice reconciled just before her death. That Miss Leonora was punished for her disrespect to the souls of the dead. And, for lack of a better explanation, that Bertrand was punished for his lack of character.'

An uncomfortable silence fell in the room, broken only by the dull drumming of the rain.

Trevelyan stared at me, his eyebrow rising very slowly as he pondered on my statement. At last he closed the file.

'I cannot mention that to the judges, can I?'

Epilogue

Katerina's reputation had been soiled forever.

There was public outrage when she was released, and the way the story was told by the press did not help at all. To add insult to injury, the London *Times* had openly mocked the Scottish High Court in a lengthy column, rubbing in their faces that the very honourable William Frey of Chancery Lane had been right all along.

Katerina's establishment was pillaged a few days later, and she immediately decided it was time for a fresh start.

We met her at Caledonian Station to bid farewell. Amidst the icy November winds, the station was like a steaming teapot, noisy and crowded. We found Katerina standing by a small pile of trunks, watching as a station worker loaded them onto the train. I had expected to see a band of reporters stalking her, but the woman was unrecognisable: she was wrapped in a fine coat, wearing a surprisingly tasteful hat decked with a garland of tiny velvet roses. Her dress had a high neck, buttoned all the way up, surely to conceal the scars from the noose.

She pulled a gloved hand out of her bearskin handlebar and waved at us.

'I'm surprised,' she said, nodding at her luggage, 'how small my life seems packed up in trunks.'

'Ha!' McGray let out. 'If only Percy here could say the same.'

I gave Katerina an approving look. 'That is a nice change of attire.'

She preened a little. 'You'll be surprised how rich I am, now that I sold the divination room and chased all my debtors.'

'Ye didnae break any legs, I hope!'

Katerina cackled. 'Oh, no. I promised myself I wouldn't do it again. Not after I sent that lad to—'

I raised a hand. 'Do not repeat it, please. That was an unnecessary—'

'Och, she did it to help ye, Percy! I'm only sorry I couldnae take care o' the carroty sod myself.'

Katerina had a wicked smile.

'What?' I asked.

'It was a pleasure to take care of that ratbag. He attacked you like a damn coward! But . . . that's not the one I meant just now.'

'Oh, please, do not tell me that—'

She rummaged through her little game bag, produced something tiny and put it in McGray's hand.

'This is for you, my boy.'

It was Pratt's tiny gold tooth.

I barely saw it, for he swiftly closed his hand around it and shoved it in his pocket.

'Och, Katerina, ye should nae—!'

But he was fooling nobody. He was as delighted as her.

'I hear he's wearing a lead one now,' she said with a wink. 'Nobody to bribe him with gold anymore.' Then we heard the sharp steam whistle. 'That's me,' and she walked proudly to her first-class compartment.

McGray opened the door and helped her step in. 'Going to see yer wee Michael?'

'Yes, but not right away. I'll visit him as soon as these fade,' and she pulled down the tight collar less than an inch. The skin was still blackened, even after all this time. 'And I need to settle down first.'

She offered me a hand and shook mine with true affection.

'Thank you – Frey. Thank you *very* much. I will never forget what you did for me.'

She settled on the cushioned seat, struggling a little with the frills of her skirts, and smiled at us as McGray closed the door. She then perched on the windowsill.

'If you two ever need something . . .' she chuckled, 'I shall know!'

The train set in motion then, and we saw the infamous, jubilant Madame Katerina be taken away to her new life in England.

'Durham, she said?' I asked.

'That's where her son lives. I don't think she'll settle there.' He gave me an impish look. 'Why? Ye want another candlelit dinner?'

'She is not that fortunate.'

McGray laughed, crossed his arms and watched the train move on. He let out a long sigh.

'What did she tell ye?'

'Excuse me?'

'The woman thought she was going to die. She must've told ye one last prophecy.'

He was right, and I saw no point in hiding it. 'Something nice and vague, as usual. She said I'd be happy.'

McGray looked down, kicking the dust on the platform.

'Why? Did she tell you something too?'

He twisted his mouth. 'She said there's a wee part of Pansy's mind that still loves me . . .'

I was expecting him to say more, but he simply raised his chin, his eyes on the railways. He noticed my puzzled look

407

'That's it. That's all she said.' He shook his head. 'I ken what it means.'

I knew what he was going to say. No wonder it took him a moment to let it out.

'Pansy will never be cured.'

The sentence lingered in the air, the racket of the station suddenly sounding dull.

'Katerina has been wrong before,' I said, and McGray simply sneered. 'Nine-Nails, she could not even predict her own death! How amateurish is that for someone who boasts having *the eye!*'

At least that made him smile a little.

'I better go, Frey. I need to apologise to Clouston. And pay him. I made a right mess o' his study. See ye later for a dram?'

'Yes. I will meet you in a few hours. I still have to arrange the orphanage for the "Mary King" girl.'

'That creature was a girl?'

'Yes. Underneath all that grime. And as soon as that is sorted, I have to see that they release Holt.'

'They're letting the weasel out?'

'Yes, but with a hefty fine. Do you mind if I give him that gold tooth?'

McGray begrudgingly agreed.

'Some sods are so lucky . . .'

It was the first time I saw Eliza Shaw in a proper dress. However, she looked weaker and paler than ever when she received me. Her parlour was crammed with boxes and trunks ready to be taken away.

'Are you moving, ma'am?' I asked as I dodged the luggage.

'We're selling the house, inspector.'

'And you are vacating the place already? It must have been a very quick sale.'

'Yes. The good Lady Anne heard of our misfortunes. She came personally and made us a very generous offer.'

I could not help shaking my head. Lady Glass had most likely been preying on their property for a while, and her 'generous offer' was, surely, nowhere near the house's real value.

Mrs Shaw read my expression. She cast me a reproachful look as we sat in her small parlour. It looked like they were not taking the furniture with them.

'Don't twist your mouth like that, sir,' she said. 'Lady Anne is a pious woman. We needed the sale. We couldn't even have afforded to heat the house this winter.'

'I am so sorry to hear that.'

Mrs Shaw looked as if about to cry. Fortunately her maid brought in a tea service, and the simple task of pouring the brew seemed to calm her down.

'It's all right,' she mumbled. 'We are not the first family to fall from grace.' She cleared her throat. 'What can I do for you, inspector? I thought the case was closed.'

There was a clear hint of resentment in her voice.

'Indeed, ma'am. I only came to give you this . . .'

I searched in my breast pocket and pulled out Leonora's gold nugget. I placed it on the tray, next to the sugar bowl.

Mrs Shaw stared at it in confusion.

'What . . . what is that?'

'You must recognise it, ma'am. Miss Leonora wore it all the time, did she not?'

'Well . . . yes. I meant to say . . . why did you bring it here? If anyone should have this it would be Walter Fox.'

I sat back after refusing the teacup she offered.

'I had another person in mind. Mr Holt.'

Mrs Shaw twitched. 'Grenville's valet?'

'Yes. Were you aware of their liaison?'

The woman slightly shook her head, but then had the good sense to tell the truth.

'Leonora mentioned it once. I kept it quiet for her reputation's sake. You'll understand. If I didn't mention it, it was because it had nothing to do with her death.'

'Indeed I do. And indeed it did not, however . . .'

From the same pocket I pulled out a few torn sheets which Mrs Shaw seemed to identify at once.

'What is that?' she asked nonetheless.

'Sheets from Miss Leonora's journal,' I said, displaying them on the table. 'Mr Holt has been letting the truth out . . . in trickles. He only just told me that Miss Leonora tore these pages out and gave them to him on the day of the séance.'

Mrs Shaw gulped at once. 'Does she . . . does she mention their affair?'

'Indeed, ma'am, and in torrid language. That is the reason she gave them to him.'

She forced a nervous smile. 'What . . . I mean, why are you telling me this?'

For a moment I looked at her in silence, seeing how her anxiety grew.

'I think you know, ma'am.'

The woman tightened her hands around her teacup. 'I'm afraid I don't.'

I flipped the first page of the lot.

'Miss Leonora wrote on both sides of the sheets. When she tore out her musings on carnal love, she also tore out the entry of the day before. When she was here.'

'She was—?'

'She came to see you. To thank you for your *advice*.'

'She did not—'

'You refused to see her, ma'am. Miss Leonora says that you asked your maid to send her away. She *heard* you give the instruction, and she also says how intriguing your behaviour was. Especially after you'd been so kind to her in the previous month.'

Her lips quivered.

'I . . . I was ill. I could not receive her.'

'Most unfortunate. Miss Leonora wrote she regretted not being able to thank you for not throwing away . . . Grannie Alice's possessions.'

The cup began to rattle in the saucer, and Mrs Shaw had to put it down.

'The next thing,' I said, 'I've had to deduce myself. Upon Alice's death the family would have given away her belongings. You and your sons were struggling, so perhaps the Grenvilles thought you'd appreciate the items. Say . . . a few old perfume bottles, a silver hairbrush . . . a . . . box of old candles?'

There was a deep silence, Mrs Shaw slowly clenching the folds of her dress, almost digging her nails into her legs.

'Those candles were in your possession,' I went on. 'They were in your hands for a long time, along with other belongings. You must have gone through them. You must have found in them evidence of what the candles contained; evidence of Alice's intentions.' Mrs Shaw looked down, unable to face me. 'You know of which intentions I speak, do you not?'

Mrs Shaw shook her head, a first huge tear rolling down her cheek.

'You were not connected to any of the victims – the *intended* victims, I mean. Who would have died that night? Your father-in-law? Your sister-in-law and her daughter? The even more distant Willbergs and the colonel? You did not share blood with any of them, but you did hold them responsible for your husband's demise.'

She gulped again, the veins on her clenched hands popping out.

'You instigated the séance,' I said. 'Walter's actions may have led to it, but it must have been you who suggested it. And then you had to distance yourself from it. You knew you could not be seen with Miss Leonora just before she died; it would only invite suspicion.

'Sadly, by doing so, you did not hear of the change of plans. You did not know about the change of location, which meant Mrs Cobbold had to take the children away, which resulted in Bertrand having to take her place. You, ma'am, by attempting to avenge your husband, inadvertently caused the death of your own son.'

Mrs Shaw was struggling to breathe. She drew in short, throttled breaths, swallowing painfully. I thought she would choke to death before my eyes. I even leaned forwards to help her, but then she let out a hiss.

'Even if I had . . . you have no proof!'

'Indeed, I have nothing but my own deductions. Leonora never mentions the candles specifically in these pages. You could always argue she was referring to other items. It is a shame most of this happened so many years ago, and all the people who could have confirmed my suspicions are now dead.'

She gave me a wicked smile, far more disturbing than a twisted hand emerging from a flame. 'You cannot touch me with your *deductions*!'

I nodded, and just as soon stood up. 'I cannot, and I do not, intend to. Ma'am, you have punished yourself enough already . . . trying to play the judge.'

There was a moment of silence, and then, in one swift movement, Mrs Shaw brushed the tea service off the table. Silver, china and brew shattered and splattered mightily all over the nearest wall. The tea was still dripping on the patched-up carpet when I heard the metallic squeak of Harvey's wheelchair.

'What is it?' he barked. He looked at the mess and then glared at me. 'Is this man troubling you again?'

Mrs Shaw said nothing. She slouched miserably on her seat, pressing a handkerchief against her face.

'I was just leaving,' I said at once. I walked to the hall, put on my hat and buttoned my coat as I cast one last look at the sorry pair. 'Good luck to you both.'

And I meant it, for their future was most uncertain.

So many things in this case would remain forever so.

As I walked down the street, I recalled Alice's portrait; that firm, mysterious stare, surrounded by black cats and arcane symbols.

I already knew I could never silence that annoying shade of doubt, telling me that she had indeed orchestrated all this from the grave. Coincidences, I'd told myself again and again, or perhaps she'd left things – her notes, the candles – in strategic places, to be discovered even in the event of her death. A contrived explanation, McGray would say, albeit not impossible.

I also thought of the . . . treasure. Perhaps Alice had indeed told young Eddie where the deeds were. Perhaps there *had* been gold hidden somewhere. Perhaps the child had seen more than he'd admit during that séance. I pictured him at his grandmother's lawns in Kirkcaldy, digging up a little hole, retrieving shiny gold nuggets or a tiny chest with the coveted documents.

And I recalled that fleeting image of Uncle Maurice, conjured so vividly, right before my eyes, in that haunted room. Whether it had been the flicker of the candles, my own grief, or something else, I would never know for certain.

I shrugged, lit up a cigar and turned my attention to the tangible world around me; the muddy cobbles under my feet, the cold wind, the drizzle, the gloomy clouds . . . but also the snug shoes and the warm clothes that shielded me from it all. And I already savoured that drink I'd share with McGray later on.

It was good to be alive.

Author's note

Pharaoh's Serpent – mercuric thiocyanate – is one of the strangest substances in Christendom. Its combustion is not only disturbing to watch, but it also produces extremely poisonous vapours and solid residues, making it sound more like something out of the seventh-level spell section in the Dungeons & Dragons manual.

Even though it was officially discovered in the early nineteenth century (briefly sold as a party trick, until users began to drop like flies), there are a few intriguing documents that suggest the compound may have been known – and used – for centuries.

If you want to see just how blood-curdling the reaction truly is (my description may not have done it justice), there are many online videos performed by people who know what they're doing. I can't stress enough how dangerous this compound is and I'd strongly discourage the amateur chemist from trying it out – sticking one's head in a gas oven would be a comparatively milder experience.

As mentioned in the text, this poisoning would have been difficult to detect in 1889, unless one knew exactly what one was looking for. Forensic and analytical sciences have gone a long way since then, and mercury and cyanide in the lungs are now very easily detected – just saying.

Now that we've all (hopefully) had some fun, I would like to draw some attention towards artisanal gold extraction, and the extremely worrying figures I found whilst researching for this book.

The process – like many extraction methods – has hardly changed over the centuries. The method described by Frey was already ancient back then, but it's still widely used today, particularly in developing countries, where the bulk of gold supply comes from. In fact, artisanal gold extraction still causes more mercury pollution and poisonings than any other human activity. Statistics differ, but at the time of publication it is estimated that as many as nineteen million people worldwide rely on unsafe gold mining as their main source of income.

Meanwhile, in Windsor . . .

11 December, 1889

The Queen's parlours always reeked, the rose water unable to mask the stench of damp tweed, old flesh and wet dogs.

The Prime Minister Lord Salisbury could sense it even from the corridors, doing his best to ignore the odours, while waiting in the small oak-panelled antechamber.

There was nobody around, so he allowed himself a long, weary sigh, which condensed in a steamy cloud before his eyes. The Queen always kept her chambers a little too cold for anybody's taste – even now, when the fields of Windsor Castle were already covered in snow.

Lord Salisbury detested these secret summons, sent out in little slips of green paper, so small that once folded there was scarcely enough space for the wax seal. He always had to burn them at once, and halt all his ministerial duties. Little did it matter that the Anglican Church was still waiting for a successor to Bishop Lightfoot, or that the tensions between the German Kaiser and his chancellor had many British interests at a stand-still. Everything became trivial as soon as one of Queen Victoria's little green notes arrived.

As usual, the message had only read 'The Queen needs you at once', but Lord Salisbury knew very well what would be discussed. He thought of the dreadful news he was about to deliver, and for an instant even the stout legs of the most powerful politician in the British Empire trembled.

He then heard a soft metallic jingling, now familiar throughout the halls of the royal residences, accompanied by slow, hefty steps.

The door to the Queen's parlour opened, and out came a towering, wide-waisted, dark man swathed in all manner of tunics and pashminas, with an extravagant turban and gaudy strands of gold and pendants around his neck.

'The Queen can see you now,' he said in a haughty voice, and after a rather long pause, added a mocking, '*sir.*'

Lord Salisbury did not even look into the Munshi's eyes. He simply walked past him, making an unnecessary racket with his walking cane, and shut the door himself, lest the nosey Indian fellow might 'forget'.

As soon as he looked ahead, Lord Salisbury felt a chill.

Entering those rooms was like walking into an icy, half-dead world. The curtains only let in a sliver of dim daylight, cast over a ludicrously small table where a young maid-in-waiting was arranging a silver tea set, the tray bursting with cakes and sweet treats. Next to it, and out of reach from the thin ray of light, sat Queen Victoria.

The monarch was a round mountain of mourning crêpe and black furs; layer upon layer of lace, taffeta and gold. A pair of chubby hands, every single finger bejewelled with at least one ring, were demurely folded on her lap. Her face, almost as white as her thinning hair, was partly concealed by the frills of tulle from a tiny black hat.

One of the chubby hands waved curtly at the maid. 'Get out. I can pour my own tea.'

The young woman curtsied, cast the Prime Minister a nervous look, and then quit the room.

Lord Salisbury, as was customary, gave a low bow and waited to be addressed. He heard the tinkling of silver and china, and smacking lips devouring pastries, before Victoria spoke to him.

'The witch has not come. What is the silly meadow flower up to?'

Lord Salisbury rose then and spoke firmly, albeit a little too fast.

'I am terribly sorry, your Majesty. Your contact has died.'

A clump of pastry fell into the teacup, splashing hot brew onto the royal hands.

'Died?' she echoed, placing the cup and saucer on the table with a clatter. 'Good Graces! How very untimely!'

'I am afraid the lady had no choice in the matter, your Majesty.'

'Everybody seems to be dying around me these days,' Victoria grieved, reaching for shortbread. She shrugged as she chewed. 'It was bound to happen soon, was it not? That ghastly woman was ancient, one can only guess.'

Lord Salisbury opened his mouth, ready to deliver the grim particulars of the death, but Victoria interrupted.

'And that silly Redfern! She has said nothing! The scolding I shall give the nasty old prune.'

Lord Salisbury cleared his throat.

'I am afraid – Redfern is dead too.'

Victoria looked up at once, her minute pupils dark against wide, bulging eyeballs; her neck, fat and slack, dangling like that of a turtle.

'What, both?'

'I am afraid so.'

The little, almost lipless mouth, peppered with crumbs, began to open.

'But I wish to talk to Albert,' she said rather absent-mindedly, like a girl who cannot understand a lesson. As she spoke, her stumpy fingers fidgeted on a golden locket, which Salisbury knew contained a miniature and a lock of hair of the long gone prince.

'I am afraid, your Majesty, that at present, communing with the late prince will be – impossible.'

And those little eyes began to burn with a wrath Lord Salisbury knew far too well.

'Impossible?' she hissed, and then screeched, '*Impossible?*'

And with a swipe of the hand Victoria tossed the little table up in the air. China, silver, tea and cakes darted across the room, crashed against the window and rolled around in deafening racket.

Victoria clasped the arms of her chair and made to stand up, but her royal weight and her cracking knees did not allow. She was fast approaching seventy-one, and almost as wide as she was tall.

'*You do not tell the Queen what is impossible!* I must talk to him! I must talk to him *now!* Fetch me someone! One of the others! *Any bloody—!*' The maid stepped in, ready to pick up the mess, but Victoria roared at her. '*Get out, you stupid cow!*'

Lord Salisbury seized the moment to interject.

'Your Majesty, the witches' coven has fallen apart. I have not been able to locate any of our previous contacts.'

Victoria pushed out her jaw, her lower teeth bare as she caught her breath. 'And your son? I know that his wife's dry womb is finally at work. I know it is the work of witches.'

Lord Salisbury gulped. 'That – that was arranged *before* the deaths. Our woman came, delivered her instructions and then vanished. All I know is from her lips.'

'Tell me.'

Again, the Prime Minister swallowed painfully. 'Their main hideaway was discovered. The two headwomen were killed. The rest have vanished.'

Victoria lounged back on her seat.

'Discovered? By whom? Who is responsible for this?'

Lord Salisbury felt a single, cold drop of sweat roll down his temple. This was the detail he feared the most.

'Two . . . two inspectors from the Scottish police.'

'Scottish po—? What were they doing in Lancashire?'

Salisbury recalled Inspector Frey calling it *The Lancashire affair* in his classified reports. Ian Frey, whom Lord Salisbury had personally appointed – a fact which Victoria must never know.

'They stumbled upon the witches whilst on the trail of a fugitive,' he said. 'Otherwise, they would have never—'

'And they killed my witches . . .' Victoria mumbled, the facts finally creeping into her mind.

'Yes, your Majesty,' Lord Salisbury said, and he had to repress a triumphant smile. He could tell where the Queen's thoughts were going. In her head the blame was drifting towards the inspectors – and away from him. He must act carefully to keep it that way.

Victoria began fiddling with the locket, so harshly she nearly snapped the thick golden chain. Her bulging eyes pooled tears of rage.

'Then I want their heads . . .' she whispered, and gathered breath for a rasping holler.

'I want them dead!'